NO
PLACE
TO
HIDE

NO
PLACE
TO
HIDE

NO PLACE TO HIDE

RUTH SEARLE

The Book Guild Ltd

First published in Great Britain in 2023 by
The Book Guild Ltd
Unit E2 Airfield Business Park,
Harrison Road, Market Harborough,
Leicestershire. LE16 7UL
Tel: 0116 2792299
www.bookguild.co.uk
Email: info@bookguild.co.uk
Twitter: @bookguild

Typeset in 11pt Minion Pro

Printed and bound in the UK by TJ Books LTD, Padstow, Cornwall

ISBN 978 1915603 180

British Library Cataloguing in Publication Data.
A catalogue record for this book is available from the British Library.

To Daniel and the future...

The first in a series featuring surgeon, Daniel Kendrick

ONE

07.30 Monday 19th August 2019

"Our beautiful daughter is dead, Daniel. You have to face up to it." Dr Fay Kendrick stood in the stark white living room of their home, scowling at her husband.

"What do you want me to do?" Daniel Kendrick was floundering as he tried to deal with another of her outbursts. "Am I supposed to get angry too? How the hell is that going to help?"

Fay bit her lip and looked away.

"Tell me, Fay. You're the shrink. Our Sophie was murdered. How are we supposed to deal with something like that?" Daniel leaned stiffly toward his wife.

Fay looked back at her husband with cold green eyes. "You think because I'm a psychiatrist, I have all the answers? There's no precedent for this, Daniel. How many people lose their six-month-old baby to a cold-blooded killer? Guess what? I'm struggling with it too." She grabbed her dragonfly tiffany lamp from the coffee table and hurled it across the room. It shattered on the floor and hit Daniel's saxophone, knocking it off its stand.

1

Daniel sighed, exasperated, but ignored it. "Don't you think I know that. We're both trying to deal with it." Daniel spoke more softly, trying to ease the situation.

"At least I'm not pretending it never happened." Fay's jaw tensed as she jabbed a finger at him. "You're a bloody mess, Daniel. You're in denial and you have to face it sometime".

"It's the only way I can cope."

Fay took two steps closer to her husband, a vein visibly pulsing in her neck. "You won't talk to me. You won't even look at her photographs and you refuse to go into her nursery. How can you be so cold and heartless about it? About her death. Sophie was our precious baby... she's still part of us." Her voice was shaking as she spat the words out.

Daniel felt the sting of her accusations but was fighting the instinct to retaliate. He looked at her. At the woman he'd loved since the day they'd met. The woman he was now afraid he was losing. "I'm not cold, Fay. I... I just don't know how to face it. You spend hours in Sophie's room. I don't know what the hell you do in there. It's like a bloody mausoleum –"

"No... it's not. It's the only place I can feel close to her. You just don't get it do you?"

Daniel could see anger turning to anguish in his wife's haunted eyes. "So, tell me, Fay, how are you dealing with it? You're not exactly coping either. You're in there brooding for hours on end. That's why we don't talk any more. You need to face things too."

"I feel her in there. It's all I have left of my baby girl... our precious baby." Fay looked away, tears threatening.

"I know... but you have to move on too. We both do." Daniel reached a comforting arm toward his wife, revealing three thin white scars across his left wrist. He instinctively tugged at his shirt sleeve to cover them.

Fay glanced at her husband's wrist but looked back into his eyes. "You haven't even started to move on, Daniel. You're stuck. You're in denial. At least I'm trying to do something... to get some sort of closure."

"What do you mean?"

"Let's talk about it tonight. We both have to get to work," Fay said dismissively.

"Fay, you have to calm down. This isn't helping."

"Calm down? You're telling me to calm down? Our daughter is dead... murdered by some sick bloody maniac... and you want me to calm down?"

"It was over two years ago. Sweetheart... you've been angry for two years. All I mean is... it's time to put the past behind us."

"How on Earth can we put a thing like this behind us? This has changed our lives forever. You just can't see it, can you? You think we can blithely carry on exactly as we were before. Well let me tell you, I don't care if you think it's time to 'move on', as you put it." Fay jabbed an accusing finger in his direction. "It's tearing me... us... apart..."

"Are you saying you want a divorce?" Daniel flinched as the words left his mouth. It was the last thing he wanted.

Fay was silent for several agonising moments before replying. "No... I don't know... all I know is that something has to change. Maybe we should get some professional help. You have to face up to the fact that Sophie is dead. She's never coming back." Fay looked up at Daniel, slowly shaking her head.

He saw the torment in her eyes. He sensed that a part of her soul had died along with their daughter on that tragic winter day. He edged forward, trying to close the aching chasm between them. He longed to hold her. To exorcise them both from the wretched demons of their grief. But Fay's rage had been building like a stony ice-cold edifice between them for the past eighteen months and he didn't know what the hell he was supposed to do with it.

"I just wish I could get hold of the bastard that killed her..." Fay said through gritted teeth.

Daniel said nothing. He moved closer to her. Longing to embrace his wife, to show her he still cared. To make her realise that they were both grieving in their own way. If he could make her see how much he loved her. How much he wanted to make things better. If only he could escape from the darkness of his own paralysing pit of fear. Fay was right. He was stuck, yet denying his grief was the only way he could function as a surgeon – as a human being.

Daniel gently touched Fay's arm, wanting more than anything for them to console one another as they had in the weeks following Sophie's murder. To be there for one another.

"Don't touch me," she hissed, as she lashed out at him – striking his face and slashing his cheek with the sharp edge of her diamond solitaire engagement ring. The ring he had lovingly chosen for her.

Daniel winced at the nauseating sting of pain but silently clutched his face. He pressed onto the deep cut with the palm of his hand as he tried to stem the warm, sticky blood that was flowing down his face and the inside of his arm, crisscrossing the scars he constantly tried so hard to hide.

"Fay… don't go… not like this," he said.

Her eyes widened as she noticed his blood-soaked shirt sleeve. Her hand flew to her mouth, seemingly horrified at what she had done. "I'm sorry, really sorry," she mumbled as she grabbed her bag and car keys before storming out of the house, slamming the door behind her.

Fay's anger had exploded once again and he hadn't the faintest clue what to do about it.

TWO

Daniel resisted the urge to go after her, knowing her temper would cool in time. He kept the pressure on his cheek as he walked out to the kitchen to find the first aid box. He could hear the growl of Fay's Mercedes and the squeal of tyres on tarmac as it sped down the road. He found a bundle of SteriStrips, some antiseptic wipes and grabbed a handful of paper kitchen towel. He took them to the hall mirror and winced when he saw the long cut running diagonally down his left cheek. He cleaned the gash and most of the blood, then applied the adhesive strips, trying to bring the wound edges neatly together. His whole cheek was throbbing like hell but it would heal in time, he thought. Unlike their psychological wounds or the yawning abyss that had grown between him and Fay. It wasn't the first time she'd lashed out at him in the past few months but he knew that retaliating would only escalate her anger.

Maisie, Fay's Maine coon, was meowing and circling his feet. Daniel poured some dried cat biscuits into her bowl and emptied a sachet of fish-flavoured Whiskas into her china dish. He stroked the silky fur on her back as she rubbed her face across his leg.

His shirt sleeve was soaked with blood. He took it off, threw it into the washing machine in the laundry room and grabbed a clean blue and white stripped one from the ironing basket, giving it a quick shake. There was no time for ironing. He could either be late for work or turn up creased. He did make time, though, to clear up the glass from the shattered tiffany lamp and vacuum the carpet. He set his saxophone back on its stand and frowned at a dent the lamp had made in its bell.

Then Daniel checked on the dogs, Chester, a harlequin great Dane and Ella, a Doberman. They slept in a double garage adjoining the house that Daniel had converted into an insulated room with raised wooden beds he had made himself. Fay had added soft, comfortable bedding. He had called it 'The Dog House'. He was greeted by two excited pooches, sprinting manically up and down the garden while he put food in their bowls. He whistled and they sat by their dishes, as he had trained them to do; their tails wagging. Chester was quivering with excitement and was first to his bowl when Daniel gave the command. The food was gone in seconds.

The floor of the huge dog's room was littered with tennis balls, some chewed and tattered. Daniel collected them up in a bucket and poured them into the dog's Deluxe Automatic Ball Thrower – one of the novelty items that Daniel had collected over the years. On the wall was a framed photograph of Ella wearing her talking bow tie and Chester wearing sunglasses. It was a portrait taken by Fay in happier times.

"Right, you two, I'm off to work. Rosie will be here for you soon." Rosie Hillier ran a local dog creche and collected the dogs every week day at 9.30 am. She returned them at 5 pm and they spent the evening in the house. Daniel liked to walk them in the woodland beyond the gate at the end of their row of contemporary detached houses. It felt like his sanctuary from the frenzied pace at work and the emotional rollercoaster at home.

He rubbed Chester's broad chest, smoothed a hand over Ella's head and looked into their trusting brown eyes. "You know, dogs have a way of finding the people that need them. Thanks guys." He flicked the switch and set the ball thrower into action. It would run on a timer for thirty minutes and keep them occupied. He smiled as they raced after the balls. He shut the door of their room with a heavy heart, wishing he could stay home, enjoy a peaceful day alone with the dogs and try to forget about the sorry state of his marriage.

Daniel grabbed his suit jacket, said goodbye to Maisie, who was chattering at a fly on the window, locked the doors to the house, then went back to double check he actually had locked them before he slid into the driver's seat of his Dravit Grey BMW 8 convertible. It was a present to himself for finally getting to consultant general surgeon – although he was beginning to regret getting the promotion. He reversed out of the driveway and drove through a narrow country lane and onto the 'A' road that led into the centre of town. He took a right-hand turn into Park Road, past Fay's private clinic – a small diversion. He could see her silver Mercedes SLK parked on the opposite side of the road. At least she'd got to work in one piece. He drove on through the town centre and within twenty minutes, he'd arrived at Riverbeke General Hospital.

He parked in his designated spot, went into the hospital via a small staff entrance and bought a take-out latte and a Mars bar at the kiosk. He took the stairs to the third floor, walked along the corridor and let himself onto the surgical ward with his swipe card. He greeted a cleaner, several of the nurses and the ward receptionist as he wove his way past the nurse's station and into his small office that overlooked the maternity department. It was where Sophie had been born and was a constant reminder that, frankly, he could do without. He took off his jacket and slung it over the back of his chair. He rummaged in his desk drawer and found a tin of 'Grumpy Old Git' mints that his son, Richard had given him. He popped one in his mouth.

"What happened to you?" Daniel's registrar, Matthew Clarke, a tall, muscular man with three-day stubble and intense blue eyes, had followed him in and was peering at the cut on Daniel's cheek.

"An argument with a cupboard door." Daniel said dismissively.

"Nasty."

"Had a haircut?" Daniel asked.

Matt ran a hand over his new textured quiff. "Yeah, actually," he said, as if he was waiting for a compliment.

"Any reason they didn't finish the job?" Daniel asked, deadpan.

Matt rolled his eyes.

Daniel smiled. "So, what have we got today?" he said, turning his attention to the theatre list Matt had given him. He offered Matt a mint and he took one.

"There's a big bowel resection scheduled for you this afternoon. Malcolm Phelps," Matt said.

"Yes, he was an urgent referral from his local practice. Came into my colorectal clinic last Friday. It looks like a pretty aggressive carcinoma." Daniel flicked through the patient's notes. Dealing with bowel cancer was his specialty, although he'd retained his general surgical skills and supported the A&E Department with abdominal trauma cases.

"I'm sure you'll do your best for him," Matt said.

"He was in pain for over a year before he went to his GP. He may have left it too late but we'll see." Daniel handed the notes to Matthew with a watery smile. "Let's get on with the ward round."

The two doctors went out in to the ward and were joined by a waiting entourage of two SHOs – Senior House Officers – three junior doctors, two staff nurses and the ward manager. Daniel could sense several of them staring at the gash on his face but were polite enough not to mention it. Daniel began his consultant's round, beginning with a morbidly obese man reclined in his bed.

One of the SHOs, Dr Steven Letts, a bear of a man with crazy hair, stepped closer to the patient's bed, holding a set of notes and an iPad showing lab results. "This is Jeffery Watkins, thirty-six. He had a laparoscopic gastric band procedure yesterday. No concerns apart from some post-op discomfort."

Daniel looked through his notes. The man had tried but failed to lose weight over a period of several years and it had been affecting his heart as well as his mental health. He looked at the patient. "Mr Watkins, we'll get you up and about today and hopefully you can go home later. Drink plenty of fluids and we'll see you in clinic in a few weeks." Daniel smiled at the man who thanked him profusely.

Daniel moved on to the next patient.

Dr Letts, once again stepped up to the patient's bed with a set of notes, which he gave to Daniel. "Niall Jackson. Incisional hernia repair after an emergency laparotomy last year. Recovering well. I'd like to discharge him today."

Daniel read the operation notes and handed the file back to the SHO. "Looks like we can let you get back home later, Mr Jackson."

"Thanks doctor."

Again, Daniel moved on to the next patient, followed by his entourage of medics. Matt pushed through to the bed holding the man's notes.

"Malcolm Phelps. We spoke in your office," Matt said.

Daniel nodded and turned to the patient. "How are you feeling today?"

The man clutched his belly and shook his head. "I'm in agony, Mr Kendrick. Not sure I can stand much more."

Daniel stepped closer to the bed. "Just relax. I'd like to examine your tummy."

The patient nodded his agreement.

Daniel placed a hand over the man's rigid abdomen and gently palpated. He could feel a large, hard lump that, on his CT scan results, had showed was originating from his transverse colon. Daniel could have sworn the tumour had grown in just a few days. He turned to his registrar. "Do we have a theatre free?"

"Yes, Theatre One."

"Bloods OK?"

"Fine. We're good to go."

"Have you eaten or drunk anything this morning?" Daniel said, turning once again to his patient.

The man shook his head, wincing with pain.

"Let's take him down this morning. No point in waiting." Daniel addressed his patient. "Alright, Malcolm, we'll get this sorted for you straight away. Nurse Foley will look after you and the anaesthetist will come and see you shortly. Are your family here?"

"Yes, they're in the relative's room."

"Can you have a word with them, Matt?"

"Of course," Matthew said.

Staff nurse Amelia Foley took the notes from the registrar.

"See you in theatre," Daniel said.

Time was against his patient now. Daniel was determined to do all he could to give him a good outcome as his surgeon. He felt an urgency to save life. He was driven and obsessive about it since he'd failed to save the life of his first wife, Susan, from bowel cancer, nearly ten years ago.

With nothing else pressing, Daniel cut short his ward round. This patient was his priority now.

He walked down the corridor to the theatre department and changed into blue scrubs, a surgical mask and his own comical dinosaur-themed theatre cap that matched his socks. There were a few glances from the staff at the gash across his cheek but nothing was said.

He scrubbed then pushed his arms into the surgical gown that a young female student nurse was holding for him. He noticed she was blushing as he snapped on a pair of sterile latex gloves.

Daniel strode into theatre to see his patient anesthetised, draped, and his abdomen painted with a brown povidone-iodine fluid. The anaesthetist looked up and acknowledged Daniel as he checked the patient's ventilator settings.

"Let's have some music, shall we?" Daniel glanced at the theatre orderly who was hovering nearby.

"Sure. The usual?"

"Yep, let's go for it," Daniel said.

An instrument trolly was wheeled next to the operating table and the scrub nurse handed him a scalpel. He began to cut through the skin and fat layers. Dr Johnathan Wilkens, an SHO, was assisting, swabbing blood from the wound.

Daniel cauterised bleeding vessels to the pounding beat of Marillion's Incommunicado. The acrid smoke from the diathermy curled up into the bright operating lights and filled the air with the distinctive, nauseating smell of burning flesh. He split the muscle layer digitally then asked for retractors. Dr Wilkens positioned the metal instruments and pulled the wound apart to gain access to the wet, slippery viscera.

"Here we are," Daniel said, his hand probing a tumour the size of a large grapefruit, that was eating away at the man's colon. He checked the abdominal cavity and felt the drag of sadness for his patient when he discovered several small sites of metastases where the cancer had spread. He smoothed a hand over the liver. It felt rough and there was a small tumour on the underside that hadn't been picked up on the scan.

It was a death sentence.

"What are you going to do?" the SHO asked.

Daniel signalled for the music to be turned off and thought in silence for a moment, noticing another small tumour erupting from the bladder. "It's inoperable. Normally it would be an open and close case but I'm thinking I could make what's left of his life a little more comfortable if I do an anastomosis and at least get the primary tumour out".

"Will that give him more time?"

"Maybe long enough to say goodbye to his family", Daniel said. He had been grateful for the time he and his first wife, Susan, had spent together after her diagnosis, even though she had suffered intolerable pain near the end. He shook his head as if to block the memories.

Both the SHO and the anaesthetist nodded pensively but said nothing. The mechanical breathing of the ventilator and the gargle of the suction in its holder were the only sounds in the theatre for several minutes as Daniel figured out how he was going to excise the tumour. Now he was a consultant, he had to make the final decision.

He turned the tumour over in his hands. "I think a right and transverse hemicolectomy with ileo-colic anastomosis should do it. There's some adherence to the main vessels, so it will be tricky. Okay, let's do it. Knife please." He held his hand out and the scrub nurse slapped a scalpel handle into his palm.

Daniel had performed countless bowel resections but each procedure presented its own challenges. He could feel the heat of the operating lamps on the back of his neck, and the cut on his cheek throbbed a little as he carefully began to excise the tumour where it had encased a large artery. As he cut into the tumour, the scalpel nicked the vessel and blood poured into the abdominal cavity. The alarm on the patient's heart monitor began its urgent bonging as the patient's blood pressure plummeted, adding to the sense of urgency that had gripped the operating room.

"Shit. Suction and mops please." Daniel put the knife down and began mopping up the blood with large gauze swabs as it pumped relentlessly from the artery.

"I may have to clip the aorta, if I can bloody find it." Daniel was struggling to see with the volume of blood that was pouring from the vessel.

The scrub nurse handed him an artery forceps but the bleeding was so profuse, Daniel couldn't see to clip it off. "Shit. He's bleeding out."

"We're losing him," the anaesthetist warned.

Daniel tried frantically to stop the bleeding, pushing mop after mop into the man's abdomen, trying to press on the artery to stem the flow. Each time the white gauze was drenched in blood within seconds.

The alarm on the heart monitor changed to one long bleep.

"Asystole," the anaesthetist said.

Daniel continued to push mops into the man's abdomen, desperate to save his life. A sea of red, sticky blood soaked the drapes, Daniel's gown, and everything else in its path. It looked like a massacre.

Through the intercom, Daniel heard his registrar's voice.

"Stop, Daniel. He's gone. There's nothing more you can do."

Daniel continued his frantic efforts to stop the bleeding; Matt Clarke's voice and the heart monitor's long, flat, piercing sound ringing in his ears.

Then Matt was beside him, pulling him away. "Daniel. He's gone."

Daniel stepped back and grasped the sickening devastation of what had happened. He felt the churning in his gut as he realised, he had lost a patient. His scalpel had cut into the main artery that had caused Malcolm Phelps' death by exsanguination. He slowly looked up at the clock on the wall of the operating theatre. "Time of death, two-thirty-five."

The anaesthetist killed the alarm on the monitor leaving an ominous silence.

THREE

Monday 19th August 2019

At 7.30 am, Jaxon Sloan walked out of his cell at HMP Gallow Hill for the last time. He'd been incarcerated at Her Majesty's pleasure for the past five months and was dying to get out. He was sick and tired of the constant violence by inmates, and overcrowding meant two or even three prisoners had to share cells originally designed for one person.

He'd been lucky to be sharing a cell with an old mate, Sully Rathmore, who was on his second stint for 'level 2' armed robbery. Lack of prison staff meant cell blocks were run on a restricted regime with inmates in lockdown for hours every day without the usual outlets for recreation, exercise and work. Sloan felt like he was trapped in a pressure cooker. He didn't mix well with the other inmates and there were frequent skirmishes among the men on his wing with near riots on occasions.

Many of the agitators were taking synthetic drugs – new psychoactive substances that only added to the violent outbursts directed not only at the screws but at other inmates. Sloan avoided taking drugs of any description. He'd seen the effects of the bad trips some of the prisoners had experienced and he preferred to keep a clear head.

He was glad he'd done his stretch and was looking forward to a decent meal instead of the tasteless, unidentifiable stews and curries that looked like they had already been eaten. Mostly, he craved peace and quiet. In prison, all he could hear was the constant banging, shouting and, at night, the cacophony of snoring blokes that kept him awake. There was barely a moment's silence.

Early in his sentence, he'd voluntarily sought out the sessions with a psychiatrist that had been on offer. Dr Fay Kendrick had been very kind to him but somehow, he'd fallen behind with his appointments and wasn't sure it had helped him understand and control his fits of rage any more than the anger management had. Maybe he should just stay away from other people – especially those that infuriated him.

Sloan waited while the barred metal doors were unlocked to let him through. He was accompanied by a squat wing officer, with a threadbare ginger combover, that had been the plague of his life. 'Red' the inmates called him after the angry cartoon bird with his ruddy complexion, red hair, beak-like nose and cynical attitude. 'Red' completed the paperwork that confirmed his name, inmate number, cell location and activity; sinisterly called 'time expired' since he was for release. Sloan was handed over to the prison officers in the reception area to be processed.

"You'll be back," 'Red' hissed sarcastically.

Sloan didn't reply. He was glad to see the back of this particularly belligerent screw.

He was strip searched and taken through pages of seemingly pointless paperwork; Sloan was deemed ready to be released back into society. He dressed in the shirt and jeans he'd worn when he was sent down; now uncomfortably tight after months of prison stodge and inactivity. His thick-set neck now carrying rolls of flab, earning him the nickname, 'bulldog'. He retrieved a holdall with a change of clothes and some toiletries that he'd brought in but wasn't allowed to use in prison. He'd been made to wear prison clothes and make do with the tiny sachets of prison issue shower gel and their cheap and nasty deodorant and toothpaste. He could have bought better toiletries from the prison canteen shop but he chose to spent his meagre earnings rather more shrewdly on sweets and cigarettes to lubricate his dealings with some of the other inmates.

"Behave yourself this time, Sloan. I don't want to see you back in here again," an older, chilled out, seen-it-all prison officer said as he handed him a clear plastic bag with the rest of his belongings: a tattered black leather wallet containing a twenty-pound note, some small change and a couple of a debit cards, along with a bunch of keys and a fully charged mobile phone with its charger. He passed Sloan his £46 prison discharge grant and waved a hand in the direction of the main prison door as if dismissing him, "go on, get out of here."

Sloan didn't need to be told a second time. He pocketed the money, his few belongings, grabbed his holdall and waited again while the large wooden door was unlocked by a willowy, raven-haired woman prison officer who could easily have been a catwalk model. "Good luck Jaxon," she said, and smiled as if she genuinely meant it.

"Thanks boss." Sloan nodded as he passed her and stepped, at last, into the outside world. He squinted into the sunlight as he found his bearings. HMP Gallow Hill was a category C prison on the outskirts of the small town of Dilport. The next major town, and where Sloan lived, was Riverbeke, 30 miles to the north east. Sloan was headed into Dilport on foot.

The early morning air was cool and smelled of freshly cut grass after a night of light rain. He drew the air deeply into his lungs as if to clean out the rank stench of prison. The leaves on the trees were greener than he'd remembered and he could hear the chattering alarm call of blackbirds being stalked by a cat in somebody's garden across the main road. The heavy wooden door of the prison slammed behind him and he released the air from his lungs with a guttural sigh. A long-awaited sense of relief washed over him as he turned and started to walk beyond the high stone walls of the prison toward the town. Sully had arranged for him to meet up with an accomplice of his, Ash 'slasher' Mateo, a burly West Indian, who was a good solid mate, according to Sully; a salt-of-the-earth type, who'd do anything for anyone, especially another convict in need of a helping hand. Sloan was to wait outside Dilport's small library on the main road, where Mateo would pick him up in his black Mercedes CLS Coupe at 9.30 am. He checked the time on his phone, 8.43 am. Perfect timing if he kept up a brisk pace.

FOUR

Damon Wixx sat in Dr Fay Kendrick's waiting room, a high-ceilinged, former drawing room in a large Victorian terrace, now decorated in contemporary white with cream sofas and a very expensive bespoke reception desk. He was stroking the black tattoos inked along his left inner forearm. The first, near his wrist, was a large death head moth, the second a smaller version of the same artwork. Reminders of who he was and treasured mementos of what he was capable of; the creepy faces on the moth's backs were waymarkers of the life's journey he had embarked upon.

Dr Kendrick was late. He'd never known her to be late before. Mostly amenable and so very sympathetic, her compliance gave him power. Control. She sometimes appeared to believe his charming charisma, friendly persona, self-proclaimed superior intelligence – his 'mask of sanity'. Sometimes but not always; and that was what kept him hooked.

She had become his psychiatrist five years ago. It was then that he had begun his campaign to isolate her from all she loved; all she held dear.

Idealise, devalue, abuse and discard.

That was the basis of the psychopathic bond that Damon Wixx had with nearly all the women in his life. Dr Kendrick had been and still was a challenge. He had idealised her – had been obsessed with her – and now, amused and delighted, he wanted to take from her the people that were most precious. He stroked the larger of the death head tattoos on his arm and smirked. Soon there would be another, even larger inking.

He looked across the room at Meredith Baily, Dr Kendrick's receptionist. She was engrossed with her phone, her purple talon-like fingernails tapping compulsively at the screen.

In his youth, she would have been just his type with her flirty makeup and skimpy outfits. She reminded him of the girl he'd raped and murdered all those years ago. Her body had never been found.

It was the first of the murders he'd got away with.

He stroked the death head moth. The one nearest his wrist. It was a tribute to his first human killing. He imagined her pale, curvaceous body rotting at the bottom of the sea, half-eaten by sharks. Had the tides and currents moved her from where he'd dropped her overboard that night, he wondered indifferently. Had the iron bars he'd tied to her shapely torso been heavy enough to keep her on the sea bed?

He'd taken his pleasure from her then exerted the ultimate control over another human life. He strangled her with his bare hands until he felt her struggles weaken and her life ebb away. In Damon's cold, calculating, reptilian brain, taking a life was intoxicating.

Wixx felt a growing emptiness in his soul that only the ultimate control of taking a human life would fill. He needed to kill again – and soon.

Damon was tired of the boredom of mundane relationships and contemptuous of the idea of love and commitment. Wixx had nothing but distain for the emotional lives of normal human beings. He was an emotional vampire, intent on sucking the feelings and passions from others so that he could toy with them. Abuse them. Manipulate them.

An emotional predator.

In Dr Fay Kendrick, he saw a feisty anger that lay just below the surface. A dark passion he needed to fully ignite, then suck from her. He needed that sustenance. He wanted to isolate her from everything she cared about.

He had watched her patiently throughout his 'therapy'. That obligatory delving into his mind for answers to his abhorrent behaviour. The endlessly tedious Hare's Psychopathy Checklists, she used to analyse him. He'd had fun with it but now he was bored and it was time to raise the stakes and make his next move. To kill her husband then feed on her deepest, most wretched emotions.

Meredith Baily looked at the clock in the reception area of Dr Kendrick's clinic, then across to Damon. "Hopefully Dr Kendrick won't be long."

Damon wasn't a particularly tolerant individual but he did want to see her again; to gaze into those beautiful eyes.

A predator closing in on his prey.

Meredith Baily stood and smiled stiffly at Damon Wixx as he sat in Fay Kendrick's clinic waiting room. Tottering on six-inch heels, her shapely arse swayed exaggeratedly in a tight skirt as she disappeared into the ladies'.

Damon noticed the door to Dr Kendrick's consulting room was ajar – a chance to look around while she wasn't there. He slipped through the gap and breathed in the smell of the room – her smell. On the coffee table between the armchairs at which they sat for their weekly sessions; he saw a sheaf of papers. He picked them up. The top page read 'Biophilia and the Healing Power of Nature'. The author was Dr Fay Kendrick. He started to leaf through them but was interrupted when the phone rang in reception.

He stuffed the papers inside his jacket and zipped it up. He couldn't resist the opportunity to take something personal of hers. This would be an interesting addition to his collection. He glanced around the room and saw a briefcase on her desk. A colourful scarf was hanging over the back of the chair. She couldn't have gone far. He wanted to grab the scarf, to indulge himself in her fragrance, to steal something of hers just for the hell of it, but the urgency of the ringing phone made him hesitate.

He crept back out into the reception area just before Meredith Baily emerged from the ladies', flicking her thick mane of chestnut hair behind her shoulders. Unable to reach his seat in time, he pretended to be engrossed in an abstract painting on the wall – a vibrant metallic swirl of colour.

Meredith eyed him suspiciously but turned her attention to the ringing phone. "Don't worry, Dr Kendrick is not here yet," she was saying in her best telephone voice, "we can reschedule your appointment." She replaced the receiver and glanced at the clock. "I think it best if we reschedule your appointment as well, Mr Wixx. I can't imagine where Dr Kendrick is but she wouldn't want to keep you waiting any longer." She thumbed through the diary. "How about tomorrow afternoon at three?" It was a rhetorical question.

Damon felt a rush of anger and contempt. Anger at Fay for not turning up for his appointment and contempt that her receptionist was thwarting his plans. Then reason kicked in almost as immediately.

He needed to keep things casual. Keep it cool. Don't ruffle any feathers.

Not yet.

He could wait to make his move and the idea of that seemed strangely alluring.

FIVE

Monday 19th August 2019

Jaxon Sloan slung the holdall across his shoulder and walked down the steep Gallow Hill, along a mile of winding 'B' road and across the recreation field on the outskirts of Dilport; stopping briefly to take in the peace and tranquillity of the river that ran along the park's eastern edge. Despite his reputation as a tough cookie, Sloan was a peace-loving character and being around nature gave him a sense of oneness with the world that had been lacking in his life for the best part of a year.

Prison had been the culmination of months of unrest at home with his wife, Lisa. The accusations, the blame games and the violent outbursts; from both of them, he had to admit. Her belligerence fuelled his own and they often ended up in a pointless shouting match, hurling insults and abuse at one another. Sometimes it had escalated into physical violence, with Lisa frequently the first to lash out. Usually, thumping him with her fists, or kicking him and spitting in his face. Mostly, he could restrain himself and take it, thanks to his training and experience as a nightclub bouncer.

He'd dealt with plenty of foul-mouthed, aggressive drunks like her over the years. He'd also attended anger management classes but his rage often got the better of him and he retaliated, usually with a sharp slap across his wife's face. He was slow to anger but when he saw the red mist, he couldn't stop himself from lashing out. Things had not been good in the Sloan household for some time but that was all about to end. Lisa had taunted him mercilessly in recent weeks, safe in the knowledge he was securely banged up. But she was about to regret her actions and the way she had betrayed him. She'd finally reached the end of her rope, Sloan thought, as his pace quickened.

Jaxon reached the library in Dilport at 9.20 am. Within minutes, he heard the screech of tyres skidding on tarmac. Ash 'slasher' Mateo's shiny black Merc came to an abrupt halt in front of Sloan. The nearside window lowered and Mateo leaned across from the driver's seat.

"Jaxon Sloan? Sully's mate?" Mateo asked above the low growl of the car's engine.

"Yeah. Ashley?"

"Get in."

Sloan opened the car door, pushed his holdall into the passenger footwell and slid in next to Mateo, the bulky West Indian filling the space; his shaven head skimming the roof of the car. He appeared to have no neck and his huge, denim covered thighs just about wedged beneath the steering wheel. He must have been at least six foot four and would have looked more comfortable in an SUV or something he could actually fit his considerable bulk into.

Mateo checked his wing mirror and without indicating, pulled out into the sparse traffic heading north east toward Riverbeke. He glanced across at Sloan. "Glad to be outa there, man?" he asked with a deep, gravelly Caribbean accent.

"Damn right," Sloan said, suddenly a little nervous and wondering if he was doing the right thing. He hoped he could trust his former cell mate.

"Know the feeling. I got out eight months ago from Gallow Hill. Did a bit of a stretch for firearms offences." Mateo shrugged as if it was no big deal.

Mateo continued without waiting for an answer. "You can stay at my place tonight. My wife is cooking us up a nice dinner and there's plenty of beer." He glanced at Sloan; a cheeky glint in his deep brown eyes.

He appeared to be the salt-of-the-earth type, just like Sully had said. Sloan started to relax.

"That's really kind of you. Thanks." With no family and a wife that had clearly transferred her affection elsewhere, Jaxon was glad of the hospitality and some friendly company.

"No problem. Sully said you were one of the good guys and I owe him a big favour." Mateo didn't elaborate and Sloan didn't ask. He reckoned it was none of his business.

Mateo slowed to a stop at a 'Give Way' sign at the edge of Dilport, then eased the Merc out onto the main 'A' road that eventually led into Riverbeke. He picked up speed as they snaked along the winding road, barely slowing for a hairpin bend.

"So, you got woman trouble, Sully tells me," Mateo said, his eyes fixed on the road ahead.

Sloan wasn't sure how much Mateo knew but he would have to tread carefully. He'd learned the hard way about divulging too much personal stuff to people. "Yeah, you could say that. What did Sully tell you?"

"Told me she didn't waste a nanosecond shagging Kieran Hook when he got out of Gallow Hill two months ago. You know him? You must have been in there at the same time."

Sloan realised Mateo knew all about his wife's adulterous behaviour – as did most of the prison population probably. She'd stopped visiting him over six weeks ago and it didn't take a genius to figure out that she'd shacked up with Hook after all the bragging he'd done about his various conquests – including Jaxon's wife. "Bitch," Jaxon muttered quietly under his breath.

Mateo just about managed to control the car as he took another sharp corner way too fast. A Range Rover coming the other way was forced to swerve as the Mercedes straddled the white line. Sloan pushed back in his seat, his foot pressing hard onto an imaginary brake pedal.

Sloan was almost chewing the dashboard as they tore along the road at high speed, barely slowing for bends, despite the near miss. After months off the roads, it was a distinctly unnerving experience. "I... know him but... we were on different wings." Sloan finally managed, trying but failing to sound nonchalant. He was loathed to admit he was such a nervous passenger.

"I've heard all the rumours about Hook, man, and he's still at it with your misses. I checked up on them for you just yesterday. Just so you know." Mateo confirmed Sloan's suspicions.

"In my house?" Sloan felt his hackles rise at the thought of Kieran Hook with his wife. In his bed.

Mateo nodded. "I have photographic evidence if you want it. Might come in handy." Mateo gestured with a twist of his head toward the back seat of the car. He seemed to be enjoying playing detective on Sloan's behalf.

Sloan looked back and saw a yellow cardboard folder among a pile of other stuff that had been left on the back seat. He hesitated, not desperate to see his wife with another man but knowing he had to confirm what had been festering in his mind for weeks. He braced himself against the door and footwell of the car as they hurtled round another bend then reached for the folder. He set it on his lap.

"Yes, that's it," Mateo said, glancing down.

Sloan opened the folder and pulled out a sheaf of photographs that had been printed onto A4 paper. Images, taken through the window of Sloan's living room, of Lisa and Hook in an intimate, partially naked embrace. It was indisputable evidence.

"You can keep them. For the record," Mateo said.

"Thanks." Sloan felt like he could do without the vivid reminder of his wife's adultery but Mateo was right, they would provide evidence for the divorce, should it be needed. There was no way he'd want her back now.

The two men fell silent as Mateo drove the Mercedes along a straight stretch of road. They were still well over the speed limit but Sloan tried to calm his nerves – they couldn't be far off now. Two miles down the road, Mateo turned left into a narrow single-track lane bounded on both sides by tall hedges. They were on the outskirts of Riverbeke. The Mercedes negotiated a couple of narrow, twisting bends before turning into the long driveway of what looked like a farm.

"This is home," Mateo said as he pulled up alongside the pine end of a large, white-painted stone farmhouse, the tyres of the Mercedes losing traction on loose chippings as he braked sharply, kicking up a cloud of grey dust behind them.

Sloan quietly breathed a sigh of relief that the dreadful car journey was over. They were in a large farm yard surrounded by high hedges and apparently isolated from other houses. There were several barns and outbuildings dotted around, some were obviously dilapidated with gaping holes in the roof and walls but others looked as if they were used for storage. Sloan glimpsed a black Land Rover Defender through one of the barn doorways. There were a few brown hens and a colourful cockerel protecting his girls as they pecked about in the yard.

"This way," Mateo said as he gestured toward the front of the house. He swept an arm around the farmyard. "It used to be my father's beef farm. He's long gone now and I have no interest in farming. Man, it's too much like hard work. But we have a couple of horses." He pointed toward a five-bar gate which led to a large paddock. A wooden, hand-written sign next to a pile of muck, read 'FREE HORSE MANURE. HELP YOURSELF'. Right behind the sign was a white, shaggy-mained pony, seemingly unashamed to be the one responsible for producing it.

Mateo guided Sloan into a storm porch, with three pairs of green wellingtons in various sizes parked along its wall, then through a red-painted door that led into the farmhouse. They emerged into a dimly lit square hallway and it took Sloan a few moments to adjust to the gloom after the bright sunshine outside. Gradually, he could see a plain wooden staircase rising from the centre of the hall, with several latched wooden doors leading off on either side. The floor was uneven and laid with old, worn slate flagstones. The place was suffused with the musty smell of old furniture.

Mateo led Sloan into a large kitchen and family room. He threw his keys onto one of the kitchen counters, a well-worn scrubbed oak worktop. "Make yourself at home, Jaxon," he said, "I'll go and find my wife." He went through a heavy wooden door, which Sloan presumed led to the garden.

Sloan tucked the folder with the incriminating photographs into the front pocket of his holdall and placed the bag on the floor. Initially he felt awkward, being a guest in a stranger's home but when Mateo, returned followed by his family, he began to relax and enjoy the experience.

"This is Charlene, my wife and my two daughters, Amba and Anisha." Mateo smiled proudly as he presented his family to Sloan.

Charlene smiled, bright white teeth flashing against her flawless black skin as she extended a chubby hand to Sloan. Her face lit up. He shook her hand firmly and returned the smile. "Thank you for having me Mrs Mateo." Sloan said, remembering his manners.

The children, aged around five and seven, held back shyly, clinging to their father. They looked adorably cute with braided hair and matching dresses. They both had their mother's big brown eyes.

"It's a pleasure," Charlene said. She seemed genuinely happy to have him there.

27

Sloane looked at what seemed to be a happy, normal family and wondered what the hell Mateo had done to get a prison sentence for firearms offences.

SIX

Monday 21st August 2019

Dr Fay Kendrick had no idea who she was. She stumbled along the overgrown pathway with no inkling of where she was going or how she got there. All she knew was that she finally felt safe. She was surrounded by acres of dense woodland that had been abandoned to nature and growing wild. Her head hurt. She touched her temple and felt the sticky oozing of blood from a wound. It was seeping into her hair and down her cheek. Her mind was blank. She had no idea if she had fallen, been involved in an accident or even been attacked. She could have been unconscious for seconds or days but she had found her way to this wilderness by following her instincts. That much she knew. Somehow, she belonged in this place. She had nothing with her other than the floral dress and leather sandals she was wearing. No bag, no phone, nothing to identify her. Nothing to show she belonged anywhere. She was bewildered, frightened and her feet hurt as if she'd been walking for hours.

Fay looked up through the tree canopy. A blazing yellow sun hung low in the sky. She guessed it was late afternoon. It was hot and she was thankful for the cool shade of the trees. She

29

felt isolated yet strangely protected, as if nobody would be able to find her or hurt her here. She closed her eyes briefly, trying to make sense of what was happening. She heard the beautiful melody of birdsong. Familiar and comforting. She savoured the earthy smell of the forest and the rustle of leaves in the breeze. She was sure she knew this place.

Then, driven by her instincts, she ventured further into the dense undergrowth, pushing back branches as she tried to follow the narrow track. Thick brambles scratched at her legs and caught her dress. She trusted a strong urge to keep going; sensed there was something up ahead that she needed to reach; somewhere safe.

Fay heard a twig snap behind her and sensed a shadow in her peripheral vision. She stopped and glanced around, suddenly feeling nervous. Had she been followed? She crouched low to the ground, staying still and silent. Then a fallow deer and her fawn trotted past, the sunlight dappled through the trees onto their backs, highlighting the subtle colouring of their coats. She sighed with relief but looked around nervously. In every direction, there was nothing but trees and dense undergrowth. For all she knew, she could be the only human being left on Earth. A shudder of fear surged through her body at the thought but she quickly dismissed it. It felt more like she was running from something, or someone. Why couldn't she remember? Whatever had happened, she sensed the need to escape. She touched her temple again. The blood seemed to have stopped oozing. She continued along the narrow path that had become almost completely obscured in places. Fay noticed a wooden sign nailed to a large oak tree. It read, 'Private Property'. Was she trespassing on someone's land? Did this place belong to her? She had no idea.

The sun was sinking toward the horizon and Fay was beginning to feel very vulnerable. She didn't want to be out in the open after dark. She still had no clue where she was headed but she sensed she would be safe and comfortable when she found it.

Fay pushed on through the undergrowth until she came to a clearing in the woodland. She gasped as she fully recognised the scene before her. This was where her instincts had led her and it was familiar; reassuring. A huge lake shimmered in the fading sunlight, with an island at one end covered in dense shrubbery and dominated by an old ash tree. Mallards dived for vegetation and there was a pair of mute swans gliding effortlessly across the water. Fay could hear the hooting of coots and beyond, she saw a wooden cabin on the shore of the lake. She remembered this place.

Mesmerised, she walked around the lake, absorbing the peace and tranquillity that enveloped her. It was her sanctuary. A memory flashed into her mind – her father thrashing her with a leather belt. His angry eyes burning into hers; then she was running as fast as she could away from him. She flinched at the recollection. She had come here as a child and not for the first time. It was her secret hiding place.

Fay reached the cabin; a modest wooden building with an apex roof and stone chimney. It had a simple door from an outside decking area into the main room of the cabin and a long picture window overlooking the lake. Adjacent, was a wooden jetty that was in a sorry state of disrepair. Fay tried the door handle but it was locked. She stood for a second then remembered where the key was hidden. She retrieved it from beneath a flowerpot – the contents parched and dead. She unlocked the door and pushed it open. The cabin felt familiar. Fay felt overwhelmed as flashes of memories flooded back to her: not recent memories but memories of her childhood escapes to the cabin. She knew she had always been alone here, apart from the family's dog, a golden Labrador named Jerry. He had been her best friend, she recalled, and was with her frequently when she ran away from her violent father.

Fay wandered around the cabin, picking up familiar items that were strewn around. A rag doll, a cushion, a china mug, Jerry's collar. She brushed the dust from a chair and sat at the wooden table in the centre of the cabin.

She hoped she would be safe here.

SEVEN

Monday 19th August 2019

Damon left Dr Kendrick's office, called into the supermarket for a few ready meals and headed back to his tower block estate in the fag-end of the town: a carbuncle perched on the landscape like a wart on a witches' chin. The graffiti covered walls and litter-strewn pavements were testimony to the depravation that surrounded him. He hated the place, had no real friends, and had lost touch with most of his family, including his adoptive parents. He maintained a relationship with a wealthy uncle, preying on him and his loneliness to procure money from him on a regular basis.

Most of the wasters he knew proudly boasted about their time in the nick, parading it like a badge of honour. Some were on parole or doing community service for some petty crime or other and the only person he thought of as a friend was still serving his six-year sentence for armed robbery in a maximum-security prison that was over thirty miles away. Damon knew he should pay him a visit sometime but he never quite got around to it. Maybe he'd catch up with him when he got out – or maybe not. He didn't particularly care.

Damon reached Bridgeman Tower, an eight-storey tower block built in the 1960s in the raw concrete, 'Brutalist' style of architecture. It was one of four tower blocks serving the north end of town. Damon took the rickety metal lift to the third floor. He walked along the landing to his front door, easily identifiable among the cloned flats by its peeling red paint and a dirty strip of blue duct tape holding the broken glass pane together. He fumbled for his key and let himself in. The smell of last night's microwaved curry saturated the air and Damon dumped his groceries on the table in the tiny kitchenette then strode across the living room, opened the window and stood sucking in the cool breeze.

From the third floor, he had a fairly open view of the estate and the town beyond but although he'd been there for three years, he couldn't settle. It was a temporary abode until he made some money, mainly from drug dealing or robbery. He was a dealer, not a user. Apart from the cannabis he smoked constantly. The urges and passions that drove him were the dark, primal urges to kill that were becoming undeniable.

He thought of Dr Kendrick again and reached into his jacket for the stolen papers.

The delectable Dr Kendrick – Fay. He closed his eyes momentarily and pictured her in his mind. Her delicate feminine features and those stunning green eyes that changed colour with the light. The curve of her waist and the glimpse of her smooth, lightly tanned thigh. He imagined what he might do to her when they were alone. Would she put up a struggle as she had a few weeks ago in her office? Undoubtedly. But that would only fuel his desire. He imagined his hand across her throat just like the girl he'd raped and killed. The girl at the bottom of the sea. And the child he'd smothered to death. He glanced at his Death Head Moth tattoos and smirked.

He felt a surge of excitement as he turned the pages of Fay's manuscript. The words were typed but the pages were littered with her own handwritten annotations – a glimpse into her mind. Words were crossed out, new ones added and there were notes in the margins. He felt as if he was part of her secret world. A world he'd never glimpsed before. Most of the writing, Damon couldn't read or understand and there were long scientific names that made no sense to him but one page stood out. Dr Kendrick had written in the margin, 'my lake, woods and cabin – biophilia and terpenes'. There were some undiscernible scribbles, then, further on, she'd written, 'Otter Brook Lake. My secret sanctuary'. He had no idea where that was but it obviously meant something to her.

Perhaps this was something else he could isolate her from.

EIGHT

Monday 19th August 2019

The rest of Daniel's day had flown by in a whirl of meetings and administration. Matt had handled the rest of the theatre list since there were just a few minor procedures. The hardest part for Daniel had been speaking to Malcolm Phelps' wife and daughters, once he had showered and washed away his patient's blood. Having to explain why the man they all loved had died on his operating table had been grim. Mrs Phelps had been remarkably philosophical about it. She found some comfort that his death had been quick and that he hadn't known anything about it, rather than the protracted period of pain and torment they had all anticipated. They were aware of the prognosis – that he had just weeks to live – but Daniel had wanted to give them time as a family to say their goodbyes. Now they had to arrange his funeral. It had been churning around in his mind all day.

Daniel had worked late at the hospital and arrived home to a dismal, empty house. There was no sign of Fay and she hadn't responded to his earlier text. He'd tried to smooth things over with a friendly message. He checked the landline answerphone. Nothing.

He dumped his briefcase in the hall and let the dogs into the house. Chester licked his hand and followed him into the kitchen, his huge claws clicking on the tiled floor. Ella made a beeline for the rug in the living room. She twirled around a few times and finally settled down for a snooze with her favourite soft toy – a teddy bear they called Eddie.

Daniel opened cupboards and the refrigerator hunting for something to eat. He found a solitary mint humbug in the bottom of the fruit bowl, unwrapped it and popped it into his mouth. On the fridge door was a wooden magnet that read, 'Today's menu choices – take it or leave it.'

He had secretly hoped Fay would be home with dinner prepared but there was no wife and no dinner. He was starving and had skipped lunch to get Malcolm Phelps into theatre. He'd felt nauseous ever since but now his stomach was growling with hunger.

He reasoned Fay would have eaten by now as she hated to eat after 7.30 pm, so there was little point in waiting for her. He seemed to have eaten dinner alone quite a lot lately. He found a loaf of sliced bread, three days past it's use-by date and a tin of baked beans. That would have to do. He tipped the beans into a bowl, microwaved them and put two slices of stale bread into the toaster.

Maisie was rubbing around his legs, meowing. He tipped some food into her bowl, which she devoured as if she was famished. Daniel rescued his toast from burning in the nick of time.

He poured a large glass of merlot and sat balancing his beans on toast, dripping with butter and smothered in ketchup, on his lap in front of the TV. Chester was stretched out on the blanket-covered sofa he considered his own. Maisie lay curled around the dog's neck like a warm fluffy scarf. Daniel settled on a documentary about the wildlife of the Caribbean. He and Fay had been planning to go there on holiday when Sophie had been three months old but they decided to wait until she was older, so she would remember it. They'd never spoken about it since.

Daniel's iPhone rang and he could see it was Oliver Davenport. Oliver was a friend and colleague at the hospital. He muted the sound on the TV.

"Ollie. How's it going?" Daniel scraped up the last of his baked beans, forked them into his mouth then placed his plate onto the coffee table in front of him. He grabbed his wine glass and leaned back into the sofa cushions.

"Fine. Busy with private patients at the moment but think of the extra money – you really ought to join me Dan." Oliver was becoming insistent that Daniel join him at his new cosmetic surgery practice, since he was about to jump ship from the NHS to make it a full-time career.

"I'm thinking about it. The money does sound good." Daniel hadn't yet discussed it with Fay. She always seemed too distracted to talk about his career.

"So, are you and Fay coming to the fundraiser tonight? Thought you needed a reminder since I haven't seen you all week."

Daniel had forgotten. He wasn't really in the mood for a formal social evening and it would be awkward with Oliver's wife, Melissa, there. She was starting to get embarrassingly overfamiliar with him. "Not sure Ollie. To be honest, I'm cream-crackered. Had a bad day. Lost a patient in theatre. Maybe I'll give it a miss tonight."

"Yes, I heard about that." He paused for a moment as if he was unsure what to say, "come on Dan, all the more reason to get out for a break. Life has to go on – you know that. You'll enjoy it when you get there."

Daniel hesitated. He really wasn't in the mood. "Not tonight, Ollie." He smoothed Maisie's back as she walked across his lap to get to the other side of the sofa.

"Come for an hour, just to show your face. People are expecting you and there'll be a buffet and free drinks." Oliver was insistent, as usual.

"Not sure I can face it."

"To tell you the truth, I could do with you there to keep an eye on Melissa. She's been a bit down lately and I'll be tied up with this ruddy auction."

Daniel didn't relish the prospect of spending an evening with Melissa but Oliver was very persuasive and the buffet sounded tempting. Daniel checked the time and did a quick calculation; 7.45 pm now. It would take him 10 minutes to change, 15 minutes to get there and he could be home by 10 pm. It would be a change from another evening getting sozzled alone in front of the box. Fay wasn't home and anyway; he could do without another argument.

"OK, I'll just stay an hour."

"Excellent." Oliver rang off.

NINE

Sloan had spent the day with Mateo and his family. They had welcomed him warmly and the girls, Amba and Anisha had forgot their shyness and were keen to show him their ponies and various dolls and teddy bears before they wandered off to play on their own. Mateo's wife, Charlene, had kept the kettle boiling practically all day, cheerily offering endless cups of tea and coffee with thick wedges of home-made chocolate cake. Sloan felt so at home with the Mateo's family, he had almost forgot he'd just been released from prison and was effectively homeless. Part of him wished he could stay here forever, cocooned from the harsh reality of the outside world; the hatred, the violence the conflict that had dogged his life. If he was honest, he hadn't felt so welcome or so valued in a long time. None of his childhood foster homes – and there had been several – had been particularly loving but perhaps he only had himself to blame for that with his constant outbursts of temper. Not to mention the turbulent relationship with Lisa.

"So, what now, Jaxon?" Mateo asked grabbing a couple of whiskey glasses from the dresser and pouring two fingers of Scottish single malt for each of them.

Sloan thanked Mateo and took a swig – and spluttered. The fiery amber liquid seared down his throat like a burst of spicy hot pepper. "Not sure really, if I'm honest, Ash," he said, trying to regain his composure; he felt like he'd been punched in the face with a brick. "I have to confront Lisa, that's for sure but what comes after that, I have no idea."

"You need to see a solicitor, man," Mateo said, draining his glass and reaching for the bottle to top them both up.

Ordinarily a beer drinker, Sloan accepted the whiskey Mateo offered, now sipping it more respectfully, "I could get used to this," Sloan said as ethanol singed his nostrils. They clinked glasses.

"Hope it works out for you." Mateo fixed Sloan with a warning etched into his eyes. "Be careful Jaxon."

Sloan nodded, taking Mateo's meaning and they fell silent as they sipped their drinks.

Sloan was reluctant to voice the question that had dogged him all day but Mateo sensed what Sloan was angling for. "The prison thing – it was for something minor, really." The big man paused to take a slug of whiskey before continuing. "I had a shotgun that wasn't registered and I happened to point it a man that was breaking into my home. Nobody got hurt, he just suffered a minor flesh wound, but I would have shot him dead. God help me; I would have done anything to protect my family." Mateo's voice was low and gravelly.

"That's understandable," Sloan said sympathetically. "I would have done the same thing. What gives anyone the right to break into your home, threaten your family, and think they can get away with it?"

Mateo fixed Sloan with deeply penetrating eyes. Sloan knew what was coming next. What had been arranged with Sully in Gallow Hill. So far it had been something of an elephant in the room.

"Come with me," Mateo said solemnly.

41

The big man led Sloan out into the rough farmyard. The light was beginning to fade and the clouds reflected a translucent orange glow as the Earth rolled into the sunset. One of the ponies watched them from the gate, his ears flicking and turning to follow the sounds of the evening. Mateo's huge frame lumbered across the yard and into the barn where the Land Rover was stored, he suddenly seemed wary. He pushed open the big wooden door and Sloan followed him inside. Mateo retrieved a key from a high beam in the barn's wall and unlocked the boot of the Land Rover. He pulled out an object wrapped in thick canvas and offered it to Sloan.

"Here – it's empty but there is a full box of cartridges. What you do with it is up to you. I know nothing, right? My prints have been wiped and I will deny all knowledge of it – it's not registered either." Mateo handed Sloan a slightly battered sawn-off shotgun.

TEN

Monday 19th August 2019

Daniel changed into a formal black evening suit with a crisp white shirt and colourful striped socks – a Christmas present from his son. He picked out a navy tie with a green turtle print design but pushed it back into the drawer, leaving his shirt open at the neck. A tie usually ended up in his pocket ten minutes after he arrived at these events anyway.

He put Chester and Ella in the Dog House, left a couple of lights on in the house for security and drove to the country club where Oliver and Melissa Davenport were hosting a charity event.

He parked in front of an imposing grey stone Edwardian vicarage covered in Virginia creeper that had been long converted into a country house hotel. The service and the food were exemplary and it was a favourite venue with some of the senior medics for special events and fundraisers.

Daniel walked through the reception area and followed the noise into the function room at the back of the hotel. Groups of elegantly dressed people were huddled in polite conversation, juggling drinks and platefuls of finger food with practiced ease.

Waitresses dressed in long black aprons moved around the room offering hors d'oeuvres, mainly canapes. Daniel stopped a woman with a plate of crab and avocado toasts and took two as he wove his way to the bar.

"A large merlot please," he asked a tall, willowy barman sporting a man bun, leaning across the bar to be heard above the clamour of voices and background music from a string quartet.

Daniel took his drink and surveyed the room. It was the usual crowd, mainly consultants and other senior medics with their wives. Everyone was cordial and well-behaved but as the evening wore on, Daniel knew these same people would become as rowdy and drunk as any other group given a free bar. He felt conspicuous on his own, wishing Fay was with him, although she had said more than once that they were too far up their own arses for her liking.

"Daniel. Good to see you, old man." Dr Kenneth Worsley sidled up beside Daniel, a fresh pint of bitter in his hand.

"Ken. Good turnout." Daniel would have to escape before the ex-army doctor got into one of his self-important monologues.

"Indeed. And where is your lovely wife tonight?"

"She had to work late," he lied.

"Kenneth, how are you?" Behind them, an elderly gentleman touched Worsley on the arm.

Daniel seized his opportunity to escape and left the two old men to a verbal battle of one-upmanship. He squeezed past a group of cackling women in search of more food. Across the room, along the length of the far wall, he found a buffet table covered in a white linen cloth and piled with dishes of salad, mini tacos, skewers of grilled shrimp or satay beef, cheese and fruit kebabs and a variety of mini sandwiches, rolls and small pastry shells with exotic-looking but undiscernible fillings. At the end of the table, there were a selection of exquisite tarts, pastries and gateaux with jugs of pouring cream. Yes, Daniel thought, taking in the delicious smells, it was worth coming, if only for the party food – the beans on toast had hardly touched the sides. A man had to eat.

Daniel took a plate and piled it with a selection of food. Someone had to be first to the banquet, he thought. He sipped his wine and ate as he meandered across the room, nodding to some and lifting a glass to others in acknowledgement as he caught their eye. Oliver Davenport waved a hand from the far side, where he was preparing his auctioneering entertainment for the evening. Daniel raised his glass in his direction. Now he'd been seen and acknowledged, he could escape when he'd finished eating. He'd sat through quite enough of these VIP auctions.

Daniel was just finishing off his last mini beef taco and considering going back for some more when he heard a familiar voice behind him. He turned to see Melissa Davenport tottering toward him; a swirl of pink chiffon and stilettos with immaculately coiffured platinum blonde hair, scarlet nails and overdone make-up.

"Darling! How marvellous to see you!" Melissa air-kissed him on both cheeks, puckering scarlet red lips. She reeked of a heavy floral perfume that was beginning to put Daniel off his food.

"Hello Melissa." Daniel knew Melissa was insincere but he had to admit, he enjoyed the attention she lavished upon him. It was a nice change from the rows and indifference at home.

Melissa stared openly at the wound on his cheek. "Gosh, Daniel, whatever happened to you? That looks ghastly."

"An argument with a broken plate." He'd forgot what he'd said to the last person who asked.

"Darling, how awful."

Daniel shrugged and popped the last few peanuts into his mouth.

"And where is Fay? Is she avoiding me do you think?" Melissa blew a kiss to someone across the room then looked at Daniel. Her impossibly blue eyes sparkled through a tipsy haze.

"Fay's just a bit busy tonight."

Daniel could see over Melissa's shoulder that a small queue had formed at the buffet table. He hoped she would move on soon.

"Sweetie, you know Oliver is simply dying to tell you more about his cosmetics practice. Did you notice I've had work done? He's a truly wonderful surgeon." Melissa patted her throat, her slender fingers encased with expensive gold, platinum and diamond rings. Her perfectly manicured nails were a glossy scarlet, matching her lipstick exactly.

Daniel twisted his head to one side as he listened to Melissa. He was slightly deaf in his left ear and with the background noise, it was difficult to catch what she was saying clearly. He peered at the side of Melissa's face and neck, noticing a faint scar beneath her make-up. It ran through the natural fold of skin in the front of her ear then curved behind it, ending at the hairline. He admired the intricate work and the sutures, that were barely visible.

"A lower facelift? That's a beautiful job," Daniel said.

"Isn't it splendid!" she said, sipping prosecco. She left a lipstick stain on the glass.

Daniel knew Melissa had regular Botox injections. The stiffness in her face gave the game away. No doubt that was done by her husband as well. It was as if he wanted to create one of those Stepford wives from the 2004 movie. Fay had insisted on growing old gracefully, although she was still in her prime at 44 years old. She was an elegant woman but unlike Melissa, he could never imagine his wife being so obsessed with her appearance to the exclusion of practically everything else.

Melissa squeezed Daniel's arm and glanced toward a group of men hooting with laughter at a joke someone had cracked. "Don't go away, sweetie, I simply have to say hello to Gerry. I'll be right back." She held up a finger as if she were disciplining a dog before she disappeared; her chiffon scarf floated across his shoulder leaving a trace of perfume in her wake.

Daniel could hear her gushing to the group as he made his way back to the buffet. He joined the queue, chatting to Charles Jameson, a cardiothoracic surgeon, who regaled him with a description of his new yacht – a seventy-eight-foot Oscar Sunseeker worth nearly half a million pounds. He tapped a photograph on his phone and tilted it toward Daniel.

"Looks great," Daniel said, eyeing the superyacht as he reached for the mini ham rolls. He took two along with a handful of salted crisps and put them on his plate.

"You must join us for a sail sometime – you are always welcome. We could get down to the Channel Islands for a few days. Jersey is always a good bet. What do you say? Rosemary would be thrilled."

"Maybe, sometime." Daniel liked the idea of a boating holiday and Charles and Rose were nice people, even if they did like to parade their wealth. He wasn't too sure Fay would go with him, though. She thought them pretentious and unbearable company.

Charles was whisked away by one of his colleagues and they said they would meet up again to discuss the holiday. Daniel knew it might never happen but it was nice to be asked.

Before Sophie had been born, he had an entirely different circle of friends – close friends that he rarely saw any more. Now, he preferred the superficial chit-chat, the pretentiousness and the shallow relationships. No one ever asked him how he felt. Nobody asked how Fay was coping. No one cared; and that's how he liked it.

"Daniel, darling. You must have another drink." Melissa was back, her prosecco had been topped up again and was bubbling in a tall crystal glass. Without waiting for a reply, she summoned a waiter with a wave of her hand and asked for a large red wine for Daniel.

He tried to protest but Melissa was insistent, as ever. "Now you must promise me you'll join Oliver at the clinic. You won't regret it. You know the money is fabulous, it truly is, and there's such a demand for cosmetic procedures these days. Absolutely everyone is having work done. You could make a fortune, darling, and get away from the dreary NHS. Oliver is giving it up before the end of the year. It's been simply ghastly for him. Will you promise you'll join him?" Melissa was squeezing his arm as if she was trying to stop him from escaping.

"I'll give it some thought," he said. Contrary to Oliver, Daniel enjoyed his NHS career, despite the grim days, but the money did sound tempting. Perhaps he could squeeze in some part-time work with Oliver and have the best of both worlds.

"Daniel, it would be wonderful to have you on board." She gave him a tipsy little wink as she sipped her drink.

He took the wine from the waiter. Sod it, he thought. He knew he was overeating again and drinking too much – it was his default when he was stressed. He checked his iPhone again. Nothing. Fay seemed to have abandoned him and he could get a taxi home later.

Melissa stood, clutching Daniel's arm as her husband started the auction proceedings. Oliver gave him a thumbs up and he knew he'd be stuck with her for a while. The room became quiet and everyone faced the stage as Oliver Davenport entertained his guests. There were polite ripples of laughter from the usual crowd. Oliver invited bids for the various items being auctioned: a dinner date with a local actor, a signed football shirt, a bottle of vintage wine, vouchers for dinner at the hotel and a variety of other items that had been donated to the cause, including a giant teddy bear from a department store in town. Fay would love that, he thought, remembering her collection of soft toys that she had placed around the spare bedroom. The money from the auction rolled in and Daniel bid on but lost a weekend trip to Italy to one of the hospital board members. He was sure she'd won something similar last year. A fix perhaps but not worth making a fuss about.

Melissa was getting more and more tipsy with every glass of prosecco, clinging onto him to steady herself, and Daniel had lost count of the number of wine top ups he'd been given by various waiters. He checked his watch. Midnight. Shit. Where had the evening gone?

"I have to get home, Melissa. I have an early start. Say goodnight to Oliver for me."

"Sweetie, must you go? It's so lovely having you around." Melissa pushed her face against his arm and looked up into his eyes. Her mascara was smudged and she was smiling seductively at him as she tried to stay upright on her stilettos.

"I have to go. Sorry." Daniel gently pushed her away, catching Oliver's eye and indicating he had to go.

She pouted at him with the little girl face she put on when she was disappointed. "Well then, we must get together soon. Are you sure you won't stay?"

"I really have to get home." Daniel inched away from her and she watched him as he disappeared through to the reception area. He placed his empty glass on a side table and asked the receptionist to call him a cab.

"I think there are a couple of taxis outside sir."

"Thanks."

Daniel went out into the cool, rose-scented air, a faint whiff of cigar smoke wafting from one of the guests that passed him on the way back into the hotel. Gravel was crunching beneath his feet. A bat fluttered past and circled him once before flying off into the trees. It felt good to be outside, away from the noise and heat of the function room. He took in a deep breath, trying to clear his head. He wished Fay had been with him.

Daniel found a cab parked at the side of the building. He slid into the back seat and gave the driver his address. He could see his BMW across the car park. He would have to call by in the morning and pick it up on his way to work.

The taxi smelled of pine air freshener which did little to cover the underlying reek of stale cigarette smoke and sweat. Daniel opened the window an inch to let in some of the cool night air. The taxi driver spoke with an eastern European accent and they exchanged a few social pleasantries but most of the drive back to Daniel's house was in silence apart from the drone of a radio with the sound turned down. Too quiet to hear what was playing but loud enough to be an irritating background noise.

"Thanks," Daniel said as the driver pulled up outside the house. He passed him cash for the tariff plus a generous tip and got out of the car, relieved to escape the smell and the noise of the taxi.

There was still no sign of Fay's Mercedes. Where the hell was she? Daniel unlocked the front door. The house was just as he left it. No sign of her having been home during the evening and it was gone 1 am. Maisie was curled up on the sofa but lazily opened one green eye to scrutinise him as he walked past her.

Whatever Fay was up to, he would have to deal with it in the morning. Daniel let the dogs out into the garden briefly before shutting them up for the night, checked all the doors were locked – twice – and went upstairs to bed.

ELEVEN

Early hours of Tuesday 20th August 2019

Jaxon Sloan had been awake most of the night. Mateo and Charlene's spare bed was soft and comfortable and his head sunk gratefully into the soft pillow, yet sleep eluded him. Maybe it was a habitual thing from months of listening to snoring inmates in prison all night long, or maybe he just couldn't stop churning things over in his mind. He knew he would have to confront Lisa, not least because he had nowhere to live.

Sloan remembered the gun Mateo had given him, which was hidden away from the children and Charlene. Mateo had warned him against using it – it was for protection only he'd said. Sloan began to feel restless as he considered his alternatives and none of them were particularly appealing. His mind was churning with unwelcome thoughts of his wife's infidelity.

Sloan tossed and turned for another hour. He could hear the ponies whinnying in the paddock and an owl hooting in nearby woodland. He'd been trapped in a prison cell for months and felt a growing need to be outside; to experience the night and the vastness of the sky. He got out of bed and dressed, pocketed his iPhone and wallet, grabbed his holdall and slipped quietly out of the room and down the stairs. He went into the kitchen and rummaged in the children's toy box for a blue crayon and a piece of paper. He wrote:

THANK YOU ALL FOR HAVING ME. JAXON

He placed the note on the kitchen table, tiptoed out into the hall, let himself out through the front door, then quietly clicked it shut behind him.

He walked across the farmyard and into the barn, where he retrieved the hidden key to the Land Rover and pulled out the gun and the box of cartridges from the boot as Mateo had agreed. He emptied the cartridges into his jacket pocket, checked the weapon, then placed it gently into his holdall and zipped it shut. Jaxon replaced the key into its hiding place and walked toward the ponies' paddock, the rubber soles of his boots crunching softly on loose chippings. The moon was waxing, almost full, and the dark shadows of night danced around the yard and over the walls of the farmhouse like a ghostly silhouette. The white pony was standing by the gate. Sloan stroked its soft muzzle but the pony jerked its head away and sauntered off. Jaxon let himself into the paddock, quietly closed the gate after him and double checked that the latch had caught. He slung the holdall across his shoulder and walked through the paddock toward the next field. He was heading in the direction of Riverbeke.

Sloan looked back at the farmhouse and was grateful for the kindness of strangers. The whitewashed house looked stark against the shimmering moonlight and he knew he must leave Mateo and his family in peace to enjoy their lives. It was time for him to move on. Time to deal with his situation and draw it to a conclusion.

Jaxon Sloan followed the North Star as he made his way toward Riverbeke. The familiar landscape looked very different from the perspective of the surrounding fields but it would be quicker to go cross-country, as the crow flies, than follow the winding road into town. He crossed the ponies' paddock and over a wooden style into the rolling countryside beyond.

Sloan slogged up the hill, keeping the pole star ahead. His breathing was laboured, his clothing clammy from unaccustomed exercise and the weight of his holdall but he made gradual progress until he reached the brow of the hill. He was grateful for a cooling breeze that gusted up and over the hilltop. In the distance, he saw the sprawling lights of Riverbeke, the town still and silent as its inhabitants slept, with just the occasional car head– and tail lights snaking their way along the roads. The town lay in a wide valley which levelled out to the north. It looked as though it had slid down the hill and settled at the bottom, spreading out like lava from a giant shield volcano.

Sloan checked the time; 02.55. He estimated it would take him about an hour to walk into town and get to his house on the north western edge. He could just make out the group of streets near his home but at this distance, the individual houses merged into a dark band behind the white dazzle of the newly installed LED streetlights. Further south there remained the gentler amber-yellow glow from the older sodium lights that had yet to be replaced. The town looked different from above, the layout seemed more elongated than his old map suggested, due to new housing developments built at either end of the town.

At the far north of the town, he could see the four ugly tower blocks, a relic of the 1960s, that dominated the skyline. The landing on each floor was brightly lit, as if the buildings were standing in bold defiance against the growing number of protesters that wanted the towers demolished and replaced with something more modern and architecturally pleasing. Sloan could see from his vantage point how overbearing the buildings actually were and knew from his own experience how, over the years, they had become a ghetto for misfits, petty villains and a smattering of dangerous career criminals. The prison population at Gallow Hill had certainly been overrepresented by residents of the towers.

Sloan caught his breath and began the decent toward the town; the smells of the countryside – even the pungent smell of recently spread manure – was preferable to the stench of prison. To his right, a small flock of sheep lay huddled together under a tree and in the gloom, they resembled a giant ball of wool. They watched him warily, a faint silvery-green eyeshine reflecting the moonlight.

Sloan had a sense of direction now and the lights of the town would lead him to his destination. From a distance, he recognised a side street that led to the main road that ran through Riverbeke. He turned and headed for it.

Eventually, he found a wooden style that led to a public footpath. He followed the signs and gradually, buildings appeared; sparsely spaced detached houses at first, then he reached a battered gate that led down a narrow lane and into a street of older semi-detached houses at the edge of town.

Sloan turned left at the end of the street. A dogleg took him into another residential street, then another until he reached the wider main road through the town, lined with Victorian terraced houses on both sides. Most of them were in darkness but there was an occasional landing or bedroom light left on. He heard a baby crying through an open upstairs window and in one house, a TV was blaring out a gristly scene from a late-night horror movie, the coloured glow of the screen flickering behind a thin curtain. Now he was on familiar territory and his pace quickened as he walked down the main street.

Finally, Sloan reached a crescent of ten semi-detached, ex-council houses, all now privately owned. Sloan stood at the end of the lane. He could see his house at the far end of the crescent; an end house, white-painted, square, with the original aluminium windows and a new navy-blue front door. Sloan slunk into the shadow of an old ash tree as he contemplated his next move. He could see Lisa's rust bucket of a blue Ford Fiesta reversed into the driveway and behind that a car he'd never seen before, a newer white Vauxhall Astra with mud splattered up the side. Probably Hook's car. His own Volvo estate was nowhere to be seen – Lisa had probably sold it while he was in prison. Sloan felt his hackles rise. His hand balled into a tight fist. Was this enough evidence, he thought? He needed to confront her – confront them – or he would never rest. He checked the time; 04.00 and the dead of night. His neighbours' houses were all in darkness apart from a landing light that Mrs Pritchel always left on at night.

Sloan walked down the side lane to the rear of the houses and along the back lane. He reached the gate of his own house and he let himself in. Even in the dim moonlight, he could see the garden was an overgrown mess. He reached the half-glazed back door and fumbled for the bunch of keys in his holdall. The door opened to Jaxon's relief.

TWELVE

Early hours of Tuesday 20th August 2019

Jaxon Sloan crept into the small kitchen. It was cluttered with dirty dishes and there was a pungent smell of last night's cooking. A pan sat soaking in the sink with a burned crust around the edges and a thick layer of grease floating on the water.

Sloan crept into the hallway, moonlight illuminating his way as it shone through the half-glazed front door; his holdall in hand. Everything seemed smaller and more cramped than he had remembered it.

Sloan moved towards the stairs. It was time to confront his wife and get some answers to the questions that had been plaguing him for weeks. He noticed a man's coat hanging in the hallway near the front door as he stood at the bottom of the stairs, his hand resting shakily on the balustrade. A knot of apprehension was forming in his gut. It felt surreal to be creeping around his own home in the dead of night as if he were an intruder.

He carried the holdall up the stairs, careful to avoid the familiar creaking stair treds. His mind was racing with the things he wanted to say to Lisa. Would he soften and want her back; would he reason with her and get her to see things from his perspective? And what about Hook? Could he bring himself to be civil to him – the waster that had stolen his wife? As Sloan climbed the stairs, he felt the familiarity of the house he'd lived in for so many years, then, the resentment of what they had done. His heart was pounding now from the effects of adrenaline. He tried to calm his mind, reason with himself; metaphorically count to ten. He was well aware of his temper and how it could flare out of control. He wanted to talk rationally to Lisa. He really did. Surely it was worth talking to his wife – to see if there was anything salvageable in their marriage. They'd known one another too long to simply throw away their relationship. Hadn't they? And yet, after the years of angst with her constant jibes and narcissistic behaviour, he wasn't sure he had the stomach for reigniting a love that had long gone cold.

Sloan was trembling as he stepped onto the landing. The door of the main bedroom at the front was ajar and he could hear the sounds of gentle snoring. It sounded like Lisa. He crept up to the door and softly pushed it open, battling to calm the knot of trepidation in his stomach. The curtains were partly open, letting in a sliver of moonlight and he could see Lisa lying in their bed, her arm draped across Kieran Hook's tattooed chest as he slept. He'd recognise him anywhere; the jailbird haircut, the grotesque tribal tattoos all across his chest and up his neck and jaw and the facial burn from the prison napalm that an inmate had thrown at him during a skirmish.

His fist tightened again as he tried to control the raw emotions that were threatening to run rampant. He looked at his wife, her pretty face peaceful and sleepy, her long chestnut hair flowing across the pillow; the smooth, soft line of her naked arm and shoulder as it lay across Hook's chest. They were lovers breathing in unison. Pure visceral rage churned in his gut like a waking giant. How could he ever reconcile this? How could he ever forgive her for such a treacherous betrayal?

57

An icy, dark corner of his heart burst in an avalanche of hatred. It was the place he fought to keep locked away; a place where all the loathing and anger had been marinating ever since he'd heard of his wife's infidelity. Now he'd reached a dangerous tipping point and there was no stopping him. Pure hatred oozed from every cell in his body. Sloan stood at the bottom of the bed, placed the holdall on the floor beside him and quietly unzipped it, his nervous trembling now yielded to a steady determination. He pulled out the sawn-off shotgun that Mateo had given him and quietly and carefully cracked open the barrel. He reached for the cartridges in his jacket pocket and deftly loaded the gun, left and right barrels. He looked at his wife and her lover, entwined together in his bed, quietly snapped shut the gun, slid the safety catch off and cocked both hammers. He took two steps toward the bed on Lisa's side.

Now, within two feet of his wife, he sensed the faint aroma of her perfume and heard gentle snuffles as she breathed in and out. Jaxon Sloan took a deep steadying breath, as if he was giving himself one last chance to stop what he was about to do but he was seething with uncontrollable rage and resentment. His mind was numb from a cocktail of adrenaline and cortisol being pumped around his body by his pounding heart. Fuelled by hatred, he felt like a zombie, only capable of obeying his primal instincts. Sloan took aim and fired one barrel into his wife's flank at point blank range; a volley of lethal pellets tore into her body as the gun kicked back hard into his shoulder. Lisa's bloodied flesh splattered out from the entry point and her body shook like a rag doll in response to the force of the shot. Sloan saw Hook's eyes wide in terror for a brief moment as he woke, then the gun kicked into Sloan's shoulder as the cartridge exploded into Kieran Hook's chest. Sloan's ears were ringing as the thunderous sound of gunshot ricocheted around the room. The sight of two bloodied corpses and the terror in Hook's eyes were etched into his brain.

Sloan stepped backward, stunned for a moment until he fully realised what he had done. The smell of gunpowder hung in the air, like firecrackers on bonfire night. All he had wanted was to be rid of the pain of Lisa's betrayal. Had he killed his wife and her lover in cold blood? Or murdered them in the passionate heat of an angry rage? He honestly couldn't say but something – a primitive sense of survival – dragged him back to reality and he quickly threw the gun back into the holdall and without zipping it up, he hurried out of the room and leapt down the stairs in three bounds to the front door.

Sloan instinctively grabbed Lisa's car keys from the hall table and let himself out of the front door. He made for her ageing Fiesta. He had to get away and fast. Someone would undoubtedly have heard the two gunshots. He managed to open the car door and threw his holdall onto the passenger seat then climbed into the driver seat. He fumbled to push the key into the ignition and made the connection on the second attempt. He revved the engine, engaged first gear, released the handbrake and floored the accelerator. He looked right as he tore out of the driveway to see Mrs Pritchel leaning out of her bedroom window in her nightie. She was staring right at him, mouth agape, a look of sheer terror etched on her face. He'd been seen and he had no doubt she would take great delight in reporting him to the police.

Sloan swerved out of the drive and onto the road – tyres screeching on tarmac. He glanced in his rear-view mirror to see several lights come on in neighbouring houses. He had to get as far away from Riverbeke as possible. His anger had cost him everything. There was no going back now.

Sloan turned out of the crescent and onto a street of terraced houses that ran perpendicular but as he reached the top of the street, the engine spluttered and stalled. He tried the ignition three times in quick succession but the engine was dead. He looked at the petrol gage – the needle was well below the red line. It felt like Lisa's last satirical act of revenge.

Sloan realised there was no time to waste. He would be forced to escape on foot. He grabbed the holdall and leapt out of the car; the door left wide open in his haste to get away. He noticed more lights coming on in the surrounding houses but sprinted to the end of the street, turning down a lane and out of sight. At the junction, he ran across the main road and on up a short hill toward the woodland that ran alongside the river. Here he would be able to hide amongst the dense forest.

In the distance, above the sound of his pounding heart, he could hear police sirens piercing the stillness of the night.

THIRTEEN

Tuesday 20th August 2019

The morning passed in a haze of patient consultations, phone calls and test results for Daniel Kendrick as he ran his six-week post-surgery clinic. He called up to the ward to check on his post-operative patients from the day before and apart from an elderly woman complaining of pain, all were making satisfactory progress. Matt, his registrar, had things under control, so he took a late lunch at a vegetarian cafe a few miles down the road from the hospital. After overindulging the previous night at the charity auction, he opted for a healthy salad bowl, a half-decent coffee and a welcome escape from his colleagues and the hospital environment. He could grab at least forty-five minutes to himself. Most of the staff ate at the hospital refectory or the McDonalds nearby but neither particularly appealed to him.

He'd been checking his iPhone periodically throughout the morning but there was still nothing from Fay. Why was she ignoring him? Surely, they were mature enough to sort things out. Maybe she had left him? Maybe she was letting him stew? Whatever it was, they had to talk about it.

Daniel ordered his lunch and found a table at the rear of the café. The tables were covered in floral tablecloths and each had a vase with a single tulip and a bunch of white gypsophilia. There was just a smattering of people in there, a couple of smartly dressed ladies enjoying what looked like a working lunch, a woman and her mother chatting over tea and scones and a middle-aged business man sitting alone near the window, gazing at the comings and goings in the street. The café smelled of coffee and freshly baked bread and there was the quiet murmur of conversation. Daniel sat facing the door as he always did. It was apparently an instinct in some men that harked back to our Palaeolithic ancestors – cavemen who guarded the entrance to the cave, protecting their family from predators. Or so Fay had told him once. It was one of her pet psychological theories. She loved analysing people's behaviour and sometimes he found it unnerving. It was as if she could read the private thoughts in his mind – like a mind-meld with Spock.

That was, until they lost Sophie.

He had picked up a copy of the Times along with his usual Mars bar from the hospital shop in the foyer. He read while he waited for his order. It was full of Brexit news and the shenanigans going on in Parliament, there had been a devastating hurricane in the Bahamas and, of course, the usual celebrity sex scandals. On page four, there was a story about the serial killer, still on the loose, near Riverbeke. There was a lack of evidence thus far but the police were widening their search and putting more resources into finding the perpetrator. Detectives were working on a number of theories in an attempt to find a motive for the killings. Daniel shook his head in disbelief. It all seemed surreal and too close to home.

A whip thin waitress, dressed from head to toe in black, arrived with his lunch order. She reminded him of Mortitia from the 1960s TV series, The Addam's Family, with her pale skin, long, raven-black hair and pillar-box red lipstick. He put down the newspaper, thanked her and stabbed a fork into his salad. He was craving carbs after a hectic morning and was tempted to order a hunk of bread. He resisted. He would eat his chocolate bar later.

He finished the salad and was halfway through his coffee when he saw Melissa Davenport walk into the café. Shit. He felt cornered. He would rather not have to endure an awkward conversation with her. Especially after her clingy behaviour with him the previous night. He opened the newspaper again and hid behind it, peeping around the side of the page to see if she had been served at the counter; searching for a way to creep past without being seen.

He drained his coffee cup, left some loose change on the table as a tip and checked for Melissa again. She was waiting to pay at the till and had her back to him. He would have to be quick. He grabbed the newspaper, stood and hurried past.

"Daniel," she said, turning to lock him with her gaze. Dressed in a fuchsia pink shirt dress, belted tightly at the waist, her face was caked in makeup; an effort to disguise her puffy, hungover eyes.

He stopped dead in his tracks. "Melissa," he said awkwardly, half turning toward her. "Sorry, I have to dash off to clinic." He started to back away, pointing to the door with his thumb.

"But surely you have time for a coffee and a chat, Dan? After all, you did run out on me last night." Melissa pouted barbie-pink lips and batted her thick false eyelashes at him. Then she swapped her Gucci handbag to the other arm and reached out to pluck an imaginary piece of lint from the shoulder of his jacket, before turning him gently to face her.

"I'd love to, Melissa, but I have a clinic and I'm meeting Fay. Better not be late." He said, a smile not quite reaching his eyes.

"Well, darling, I hope you have better luck than I did this morning. She didn't turn up for our meeting. Rather rude, don't you think, sweetie?" Melissa turned and tapped her platinum credit card on the payment terminal.

"Fay?"

Daniel was puzzled. Why would Melissa Davenport be meeting his wife? A stab of apprehension shot through him. Was this one of her ploys to corner him? What had she been telling Fay? She may have lied and implied they were having an affair, which was simply not true. Daniel felt mortified. She could be extremely manipulative at times.

"Of course, dear. Everyone has a psychotherapist. Don't you? I see darling Fay regularly for therapy." She smiled thinly, almost patronisingly. "I just hope she won't miss another of my appointments."

Daniel was tempted to point out that Fay was actually a psychiatrist. She was not there to listen to her superficial problems but decided against it. No point in antagonising Melissa.

"Fay has been very busy lately," Daniel said politely. The mood felt distinctly different from the previous night, when Melissa, playing to the gallery, had been drunkenly fawning over him. He had hardly resisted, to his embarrassment.

"Not your fault, darling. Are you sure you won't join me for coffee?" Melissa squeezed his arm.

"I'd better get back," Daniel peeled back his sleeve and looked at his watch.

"Well, another time then." Melissa fixed him with her impossibly blue eyes, kissed his cheek and whispered. "I know you're playing hard to get but you won't be able to resist forever. You'll see."

Daniel backed away. The heavy scent of her perfume lingering unpleasantly in his nostrils. "Bye," he said simply and walked out of the café.

FOURTEEN

God, he could do without this right now, Daniel thought. Melissa was becoming persistent and why was she seeing Fay as a private patient? Fay hadn't said anything about it to him but why would she? She kept her patient's confidentiality, even with him, and he admired her professionalism. Maybe it was more of a status symbol for Melissa to be seeing a psychotherapist, as she'd called her, although in his opinion, she was probably was in need of some sort of therapy – a personality transplant would do it. He felt a little guilty. He enjoyed Melissa's attention when he'd had a few drinks. It was just harmless flirtation. But stone-cold sober, it could be awkward and irritating. He shouldn't be encouraging her, especially if he was contemplating working with her husband in this new cosmetic surgery clinic of his.

As Daniel walked back to the hospital, he tried to call Fay and once again, the call went straight to voicemail. He left another brief message asking her to call him as he was getting worried.

He'd been dismissive of his wife, thinking she was reacting to their row but was she alright? Why had it taken him so long to start worrying about her welfare? There was a bloody serial killer on the loose around this town and his wife had gone missing – why was it only now he was becoming concerned? She hadn't been at her clinic this morning, according to Melissa. Her mother hadn't seen her and neither had Ginny, his daughter-in-law. He should check with Meredith at Fay's clinic. Maybe she had turned up there.

He called the clinic landline number.

"Dr Kendrick's clinic. Meredith Baily speaking, how can I help you?" She sounded flustered.

Daniel switched the phone to his good ear. "Meredith, it's Daniel. Is Fay there?"

"No, Mr Kendrick, I haven't seen her since yesterday morning. I've had to cancel her appointments and some of the patients are not happy about it."

"Can you stay there and hold the fort? I will try and get down there later. Thanks Meredith." Daniel thought there might be a clue to her whereabouts in her office.

"I'll do my best," Meredith said before they rang off.

So, she wasn't at her clinic. Perhaps she was working at the prison? As Daniel walked toward the hospital, he searched the contacts in his phone for the number of a colleague and friend of Fay's. Perhaps she had seen her. He found the number and tapped 'call'.

Dr Shelly Winters answered after three rings. "Hello Daniel. How are things." She sounded as if she was eating her lunch.

"Shelly. I was wondering if you'd seen Fay in the last couple of days?" Daniel skipped the social pleasantries. He knew Shelly would understand.

"No Dan, I haven't seen her for a few weeks. What's the problem?"

"Probably nothing but she didn't come home last night and she hasn't been at her clinic either. I'm just trying to track her down." Daniel tried to sound nonchalant but he had to admit to himself, he was starting to feel anxious.

"Hang on I'll ask Doug – he's liaised with her recently."

Daniel could hear Shelly calling to Dr Doug Winters, another of Fay's psychiatric colleagues and Shelly's husband. He heard Doug's voice in the background but couldn't make out what he was saying above the roar of traffic. He covered his free ear with the palm of his hand.

Shelly came back on the line. "Dan, Doug said he saw her a few days ago to discuss one of his patients but not since. Have you tried calling Charlotte or Delyth?"

"No but it's worth a try. Thanks Shelly."

"Let us know how it goes."

Daniel said he would and rang off. He didn't have numbers for Fay's friends but they could be in her address book at home. He would try later. He crossed the road, wove through the car park of the hospital and in through the back door of his clinic. There were several patients queuing at the reception desk and others sat in a large waiting area, lined with blue plastic hospital chairs, vacantly staring at the television mounted on the wall. The BBC lunchtime news was just starting. Daniel felt agitated. The last thing he wanted to do was plough through a list of appointments. He didn't enjoy running clinics at the best of times. He'd much rather be operating – being at the coal face of surgery. But right now, he should be trying to find Fay.

Daniel smiled at one or two of the patients he passed as he strode into his office. One of the nurses had left a fancy, chocolate sprinkled cup-cake on his desk. He assumed it was for him and ate it gratefully, binning the wrapper and wiping his mouth with a paper towel from the dispenser.

The first patient on his list was David Jones. He was a proud, stoic man in his seventies recovering from a procedure to repair an inguinal hernia. Daniel had warmed to the man. Like him, he had nursed his wife through a terminal illness. Now living in a care home, he seemed to spend much of his time at the pub with his dog and, Daniel sensed, was probably lonely and seeking company and a sense of normality.

Daniel stepped out into the waiting room.

"David Jones, please." He waited. No response. "Mr Jones; David Jones." He saw the world-weary gentleman rise from his chair and waved his hand in acknowledgement before making his way, stooped in pain, into Daniel's consulting room.

"Hello doctor," David said breathlessly as he shuffled into the room, closing the door behind him. "How are you?"

Daniel's heart went out to him. "I'm fine Mr Jones. More to the point, how are you?" Daniel indicated for him to take a seat adjacent to his desk.

"Not so bad." David sat heavily, seemingly relieved to take the weight off his legs. He had obviously dressed smartly for his appointment. His usual donkey jacket replaced with an ancient but serviceable charcoal suit over a loud checked shirt and clashing red, patterned tie, mostly hidden behind a grey, grow-your-own-scarf kind of beard. He removed his flat cap, smoothed a hand over sparse white tufts of hair and smiled at Daniel.

Daniel could see he was in pain. "How have you been since I repaired your hernia?"

"The operation was fine – healed up nicely. It's just my arthritis giving me gip." David rubbed his knees and showed Daniel his gnarled hands.

"Are you having any treatment for that. With your GP perhaps?"

David waved a livered hand dismissively. "It's just old age. I'm fine." David was never one to make a fuss.

"Let's take a look at your wound. It's six weeks post op now, so hopefully, we can discharge you." Daniel indicated for his patient to lie on the paper-covered examination couch.

David got up from the chair and limped over to the couch, unzipped his trousers and lay down, pulling up his vest and shirt to expose a six-centimetre-long operation scar along his lower right abdomen. Daniel examined it and gently palpated around the area. The scar was a little lumpy but had healed well and there was no sign of the hernia re-occurring.

"That seems fine, Mr Jones." I think we can discharge you now. Daniel washed his hands at the basin in the corner of the room and dried them on paper towels from a dispenser.

David got up from the couch, tucked his shirt back into his trousers and zipped up.

"Any problems, come back and see us, but you should be fine now." Daniel smiled at his patient.

"Thank you, doctor. No offense but I hope I never see you again." David grinned and headed for the door.

Daniel returned a watery smile. He'd heard that joke a million times. "Goodbye Mr Jones, and see your GP about that arthritis."

David Jones waved another dismissive hand as he shuffled out into the waiting room.

Daniel looked up at the clock. It was 1.20 pm. It would take him at least three hours to get through the rest of his clinic appointments. Maybe he could call in a favour. He really needed to be looking for Fay and was feeling jittery from another evening on the booze.

Daniel called Matthew Clarke, his registrar, on the ward.

"Matt. How are things up there?"

"Pretty quiet this afternoon, so I thought I'd do a teaching session with some of the F2s," Matthew said.

"Excellent. Look, could you do me a favour and cover my afternoon post-op clinic. Should be straightforward and I'm on the other end of the phone if you need me. I think Colin is around too if you need a consultant."

Matthew hesitated for some moments then sighed. "Sure Daniel, I'll be right down. I'll take my bleep and be on-call for the ward. Is everything alright?"

"I hope so." Daniel didn't feel like explaining.

They rang off and Daniel went into the treatment room and told Debbie, the clinic nurse, that Dr Clarke would be covering his clinic. He thanked the nurses for the cake and went out into the waiting room. What he heard made his blood run cold.

FIFTEEN

Daniel stopped and turned to look at the TV. A news reporter was saying that there had been a double murder in the early hours of the morning – in Riverbeke. Two people, a man and a woman, had been shot and killed in their bed with a sawn-off shot gun by the woman's husband. A recently released prisoner from HMP Gallo Hill. His name was Jaxon Sloan and although police were searching for him – he was still on the run. Police, the reporter said, had put out a warning not to approach him as his prison mugshots flashed up on the screen. He looked a right thug, thought Daniel with his thick neck, piggy eyes set too close together in a square-looking head, accentuated by a close-cropped jailbird haircut. A Detective Chief Inspector was being interviewed and assured that everything was being done to find Sloan and get him back into custody. Resources were being drafted in from other areas and a police surveillance helicopter was searching the area. It was hoped that the new drones bought by West Midlands police could be brought down to help with the search. The reporter handed back to the studio and the newscaster went on to another story.

Shit.

Daniel felt a rush of anxiety. There was now a second murderer on the run around Riverbeke and his wife was missing. What the hell was going on? Could this killer be the same person that had killed those other four people?

No. Daniel remembered that the serial killer case had been ongoing for weeks now and this man, Jaxon Sloan, had apparently only just been released from prison. It seemed impossible that the killings were connected.

Daniel began to worry about Fay. He had to find her; to make sure she was safe. For all their disagreements and the distance between them lately, he still loved her. He slipped out through the back door of the clinic and headed for his car, parked in the consultant's bay.

Daniel eased the BMW out into the traffic and headed for home. First to check if Fay was there and then to go through her address book and make a few calls. If he had no luck there, he would go straight to her clinic in Park Road and talk to Meredith. Perhaps it was time to call the police and report her missing?

He pulled into the drive – still no sign of Fay's Mercedes. Maisie was meowing on the doorstep. She trotted over as he got out of the car; her tail held high as she greeted him.

"Hello, you," he said, bending to tickle under her chin. She responded by rubbing against his leg. "Are you missing your mum? I bet you are. Me too." He felt an unexpected rush of love for his wife.

They went into the house and Daniel poured more biscuits into Maisie's bowl and changed her water, which now had a film of fluff and cat hair floating over the surface. "There you go. That ought to keep you quiet." Maisie settled down and began to eat, crunching noisily and spilling bits of biscuit on the floor around her dish.

When Maisie had finished eating, he let Chester and Ella into the house, Ella was carrying her teddy bear, Eddie, in her mouth. They gave him their ritual, enthusiastic greeting and then settled down in the living room.

Daniel grabbed a Penguin from the biscuit tin, tore off the wrapper and ate it in three bites. He fished out Fay's address book from the kitchen drawer and flipped through the pages. He found Charlotte's number and then Delyth's. He called them both but neither of her friends had seen Fay in over three weeks.

Daniel decided to call his son, Richard. Maybe Fay was there or had said something that would give him a clue as to where she might be. He speed-dialled on the landline while he charged his mobile. The call was answered after five rings.

"Dad. How are you?" Richard sounded tired, his voice languid and monotonous.

"I was just calling to see how you and Ginny and my little grandson are doing." Daniel didn't want to worry the kids. They had enough on their plate with a young baby to take care of.

"We're fine thanks. Jon is keeping us awake at night but I guess that's OK. He's taking his feeds well and putting on weight. Ginny is taking him to the park in his new stroller this afternoon."

"Sound good. Fay's mother was asking when you are all going to visit."

"Well, one day, I guess. Things are a bit full-on at the moment. You know how it is."

"Sure, but make the effort, OK? She'd really like to see you and she's been very generous. Don't take it for granted." Daniel put his dad voice on.

"I'll do my best."

"By the way; have you seen Fay the last couple of days." Daniel tried to sound casual.

"No. Haven't seen her in a while. Not since we came over to your house for dinner. Must be three weeks at least. Is she still busy with work?"

"Yeah, always busy. Look, I'll leave you to it. We'll catch up soon alright and don't forget – visit your grandmother."

"Step grandmother."

"Whatever. Just visit."

"OK Dad."

Daniel raked his hair with his fingers. What to do next? He flipped through Fay's address book once more, searching for inspiration. Most of the numbers were for psychiatrists she worked with, a couple of hairdressers, the vet's, the cat groomer, the GP surgery, a taxi company, a few of their favourite restaurants, an electrician and the car mechanic.

He was out of ideas. It was time to call the police.

Daniel tried once more to call Fay's mobile but again, the call went to voicemail. He hung up without leaving a message. Then he looked up the number of the local police and was directed to the 101 non-emergency number.

"Sergeant Trevor Williams speaking. How can I help?"

"Sergeant, I need to report my wife missing." Daniel tried to stay calm. Calling the police suddenly made it seem all the more serious. He paced the floor as he spoke.

"Can you give me some details please?"

"Yes, of course."

"Firstly, can I take your name, address and telephone number."

"Dr Daniel Kendrick. Number 5, Bramble Lane, Riverbeke. 074089 40066."

"And you say your wife is missing?"

"That's right, her name is Fay Kendrick. Dr Fay Kendrick. She's a forensic psychiatrist."

"Where does she work?"

"She has a private clinic at 107, Park Road, Riverbeke, and she also works at Gallow Hill and Ravenwood prisons and at the psychiatric hospital." Daniel wandered across to the window. Still no sign of her coming home.

"Thank you. And can you give me a description of her appearance."

"She is around five foot five, slim, long blond hair, which she usually wears up. She's a very beautiful woman." Daniel held an image of her in his mind; beaming with happiness on their wedding day. He could hear the tapping of keyboards.

"What was she wearing when you last saw her?"

Daniel had to think. Was it the floral dress or the linen skirt and blouse? "I'm pretty sure she was wearing a floral dress. Pink colours. And sandals." He paced back and forth the living room.

There was a pause while sergeant Williams recorded the information with more tapping of keys. "Now, how long has she been missing?"

"Since yesterday morning."

"And have you asked around her family and friends and checked the places she may have visited. Her workplace, for example?" The officer sounded polite and professional.

"Yes, I've called around everyone I can think of. I'm going to go to her clinic this afternoon." Daniel wandered into the kitchen, opened the refrigerator, took out a carton of orange juice and drank from the carton, spilling some down his shirt.

"That's a good idea. Now, does your wife have any medical conditions?"

"None that I know of."

"Has she ever gone missing before?"

"No. Never."

"Now, could I take the registration number of her car."

Daniel had to think again, but remembered Fay's number plate and gave it to the sergeant.

There was a pause while the police officer accessed Fay's number plate in the DVLA – Driver and Vehicle Licencing Agency – database.

"That's coming up as a Silver Mercedes SLK convertible. Is that correct?"

"Yes, that's Fay's car."

"Right, well it's not been reported stolen and there's no record of a road traffic accident."

"That's a relief," Daniel said, perching on a stool in the kitchen and taking another swig of orange juice. Maisie jumped onto the counter and Daniel stroked her back.

"That's it for now. Perhaps you'd send me a photograph of your wife and I will record her as missing and get this information circulated around other UK police forces in the next 48 hours."

"Can't it be done any sooner?" Daniel was anxious and 48 hours seemed way too long to wait.

"I'll try my best, sir, but we are extremely busy at the moment."

"I understand, but there's a murderer with a sawn-off shotgun on the loose in the area, so I'm sure you will realise how worried I am for my wife's safety." Maisie jumped down onto the floor and went over to her dish for more biscuits.

"Yes, sir. I can assure you we are doing our utmost to apprehend the perpetrator of the shootings and I will get these details circulated as quickly as I can. These things take time. Please let us know if the situation changes or if you think of anything further that might assist us in finding your wife."

"Thank you. I will."

The sergeant gave Daniel the email address to send the photograph and they ended the call. What more could he do? He felt helpless. He walked over to his laptop, opened the lid and searched for a recent photograph of Fay. He found three that were suitable, two headshots and a full-length picture, taken at a friend's wedding ten months ago. He emailed them all to the address he'd been given.

Daniel looked at the photographs of Fay, he realised the cracks had already begun to show in their relationship. Why hadn't he seen it? Why hadn't he done more to keep their marriage together?

SIXTEEN

16 days ago

Jack Butler couldn't have known he was about to die as he sat in his local pub. It probably wasn't the way he would have chosen to spend his last day on Earth. Neither would he have chosen the distressing way he was about to die.

Jack Butler was a liar. He lied about anything and everything – a pathological liar his parole officer had called him. He compulsively lied to his victims before raping them. For him, it was ludicrously easy to invent a new persona; a new life story where he could be whoever he wanted to be as the fancy took him. Once he'd pretended to be an airline pilot. That had been fun, and the women he targeted had lapped it up, imagining a life of jet-setting luxury if they were fortunate enough to get involved with him. So gullible. So easy to impress. Over the years, he'd developed a nose for sniffing out the gold-diggers, the shallow, insipid harlots that prostituted themselves to gain financially from him; or rather the character he pretended to be. They had never suspected the truth; that he was a loser, interested only in boundless self-gratification. He'd been too shrewd and elusive to allow anyone to uncover the truth. Although the harlots had been fun to begin with, there was no contest, his primal instincts to hunt and pursue had remained unchallenged. And so, he had begun to find another breed of prey; women who put up a fight. They were far more exciting and satisfying to conquer. He liked them young and innocent too. It gave him a sense of power; of exploration. Surprisingly few had complained – especially the young ones. Instead, they avoided him afterwards, silenced by their own sense of humiliation. That suited him just fine. Once he'd raped his victim, he preferred to move onto the next conquest anyway. Someone new and different every time.

Butler sat in the far corner of the beer garden nursing his pint of local brew, the cocaine he'd snorted earlier had kicked in nicely. It was a perfect spot for selecting his next victim. It was a good vantage point, semi-hidden in the corner by tubs of giant foliage. The place was filling up with people; mainly groups of young women; friends meeting for a drink before moving on to the nightclub in town. The noise level increased as more people joined the throng of happy, jovial partygoers. He would take his pick of the women with any potential and follow them later in the evening: he already had his sights set on a slim young blonde with endless tanned legs, covered only by a skimpy skirt. He could barely tear his gaze from her as she chatted animatedly with a group of friends. He would pursue her and make his move but for now, he was enjoying the view and the charged social atmosphere.

It was unfortunate that his latest victim had been injured so badly. He didn't think he'd been more rough than usual but she had put up an admirable fight. He hadn't even realised she had taken herself off to the hospital A&E until the police came knocking on his door late at night. The court case had been unpleasant to say the least and the judge had been unfairly biased in her sentencing but he'd served his time as a model prisoner and been released early for good behaviour. He'd learned new skills in brick-laying and even came out with an

NVQ qualification that would set him up in a new job with a local company. All in all, that had proved worthwhile but he would be careful not to get caught again. He didn't relish the prospect of another custodial sentence. Maybe he should return to those women that were easier prey; for a while at least.

Butler sat sipping his final beer, oblivious to the fact that he would never again rape another woman – easy prey or otherwise. The killer had followed Butler to the pub and had come well prepared and ready to strike. Weaving stealthily through the crowds and careful to blend in, the killer approached Butler with a smile. Butler reciprocated with a thin smile of his own. It was only polite to acknowledge someone you knew after all. They exchanged a few pleasantries before the killer pretended to stumble, spilling iced lemonade on Butler's chinos and shoes. Butler bent to see what had happened, attempting to mop up the cold, sticky liquid and prevent any damage to his best threads.

The victim was now conveniently distracted and the killer took the opportunity to slip a mega-dose of powdered ketamine from a small paper pouch into the victim's beer. It was ironic that the drug was used by veterinarians to anesthetise animals, since in the killer's opinion, Butler was nothing more than an animal driven by his primal instincts and devoid of any kind of human moral compass. It was also, poignantly, a drug used in date rape. A pertinent ending for him then. The killer had to stop him before he harmed another innocent young woman; robbing her of her self-esteem and forever tainting her perception of men, however decent they were and however hard she tried to overcome it. The killer made the appropriate fuss over the spilled lemonade before retreating unnoticed by others from the pub's beer garden. It was about to become a murder scene.

Butler cursed after his killer for the spilled lemonade but soon settled to continue his vigil, oblivious to the fact that he was about to die. Irritated by the incident, he took a long swig of his beer, followed by another. The ketamine had been ingested just as the killer had intended. Within minutes, Jack Butler became woozy and disorientated, at first putting the effects down to the beer. But as he reached for his pint once more, his arm shook uncontrollably and he was unable to grip the glass with his hand. He felt a tremor in his legs and before him appeared the ghostly image of countless women reaching out to him, knives prodding at his face; their faces angry and vengeful. The hallucinations solidified and lurched alarmingly at him as Butler became further disorientated and disassociated from his own body. He was aware of the people around him, chatting and laughing, yet he was completely unable to move or call for help. His body was paralysed and horrifyingly, he felt the paralysis creep up through his chest. His breathing became shallow, yet even as he fought for air, his lungs refused to inflate, as if the life was being crushed from him by a giant boa constrictor. For long minutes, Butler watched, helpless and incapacitated as the sinister hallucinations that had welled up from his subconscious tormented him. Finally, the synergy of alcohol, cocaine and ketamine played out and the welcome blackness of unconsciousness and death released him permanently from his suffering.

SEVENTEEN

Tuesday 20th August 2019

It was late in the morning and the sound of the postman pushing a few envelopes through the door of Damon Wixx's flat roused him from a deep slumber. He must have fallen asleep on the sofa, having sunk more than a few cans of lager the previous evening as well as over half a bottle of vodka. Sure enough, the evidence was strewn around him as he glanced around his living room.

Now he had a crick in his neck and a thick head to go with it. The TV was churning out a news story. Oblivious to the noise in his drunken stupor, it must have been on all night with the surround sound reverberating through his cramped maisonette.

There had been no further developments on a murder case. A man had been found dead in the beer garden of a trendy pub in the town under suspicious circumstances. A barmaid had discovered him slumped in his chair while she had been collecting glasses and was being comforted by her employers. None of the pub's clientele had noticed anything untoward throughout the evening – they had probably thought he was drunk. The screen flicked to a photograph of the dead man and Damon's eyes widened.

"Shit, that's Jack Butler," Damon said aloud. He'd known him in prison a few years back and they were both in Fay's group therapy sessions. Convicted for paedophilia and GBH if he remembered rightly. Never liked the guy. He was always an arrogant know-all, forever brawling with the other inmates. No finesse. Damon thought he deserved to die.

The newscaster turned to the next story and Damon shrugged and flicked the TV off with the remote control. What did he care about a dead paedo – probably got what he deserved, Damon thought sarcastically. He tended to look for the bad in everyone. It was why his many casual relationships never worked out.

He rasped a hand over his stubbled chin. His body was aching and stiff and his mouth was bone dry. He grunted, hauled himself from the sofa and went into the bathroom. A brief glance in the mirror revealed how dreadful he felt. Dishevelled hair, grey eyes sunken and bloodshot. He combed his hair with his fingers and scowled at his reflection. He was a mess. His whole life was a mess. He believed the world was against him and it was anyone's fault but his own that he'd failed to achieve even a modicum of success.

Yet, he was blind to the oxymoron that had defined his life. In his delusional contempt for others, he believed he was a superior human being to almost everyone he met. Envy and contempt were polar opposites that sprang from the narcissism that formed the basis of Damon's state of being. He wanted what others had yet at the same time, distained it.

Damon brushed his teeth and drank from his cupped hands – a long slurp of cool water that chilled his stomach but barely began to quench his thirst. He took a fifteen-minute shower, shaved, then dressed in faded denim jeans and a black T-shirt. He made a mug of strong tea, stirred in three heaped sugars and strolled into the living room. He picked up Dr Kendrick's manuscript and wandered with it into his bedroom. The tiny room was cluttered and stuffy, the unmade bedsheets grubby and stained. Dirty clothes were strewn everywhere and the carpet was sticky from larger spills.

Damon placed the manuscript on the bedside cupboard and looked up to admire his handiwork. Covering the walls was a collage of tattered photographs, printouts and press clippings of Dr Kendrick. They had been stuck straight onto the damp-stained magnolia emulsion with Blu Tack. Most of the photographs had been copied from her infrequent social media posts but some he'd taken surreptitiously with his mobile phone camera during their sessions.

Damon scanned the wall to find a snapshot of her husband; Daniel Kendrick. His dark eyes narrowed as he reviled the surgeon; a feeling of utter loathing welling uncontrollably in his gut. He hated the fact that Daniel had something – someone – that he wanted for himself. What was so special about him – apart from his money and his privilege – that he deserved to have her as his wife? Soon, he consoled himself, Daniel Kendrick would be dead and gone.

Damon turned his attention to Fay Kendrick's photograph – the one he'd taken in her office when she'd been preoccupied on the phone. She looked feminine; vulnerable. It would be incredibly easy for him to physically overpower her.

Those familiar emotions surfaced again – a predator's obsession with its prey. It was a game he liked to play with Dr Kendrick. She would ask him questions about himself and he would smirk smugly as he evaded them. He knew just how to use his glib charm to manipulate her into feeling sympathy for him. He was the supreme master of smoke and mirrors; of getting her to see only what he wanted her to see.

He became bored and frustrated with the psychobabble and questionnaires attempting to assess his personality. What did it matter how securely or insecurely attached to his mother he was, for god's sake? He didn't give a damn that his psychopathy scores were through the roof. He didn't give a toss about that stuff and always lied about it anyway. He could easily waste a whole session playing on her emotional reactions and leading Dr Kendrick down the proverbial garden path with his cunning convolutions and fabricated answers to her questions. He enjoyed being around her with the thrill of luring her in with his charm. An educated woman like that was a challenge, for sure, but he knew how to play on her professional concern for his welfare. He would give her a few crumbs of hope that she was making progress with his so-called therapy and she continued to 'help' him. He knew it was all based on lies. He had absolutely no intention of changing. Why would he? He liked the person he was. He simply enjoyed fuelling his fantasies of possessing her. She was no more than a pleasant diversion for him. Once he tired of the game, he would dispose of her.

Damon ran his scabby-nailed fingers along the photographs of Dr Kendrick he had amassed over the years that he had been seeing her. It had almost been worth doing time in prison, as he would never have had dealings with Dr Kendrick outside of the forensic psychiatry department. How would their paths ever have crossed? He had to admit, he'd become obsessed with her. She intrigued him like no other woman ever had. She had been the only person in his life that had shown him compassion.

What he enjoyed the most was seeing her expression turn from dispassionate and sombre to one of sympathetic concern as he faked some tragic childhood experience that was allegedly haunting him. Some of it had a grain of truth, like the verbal and physical abuse he'd suffered as a child at the hands of his drunken father. Yet his exaggerated storytelling elevated his suffering way beyond the truth. He had made it the scape goat for his abhorrent psychopathic behaviour as an adult. He could pretend it wasn't his fault, just as every other misfortune that had ever happened in his life was not his fault. He seemed to be pretty effective at convincing her of that. He also found it ridiculously easy to complicate the issues and draw her away from her pet theories about his deviant personality.

He liked to turn on the charm and play on her empathy. He could sense her softening toward him and knew she was searching for reasons to absolve him of the evil motivations so many others accused him of. Was that why he'd become so obsessed with her? She had seen into the blackness of his soul, yet she had not turned away like others had done. She sought the good in him, looked for reasons to believe in him. He managed to convince her that he was capable of changing. That was her mission, she was a doctor driven to cure him and prevent him from re-offending. He'd been given a label; a psychopath, but he didn't believe it was true. If it was, he didn't care. It was just a label.

He was looking forward to their appointment.

Damon left his flat, squinted against the bright sunshine and walked along the landing toward the lift. The Bichon Frise from the flat next door leapt out of a doorway and stood its ground, growling and yapping like a demented Tasmanian devil. What should have been a snow-white silken coat was badly matted and filthy, its corkscrew curls long and tangled from a lack of grooming. His face had black tear stains from weeping eyes and the hair around his mouth was stiff and brown with dried-on food. What had once been a gentle, sweet-natured and affectionate puppy, had become a frightened and self-defensive adult, dripping with feisty arrogance through no fault of his own. The dog went for Damon's ankle and he roughly shoved him aside with his boot. He'd often fantasised about drowning the creature in a bucket or slitting his throat.

"Shut up Gizmo," a woman's gravelly, irritated voice emanated from the flat next door.

The dog rebounded and continued to yap and nip at his heels as he followed Damon along the landing. Damon turned and kicked it hard across its flank and this time it retreated, yelping in pain. A self-satisfied smirk played across Damon's lips and he shrugged when an old woman scowled at him as she passed, intimidated into silence.

EIGHTEEN

Tuesday 20th August 2019

Daniel shut the dogs into the Dog House, double checked the house was locked and drove through their village, skirting around the middle of the busy town to Park Road. He managed to park sixty yards from Fay's clinic in the tree-lined street of large, three-story Victorian houses. He scanned up and down the street. There was no sign of Fay's Mercedes. He entered the clinic to see Meredith scribbling in the appointment book. She looked up when she heard him close the door.

"Mr Kendrick." She sounded relieved to see him.

"Any news?" He caught her staring at the gash on his cheek but nothing was said.

"No, nothing. I can't understand where Dr Kendrick could have gone. She always lets me know what's happening or if she's going to be late." Meredith was uncharacteristically dressed in casual clothes. No sign of the thick make-up, tottering heels and short skirts that she usually wore. Now she wore skinny jeans and a loose white cotton shirt with flat strappy sandals. She was obviously struggling to field calls from patients, parole officers, Fay's colleagues as well as juggle appointments.

"I've called the police and reported her missing. In the meantime, can I have a look at her appointments for the past few days? Maybe there's a clue there somewhere." Daniel walked behind the reception desk and Meredith passed him the book.

He flicked through the pages for the past week. There were several patients booked in, taking up most of each day.

"What does this 'PP' mean next to some of the names?" Daniel asked, pointing to Melissa's name. Daniel twisted his head toward her. There was a slight but distracting buzzing in his left ear.

Meredith looked closer. "That's our code for Private Patient."

"And the other codes?"

"Mostly psychiatric patients from the hospital or the prisons." Meredith said. "The 'GH' next to the name is Gallow Hill and the 'RW' is for the Ravenwood prisoners. The others are usually from the psychiatric hospital. We put their appointments in the book but obviously, she goes out to see them. Only the ones who have been released from prison or discharged from hospital come here.

"But I thought she mostly saw private patients now." Daniel, with the help of her mother, had persuaded Fay to build up her private clientele rather than put herself at risk by treating dangerous criminals. She had agreed after an incident at the prison where one of her colleagues, Norman Ridley, had been potted – had faeces thrown at him – and an inmate had tried to strangle him with his bare hands. It had taken four prison officers to release Norman from the stranglehold.

"No, most of her patients are prisoners or ex-convicts." Meredith looked up at Daniel with a small frown, as if he should have known that.

Daniel felt resentful. Fay had assured him she was seeing more private patients these days. The likes of Melissa seeking psychotherapy, he'd assumed. He flicked back further in the appointment book and there were a few marked with a 'PP' but many more with 'GH' or 'RW'. Quite a few were hospital patients too.

Daniel was checking through the appointment book as the main door opened and a man walked into the reception area. He was in his thirties, average build, around five foot eleven with sandy coloured close-cropped hair and arms plastered in tribal tattoos. He glared at Daniel then turned his attention to Meredith.

"I'm here for my 3 pm appointment." He said flatly.

"Mr Wixx. I've been trying to call you but you don't seem to have a signal."

Damon reached for his phone to check his signal as if he didn't believe her. After a few moments, he asked, "What's up?"

"I'm afraid I have to cancel your appointment again. I'm sorry you've had a wasted journey." Meredith said apologetically.

"What am I supposed to do now?" Damon Wixx squared up to Meredith. He wasn't a happy bunny.

"I'm sorry, I wish I could have saved you the journey here. I can only apologise."

Daniel looked up from the appointment book and scowled at Wixx. The man narrowed his eyes and stared back at Daniel with pure venom, as if he hated him to the core. Daniel looked away. He was one angry son-of-a-bitch and the last thing he wanted to do was provoke him. So, this is the type of patient Fay is seeing all day every day, is it? Daniel thought. Aggressive, arrogant and rude. No wonder she's so stressed.

"Yeah, well, that would've been good. So, where is she?" Wixx was saying, a gratuitously arrogant tone to his voice.

The tension in the room intensified.

"I'm afraid I can't say," Meredith said politely and calmly. "Shall I call you when we have an appointment for you. That would save you another wasted journey."

Damon shrugged his shoulders. He just stood there defiantly. "So where is Dr Kendrick? I have a right to know."

Meredith looked decidedly uncomfortable. "She's missing. The police have been informed."

Daniel glared at Meredith, warning her not to say any more. He didn't want that arrogant little twerp knowing his business and it was certainly not his right to know.

"What do you mean missing?" He persisted.

"I can't say any more, I'm sorry. I'll call you in a few days." Meredith was visibly squirming now.

Damon Wixx simply scowled at Daniel, turned on his heel and walked out. The relief in the room, after he left, was palpable.

"Who the hell is that?" Daniel asked.

"Damon Wixx. He's one of Fay's ex-convict patients. He was sent by his parole officer to have therapy but he's a no-hoper I think."

"No kidding." Daniel rolled his eyes and ran a finger down the list of appointments.

He found the name Damon Wixx written in for several appointments over the past few weeks. Then there was one for yesterday, late morning, and now this afternoon. Could he have had something to do with her disappearance? But why would he turn up here for an appointment yesterday and again today if he knew she wouldn't be here? He could be covering his tracks – it could be an act to give him an alibi, Daniel thought cynically. As a criminal, he would be up to all the tricks.

"So, what's his story?" Daniel asked.

Meredith shrugged. "All I know is that he's a psychopath. Don't think much can be done to change that from what Dr Kendrick has said. She's had dealings with him for years and tried her best with him but I can tell she doesn't like him. He scares the life out of me, to be honest." Meredith shivered exaggeratedly.

"I'm not surprised," Daniel said staring at the door as if he might walk back in itching for a fight.

Daniel thought for some minutes. "I'll have a look in Fay's consulting room." Perhaps he would find clues there.

Daniel went over to Fay's office and pushed the door open. The room was light, bright and welcoming, with cream-painted walls and a patterned burgundy carpet. Two large armchairs were turned toward one another with a low round wooden coffee table between them. A box of tissues and Fay's reading glasses lay on the table. A walnut desk, a gift from her grandmother, was positioned near a bay window at the other end of the room. The Victorian window had authentic-looking white shutters installed on either side. On the desk was her briefcase. Daniel walked over to it and lifted the front flap. Inside were a sheaf of papers which he pulled out. The top one was a referral letter from the court for a Mrs Amanda Huntly who was depressed and suicidal after being sentenced to three years in jail. Daniel placed it on the desk. Next, a letter asking her to be an expert witness at a trial, something she did regularly. Then, he found some handwritten notes about another patient, Justin McCartney.

REFERR TO DR MADDISON. LIKELY
DISASSOCIATIVE IDENTITY DISORDER.
TRY FOR AN URGENT SECTION –
PSYCHOTIC EPISODE?

Daniel placed the notes on the desk. He dropped the pile of papers when he saw what was up next.

YOU MUST DIE YOU WORTHLESS PIECE OF CRAP

Each chilling word had been cut out from newspapers and magazines and glued onto a sheet of paper like some sort of cliched scene from an old crime movie. Daniel stepped back in horror. This looked like a death threat aimed at his wife. All the warnings that he and her mother had given her came rushing back to him. Now her life actually could be in danger. He felt sick with worry, putting his hand out to steady himself on the chair. He touched Fay's colourful chiffon scarf and recoiled in horror as he realised it was covered in coagulated blood.

NINETEEN

Damon stood in Fay's clinic and automatically searched his mind, checking what he'd been up to recently that might attract the attention of the police. What if Dr Kendrick had reported him for stalking her? He had been careful not to be seen but he had a feeling she knew he'd been following her and it had been going on for a while. He'd made that clumsy premature pass at her just days ago at their last meeting. People – society – didn't like that.

While on parole, Damon knew his every move was being scrutinised. One slip-up could land him right back in the slammer. Even if Dr Kendrick hadn't reported him to the police, she could have written derogatory comments in his notes and if he was suspected of having something to do with her disappearance, they would have the right to access his medical records. Not that he cared a damn but his plans for Dr Kendrick would be in tatters if he ended up behind bars again. It was an inconvenience he would rather avoid.

Damon suddenly felt the need to get out of there.

He turned and walked out of Dr Kendrick's office and into the leafy, sunlit suburb. He had to get back to the flat. The police

93

would find out he was one of the last people to see her and would likely be paying him a visit. He thought of the wall filled with photographs of Dr Kendrick that no doubt they'd consider creepy. People tended to think of him like that. Then there was her manuscript that he'd stolen and the modest stash of drugs he had hidden in his bedroom – some of them class A cocaine and ecstasy that he was selling on the estate. Bad news if he was found in possession. It would be obvious he was dealing.

Damon rolled a joint, lit it and walked back to his flat on the other side of town. The police were on their way to Dr Kendrick's office and no doubt they would want to talk to him given his criminal record and his association with the doctor. He knew the police had every right to search his flat without a warrant and he had stuff to jettison.

Damon negotiated his way through the crowds along High Street. There was a public demonstration taking place – something about animal rights, as far as he could gather. It seemed peaceful enough with a large crowd of high-spirited people dressed in farm animal costumes and carrying placards with 'Stop Live Transport' plastered all over them.

Damon sneered at the protesters, tossed the butt of his splif in the gutter and weaved his way between them, deftly avoiding the leaflets that were being handed out. Finally, he managed to get clear; dodging a group of police officers that had been keeping a friendly eye on the demonstrators. They seemed to be engrossed in conversation and happily enjoying the warm sunshine but he still gave them a wide berth. His inherent contempt for the authorities put the police at the top of his hate list.

Damon reached his estate, walked along the precinct past Richie Finch, squandering his benefit money in the betting shop, and turned into Bridgeman Tower. He rode the foul-smelling elevator as it rattled its way to the third floor and let himself into his flat. He had work to do if, as he suspected, the police were planning to pay him a visit.

Gizmo, the grubby Bichon Frise from next door was yapping and whining as usual and Damon could hear him clearly through the thin walls of the flat. He guessed the dog had been shut in while his owner was out. He hated the scrawny animal with a vengeance, especially when it crapped right outside his front door. He vowed to do something about it, and soon. For now, he had to focus on disposing of any incriminating evidence before the police arrived on his doorstep.

Damon took one last look at the photographs of Dr Kendrick. The infatuation and yearning he'd felt for her was turning to irritation. He pulled the photographs from the wall, ripping some of them into tiny pieces. His eyes rested on a photograph of Daniel Kendrick and he felt pure jealous anger and hatred swell in his gut. He ripped it from the wall and crumpled it into a tight ball. Daniel Kendrick had to die.

He took the other the photographs down, not noticing that one, of Fay, had fallen onto the floor, partially hidden under the bed. He grabbed the pile of photographs and took them into the bathroom. One by one, he tore them into tiny pieces and tossed them into his filthy, shit covered toilet bowl.

TWENTY

Tuesday 20th August 2019

Where was she? Was she even still alive? Dear God what the hell had happened to her. Daniel felt the nausea rise in his throat as he grabbed his phone and tapped out a number. His bloodied fingers were trembling.

"Sergeant Trevor Williams please. I have to speak to him urgently."

"Sergeant Williams. How can I help?"

"Sergeant, it's Daniel Kendrick. We spoke earlier about my wife, Fay. She's gone missing."

"Yes, Mr Kendrick. I remember. Have you found her?"

"No but I'm in her office and have just found a death threat from one of her psychiatric patients. Her life could be in danger. I also have her scarf and it's covered in blood." Daniel was shaking as he waited for the police officer to respond.

"Alright Mr Kendrick. Please don't touch anything. Leave everything as you have found it and don't let anyone else disturb anything. You are in her office, you say?"

"Yes, at 107, Park Road, Riverbeke."

"Ah yes, I have that on my records. Wait there and I will send an officer out to see you. Hopefully in the next hour or so."

"Thank you. Please hurry."

Daniel rang off and rushed straight out of Fay's consulting room, through reception to the men's toilet and vomited into the bowl. He felt like his whole stomach had turned inside out. He wiped his mouth with the back of his hand, the reek of puke and bile in his nostrils. He flushed and went to the basin to rinse his mouth of the acidic taste, wash the blood from his hands and splash cold water on his face.

His mind was racing. Where the bloody hell was she? What had happened to her? Was that psychotic patient responsible? Had he carried out his death threat and killer her? Was it that arrogant bastard Wixx? Could he even be the serial killer that was on the loose? Questions hurled through his brain as he tried to get control of his thoughts. He looked up to see his own reflection in the mirror. His eyes had become dark pits of dread. Tension was etched into his face and the cut across his cheek was a stark reminder of the discord in their marriage. Yet despite all their problems, all he wanted was to hold Fay in his arms and tell her he loved her. That he was sorry they had rowed and that he wanted to shield her from all this. He felt he couldn't protect her when she was out there, putting herself in danger. In his distress, he just wanted to wrap her in cotton wool and keep her at home where she would be safe.

Daniel grabbed a paper towel from the dispenser and wiped his face. Hadn't they been through enough? Their baby girl had been abducted and murdered and their lives as well as their marriage ruined because of it. Wasn't that more than enough for any couple to take? As he looked into his own eyes, he felt lonelier than ever. He couldn't lose Fay. He had lost his first wife to cancer. That had been traumatic enough. But then to lose his baby and now the distinct possibility of losing Fay. That would be more than any human could be expected to endure. Wasn't it?

Daniel gripped each side of the cold porcelain basin and stared into his own hazel eyes. He had to get control. He had to be strong for Fay. He would help the police to find her and do everything he could to bring her back to him safe and alive. And when she did return to him, he would hold her tight and never let go.

Feeling stronger and buoyed by his determination to find Fay, Daniel straightened his shirt and went out into the reception area. Meredith was just finishing up a call.

She looked up at him with concern. "Are you alright Mr Kendrick?"

Daniel shook his head. "I've just found something in Fay's office. I've called the police again. They're on their way."

"Oh my god. What is it?" Meredith's eyes widened.

"I found a death threat. I think it was from a patient."

Meredith opened her mouth to speak but no words came out. Her hand flashed to cover it.

"That's not all," Daniel said sombrely. "Her scarf was covered in blood."

Meredith stood in shock, unable to speak for several moments. "Oh, my god. That's awful." She sat at the reception desk, visibly shaken, her face suddenly drained of colour.

"We'll have to wait for the police."

"Yes, of course," Meredith said, her voice quivering.

The next thirty-five minutes passed agonisingly slowly as Daniel waited for a police officer to get to Fay's clinic. He had called around all the local hospitals but there was no sign of her. He paced in the reception area, then he paced back and forth to the window in Fay's consulting room. He had been told not to touch anything and although he was dying to take a look through the rest of the papers on her desk and through the drawers for possible clues, he resisted. His fingerprints would be over everything and that might jeopardise the police investigation.

He decided to call his surgical registrar to check all was well at the hospital. He should have finished the clinic by now.

Matthew answered the call. "Daniel. How are things?"

"Not good to be honest, Matt. Fay has gone missing and I'm waiting for the police."

"Hell – I didn't expect to hear that. Do you think she'll be OK?" Matthew sounded shocked at the news.

"Hope so. We'll have to see. I trust you'll keep this to yourself." Daniel already regretted giving Matthew information. He knew how rapidly gossip travelled among the hospital staff. He paced to the window for the umpteenth time.

"Of course."

"How are things there? How was the clinic?"

"Fine, pretty routine. One nasty wound infection and someone swinging the lead wanting more time off work but mostly straightforward. I discharged a few patients for you. Hope that was in order."

"Of course. Thanks Matt. How about the ward. Any problems there?" Daniel paced back out to the reception area, where Meredith was sat at her desk watching him; obviously still shaken by the development.

"Nope. All well up here. By the way, there was a visit from the consultant anaesthetist – Dr Khan, asking about those missing drugs from the anaesthetic room and whether we'd heard anything more. I told him no. Apparently, he's doing his own investigation. He's like a bloody dog with a bone – this happened at least a month ago. I thought it would have been sorted by now."

"Yeah; Kahn can be pretty determined. Still, it's a serious incident with pancuronium and ketamine missing but I would have thought they'd found the culprit by now." Daniel sat briefly but stood again, like a loaded spring.

Matt sounded like he was speaking to someone on the ward with his hand over the receiver. There was a delay of a few moments. "Sorry, Dan. Yeah, sounds like someone is having a nicking spree for some reason."

"Sounds like it. Anyway, you seem to have things under control. I can't see me getting in tomorrow – I have to find Fay. Can you rearrange my theatre list? Apart from a few electives, I don't think there's anything that requires my attention for a day or so and Colin will be around." Daniel walked back into Fay's office, peering through the window again.

"Will do. Hope they find Fay soon."

"Me too. Thanks Matt. You know where I am if you need anything."

Daniel ended the call and walked back out into reception.

"Shall I make some coffee?" Meredith asked, seemingly at a loss to know what to do.

"That sounds like a good idea." Daniel gave her a thin smile and resumed his pacing back and forth.

Daniel flicked through the appointment book again, trying to find something – anything – that might provide a clue as to what had happened to Fay but there was nothing that jumped out at him. Instinctively, he grabbed a scrap of paper and made a list of all the patients she had seen over the past two weeks. He pocketed the note.

"There you go Dr Kendrick." Meredith handed Daniel a steaming mug of coffee. She offered a packet of Hob Nobs.

Daniel took his coffee, declined a biscuit, wandered into Fay's office and looked out of the window once again. A smartly dressed man was walking up the front steps, carrying a folder. He went back out into reception and put his coffee mug down on the desk. The policeman walked in through the main door and closed it behind him. He was well over six-foot tall with thick greying hair, average build with a slight paunch. He wore an immaculate charcoal grey suit over an open necked white shirt and wore highly polished black shoes. He exuded an aura of authority and smelled faintly of expensive cologne.

"I'm looking for Mr Daniel Kendrick," the officer said.

Daniel stepped forward and extended his hand. "I'm Daniel Kendrick."

The policeman's warm hand engulfed his own with a firm handshake. He glanced at the cut on Daniel's cheek. "Detective Sergeant Ian Harper," he said. "I'm your initial investigating officer."

"Good to meet you."

The DS looked at Meredith.

"This is Meredith Baily; my wife's receptionist," Daniel said. They too shook hands.

"Please; come into Fay's office. I'll show you what I've found."

DS Harper followed Daniel into the consulting room. Meredith held back for a few moments then hovered near the door.

Daniel showed him the briefcase and the death threat, then Fay's scarf, still over the back of the chair. They avoided touching the items at DS Harper's request. Daniel was asked to stand back.

The DS took a pair of blue latex gloves from his pocket and snapped them on. He moved around the desk, then the room, assessing the situation. Then he crouched low to the ground peering at the carpet at the side of the desk.

"Looks like we might have blood on the carpet as well."

Daniel felt his stomach clench then plummet. It felt as if he'd swallowed a brick. He hadn't seen any blood against the burgundy carpet and had probably walked right through it – several times. He tried to see over the DS's shoulder but the policeman stood, causing him to step back.

"How did you find these items initially?" Harper asked.

Daniel explained that the briefcase was on the desk and that he had opened it and removed the papers. He didn't know what lay beneath the note containing the death threat.

"But you touched it?"

Daniel thought for a moment. "I probably touched it at the edges but dropped it when I saw what it was. It was underneath a note in my wife's handwriting about referring a patient named Justin McCartney. It seems like he was having a psychotic episode."

"OK, sir, we should take this death threat seriously and get an investigation underway. I'll get the SOCOs – Scenes of Crime Officers – in here to process and document the crime scene. Then we can get to the rest of these papers. I'll take down some more details and I will get this reviewed with a detective inspector as soon as possible," DS Harper said.

They closed the door to Fay's consulting room as they left then sat in reception while DS Harper made a few calls.

"The SOCOs are on their way and I've informed Detective Inspector Emma Oakes that we have a potential risk of harm to your wife."

Suddenly, the danger to Fay became very real. Meredith sat silently watching the detective, her face ashen.

"Let's get some details from you Mr Kendrick and from you Miss Baily." The detective opened his folder and began to write. He reiterated some of the information Daniel had given Sergeant Williams, which Daniel confirmed.

Daniel took a deep breath, trying to steady his tattered nerves.

"Which of you was the last to see Dr Kendrick?"

Daniel and Meredith looked at one another. Daniel indicated for Meredith to say something first.

"I saw her last Friday evening about 5.30 pm, when I left work for the weekend. I worked a half day yesterday, starting at 1 pm." She was wringing her hands as she spoke.

"And she was gone by then?" The DS didn't look up from his folder.

"Yes."

"Thank you. Now, was there anything about Dr Kendrick's behaviour or anything she said that was out of the ordinary?"

Meredith tilted her head and looked up at the right-hand corner of the ceiling as if she was searching her mind. "Well, when I arrived today, the main door was unlocked. Dr Kendrick always checked the front and back doors were secure. She often checked them several times. The door must have been unlocked all night."

Daniel nodded. "She is the same at home. We both are." He didn't add that their obsession with security started after their baby, Sophie, had been abducted.

"You had no inkling that there might be anything worrying going on with her patients?" The DS asked.

Meredith shook her head. "No, not at all. Except...."

"Except what, Miss Baily?"

"I heard a scuffle going on in Dr Kendrick's room a couple of weeks back and I heard Dr Kendrick shout 'GET OFF'. Damon Wixx went off in a strop and slammed the front door. Dr Kendrick didn't say anything to me but she looked... well, sort of shook up."

"And what do you think happened?" The DS asked.

"Personally, I think Damon Wixx had tried to assault Dr Kendrick. He tried it on me once too." Meredith looked at Daniel nervously.

He smiled and nodded, trying to reassure her.

DS Harper scribbled more notes. "Was this an attempted sexual assault?"

Meredith blushed and nodded. "Yes, that was his intention, I'm sure."

"Thank you, Miss Baily." He then turned to Daniel. "And when did you last see your wife, Mr Kendrick?"

"Yesterday morning, before we both left for work," he said decisively.

"And she arrived here at the usual time?" The DS asked.

"Yes, I saw her car parked outside as I drove past to get to the hospital. It was around 8.30 am."

DS Harper wrote again. "So, the last sighting of Dr Kendrick was yesterday morning at your home, Dr Kendrick, and there has been no communication with her since from either of you. Is that correct?" He looked back and forth between Daniel and Meredith.

They both nodded their confirmation.

Harper requested Fay's laptop, other clinic computers, diaries and appointment books then asked how he could access her patient's notes.

Meredith gathered the items he'd requested and showed him the patient database on Fay's desktop computer. She scribbled down all the usernames and passwords she knew.

"Thank you, Miss Baily," DS Harper said. "I don't think we need anything further from you at this point but we have your contact details should we need to speak with you again." He looked at Daniel as if to check it was in order to let the receptionist go home.

Daniel walked Meredith to the door. "I'll deal with things from here. You go home and get some rest. You look shattered."

"Thanks Mr Kendrick. I've already cancelled all the appointments for the next week." Meredith picked up her handbag and left, dodging three men in white boiler suits in the doorway. The SOCOs had arrived.

Daniel walked back in with the men. They exchanged words with DS Harper, then got to work photographing the scene, bagging up Fay's scarf, the death threats and other items. One of the men found her mobile phone in the desk drawer and handed it to Harper.

DS Harper searched through Fay's mobile, playing the voicemail messages Daniel had left. There was a message from her mother, Emily, asking her to call her back along with ten missed calls. All from Daniel. There was a partial text message from Fay.

We need to talk...

Daniel's heart sank. Fay, he realised, was out there somewhere with no phone. No way to call for help. She had wanted to talk to him – he hoped it wasn't to tell him she was leaving him.

"I think we have your wife's handbag as well," Harper said as he took a large brown leather bag from one of the SOCOs.

"Yes, that's Fay's."

The DS looked through the bag in front of Daniel, pulling out a personal diary, a purse containing all her credit and debit cards along with various membership cards and £54.83 in cash. There was a hairbrush, lipstick, paper tissues, indigestion tablets and a few old mint humbugs, covered in fluff stuck to the bottom of the bag. She was out there with no phone and no money.

"Her car is missing and no sign of her keys," Daniel said. His mood sombre.

"And has she taken her passport?" Harper asked.

"I don't think so but I'll check when I get home and let you know if it's missing." Daniel couldn't imagine Fay skipping the country but the way the day was going, anything could happen.

Harper asked if Daniel had contacted his wife's family and friends, colleagues and associates. Daniel said he had, with no success. He realised he should inform her mother and his children, Richard and Ginny.

"Thank you, Mr Kendrick. I think I have all I need for now. I'd like to get the investigation underway asap."

"Do you think she could be in danger, detective? I mean with two killers on the loose."

"Too early to say. We'll keep you informed. I'll get this information circulated right away. Please try not to worry." The DS gave Daniel a bland smile.

This was beginning to seem familiar to Daniel. When their six-month-old baby had been abducted, they went through the same process. But in the end, they had found nothing but

Sophie's dead body. Perhaps if they had started the search earlier; had more officers on to it. If they had done more to find her...

Daniel nodded. "Thank you." He felt helpless and empty.

"Go home Mr Kendrick. There's no more you can do here. I'll let you know how we are getting on." Harper extended his hand as if to conclude their meeting.

Daniel shook the detective's hand, his own trembling. He turned and walked out of the room, dodging one of the SOCOs who had found blood on the door frame of Fay's office. He knew he would have to let them do their job. More police officers were arriving and cordoning off the area with tape. Fay's clinic was beginning to look like a murder scene.

Daniel went into the reception area and grabbed a bunch of keys for the clinic. DS Harper would need a set, so he handed them to him before the detective left. Separately, he found a mortice lock key for one of the internal doors. It had been lying under the clinic appointment book that was now with DS Harper. Daniel knew it was for a small cupboard off the coffee kitchen at the back of the reception area. He'd hung the door himself one weekend last summer when Fay was decorating and updating the room. Perhaps there would be more of Fay's belongings in there and maybe some clues. He walked through into the kitchen.

The room was around ten-foot square and lined with white units beneath a dark blue worktop, flecked with silver. The room was clear of clutter, unlike their kitchen at home. At one end was a breakfast bar style seating area with two pine stools pushed beneath the worktop. There was a small window above a stainless-steel sink, which was gleaming. A mug rack held a collection of mismatched mugs, one of them had 'Fay's 40th Birthday' written on it in pink, a present from him, and an electric copper-coloured kettle stood next to it. Shiny-clean white splashback tiles ran along the length of the work surface.

On the back wall was an outside door that led to a small yard and rubbish store at the rear of the buildings and beyond that a gate leading to a narrow lane, which ran behind the street and T-junctioned with the main road a few blocks down.

Daniel glanced around the kitchen, finding nothing unusual before unlocking the door to the windowless walk-in cupboard that ran along the partition wall with the reception room. The cupboard was used for storage, with coats hanging on one wall. He reached behind the coats and flicked on the light switch. There were various cardboard boxes stacked against another wall and at the far end stood a four-drawer office-style metal storage cabinet. Daniel tried to open one of the drawers but it was locked. Fay must have kept the key on the bunch or in her handbag, which DS Harper had taken for forensics.

Daniel had no idea what was in the cabinet. It was probably used for storage since Fay's patient's notes were kept on the database which Meredith had shown Harper. Daniel rummaged through the boxes. There was nothing of interest; mostly old papers, receipts and old copies of psychiatric journals. Nothing that gave any clue as to her whereabouts.

He should go home, as the detective had suggested, then call Fay's mother and the children and tell them that Fay had gone missing.

TWENTY-ONE

27 days ago

Robert Horton had finally been released from prison. He was sipping beer in the ramshackle garden of the small cottage that he'd been assigned by a team of police, prison and probation officers as part of his expensive new identity, such was the public outcry against his release. He pondered just how much he was looking forward to life on the outside after fifteen miserable years of incarceration. He'd managed to persuade the parole board he was a changed person, safe to be let loose in public again and had demonstrated an appropriate level of remorse for the heinous crime he'd committed. He'd done extremely well to be released after serving his minimum term on a murder charge, although he would remain on parole and under his new identity for what remained of his life – which was about to become shorter than he could ever have imagined.

Horton knew he would have to live with the fear of an assassin's bullet or a contract killer, the price he would pay for killing an innocent four-year-old boy, an only child. But here in the enveloping stillness of the night, in the comfort of his new home at the edge of the village as he had requested, he'd found the peace to think; to contemplate.

The urge to kill children was still there. He couldn't deny that, nor could he explain what drove it. In the depths of his soul was a dark secret that lay hidden beneath the façade he presented to the world. But when the rigorous scrutiny of the authorities diminished, and the media turned its attention elsewhere, as he knew it eventually would, he'd evaluate his life and the direction he would take next. He'd been promised anonymity and been given a new identity and for that he was grateful. It had meant he could never again see his family or the few friends he'd once had but he'd accepted that as the price of his freedom and had left them all behind in the past, where they belonged.

Horton sat in his deckchair, finished his fourth beer and reached for a fifth, cracking open a chilled can from the ice bucket beside him. It was good to taste the small pleasures of life again. A few beers and the vast expanse of the night sky replete with the twinkling stars he thought he might never see again. He glanced into the bushes behind him. He thought he'd heard a twig snap. Probably badgers out here in the countryside, he reasoned. It was a world away from the tight confines of his prison cell; drab, dank and claustrophobic. Here, he could breathe again. He'd done his penance, truly believing he deserved his freedom. He could have died an old man languishing in that soul-destroying jail but now he had an unexpected chance at life again.

Could he quell the dark compulsions he'd experienced since adolescence? The sheer thrill of taking a young life? The first time had been a fumbled, nervous experience but by the second and third, he'd gained his confidence and had honed his skill as a killer. Would he have the self-discipline to control his primal urges in the future? He wasn't sure. He'd literally got away with the murder of two children until he'd made a stupid amateurish mistake, leaving his DNA at the scene, which lead to his arrest and subsequent conviction for his latest killing. But the previous murders had never come to light and he'd been grateful for that. Two young children had gone missing over twenty years ago and their bodies had never been found; no evidence to trace a cause for their disappearance or a perpetrator of it. Horton hadn't even been a suspect, yet he alone knew how they had been butchered to death and where their small bodies were buried. They were lost forever beneath dense and now inaccessible scrubland; their remains destined to become fossilised into the landscape of some distant future.

Horton sensed a presence behind him, the rustling of leaves in the undergrowth. There had been something or someone there. He turned slightly in his seat and looked into the familiar eyes of someone he knew before they lurched unexpectedly at him, slicing viciously into his throat with a Santoku knife. His self-protective instincts were vastly diminished by alcohol but he saw, seemingly in slow motion, the glint of the steel blade in the moonlight then felt the searing pain as the knife sliced through his jugular. Then, with surreal perception, he felt his own sticky blood soak through his clothing and watched helplessly as it pooled sickeningly on the ground around him. He looked up to see his killer observing him with callous detachment as he flailed and clutched at his wound trying desperately to staunch the flow of blood. He gasped for breath as warm liquid gurgled into his lungs, preventing him from calling for help. He stared into his killer's ghoulish eyes, searching for meaning as his skin became cold and clammy, his heart began to fail and the world around him faded into darkness. The last thing he saw before the terrifying oblivion of death took him was the twisted, gratified smirk of his killer.

TWENTY-TWO

Tuesday 20th August 2019

Daniel sat in the kitchen at home, called Fay's mother, Emily Rowan, and told her that her daughter was missing. She hadn't taken it well and wanted to know why Daniel had said nothing to her when she had phoned last evening. At that point he hadn't realised his wife was missing and he wasn't about to tell Emily about the relationship issues they were working through of late; or of the heated rows they'd been having. He declined her offer of help but promised he would let her know the instant he had any further information. He knew she would be facing a sleepless night of worrying.

His son and daughter-in-law, Richard and Ginny had been more relaxed about the news. They had enough on their plates with a new baby to deal with and Fay wasn't even Richard's mother. His mother, Susan, had died seven years ago and he'd had a hard time coming to terms with her death. He'd never really taken to Fay, not because he didn't like her, or that she'd done anything to upset him – quite the contrary – but because she had stepped into his mother's place.

Normally in the habit of drinking red wine to excess, Daniel poured himself a large single malt whiskey. He'd called into a pizza takeaway on the way home but now, he had no appetite. He let Maisie lick the cheese from his pizza and Chester and Ella sat, watching her, their eyes darting between their master, the pizza and Maisie in the hope they would get a share. Fay would have told him off for letting Maisie on the table but all that was on his mind was agonising over why Fay hadn't come home. Had it just been in been retaliation because of the almighty row they'd had the other night or should he be worried? Surely, she wouldn't have gone off without her bag or at least some cash. They had separate bank accounts and no doubt the police would be monitoring hers but her bank cards were still in her purse. Was she eating? Where had she been sleeping?

Daniel felt restless and useless. He had to trust that the police would do all they could to find her but there was a nagging doubt in his mind. They had failed to find their little Sophie in time to save her life. He would call DS Harper later. At the very least he could put pressure on them to act more quickly.

Daniel sloshed back his whiskey and poured another. The fiery liquid burned all the way down his gullet and was beginning to numb the anxiety that was cascading through his mind. The dogs had given up their quest for pizza and he flicked on the TV for the early evening news, turning the sound up as images of Robert Horton flashed onto the screen. The newscaster was reporting that police had no leads as to the perpetrator of his murder.

Daniel's iPhone rang and he could see it was Matthew Clarke, his registrar. He muted the sound on the TV before answering.

"Matt. What's up?"

"Daniel, sorry to bother you. We've just had an emergency admitted and it looks complicated. We could do with some help."

Daniel's heart sank. The last place he wanted to be this evening was in work. "Go on," he said, switching the TV off and placing his just-poured whiskey on the coffee table.

"A young man has been brought in with a large hunting knife hanging out of his gut. Looks like it's gone through his stomach and spleen. Possibly punctured his diaphragm as well but he's not showing any respiratory symptoms as yet."

"Isn't Colin around?" Daniel thought consultant, Colin Mathias, his opposite number, would be on call.

"He's tied up in theatre with a complicated bowel resection. Won't be out for another couple of hours. I don't like to disturb you, especially with Fay missing but this guy, Justin McCartney, is in a bad way. The paramedics called in a Code Red. He's also a psych patient, I think. We've sent for his notes."

Justin McCartney. Daniel recognised that name. It was the name on Fay's note – the one he'd pulled from her briefcase. He tried to remember the exact words.

REFERR TO DR MADDISON. LIKELY
DISASSOCIATIVE IDENTITY DISORDER.
TRY FOR AN URGENT SECTION –
PSYCHOTIC EPISODE?

He was definitely one of Fay's patients. Someone with a personality disorder and potentially dangerous if he was psychotic. Not that he would be a danger to anyone in his current state by the sound of it but he would certainly need to be dealt with by the psych team.

Justin McCartney. Could he be tied in with the death threat Daniel had found? Could he have harmed Fay while he was psychotic? It was a distinct possibility. Daniel would have to go into the hospital, if only to question McCartney and hand him over to DS Harper as a possible suspect when he came around from surgery.

"I'm on my way. Let's also call in Dr Maddison from the psychiatric unit."

"We'll get him prepped for theatre."

Daniel hung up, put the dogs out into the Dog House, tossing them the rest of the pizza, checked the back door was locked, flicked off the lights and went out to his car, leaving a security light on over the front door.

His stomach was churning like a cement mixer as he drove to the hospital. Could Justin McCartney be responsible for Fay's disappearance? Daniel had images of his wife tied up in some dank dungeon while McCartney was on the rampage with a knife. God – anything could have happened.

Daniel swerved to avoid a bicycle he'd failed to see. It had started to rain and his windscreen was misting over. He turned up the fan and it started to clear just as he pulled into the hospital carpark. Some cheeky so-and-so had parked in his designated space but he managed to find another close by. He locked up and rushed into his theatre department, changed into scrubs and a theatre cap and went into the scrub room.

Matt was already scrubbing.

"What's the latest?" Daniel asked as he removed his watch, pocketed it, tied on a surgical mask and grabbed a brush loaded with Hibiscrub. He wet his hands and arms under a running tap and began to scrub furiously. He could see through the window into the anaesthetic room that McCartney was being intubated and anaesthetised using a rapid sequence induction. The anaesthetist was applying cricoid pressure and barking orders to his assistant to administer a sedative and the neuromuscular-blocking drugs that would promptly induce unconsciousness and paralysis.

Matt's voice was a little muffled as he spoke through a green surgical mask.

"Thanks for coming in Daniel. We've got a stabbing here: a large knife lodged in the left subcostal margin. The blade is angled upwards and it looks as if he's either stabbed himself with some sort of hunting knife or someone else has stabbed him in the upper abdomen from behind. That's according to the copper who saw him in A&E. We'll know more later. First, we have to get the knife out of his gut without him bleeding out. We have six units of blood cross-matched."

"Is there a bed on ICU? They were full to the gunwales yesterday."

"Yes, a patient went to HDU this afternoon, I checked and they're keeping it for our patient unless something more urgent comes up in the meantime."

Matt finished scrubbing and began quickly drying his arms with a sterile towel from a pack a nurse had opened for him.

Daniel glanced at Matt. "He's also a psych patient. One of Fay's. From what I can gather, he's psychotic and was about to be referred to Dr Maddison. Looks like he has some sort of personality disorder."

"Never could understand psychiatry. Give me surgery any day," Matt said as he finished gowning up.

"Same here," Daniel said as he rinsed Hibiscrub from his arms and went through the same ritual of drying with sterile paper towels.

Daniel plunged his arms into a green cotton theatre gown that an operating room orderly was holding for him. He turned to allow the man to tie the gown at the back and snapped on a pair of sterile, latex surgical gloves, deftly tucking the ends of his sleeves into the cuffs of each glove.

Matt was already prepping the patient on the operating table as Daniel strode into theatre, the orderly trudging behind, fumbling to finish tying his gown.

"You know he's not long out of prison for manslaughter? He was in Ravenwood, I think," the anaesthetist said as he attached the monitor leads to the patient's chest.

"Bloody hell," Matt said. "Wouldn't want to meet him in a dark alley."

Daniel looked at Justin McCartney's face, partially hidden by the endotracheal tube. He was in his early thirties with weaselly-looking features, grey, pimple-ridden skin and colourful face tattoos. There were grimy-looking piercing holes either side of his right eyebrow and a number of red bumps in the surrounding skin caused by infected hair follicles. His light brown hair was long, matted and greasy. Even anesthetised and spark out, the man looked menacing.

Matt indicated he'd finished prepping and the scrub nurse wheeled a stainless-steel trolley, laid out with surgical instruments, to the operating table. The patient was covered in autoclaved green cotton drapes. A theatre orderly adjusted the HD-LED operating theatre lamps. The six-inch handle of the hunting knife and part of the blade that was lodged vertically in McCartney's gut glinted in the bright light.

Daniel took the scalpel that was being offered by the scrub nurse. He badly wanted to talk to this dubious McCartney character but first he would have to save his miserable bloody life.

TWENTY-THREE

Justin McCartney's blood pressure was plummeting as he lay on the operating table with a hunting knife lodged in his upper abdomen. His central pulse was unreadable and the electrocardiogram – ECG – showed a sinus tachycardia. A ventilator delivered ten breaths a minute via an endotracheal tube.

"Shit," Daniel said, "we'll have to resuscitate. Hold the knife steady, Matt. I don't want to remove it until I can see where it's going."

Daniel began chest compressions at 100 per minute, while Matt held the six-inch handle of the knife as steady as he could with both hands. The anaesthetist hastily injected 1 mg of adrenaline into a venous canula on the back of McCartney's hand.

"Aren't we going to risk further damage if we leave the blade in?" Matt asked.

"It's a risk we'll have to take."

Ninety seconds later, Daniel stopped chest compressions and checked the monitor.

"Still in ST," the anaesthetist said.

Daniel continued pounding on the man's chest. He couldn't lose him now. Not if he had anything to do with Fay's disappearance. "Don't die, you bastard," he said breathlessly.

Matt kept hold of the handle of the knife. "Do you think we should stop?" he said, looking first at Daniel, then at the anaesthetist.

The anaesthetist shrugged.

Daniel continued for a further minute, then stopped to check the monitor. Still nothing. He began chest compressions again, desperate to save his patient. Desperate to know if he was involved in his wife's disappearance and if he could lead the police to her.

"Daniel. I think we should call it a day. He's probably suffered catastrophic internal blood loss." Matt looked at the anaesthetist, who finally nodded his agreement.

Daniel ignored his registrar and continued with chest compressions. He wasn't about to let this scumbag die before he had a chance to question him.

"Daniel. Please. Call it," Matt said, still holding the knife handle steady against the rhythmic movement of the man's body as Daniel worked on his chest.

Daniel continued with chest compressions for a further minute, then stopped to check the monitor. McCartney's heart was once again beating normally and his blood pressure was 82/42 mm Hg. Low, but he was alive.

The anaesthetist squirted noradrenaline into the venous cannula to stiffen the man's blood vessels, increasing his blood pressure. He adjusted the ventilator settings.

"Sinus rhythm," Daniel said, trying to catch his breath. "We've got him back." He stood and stretched his back then rotated stiff shoulders.

"You can never let them go can you Dan?" Matt said. He knew his consultant well. Daniel was always the last to give up on a resuscitation attempt.

"Hippocratic Oath, Matt. Just trying to save a life." Daniel changed his surgical gloves for the new sterile ones that were being offered by a theatre orderly.

"Even a scumbag like this? You know how hard pressed the NHS is. Nobody will miss the likes of him. A bloody murderer, for God's sake." Matt never shied away from giving his opinion and could be blunt at times.

Daniel glared at Dr Matthew Clarke and shot him a warning look. They said no more about it, neither of them wishing to sour their professional relationship. Yet the atmosphere in theatre was tense.

The anaesthetist stayed out of it, busying himself with getting the patient back into haemostasis. McCartney's blood pressure was beginning to recover and normal cardiac rhythm, although tachycardic, was being maintained.

"OK, let's get this knife out," Daniel said, taking a scalpel from the scrub nurse.

Daniel performed a laparotomy to visually inspect the course of the knife blade. It had perforated the man's stomach and slashed through his spleen but it had missed his aorta. Just.

"OK, Matt, pull the knife out slowly. I'll tie off the bleeding vessels."

Daniel waited while the registrar gripped the handle of the knife and extracted a bloodied eight-inch-long, non-serrated blade from McCartney's abdomen.

"Suction and mops," Daniel called as he worked quickly to get the bleeding under control.

Matt assisted, mostly in silence, apart from an occasional comment on the procedure. The rhythmic sound of the ventilator delivering breath to the patient was becoming almost hypnotic as they worked to repair the damage done by the knife blade.

Daniel knew full well that the registrar hadn't approved of his efforts to resuscitate. Matt was generally a good doctor, although he did have a tendency to play God. Daniel hadn't felt like explaining the situation or discussing ethics. For Daniel, judgement calls on whether a patient deserved to be saved didn't come into it. For him, all patients were human beings and life was sacred. Everyone deserved a chance to live, whoever they were. This time, though, Daniel had an additional motivation to save McCartney. He could very well be responsible for his wife's disappearance and heaven forbid, even her death if his worst fears materialised. He desperately needed to talk to him.

An hour and fifteen minutes later, Daniel had repaired Justin McCartney's stomach injury and ligated the splenic vessels that had been slashed. The patient was, so far, out of danger and his decision to leave the knife in during cardiac compressions had been justified.

"Right. Let's get him into recovery and then up to ICU. Can I leave that with you Matt?" Daniel glanced at the clock in theatre. It was 9 pm and time to write up his notes and get home. He hoped, more than anything, that Fay would be there and life would get back to normal.

TWENTY-FOUR

Tuesday 20th August 2019

Daniel had hoped during his drive home from the hospital that he would walk in and find Fay safe and well, so he could call DS Harper and tell him to call off the investigation. Instead, he got home to a dark, empty house with no sign of his wife. Maisie was curled up on the sofa and lifted her head briefly and squinted when he flicked on the bright overhead spotlights. Daniel reached for the glass of whiskey he'd left on the coffee table earlier. He took a swig before grabbing for his iPhone. There were four missed calls from Emily Rowan, Fay's mother. Daniel found DS Harper's number and pressed 'call'.

The phone was answered by the detective.

"Any news detective. It's Daniel Kendrick."

"We are checking our ANPR – Automatic Number Plate Recognition – system to try and trace your wife's car. Nothing so far. We're also waiting on fingerprints and blood analysis at the moment Mr Kendrick. First thing, we will be holding a briefing with Detective Inspector Emma Oakes and her team and we'll go from there." His voice was calm and steady.

"How long will the fingerprints take?"

"Usually between 24 and 72 hours. I've requested results urgently but we won't know any more until at least tomorrow; late afternoon."

"Listen, sergeant, I had to operate on one of Fay's patients this evening. A knifing that could have been self-inflicted or an attack from behind. It was Justin McCartney. If you remember, Fay had written a note about him needing an urgent assessment for a psychotic incident. He's also been an inmate at Ravenwood prison for manslaughter."

"Yes, I do remember and I'm aware that he has a record. What else can you tell me?"

"He's still recovering in ICU but the note was in Fay's briefcase right on top of the death threats. He could have sent the threats to my wife." Daniel was desperate for DS Harper to drop everything immediately and investigate McCartney.

"Right, well I'll relay that to the team in the morning and we'll look into it. The death threats may have been for McCartney, not your wife. He has some rather nasty associates. Try not to worry," Harper said.

"Can't you do something tonight?"

"I'm afraid not, Mr Kendrick. The investigating team are tied up with trying to track down this serial killer, not to mention trying to find Jaxon Sloan – another murderer on the run. We have our hands full at the moment. I'm afraid it will have to wait until the morning." The detective sergeant's voice was beginning to sounded terse.

"But Fay could be in danger." Daniel was struggling to keep calm.

"You say this patient, Justin McCartney is in ICU recovering from surgery?"

"Yes, that's right."

"Then we should let him recover and pay him a visit tomorrow. There's nothing to be gained by talking to him tonight."

Daniel conceded. McCartney wasn't going anywhere. "Alright, sergeant, let's speak again tomorrow."

They hung up and Daniel poured himself another inch of whiskey. He was feeling agitated and helpless. He felt sure that McCartney was involved with Fay's disappearance but he knew there was no more he could do. He had to let the police do their jobs.

Daniel thought about Justin McCartney and decided to call ICU to see if he was awake. Matt would have gone off duty by now. He dialled the direct number and got through straight away.

"Intensive Care, staff nurse Wilkens speaking." The woman's voice was light and feminine. Daniel didn't recognise it or the name she gave but she would have been one of the night staff at this hour.

"It's Daniel Kendrick. I operated on Justin McCartney this evening. Just wondering how he's progressing."

"Just a minute, I'll check." The phone went silent apart from the sound of bleeping monitors in the background.

Daniel took another swig of his drink and waited. Fifty seconds later, the nurse was back on the line.

"He's spark-out at the moment. We'll keep him sedated until the morning to give him a rest then extubate."

"Thanks. I'll come up and see him mid-morning then." Daniel knew there would be no point in talking to him now. Reluctantly, he conceded; the DS was right.

Daniel felt restless. Where was Fay? He felt empty. The house felt empty. He had become used to her being late home over the past few months but this felt totally different. She could have been abducted. His head was suddenly full of unwanted, distressing images.

His phone rang. It was Emily. He should speak to her. He answered to an agitated mother-in-law blaming him for Fay's disappearance.

"You're always out with those so-called friends, Daniel. I'm sorry to say it but I've bitten my tongue for too long. You drink too much and you've neglected Fay just when she needed you in favour of those shallow people and their money." Emily's voice was edgy and tense.

"Look, I'm sure she'll be fine. The police are on to it and I'm trying my best to find her. Try not to worry." Daniel thought better of retaliating against Emily's accusations.

"What's happening? Are they searching for her?"

"They are waiting for forensic tests to come back and they will put together a proper plan once they've had a briefing in the morning. I'll let you know as soon as I find out anything. I promise." Daniel omitted to tell Emily about Justin McCartney. He was trying to reassure her; not give her a reason to get even more wound up.

"Well, see to it that you do. I'm really worried about my daughter." Emily's voice was breaking as if she was about to cry.

"I'm worried too Emily. I'll call you; I promise."

Emily hung up on him, leaving Daniel down-hearted. She obviously didn't have a very high opinion of him and it sounded like she had a lot of pent-up resentment against him. But there was nothing he could do about that now. He would just have to remember to call her tomorrow.

He let the dogs into the house. Their limitless devotion and enthusiasm for life always cheered him up. But he was worried about Fay and hurt at Emily's attitude, not to mention the investigation at the hospital into Malcolm Phelps' death on his operating table. Even Chester's playful tug-of-war game failed to raise his spirits.

Daniel's restlessness took him to the kitchen where he wandered around the room opening and shutting cupboard doors looking for something to eat, as if there would miraculously have been a delivery by the grocery fairies while he was out. He wanted something to comfort his agitation more than to satisfy his hunger.

He found a piece of cheddar that had gone hard on one side where he'd left the wrapper open. He cut a chunk from the good side and found some crackers in the bread bin – on the soft side but edible. He poured himself another whiskey and sat on the sofa next to Maisie, absently stroking her soft fur.

He switched on the ten o'clock news. More Brexit chaos, more accusations about Boris Johnson's private life and then, a piece about Robert Horton, his unknown assassin still on the loose. The trail had gone cold.

Another unsolved murder, Daniel thought. Shit. If they really are tied up with these murder investigations, how much time and resource will they have for a missing person?

TWENTY-FIVE

Wednesday 22nd August 2019

Jaxon Sloan was on the run. He'd just shot his wife, Lisa, and her lover, Kieran Hook at point blank range with a sawn-off shotgun. He'd shot them both dead in the bed he and his wife used to share before he got sent down to Gallow Hill prison. If he was caught, he'd end up in that shit-hole again, or worse and more likely, at the category A Ravenwood prison for the rest of his natural life and he couldn't let that happen. Ever. He'd rather die free on the run, than be trapped in the big house for the rest of his days like a caged lion.

The sound of sirens had eventually died down. He guessed the police and ambulance had been called to his home. He imagined the crime scene and a bunch of detectives scratching their heads, the SOCOs carrying out their investigations dressed in white, protective suits and masks, gathering forensic evidence into plastic bags and taking endless photographs of the scene. The pattern of blood spatter on the bed and up the walls; the lifeless bodies of his two victims. He imagined the murder squad interviewing Mrs Pritchel in her nightie and the police cordon around the house; the nosey neighbours' curtain twitching to see what was going on in their generally uneventful street. Adrien Smith from number six had come home drunk and disorderly one night and the police were called by his neighbour but there had been nothing like this – a double murder in the dead of night. In Riverbeke. It would be all over the national news and there was no doubt who the killer was. He'd been seen by Mrs Pritchel and no doubt by others as he made his getaway. He also had motive. Plenty of motive to commit murder. Jaxon Sloan knew he would never see his home again.

Now, Sloan lay inside an old lime kiln that was built into the side of a hill. It was like looking out from a stone age cave and felt just as primitive with its arched stone roof and bare earth floor. It smelled of moss and mud. He needed to rest; to take stock of his situation and decide what to do next. He had managed to get as far as the woodland just over six miles north west of his house. It had taken an hour, alternating spurts of running with brisk walking. He knew the police would be searching for him and the sooner he got somewhere safe, the better. He checked the time on his phone; almost 05.30. It would be starting to get light soon and he knew he would be safer to move around at night and go to ground during the day. The police would use all the technology at their disposal to track him down, including drones equipped with high definition and thermal imaging cameras. He'd read on the Internet about how drones were the mobile equivalent of CCTV and how they had helped, with thermal imaging, to rescue a man lying in a ditch at night with hypothermia. They had also tracked down a hit and run driver. He had to stay hidden, undetectable and out of reach. The good thing was that each flight of a drone was limited by its battery life to around twenty to forty-five minutes, so if he stayed vigilant, he reckoned he could avoid them.

Sloan knew he had to start planning carefully. He had very little cash – just over £60 – and it would be foolish to try to obtain cash from an ATM or use his debit card. Not that there was much money in his account but he knew that any activity would be tracked by police. Locals would be on the lookout for him, and his mugshot would be all over the media. He would be best to stay away from towns and villages. He would have to stay out in the woods – away from where people were likely to be.

Sloan looked up into the sky. There was a faint light that signalled dawn was approaching. Could he stay here, in this virtual cave? It was an option but he still felt vulnerable and too close to town. He remembered the 1990s film, 'The Fugitive' and how detective, Tommy Lee Jones, had ordered a search of every gas station, residence, warehouse, barn, farmhouse, outhouse, henhouse and dog house in the area. He had calculated the average footspeed at 4 mph, barring injury, and since the escaped prisoner had been on the run for ninety minutes, he ordered a search for the escaped convict within a radius of six miles. Sloan reckoned he'd covered over six miles already. Neither did he have the incumbrance of a metal ball around his ankles to slow him down like Harrison Ford, the escaped convict. But unlike Ford, Sloan *was* guilty of murdering his wife. The police would be working quickly and tirelessly to bring him down.

He couldn't risk trying to shelter in barns, outhouses, sheds – nor dog houses. He would have to survive outside, in nature. He went to check his phone and stopped himself. The police would be able to trace it if he tried to use it. He'd be caught in minutes. He would have to ditch it. Who would he contact anyway? Mateo? He couldn't put him and his family at risk. They had done more than enough for him already and didn't deserve to be dragged into his problems. His cell mate, Sully? That would trace him back to Mateo. He was on his own. The police would be monitoring his family and waiting for him to get in touch. There was no way he could contact them except through a middleman – and why would he want to contact them anyway – he couldn't believe any one of them would want to help him. Not even his crooked brother Liam, who was well used to evading the police, usually for fraud or burglary. None of them would want to help or harbour a murderer. Especially if it was him.

Sloan felt vulnerable and exposed. He had to get further away from the scene of the murder. He reached into his holdall and pulled out the gun. It wouldn't hurt to keep it loaded for protection, he thought. He remembered Mateo's warning to him about using the gun and part of him wished he'd heeded his advice. But there was no going back now.

Jaxon cracked the gun and tipped out the spent cartridges, the smell of gun smoke and burnt oil evoking images of the crime he'd just committed. A new rush of hatred gushed through his veins as he thought about his wife's betrayal but although he thought he should, it was still too raw and too immediate for him to feel even a shred of remorse for murdering them. Perhaps that would come later – he didn't know – but for now, it was all he could do to focus on evading capture by the police. Sloan pushed the spent cartridges into the bottom of his holdall, careful not to leave even the smallest trace of his whereabouts. He reached into his coat pocket and brought out two fresh cartridges, loading them into the gun, slipping one into each barrel. He snapped the gun closed and slid the safety on before replacing it in his holdall. If he ended up being cornered, at least he had some defence and possibly bargaining power. But he had absolutely no intention of getting caught. His survival instincts were strong; he would protect his freedom, whatever it took.

TWENTY-SIX

Wednesday 21st August 2019

Daniel had slept reasonably well, all things considered. Mostly thanks to the excess booze he'd consumed the evening before. Now he was anxious to get to the hospital and ICU to confront Justin McCartney. Maisie was meowing and rubbing around his legs. He put down some food for her, which she ate ravenously.

He checked his iPhone. There was a curt text from his mother-in-law reminding him to keep her informed.

Don't forget to call me. I'm worried about Fay

Daniel sent a brief reply.

I will x

Daniel let the dogs out and fed them. He knew Rosie would be there to take them to the dog creche soon.

He fished out a crumpled shirt from the wardrobe. He didn't have the time or inclination to iron it. He was running low on clean clothes and hadn't thought to put a wash on. He went downstairs with a towel around his waist, put the shirt in the tumble dryer on the highest heat setting for five minutes, took it out, gave it a good shake, let it cool slightly and put it on. It was a tip Matt had given him once. It would have to do.

He found a clean pair of boxers that Fay had given him for their wedding anniversary that read 'Two down, seventy years to go'. He put them on with his favourite cartoon dinosaur-themed socks and black chinos.

He would call to ICU to see McCartney, then get to the ward to check his schedule.

After locking up and double checking the back door was secure, Daniel checked the front door had shut properly and slid into his BMW. It didn't seem right that his car was sitting there without Fay's Mercedes next to it. He looked across to see Jane Hopkins, one of his neighbours getting into her car, a brand-new Astra SRI in gleaming black. She glanced toward him but didn't acknowledge him. It looked like a snub but he couldn't think why. He reversed off the drive as she was checking her lipstick in her rear-view mirror. He could have sworn she was watching him.

Daniel turned the car and headed through the centre of Riverbeke toward the hospital. He wove through the morning traffic, accelerating through a traffic light just as it was changing to red. Someone blasted a horn at him but he ignored it and drove on. He took a different route down Park Road, past Fay's clinic. He slowed right down to 20 mph and scanned the parked cars. None were Fay's. As he passed the clinic, he saw the yellow plastic police tape across the front door of the building. He would call DS Harper this morning to find out what had developed from their briefing.

Daniel drove on to the hospital car park, munching Jelly Babies from a family-sized bag he'd found on the back seat. He was anxious now to speak to McCartney. It was chock-a-block; not a parking place to be had due to the sheer number of outpatient clinics being held. Daniel was relieved to see his designated space had been left empty. One of the perks of getting to consultant, he thought. He parked, locked the car and walked toward the front entrance. He took the stairs to the second floor and along a blue-painted corridor to the Intensive Care Unit, dodging groups of visitors, patients being wheeled on trolleys, a cleaner operating a polishing machine and staff on their way to various wards and departments. All seemingly lost in a world of their own private thoughts.

A pharmacist was just exiting ICU as Daniel arrived, so he grabbed the door and let himself in before the automatic lock tripped. At the end of the corridor, he saw the unit manager, Angela Edwards, standing at the nurse's station with her back to him. He recognised her instantly. He had worked with her when she was a senior staff nurse on his surgical ward but had not seen her since she moved to ICU.

"Angela. How are you. Missing us yet?"

Angela turned to face Daniel and her face lit up. "Daniel! I'm fine thanks – loving ICU. How are you?" She peered at the cut on his cheek. "That looks nasty."

"I'm alright." He ignored the comment about his wound. "Listen, I've come to see one of my surgical patients from yesterday. The stabbing – Justin McCartney. What's the latest?" Daniel leaned nonchalantly on the nurse's station, rolling up his shirt sleeves, his jacket thrown over the back of a chair.

"It's not like you to come up here just for a visit."

"A long story." Daniel rolled his eyes, not wanting to get into lengthy explanations. He was anxious to talk to the person he suspected might be involved in Fay's disappearance.

"We reduced his sedation over the last few hours and he's fully awake now. Dr Jameson, our new SHO extubated him this morning. He seems a bit strange though – maybe the after effects of the sedation. His wound seems intact and he's doing well physically, so I guess he can go to the ward this morning, all being well. We need the beds."

"You know he's a psych patient?" Daniel asked.

"Actually, I was just reviewing his notes when you came in. Makes for interesting reading." Angela touched a set of open notes on the counter.

"Mind if I take a look?"

"Be my guest." Angela handed him the notes.

Daniel flicked through. He could see Fay's writing and that of several other psychiatrists. He recognised Shelly Winter's signature and saw Dr Maddison had been involved in his treatment at the hospital. He noticed that McCartney had been prescribed antipsychotics, which block some of the dopamine receptors in the brain; reducing the flow of messages. He had apparently been having episodes of hallucinations, delusions and hearing voices. He had been referred to Fay to try Cognitive Behavioural Therapy – CBT. McCartney had been poor at taking his medication for some time and was about to start on depot, or slow-release injections just before his appointment with Fay.

Daniel flicked further back through the notes. Dr Maddison had written, in spidery handwriting, that he believed McCartney had strangled a woman in a supermarket while he was psychotic. Apparently, the grip of his arm around her neck had been so tight, it took three men to get him off her. She died later in hospital from a heart attack, thought to have been due to the stress of the attack. McCartney had been hearing voices before the incident. Mad, not bad was the conclusion of the psychiatrist. Even so, he had served time for manslaughter as the jury were unconvinced. He had served less than half his sentence before being released into the community.

Angela had been getting organised for the doctor's round and was the other side of the nurse's station, hugging a pile of patient's notes. "Interesting character, isn't he."

"You could say that," Daniel said.

"I think Dr Maddison is on his way in to see him."

"Mind if I go and have a word with him?"

"Sure. He's in the far corner on the left. Next to the window." She pointed in the direction of the patient.

"Thanks Angela. Nice to see you again by the way." Daniel gave a friendly tap on the nurse's arm and started to walk away toward Justin's bed.

"You too. Don't be a stranger," she called after him.

Daniel walked through the unit, past several well-spaced specialist ICU beds. Most patients were sedated or comatose and being ventilated, surrounded by equipment, monitors and banks of syringe drivers delivering a plethora of life-saving medications. Nurses were on a ratio of one-to-one with their patients; constantly monitoring and recording vital signs. The sounds of machines bonging their alarms echoed through the room and Daniel could smell the familiar hospital disinfectant mixed with the enticing aroma of coffee as he passed a small side office.

He reached McCartney's bed. The man was awake, sitting up coughing and clutching his throat. The SHO, an efficient doctor with a pleasant bedside manner, had just finished re-siteing an intravenous canula in the back of his hand. Daniel recognised him and nodded an acknowledgement.

"Rick. How are we doing here?" Daniel said.

"He's fine. Can go to the ward soon. I think his psychiatrist is on the way up. He's got the all clear from me anyway."

A monitor on the far side of the room resounded a high-pitched alarm and three nurses ran to the patient.

"Rick!" one of them called, "respiratory arrest."

"Have to go," the SHO said as he snapped off his gloves, squirted alcohol gel onto his hands and hurried to the patient's bedside.

Daniel approached McCartney. The lanky, pasty-faced man looked like he had the weight of the world on his shoulders. He looked up at Daniel, his eyes wild and staring.

"Justin, I'm Dr Kendrick. I operated on you yesterday to remove the knife in your abdomen." Daniel wondered if the man had heard him. He continued staring, unblinking.

"Can you remember what happened?" Daniel continued.

Justin coughed and slowly, a glimmer of recognition passed over his eyes. "They told me to kill myself. Said I deserved to die." His fingers began anxiously fiddling and plucking at the bed sheet.

"Who told you that, Justin?" Daniel asked gently, twisting the right side of his head toward him, so he could hear more clearly what he was saying.

"Them. Those buggers. They want me dead. There's three of them, all telling me I deserve to die." Justin's fingers moved faster and began plucking the air then back to the sheet.

Daniel could hear the team working on the patient across the room. He glanced over to check if they needed help. They had things under control. He leaned closer to Justin to hear him above the din of alarms and people barking orders.

"But who are they. Who wants you dead?"

Justin stared into the distance but didn't answer. He swallowed hard as if his throat was sore.

"Do you remember Dr Fay Kendrick? She's your psychiatrist. You saw her the other day at her clinic."

McCartney continued to stare, plucking at the sheet.

"Justin?" Daniel prompted.

McCartney turned his face slowly to Daniel's. His eyes looked wild and vacant but he whispered, "yes. Dr Kendrick. Dr Fay."

"Do you remember what happened in Dr Kendrick's office the other day?"

Justin McCartney suddenly stopped plucking at the sheet, his hands stayed motionless in mid-air. His eyes looked to the right, as if he was remembering something, then back to Daniel's. "She tried to help me. They were sending death threats and she tried to help."

"Tell me about the death threats, Justin. Did you send them to Dr Kendrick?"

Justin held Daniel's gaze. He was frowning now and shaking his head slowly. "No... no. The death threats were for me. I told you, those buggers want me dead. They said I had to kill myself."

"Let's be absolutely clear. Are you telling me the death threats were for you?"

"Yes, for me. They told me I must die." Justin was searching Daniel's face with wild and desperate eyes.

"What Happened to Dr Fay, Justin?"

"She tried to help me. She said I would have to go to hospital again to see Dr Maddison. That I would have to have injections but they would help me with the voices."

"Do you know where Dr Fay is?"

"No. She was in her office when I left."

"When you left on Monday?"

"Yes, I ran away because the voices told me to." Justin looked away, staring wildly once again into the distance. Once again, his fingers began the incessant plucking on the sheet.

Behind him, Daniel sensed someone approaching. He straightened and turned to see a tall, distinguished-looking man in his fifties, in a crisp grey suit over a pale blue open-necked shirt. His tan leather shoes were old but polished.

"Good morning, Dr Kendrick." He extended his hand toward Daniel. "I'm James Maddison, Angela told me you are here to see Justin. Sounds like you saved his life yesterday."

"Nice to meet you, James." Daniel said, taking the psychiatrist's hand and shaking it firmly. "You heard he had a knife in his abdomen?"

"Yes, I did. I'm afraid it could have been a suicide attempt. Justin has tried to take his own life in the past." The doctor's voice was low and full of concern.

They both looked at Justin who was now staring back at them. His expression was unreadable.

Dr Maddison moved next to the bed and stooped toward McCartney. "Justin. Do you remember me? Dr Maddison?"

Justin nodded, staring vacantly at the doctor.

"What happened with the knife yesterday?" He asked gently.

Slowly Justin started mouthing words with no sound. He was still plucking at the sheet.

"Tell me what happened with the knife, Justin," Maddison prompted again.

Justin blinked a few times then said in a whisper, "they told me to do it. To stab myself. They want me dead." He was watching the psychiatrist steadily now, bewilderment etched on his face.

"Are you telling me you tried to kill yourself with the knife?"

Justin nodded solemnly. "Yes. I stabbed myself. They told me to do it."

James Maddison stood to his full height of over six feet and rubbed a hand along his jaw as if trying to make a decision.

"Do you believe him?" Daniel asked.

Maddison turned to look at Daniel. "Sadly, yes. It would be in character for him to do such a thing. Is he physically fit enough to be moved to the psychiatric ward? I think we need to keep him in for an urgent assessment and medication."

"I would prefer him to stay on a surgical ward for a few days but I guess we can manage him on the psych ward. Maybe he could have a side room."

Maddison nodded his head slowly, again rubbing his jaw.

Justin began plucking wildly at the sheet, then at the air and began grunting, his jaw clenched tight. He was staring, his eyes glaring; darting back and forth at some unseen entity.

Maddison went to comfort his patient but Justin began clawing at him, now screaming and shouting obscenities. Two nurses came running, followed by Angela. They stopped at the foot of the bed, watching in horror as Justin's psychosis escalated.

Maddison tried to calm him but Justin pulled back the sheet and dived out of bed, pulling his intravenous canula and the attached drip from his hand. Blood and saline fluid spurted across the bed and over the floor as he flailed frantically on the other side of the bed. It was as if he was trying to push someone away. "Get off... get off, you bastards," he was shouting, over and over again. Daniel, Maddison and Angela were reaching out to Justin, trying to sooth him but he continued to shout and flail his arms, oblivious to their voices. His mind was hallucinating and Justin had become unreachable.

"Call security," Angela called to a nurse behind her.

Then Justin leapt onto the window sill and tried to open the window as if he was trying to escape some unseen pursuer. The window, thankfully was deliberately and permanently jammed so that it would only open a couple of inches. He jumped down, still flailing his arms and shouting obscenities. Maddison tried to grab him but he slipped away and started to run down the unit past the row of comatose patients. Maddison, Daniel and four nurses ran after him, calling his name and trying desperately to calm him down.

Justin stopped next to the patient that had suffered a respiratory arrest, now thankfully resuscitated and being artificially ventilated via an emergency tracheostomy. A trolley with a dressing pack and various instruments still stood at the end of the bed, waiting to be cleared away. As if in slow motion, Justin turned his head toward the trolley, caught sight of a scalpel and grabbed it before Daniel could stop him.

Maddison lurched toward Justin, trying to grasp his arm but missed. Daniel called out to Justin to stop as he too made a grab for Justin's arm. Justin turned; his eyes wide in terror; the scalpel in his hand. He jabbed at Daniel, cutting his forearm; pain searing through skin and muscle. Blood gushed from the wound, soaking Daniel's shirt and dripping onto the floor.

Daniel stood back, instinctively grabbing his arm with his free hand, trying to stem the flow of blood.

Justin stood; the scalpel poised in his right hand. The fingers of his left hand plucking uselessly at the air. His eyes were wide and staring, darting back and forth as if listening to invisible beings.

Justin turned the knife on himself. He brought his free arm up and bent the blade toward it, slashing at his wrist once, then again. Blood spurted freely from a severed artery. He was screaming and crying pitifully like a wounded animal.

Daniel managed to work his way behind Justin, closed the gap between them and made a grab for both his arms; blood still seeping from his own wound. He managed to squeeze Justin's wrist, forcing him to drop the scalpel. Maddison grabbed Justin's legs and between them, they wrestled their distraught patient to the ground.

Two uniformed hospital security guards came running around the corner, a portly older man, wheezing for breath and a young trainee, barely out of school, trailing behind him. The older man went forward to help Maddison restrain Justin, while Daniel stood, his wound still dripping blood. Angela had brought a wad of sterile swabs and pressed them onto Daniel's forearm. Another nurse went to Justin to tend to his wounds.

Maddison turned to Daniel. "Let's get him sectioned urgently."

TWENTY-SEVEN

Wednesday 22nd August 2019

Sloan glanced up at the sky again. Black was slowly turning to blue; the moon had set in the west and the stars were losing their intensity. A slash of red light began to glow on the eastern horizon. He had to make his move now before first light – before the police began a search for him: a murderer on the run.

Sloan pictured a map in his mind. He was north west of Riverbeke. It couldn't be far to the river. If he could get there and cross the river, he would be in the heart of the countryside. It was a farming area with a few remote farmhouses but much of the landscape was covered in stands of dense, ancient woodland, mostly inaccessible to vehicles. It would be a perfect area to hide and would give him time to think; to plan his next move.

Sloan looked around. There was no sign of movement. No aerial surveillance, no torchlight, no dogs pursuing him. It was still and silent. He would aim to get to the River Beke. There would be no bridges to get him across the river for miles; he would have to go back to Dilport for a road bridge and that was far too dangerous. He would be exposed. He would have to wade across the river on foot but that would be to his advantage.

He would put any tracker dogs off his scent and give him a head start. Sloan crawled out from the relative safety of the limekiln, slung his holdall over his shoulder and strode through the undergrowth with the red gash of the breaking dawn behind him.

Sloan pushed through dense parts of the woodland; hundreds of acres of land that had been unmanaged for decades. It had been deliberately left to nature to encourage wildlife. He carefully avoided several badger holes and climbed over an ancient, moss-covered dry-stone wall that had fallen in places, making it easier to traverse. When Jaxon came to an open field, he skirted around the edges, careful to stay hidden in the shadow of the trees. He must have covered less than a mile over difficult ground but the sky was becoming lighter with every minute that passed. Soon he would have to go to ground and hide during the day when he would be easier to track.

Sloan reached a stream and disturbed a small rabbit that turned and hopped away from him. The river couldn't be far now. He cleared the stream with one stride and just ahead, he saw a grassy clearing with several wooden tables and benches. He recognised where he was. He was in the grounds of a National Trust stately home and just one hundred yards ahead was the Riverbeke Falls tearoom, still closed up and in darkness, He and Lisa had visited it a few times over the years. Usually on a Sunday afternoon. It would be at least two, maybe three hours before anyone would turn up to open up the place ready for business. Sloan scanned the area thoroughly in the still, gloomy light just before dawn. There was no sign of anyone; no gardeners or handymen; no early morning cleaners. He skirted around the edges of the clearing. It was an ideal opportunity to stock up on food and water.

Sloan approached the back of the tearoom, a solitary, detached corrugated metal building painted dark green. It was a converted barn that looked easy enough to break into with no security shutters, old wooden-framed windows and a single-glazed door. Jaxon found a large stone, put his holdall down on the grass, took off his coat and wrapped it around the stone; then crept up to the back door of the kitchen. He took a good swing at the single-glazed glass of the door near the handle and it shattered easily, the sound of glass tinkling in the still air. He froze for some moments, listening for a reaction but all he heard was the flapping wings of a bird flying off from a nearby tree. No voices, no dogs barking. Just a gentle breeze whispering through the leaves. He disentangled the stone and threw it down, put his coat back on, then retrieved his holdall. He reached in through the broken glass of the door and unlocked it easily. Boots crunching into the broken glass, he let himself into a tiny back hall and into the kitchen. The kitchen was small but well equipped with spotless stainless-steel counters and shelving for pans and crockery. He found a long magnetic knife holder attached to the wall next to the cooker with a row of gleaming knives; arranged in size from a small paring knife to a butcher's cleaver. He ran his finger lightly along the display and plucked off a chef's knife, a paring knife and a large cleaver; placing them in his holdall.

He looked through some of the cupboards, grabbing a few plastic bags and a kitchen roll, a box of cook's matches, a small torch, then crossed the kitchen to the refrigerator; passing a cash register beneath the serving hatch with the drawer left open. It was empty of cash. Sloan opened the fridge and the shelves were groaning with food. He rummaged and found some cheese, butter, ham, tomatoes, a bowlful of cooked pasta covered in clingfilm – items that wouldn't need to be cooked. He crammed a leftover pork and apple sauce sandwich into his mouth and chewed as he put as much food as he could into his holdall; then he walked over to a large pantry, checking through a window that he was still alone. It was deserted outside but the sun was just starting to rise above the horizon. It would be a race against time to get across the river and well away into the cover of dense woodland before people started arriving to open up the tea rooms. He quickened his pace.

The pantry was the size of a small room and was lined with metal shelves filled with bread, dry rice and pasta, flour, trays of eggs, fruit and a variety of packaged goods. Sloan grabbed a loaf of brown bread and a packet of soft white rolls, a few handfuls of nutty breakfast bars and some chocolate. He stuffed them into his holdall, filling the space around the gun. Under one of the shelves were trays of bottled water. He grabbed a few and tucked them down into the sides of the bag. It was crammed and heavy now but Sloan reckoned the opportunities to stock up on food like this would be few and far between. At least he had enough to last several days, maybe a couple of weeks if he rationed himself.

Sloan glanced around looking for anything else he might need. He slung his holdall over his shoulder. It would slow his progress if he tried to carry too much and decided to call it quits. He retraced his steps through the kitchen and out into the grassy clearing. He slipped into the shadow of the surrounding trees and hedges, disappearing like a chameleon. Resuming his journey west toward the river, he wanted to get well past the stately home and the prospect of people milling around before he could rest again.

TWENTY-EIGHT

Wednesday 21st August 2019

Angela Edwards, the ICU manager had sutured the slash wound to Daniel's arm, which had cut deep into the muscle, and had insisted on wrapping a white gauze bandage around it on top of the dressing. She said it would help protect it and keep it clean. Daniel hadn't protested.

She'd given him some painkillers, 400 mg of ibuprofen from the drug trolley, and they were starting to take effect. Now he was on his way to the ward to check his schedule. He'd grabbed his jacket but thrown his bloodied shirt and trousers in the medical waste bin and found a pale blue scrub set to wear. He'd taken a quick shower in the ICU changing rooms to wash away the blood – his own and Justin McCartney's.

He took the lift to the ground floor and walked the length of the corridor to the general surgical ward. He thought about Justin and whether he could have been responsible for Fay's disappearance. Justin was more of a danger to himself than to anyone else. He was ill but at least now he was getting the help he needed. The help that Fay had been trying to give him. He'd had a small glimpse into Fay's work life and felt a small pang of regret that he hadn't taken her career more seriously. He'd spent a lot of time focusing on what he wanted and what was best for him but not nearly enough on trying to understand her needs or her ambitions for her career.

Daniel tapped his ID badge on the door entry pad. He let himself in and was treated to the smell of vomit as he passed one of the side rooms. A trainee nurse was holding a kidney dish for one of the post-op patients. He dodged a woman in a burgundy uniform pushing a drinks trolley through the ward, the cups and cutlery clattering as the wheels bumped over the tiled floor. The ward looked pretty full with every bed occupied except one, which was kept for emergencies. There was a cacophony of ward activity against a background murmur of umpteen different conversations.

"Daniel. What's the news? We heard Justin McCartney had a bit of a meltdown on ICU." Matt Clarke had his sleeves rolled up and his tie tucked in between the buttons of his shirt. He was wearing surgical gloves and about to put in a chest drain for one of the new admissions. A nurse was preparing a sterile pack on a stainless-steel trolley.

"You could say that," Daniel said, giving his registrar a look of incredulity.

"Looks painful," Matt said pointing to Daniel's bandaged arm.

"An argument with a scalpel. It'll be OK." Daniel touched his arm, checking the bandage was in place. "Not so sure about Justin though. They patched him up and got him to psych. Apparently James Maddison is treating him with antipsychotics and he's beginning to respond."

"I knew he was bad news," Matt said shaking his head slowly.

"He's very sick, let's hope he'll recover. Mental health is important." To his surprise, Daniel realised he was echoing Fay's frequently expressed sentiments.

"I guess. By the way, the boss wants to see you when you have a minute," Matt said, returning his attention to his patient.

"Catch you later," Daniel said as he walked toward his small office adjacent to the nurse's station. He wondered what Colin Mathias, the senior consultant wanted, although he could make a good guess.

Daniel went into his own small office and closed the door behind him, shutting out the noise from the ward; the constant sound of ringing phones, monitors beeping and bonging; the hubbub of voices and the incessant rattling of trolleys. He sat at his desk and looked at the theatre list he had for that afternoon. Usually, he enjoyed his work, loving the atmosphere of the theatre, the challenge of performing complex surgery and the reward of helping patients recover; often from serious illness. Now, all he wanted was to be at home with Fay. For his life to return to normal. He realised he missed her. But more than that, he missed the couple they used to be before their baby had been abducted and murdered by the evil bastard that was still at large.

Daniel decided to call DS Harper. Surely, they would have had their morning briefing by now and have a solid plan to find his wife. He also needed to update them on the developments with Justin McCartney. He pulled his iPhone from his pocket, found the detective's number and called.

"DS Harper," the detective sounded harassed.

"It's Daniel Kendrick. Any news on the investigation?" Daniel was absently tapping a biro on his desk.

"I have officers following a few lines of enquiry, Mr Kendrick," he said flatly.

That sounded way too vague for Daniel's liking. What exactly were they doing and what lines of enquiry were they following? "Have you had results from the fingerprints back yet? Were there any from the death threats?" He asked.

"Actually, they were rushed through about ten minutes ago. The only prints that were found were those of your wife and Justin McCartney."

"Yes, I meant to let you know about developments there." Daniel told the detective about Justin's self-inflicted injury, about his breakdown on ICU and subsequent admission to the psychiatric ward.

"You say he sent the death threats to himself?" Harper asked.

"Yes, he was hearing voices and hallucinating. Fay had been trying to treat him when she disappeared. Apparently, according to him, he ran off during their last meeting."

"Sounds plausible but it doesn't explain the blood stains on the desk, your wife's scarf and the door frame. We also found blood near the handle on the inside of the main door. It looks like someone was bleeding as they left the building."

"Do you think it could have been Fay?" Daniel's pen tapping accelerated.

"It's possible. Of course, if McCartney is suicidal, it could be his blood if he'd harmed himself prior to the stabbing."

"I didn't see any evidence of that when I operated on him. I think someone would have noticed a fresh wound."

"We're still waiting on the DNA results. We have your wife's DNA on record, along with several of her recent patients'. Some of them had been prison inmates. I'll let you know if we get a match."

"We need to find out why she left her office and disappeared." Daniel was becoming tense. There were so many unanswered questions.

"Yes, we do, and we're following that up. I'm sorry, I'm afraid I have to go. I'll keep you informed."

They hung up. Apart from the fingerprint results for the death threats, which he suspected anyway, he was none the wiser. He was feeling agitated. Things were not progressing fast enough for him. His wife was missing, with no money, no phone and a serial killer on the loose. No; make that a serial killer and a murderer armed with a sawn-off shotgun.

Maybe it was time he made a few enquiries of his own.

Daniel looked again at his surgical list for the afternoon. He couldn't face being stuck in theatre for hours when he should be focusing on finding his wife. Maybe he could get cover. He was long overdue some time off. Daniel went out into the ward, passed the nurses' station. He knocked on Colin Mathias' office door, beginning to feel a little nervous, not knowing why he wanted to see him but suspecting he wasn't going to like it.

"Come." Daniel heard Colin's booming voice through the door.

He opened it and went into a large, sparsely furnished room to find Colin Mathias checking emails. A short, heavy-set man with a shirt-busting paunch and a ruddy complexion that made him look like the perfect candidate for a stroke. He turned in a squeaky swivel chair to face Daniel.

"Dan. Good to see you. Any news on Fay?" He was smiling, his thick, bushy brows rose above the frame of his reading glasses.

"How did you know?" Daniel felt a little irritated that his personal business was being talked about around the hospital.

"News travels fast in this place. You ought to know that."

It must have been Matt Clarke or that chopsy theatre orderly who had been earwigging on their conversation. "Yeah, I walked right into that. No... no news. She still hasn't come home but the police are investigating. That's what I came to see you about actually."

"You need some time off and you're looking for cover. Am I right?" Colin was, as ever, perceptive.

"Yes... plus, I have a nasty gash on my arm which could be a problem in theatre." Daniel held out his arm for inspection. It was beginning to throb.

"Ah yes, I heard about that too. You were lucky to get away with a clean cut. Any nerve damage?"

"No, it seems fine." Daniel wiggled his fingers.

Mathias got up and closed the door of his office. He slowly sat back down, removed his glasses and placed them on his desk. He gestured for Daniel to sit.

Daniel took a seat adjacent to Mathias' desk. He knew what was coming.

The senior consultant looked at Daniel – his expression had become sombre. "Look, Daniel. I'll level with you. We've had complaints that you've been coming to work reeking of alcohol and you're not exactly giving your best performance at the moment. You hold a senior position here and I'd hate you to wreck your career because of a booze problem."

Daniel looked down at the floor, unable to hold Mathias' gaze. He knew he was referring to the death of Malcolm Phelps on his operating table.

"Want to talk about it?" Mathias said, concern in his eyes.

"Not really, Colin." Daniel wouldn't know where to start but he suddenly realised he would have to face up to it if he was to avoid losing his job.

"I know things have been difficult for you since… well, you know… you lost your daughter and I understand it takes time to come to terms with. God knows what I'd do in your shoes. The thing is, you have to get on top of it or the board will be forced to consider your position here." Mathias replaced his spectacles.

All Daniel could do was nod slowly, unable to find the words to respond.

Mathias sat forward in his chair. "Look, Daniel, this is a friendly chat, OK? Take some time off, get your act together and we'll review things in a few weeks. The board have cut you some slack but they won't hold off for long. You're a surgeon in a senior post and it's a serious issue that won't be tolerated. There will be an investigation into Mr Phelps' death. You know that."

Daniel looked at Mathias, who was regarding him with concern in his eyes. He nodded his agreement. "I understand. Just let me take some time off, sort things out. I'll sort it. I will."

Daniel felt mortified, not realising his heavy drinking had become so noticeable at work, or that, aside from the death of Malcolm Phelps, his performance as a surgeon was being questioned. He had to admit he wasn't surprised but like everything else in his life, he was in denial about his problems.

Mathias sat back in his chair. It gave a metallic clang. "Look, I'm free now this afternoon. My big AP resection patient sadly died overnight so I could take over your theatre list. I was going to take a few days off for the golf tournament but I guess your need is greater than mine. Got any annual leave left?" Mathias was swivelling back and forth in his squeaky chair, pale hairy legs appeared between black socks and trouser legs.

"Yeah, plenty. I don't think I've taken any leave this year. Just don't seem to have got around to it yet." Daniel felt strangely relieved. He would be better off at home.

"Then take some gardening leave during the investigation and use the time to sort your life out. And let's keep this to ourselves. No need for the whole hospital to know."

"I will. And thanks Colin – I owe you one."

"It's a pleasure my friend. Get home and do whatever you have to do. We'll hold the fort." Mathias was waving a dismissive hand and swivelled back to his emails.

Daniel stood and went back to his own office to collect his jacket and car keys when his phone rang in his pocket. It was Emily, his mother-in-law. Shit, his instincts were to ignore it but he knew it would be easier just to get it over with.

"Emily," he said, realising he'd forgotten to call her.

"What's happening Daniel? I'm going out of my mind with worry here. Why didn't you call me? You promised you would." She sounded irate. He couldn't blame her.

"I've only just come off the phone to the police. There's nothing to report yet but they are making all the necessary enquiries." He didn't see the point in worrying her further by telling her about Justin McCartney, or about the blood in Fay's office.

Emily sighed. "This is just awful. Awful. My poor Fay. It's not like she hasn't had enough to contend with over the past few years with... you know little Sophie and everything. It's just not right."

Daniel wanted to remind his mother-in-law that Sophie had been his child too but thought better of it. He knew she'd have something to say about that as she did whenever the subject came up. She liked to accuse him of being inadequate and uncaring where Fay was concerned. She thought him a bad husband but, frankly, he could do without it right now. He was on the verge of losing his job – his career, as well as his marriage.

"Emily. I promise we are doing all we can. I'm taking some time off work to look for her and I'll keep you up to date. OK?" Daniel just wanted her to leave him alone but he knew she was as worried as he was.

She sighed again. "Alright but you must promise you'll call. I'm worried sick."

"I promise," Daniel said before he ended the call.

Daniel explained simply to Matt that he was taking some time off and left the ward, still in his borrowed scrubs. He walked down the corridor to see Oliver Davenport strolling toward him. He raised a hand in acknowledgement, hoping he wouldn't keep him with a long conversation.

"Daniel – good to see you at the do. Sorry about Melissa – she did overdo it with the bubbly, I'm afraid." He was well aware of his wife's flirtatious behaviour with many of his associates but did a good job of hiding his real feelings on the matter. "Still, it was a good fundraiser and we're still clawing in donations. How are things?" Oliver seemed to be in a jovial mood.

"No problem. I think everyone had a few too many." He hesitated to tell Oliver about Fay's disappearance or the threat to his career and decided to keep quiet.

"Listen, are you still considering coming into the clinic with me? It would be good to have you on board. I think we'd make an excellent team and think of the dosh we could make. Far exceeding NHS salaries that's for sure." Oliver chortled, obviously brimming over with excitement about his new venture into the cosmetic surgery industry.

"Considering it, yes. It sounds tempting but I do enjoy my role here. Maybe on a part-time basis?" Daniel realised he had more urgent things to think about at the moment but he was reluctant to close the door on a lucrative opportunity. Especially if his career really was on the line.

"I'm sure we could work it out. Don't leave it too long though. I'll need an answer in the next few weeks. Gerry Sandbrook is also showing an interest so it'll be between the two of you." Oliver took a sharp intake of breath and gave Daniel the sort of look a builder gives you when haggling on price.

Daniel wasn't surprised Sandbrook was interested. He was a good surgeon with the right sort of experience but had always had been more interested in making money than in the welfare of his patients. He'd taken on private patients for years as well as moonlighting at a Botox clinic.

"I'll give it some thought," Daniel said.

They promised they would keep in touch and Daniel made his way out to his car, sad at the threat of losing his career in the NHS. He would get control of his life, he thought. He would have to.

Daniel eased the BMW into the busy traffic and headed for home. It was almost lunchtime and not wanting to be seen out shopping in scrubs, he turned into the drive-through McDonalds and ordered a cheeseburger and fries with a coffee. He needed comfort food and ate as he drove, thinking about Justin McCartney and whether he really could have been involved in Fay's disappearance. It seemed unlikely but he couldn't rule it out. He was anxious to know whether the blood found at the clinic was, in fact, Fay's, or the blood of one of her patients.

One of her patients...

TWENTY-NINE

Wednesday 22nd August 2019

Sloan pushed his way through a dense wooded area and could hear the faint sound of running water up ahead. He followed the sound and soon he was standing on the river bank; a wide pebbled flank of the river that curved around a deep pool. He remembered his phone and the possibility that it could be traceable. It wasn't worth the risk, Sloan thought. He resisted the urge to check his phone one last time before he crunched his way across the pebbles and tossed it into the deep water. He briefly thought of the photographs and messages that would be lost forever. They disappeared instantly beneath the water with barely a splash and he felt surprisingly alone. There would be no phone calls, no news, no more social media. Not while he was on the run. All he had now were the wilds of nature and his instincts.

The other bank of the river was steep, inaccessible and peppered with otter holts. Sloan began following the river upstream heading north once again. If he could cross the river, he could find a sheltered area and rest up for most of the day, hidden by trees and the dense undergrowth.

Sloan negotiated the river bank for over half a mile before he found an easier place to cross. The river narrowed as it flowed past a rocky outcrop and the water was faster but shallower here. He stood for some minutes, contemplating whether to cross. The river bed was covered in rounded pebbles, green with slippery algae, and he wondered if he would be able to keep his footing in the fast-flowing current. He decided against it and walked further up river to a place where it diverged around a sandy spit. The bottom looked smoother, sandier and easier to traverse than it had been down river, although it was a little wider on each side of the spit. He decided to cross here to avoid the uneven bottom. Sloan jerked his holdall as high as he could on his shoulder and stepped into the river, his boots filling quickly with cold water. He took another step into the river and felt the full force of the water as it rushed past his legs. He took a moment to adjust his gait and took another step, his foot pushing hard against the fast-flowing river. The water splashed around his knees and he slid his foot forward, tentatively feeling the riverbed beneath him. He couldn't see where he was stepping through the turbulence but he could feel stones and a few boulders with his foot. Stumbling slightly, and unevenly balanced with the weight of his bag on one side, he took another step, then another and gasped as he stepped into a dip in the riverbed, the cold water reaching the top of his thighs. He managed to pull his foot free and take another step toward the sandy spit by jerking his body forward. The water was pushing hard against the weight of his body. Feeling a little disorientated, he held tight to his bag as he took another step through the fast-gushing water. He stood for a moment, fine tuning his balance before taking several strides and stepping out onto the sandy spit. He was halfway across.

Sloan again hoisted the holdall high on his shoulder and walked across solid ground to the last section of river, leaving wet boot prints in the sand. This part was narrower and he made it across in ten careful steps, the water flowing well over his knees. There were fewer rocks to negotiate and soon he stood on the other side of the river, dripping wet. He stepped up onto a low bank and could see dense woodland ahead. Now, he felt safer and less vulnerable to capture. Here, it would be completely inaccessible to vehicles. He pushed his way into the woodland, catching his holdall on branches and stumbling on stones and logs. After two hundred yards, he stopped, desperate to rest. His throat was dry with thirst and his belly rumbling with hunger. He found a fallen beech tree and sat on the soft, damp ground, leaning against its trunk. He put the holdall on the ground next to him, tucked up and hidden against the trunk, and sat for long minutes as he caught his breath and calmed his senses.

In every direction he looked, there was no sign of any woodland management. Dead trees lay where they had fallen and he was surrounded by scrubby, untamed undergrowth with no visible paths that people or animals had trodden. The tree canopy was thick with leaves and through it, he could see only small patches of sky, now blue in the morning light. A few white clouds drifted by. There was nothing but the soothing sounds of nature; bird song, the odd rustle of rabbits foraging in the undergrowth and above him in the branches, the mournful cries of squirrels. No search helicopters, no police sirens. It would be safe to stay here for a while, he thought. He kept his wet jeans on but reached down and untied his bootlaces. His feet were sodden from the river and he kicked his boots off and peeled off wet socks, placing them over the tree trunk to dry. Cool air dried his bare feet.

He unzipped his holdall and pulled out some cheese, ham and bread rolls. He grabbed a bottle of water, unscrewed the lid and drank most of it in several big gulps, finally quenching his thirst.

As he sat eating the stolen food, the sound of birdsong and the breeze through the trees calmed his mind like a nature meditation.

THIRTY

Wednesday 21st August 2019

Were the police investigating her patients? Daniel had the list of all Fay's recent appointments back at the house. They could all be suspects. Every one of them. He was intrigued to know more about them but how would he find out? DS Harper had their medical notes on Fay's computer and anyway, they were unlikely to share that information with him. He remembered the frustration and helplessness he felt during the investigation into Sophie's abduction. He couldn't face that again. That dreadful sense of powerlessness.

Once home, Daniel had changed out of his borrowed scrubs and showered again, washing away the grime and the smells of the hospital and the awkward conversation with Mathias. He removed the bandage on his arm – the underlying dressing was perfectly adequate, although he knew Angela had meant well. His wound was sore but he decided to manage without more analgesics. He dressed in navy chinos with a colourful checked shirt that Fay had bought him for his birthday a few years ago – all he could find that was clean.

Maisie was parading around the kitchen. He fed her, let Chester and Ella into the house and spent the next fifteen minutes cleaning up, putting on a clothes wash, hunting for bin bags and tidying up the disarray in the living room. He realised he never did any of this stuff. Fay had always dealt with everything around the house. Maybe Emily had a point.

Daniel remembered that DS Harper had asked whether Fay had taken her passport. He should check, although he doubted that she would have left the country without her handbag and debit cards. He tried to remember where it might be. He tried the kitchen drawer that was the depository for all the useless bits and pieces they gathered but couldn't throw away; mystery keys, Daniel's book of practical jokes, a sewing kit, packets of lettuce and sunflowers seeds, paperclips, various receipts, pens, an unused voucher for 'swimming with crocodiles for two', a present he'd given Fay, a stapler, standby birthday cards, an 'adopt a donkey gift pack' and a collection of foreign coins. There was no passport.

He checked the box of papers and invoices in the utility room, then the cupboard in the hallway but found nothing. He wondered if she really had gone abroad and simply left her old life behind, like Shirley Valentine. People did that. Had things really become that bad between them? Was he denying the problems in their relationship to the extent that all that was left for Fay was to leave?

Daniel ran upstairs and checked Fay's wardrobe. He found a box marked 'important documents' that she kept on the top shelf. In there were both of their birth certificates, their marriage certificate, a copy of their respective wills, papers to do with their pension arrangements and Daniel's passport. But not Fay's. He flicked through the rest of the papers and stopped dead in his tracks when he found Sophie's birth certificate.

Number 319.
Born on 22nd August 2017 at Riverbeke General Hospital.
Girl.

Name if any: Sophie Amelia
Father: Daniel Douglas Kendrick.
Mother: Fay Esther Kendrick, formally Rowan
Occupation of father: General surgeon
Registered by Fay Kendrick, mother, on 28th August 2017.
Signature of registrar: H. Harris

Daniel stared at the certificate for some minutes, tears welling in his eyes. His mind was flooded with images of their baby daughter. Unwanted images. Daniel closed his eyes, wiping away falling tears with the back of his hand. He remembered the day she was born, taking her home to the nursery he had lovingly decorated for her, her soft, golden hair, her fragrant, baby-soft skin, her first smile, the police officer telling them they had found her body...

Daniel opened his eyes and blinked hard, shaking his head as if he was trying to rid his brain of those painful memories. He folded the certificate and replaced it in the box. He put the lid on firmly and pushed the box to the back of the shelf, closing the wardrobe door tight. Across the bedroom, he saw the framed photograph of Sophie that had been Fay's favourite. The picture was of their baby, at three months old, lying on a rug in their sunlit garden; it was her first summer. And her last. Fay kept the photograph on her dressing table. He walked across, picked it up and gently laid it face down on the dresser. He couldn't cope with the constant reminders, as Fay did. She had kept Sophie's nursery as a shrine and spent hours in there sometimes. He couldn't bring himself to go in. He couldn't afford to let those feelings of grief gather momentum as they had in the months following Sophie's death. He had to keep them under control if he was to function as a human being.

Don't fall apart...

Daniel turned and walked toward Fay's bedside cupboard. Perhaps her passport was in the drawer. He opened it and beneath a pile of envelopes, he found it. She couldn't have left the country. He went to replace it but couldn't help looking at the return address on one of the envelopes. It was from Scottish Widows. He had never heard Fay mentioning any correspondence with the company. Intrigued, he pulled out the contents of one of the envelopes. There were several sheets of paper with Fay's name and address and there was a plan number in bold. As he read on, he realised it was a statement for a savings plan. The total invested was £62,240.

Daniel frowned. He knew nothing of this. They had always shared information about their finances and pooled their resources but Fay had withheld this. She had been saving in secret for some time by the look of it and there had been several lump sums invested over the past couple of years. Why hadn't she told him? He wasn't after her money; she knew that surely. They were both professionals on good salaries. They were comfortably off and had provisions for their retirement. Why keep it a secret from him? He felt a sudden wave of sadness. Perhaps, she had, after all, been planning to leave him.

Daniel sat for some moments on the side of their unmade bed. Was it too late to reconcile their marriage? He didn't want to lose her – especially if it really had been his behaviour that had pushed her away. He realised he'd been distant since Sophie's death but they had a good life as far as he was aware. It could be better, sure, but was it bad enough for her to consider leaving him?

He hoped it wasn't too late.

THIRTY-ONE

Wednesday 21st August 2019

Daniel found the list of Fay's appointments that he'd written out at her office in a crumpled heap on the coffee table. He read it. Damon Wixx had several appointments over the past few weeks, Tracey Goodwin was another regular and Melissa had seen Fay a few times in recent weeks. She had also seen several inmates at Ravenwood and Gallow Hill prisons and had visited the psychiatric unit at the hospital. He hoped DS Harper was investigating these people. He would mention it when he spoke to him next.

The dogs woke from their nap and barked. Then he heard a car pull up in the drive, pocketed the note and darted across to the window thinking it was Fay coming home. His heart was racing with anticipation. Then he saw Melissa Davenport parking her brand-new white Range Rover in his driveway. She gathered her things and opened the car door.

Shit.

She was the last person he wanted to see at the moment. What the hell was she doing coming here? She'd never come to the house before. Maybe he could pretend he wasn't in –

he could have left the car and gone for a walk. That would be plausible.

But it was too late. She'd seen him through the window. He watched as she waved to Jane, his neighbour – the one who had snubbed him for some unknown reason the other day. He vaguely remembered that she and Melissa were friends and went to the same coffee mornings together. Both as shallow and empty-headed as one another Fay had said once in a snarky remark.

He heard a car door thud, then Melissa was walking up the driveway to the front door. There was no escape.

Daniel shut the dogs in the garden and answered the door to see that Melissa's eyes were reddened from crying. Her mascara was a little smudged and her loose platinum hair less well-groomed than usual, kept off her face by huge movie star-style sunglasses. She was wearing a strappy, low cut fuchsia sundress that left little to the imagination and high-heeled fuchsia court shoes. Her Gucci bag was slung over her shoulder. Her bare arms and cleavage were deeply tanned and freckled from too much sun.

"Melissa," Daniel said, standing in the doorway as if to block her entrance.

"Darling, I just had to see you. Can I come in?" She tilted her head, gazing at him with those impossibly blue eyes.

Daniel felt obliged to invite her in, even though her timing wasn't great. He should be looking for Fay and trying to rescue his career, not making small talk with Melissa. He stood aside and gestured for her to go in before closing the door.

Melissa stepped into the hallway, leaving behind a whiff of her signature floral perfume. Her eyes were darting everywhere, taking in the house, it's décor and furnishings, the framed art on the wall. Uninvited, she walked through the open living room door, turning on six-inch heels to take in everything in the room.

Daniel felt a little irritated. What did she want with him now?

"Lovely home you have Daniel. I love the art – it's so you."

"Fay chose most of it actually," Daniel said flatly. He was about to ask her why she was there when Melissa cut in.

"I don't do cats, I'm afraid. Do you mind?" She gestured toward Maisie, who was making her way over to greet their visitor.

"Come on puss," Daniel said as he scooped her up, carried her to the back door and put her out into the garden with the dogs.

He returned to the living room to see Melissa eyeing the furniture. "Do you have an allergy to cats?" he asked, a little taken aback at her blatant assertiveness in his home.

"No, darling, I just don't do animals – or children. Just not for me." Melissa placed her bag on the sofa and sat next to it. She took the sunglasses from her head and placed them in the bag. Her platinum hair tumbled around her shoulders. Melissa patted the seat next to her, gesturing for Daniel to sit.

He stood several feet away, his hands in his pockets, his right hand fiddling with the note he'd put there earlier. "So, what can I do for you, Melissa?"

She sighed deeply, looked down at the carpet, then back at Daniel. "I'm leaving Oliver," she said, flicking her hair and pausing for effect.

Her announcement took Daniel by surprise. "Oh... really?"

"Yes, we haven't been getting on for a while and I've decided to leave. He doesn't love me – he said as much and I just can't go on any longer. We've been living a stupid, ridiculous lie – especially with this new business. He's cutting me out of it. I can't believe it. I was supposed to have been a director. He promised." Melissa's voice was breaking as she reached for a tissue from her bag.

Daniel wasn't sure what to say. He stood awkwardly, his arms now folded across his chest, trying to protect the wound on his forearm.

"Please, sit down Daniel," Melissa blubbed.

Daniel stayed where he was, unsure how to handle her. Unsure what her intentions were but sensing something awkward and unwanted was coming.

Melissa sobbed quietly for some moments, then blew her nose and dabbed carefully at her eyes, trying to avoid smudging her thick mascara any further. "The thing is… oh how can I put this…" She took a deep breath. "I've realised I love you, Daniel." She looked up at him, fixing him with her watery, intensely blue eyes. She was watching him, head tilted to one side; waiting for a response.

Daniel froze, staring back at her, unsure what to say. His head was shaking slightly, trying to make sense of her words. She looked vulnerable – so different to her usual seductive demeanour. There was an awkward silence between them.

Melissa watched Daniel, as if she was trying to read his expression, then suddenly stood and closed the gap between them, the whiff of her perfume stronger now. She trailed a scarlet manicured fingernail along his forearm. She locked his eyes with hers. "Is there a chance we could be together, Daniel? I think we'd be good for each other, you and I. What do you say?"

Daniel felt the hairs on the back of his neck prickle. He was still unsure how he should respond. He could see the little-girl-lost expression on her face and her eyes, wet with tears, were pleading with him.

Melissa smiled, buoyed by Daniel's lack of response. She seemed to be assuming far too much. She pressed herself closer to him, gently unfolding his arms with her hands and placing them around the curve of her waist.

He wasn't resisting.

She tilted her chin up toward his face. "We could run away together. We could go to the Caribbean, to the beach house. We could be happy, darling, I know we could. We could be free there. Just you and I." Melissa placed her hands one each side of Daniel's face, rose up on the toes of her fuchsia shoes and kissed him.

Daniel could taste the sweetness of Melissa's lips against his own; could feel the urgency of her mouth and the warmth of her body next to his. For a moment he melted into their embrace and pulled her closer to him. His troubled marriage, Fay's disappearance and the paralysing grief of losing his baby daughter fell away and for just a fleeting moment, he felt wanted and at peace.

But then, Daniel came to his senses. He pulled away from Melissa's kiss – their kiss. He took his arms from around her waist and pushed her gently away from him. What the hell was he thinking?

Melissa looked at him with confusion etched into her delicate face. "What's the matter, darling?"

"I can't... can't do this Melissa. I'm sorry." Daniel held her away from him at arm's length, the wound on his arm beginning to throb again.

"What do you mean? I thought you liked me, Daniel." Her lips were pouting now.

"Not enough to run away with you." Daniel was pushing her from him, gripping her upper arms, afraid that if he let go, she would kiss him again and he would be unable to resist.

"Or to make love to me?" Melissa said, still pouting her scarlet lips at him.

"That's not going to happen, Melissa." Daniel shook his head decisively now.

Melissa pouted again. "Why can't we be together Daniel? What's stopping you. We'd be so well suited."

"What's stopping me?" Daniel said. "What's stopping me is that I'm married and so are you. And I'm not so sure we are as well-suited, as you seem to think." Daniel realised with a flash of cognizance that he and Melissa were actually poles apart. Why hadn't he seen it before?

Well, I won't be married for much longer and if Fay has left you, then you're free too." Melissa pulled away from Daniel's grip indignantly.

"Fay hasn't left me." Daniel wasn't sure if that was true but he realised he wanted it to be.

"Well, where is she then?" Melissa said challenging him.

"That's what the police are trying to investigate."

"While you're here, kissing me," Melissa said, a self-satisfied smirk spread slowly across her scarlet lips.

"I think you should go." Daniel said, backing away.

Melissa fixed Daniel with her impossibly blue eyes once more.

"Are you sure there's no future for us Daniel? I do love you. Really, I do. More than I've ever loved Oliver. I could make you happy. I could be the sort of wife you've always wanted." There was a softness to her voice and a sadness behind her smile, that told him she already knew that she'd been defeated.

"I'm sure. Absolutely sure. I love my wife and I'm going to find her and bring her home. Please don't come here again." Daniel's voice was resolute.

Melissa scowled, her demeanour suddenly changing. The softness had gone from her eyes. "If that's what you want," she said acidly.

Daniel nodded. "Yes, I do. I want you to leave me alone. I'm not interested in you, Melissa. Not interested in the least."

Melissa turned and grabbed her bag from the sofa. She walked toward the front door and Daniel followed. As he opened the door for her to leave, she stopped and turned to him, her face now a picture of anger and indignation.

"I'll make sure you pay for this Daniel. You've embarrassed me and I could make your life hell – absolute bloody hell…" She put on her sunglasses and strode toward her car, got in, revved the engine and sped away, leaving a cloud of dust in her wake.

THIRTY-TWO

Wednesday 21st August 2019

Damon Wixx had called one of his drug-dealing accomplices and managed to dispose of the stash he had at the flat. He'd lost out financially but if the police had caught him with class A drugs in his possession it would only mean one thing, given his criminal history. Another jail term. He didn't really care that much – he cared less about most things – but he could do without the palaver.

After stashing Dr Kendrick's manuscript in the glove box of his mate's Ford Focus, Damon sat in his flat, smoking weed.

Sure enough, as he'd suspected, the police paid him a visit.

Damon answered the loud knock at his front door to find two plain-clothed detectives standing on the landing.

"Damon Wixx?"

"Yes. What can I do for you?"

"Detective Sergeant Harper and this is Detective Constable Coombs. We'd like a word." The two detectives flashed their warrant cards.

"Come in detectives," Damon said casually as he stood aside; a superficial charm disguising the contempt he felt for the authority of the police.

The two policemen filed into Damon's flat, DS Harper dressed in a dark suit over an open necked blue shirt while DC Coombs was more casual in beige chinos and a black polo shirt.

"Can I get you a drink?" Damon gestured for the men to sit.

They both perched on the edge of a tatty sofa but declined a drink. Damon slouched on an armchair near the window.

DS Harper was the first to speak. "Mr Wixx, can you tell us your whereabouts this Monday?"

Damon thought for a moment, his eyes swivelling to the right as he recalled what happened that day. "In the morning I had an interview at the job centre, then lunch at the Red Lion. In the afternoon, I had an appointment with Dr Kendrick at her clinic in Park Street." He looked at DS Harper. "She never turned up, so I went back to the Red Lion and stayed there until late in the evening – why?"

"And you have witnesses to verify all this?" DC Coombs asked.

"Yes, of course." Damon said indignantly. He was unfazed by their questions, since for once, he was telling the truth.

"And you attended Dr Kendrick's clinic yesterday?" Harper asked.

"Yes. I had another appointment but again, Dr Kendrick wasn't there, so I left and came home."

"Did you know why she wasn't at the clinic?" DC Coombs asked.

"No." Damon omitted to tell them that Meredith had spilt the beans that the doctor had gone missing.

The two policemen stood, thanked Wixx and left.

That was it. No search of the flat. No further questions. Damon knew he had a watertight alibi and that they were unlikely to be back. He may well have his own plans for Dr Kendrick but he genuinely had nothing to do with her disappearance and the police knew it.

As he closed the door, he felt the warmth of smug satisfaction.

THIRTY-THREE

Wednesday 21st August 2019

Daniel had watched Melissa tear away from his home in her Range Rover, her bitter words ringing in his ears. *"I could make your life hell – absolute bloody hell,"* she had said. He had no idea what she meant by that but he knew from her behaviour earlier, that she could be extremely manipulative and vengeful. He mentally dismissed, once and for all, the idea of ever going into partnership with her husband Oliver Davenport – even if his career as an NHS surgeon was on the line. And anyway, he wasn't sure he wanted to become a cosmetic surgeon. His rightful place was at Riverbeke General, saving lives. He hoped it wasn't too late to redeem himself.

Melissa had said she could be the sort of wife Daniel had always wanted. What did she mean by that, he wondered, as he let Maisie back into the house. He looked around their messy kitchen and realised he had longed for a wife that would be at home for him; would look after him and his every need. But what about Fay's needs? What about her career? He had rarely thought about that, he realised, with a flash of guilt. He hoped that if she had been contemplating leaving him, it wouldn't be too late to put things right.

Maisie was meowing for food again and he fed her, then stroked her back and scratched behind her ears. She responded by rubbing against his leg, purring, her tail held high. He let Chester and Ella back into the house and Ella made a bee-line for Maisie's dish but Daniel grabbed her collar and scolded her. The dogs wandered into the living room to their favourite places. Chester on his sofa and Ella on the rug.

It had only been a few hours since he'd spoken to DS Harper but he was anxious for news. Anxious for them to make progress with their investigation. He wanted Fay home, unharmed. For their lives to return to some sort of normality. For them to be happy, as they had been before Sophie had been murdered. He pushed his hand into his trouser pocket and pulled out the note he'd put there with the list of patients that Fay had seen recently. Melissa, Damon Wixx, Tracey Goodwin and inmates at Ravenwood and Gallow Hill prisons along with a few patients at the psychiatric unit at the hospital. Justin McCartney had been one of the last to see her but in his mind, Daniel had now ruled him out. He was psychotic and could be dangerous but didn't seem to have the wherewithal or the motive to kidnap Fay or harm her deliberately. He was a sick man needing help – the help he was now getting from Dr Maddison.

Daniel studied the list. Damon Wixx troubled him. He was an arrogant thug and had tried to assault both Fay and Meredith Baily but he hadn't appeared to realise Fay had gone missing. Why would he go back to her office twice for his appointments if he knew she wasn't there? It didn't make sense. Surely, he would be taking a risk to return to the scene of a crime when he could be long gone. No, as much as Daniel disliked the man, he seemed an unlikely candidate too and wasn't even one of the last to see her. The prison inmates were safely behind bars and unless they had accomplices on the outside to do their dirty work, it was unlikely they would be in a position to abduct her. Similarly, the hospital inmates would be safely tucked away on a hospital ward. It would be more likely to be a patient that had visited Fay's office. An attack was likely as the blood on her scarf and the carpet indicated.

Melissa? She had seen Fay at her office recently and, as Daniel had just witnessed, she could turn from sweetness and light to spitting venomous hatred in a flash. Did she have a motive to be rid of Fay? Yes, it seemed she did, judging from her performance earlier. Had she planned to dispose of Fay before making a move on him, making out that Fay had left him? It was possible, he supposed, although he wasn't completely convinced.

Most of Fay's patients he knew nothing of. He knew little of his wife's day to day work either, he realised. She had saved over £62,000 in a secret savings account. For what purpose, he wondered. Was she saving with plans to leave him? He found it hard to believe since she must have begun saving several years ago to have built up such a substantial amount. They had been happy before Sophie's death. He couldn't believe she'd been planning to leave him back then.

Daniel knew he would need more information. He needed to pay some of these patients a visit, or at least find out more about them. Perhaps Meredith could help him.

Hesitatingly, he picked up his iPhone and searched for her number. Should he call her? Shouldn't he be waiting for the police to run their official investigation? Yet he couldn't sit back waiting for news – it was driving him nuts.

He found Meredith's number and hit 'call'. She answered almost immediately.

"Hello?" she said apprehensively.

"Meredith, it's Daniel Kendrick."

"Have they found Fay?" she said, concern etched into her voice.

"No. Not yet but I want to help the police to find her. I need some information."

"What do you need? I'll do my best," she said.

"I need more details of the patients Fay has seen recently. The police have their medical records but I need to find out more about them. Do you know anything about them? Where I could go to see them and talk to them, perhaps?"

There was a pause for some moments before Meredith answered. "I know that Fay kept a separate set of notes on her patients. They are her personal, hand-written notes which she doesn't show to anyone." She paused, "I'm not sure if I should be telling you this."

"Please, Meredith, go on. It's vital we find Fay. Anything you can tell me could help to find her and bring her back safely."

"She keeps them locked away and I've never seen them but I know they are for her own benefit – you know, so she can write things that she wouldn't necessarily put in their official medical records."

"Like the attempted assault by Damon Wixx, for example?"

"Yes, I guess. She might have been worried about what he might do if it was made official. I know she was trying to deal with him without provoking him."

"Where can I find these notes, Meredith?"

Again, there was a long silence.

"In the filing cabinet in the kitchen cupboard."

Daniel thanked Meredith and hung up. He knew he had to get the personal notes that Fay had written on her patients. They could hold valuable clues to her whereabouts and the person that could be responsible for her disappearance. He had been told to stay away from the office – the scene of a possible crime – but somehow, he had to get in there and recover those notes. If there was anything of interest, he could inform DS Harper but he wanted access to the information first. Daniel had a set of keys for the clinic but he would have to avoid the front door. If the police were there, he would be seen. He would have to get in another way.

Daniel changed his bright checked shirt for a black T-shirt to go with the chinos he was wearing. No point in being too conspicuous, he thought. He decided to let the dogs stay in the house. He wasn't planning to be out long. Then he grabbed his car keys, checked the back door was locked and threw a few items from the garage into a grey canvas tool bag and put them into the boot of the BMW before sliding into the driver's seat. He reversed out of the driveway, his neighbour, Jane was curtain-twitching a few doors down, which he ignored. He pulled out of the street and onto the main road toward Riverbeke. The traffic was light as he drove through the town and he turned down several side streets before driving slowly along Park Road, past Fay's clinic. He drove past the large Victorian building, police tape still in situ indicating a crime scene. He could see no activity or marked police cars from the road but that didn't mean there was nobody there. He parked a block away.

Daniel grabbed the tool bag from the boot of the car and walked back along the street toward the clinic, dodging up a side lane and along the back of the buildings. He recognised the back of Fay's clinic, which was situated on the ground floor – the two floors above were occupied by an accountancy firm. He opened the lane gate and walked the length of the back yard, stopping at the kitchen door. He looked through the bunch of keys he'd retrieved from his pocket and found a mortice lock type key that looked promising. The key fitted the lock and it clicked open. Daniel hesitated before opening the door, unsure as to whether the police would be in there, still working the crime scene.

After a few moments, he quietly opened the back door and let himself into the kitchen, closing the door behind him. There was no sound from the rest of the building but he waited, ear to the closed kitchen door that led to the reception area and Fay's consulting room. Nothing. He waited two full minutes. Still no sound. The place seemed to be deserted but he didn't want to risk opening the kitchen door. Instead, he quietly located the key for the walk-in cupboard and unlocked it, reaching behind a pile of hanging coats for the light switch. Flicking on the light, he placed his tool bag on the floor and closed the cupboard door behind him.

Daniel tried the drawer on the filing cabinet. It was still locked. He checked the bunch of keys again, but there was definitely nothing that would be a fit. He reached into the tool bag and pulled out an iron crowbar. He pushed the flat end of it into the top of the first drawer behind the lock and forced it. The metal buckled but gave way and the drawer opened. He replaced the crowbar into the bag, fully opened the drawer and peered inside. Sets of folders were pushed into separating cardboard hanging compartments, all labelled with the names of patients. Bingo! This was exactly what he was looking for. He pulled out one folder, marked Juliet Sharpe, a name he didn't recognise from his list. He flicked through the pages of Fay's handwriting. The last entry had been over seven months ago. Fay had discharged her patient and had been pleased with the results of her therapy. She had asterisked a comment:

*'A very nice lady. Hope she will do well'.

Daniel replaced the folder in the drawer. He searched through the other compartments and found several names he didn't recognise. Then he saw a file for Melissa Davenport. He couldn't resist a look and took the folder out, flicking through the pages. Fay had remarked over and over how shallow Melissa was and how she was only interested in Oliver for his money. Daniel placed it on top of the cabinet and looked through the rest of the compartments. He was looking for a file marked Damon Wixx but didn't find it. He pulled out Tracey Goodwin's file and several others, including Justin McCartney's and piled them on top of the cabinet. He closed the top drawer then pulled open the second and grabbed a few folders, adding them to the pile. Possibly, amongst that lot, there might be some clues, someone that might have been harbouring bad intentions toward Fay. If Fay had been aware of something amiss, surely it would be here, in her private notes, that she would write about her concerns.

Daniel heard a thump from behind the partition wall with the reception area, then footsteps. He froze, listening intently, his heart racing. The footsteps seemed to recede away toward Fay's consulting room. He should get away quickly before someone came into the kitchen – if it was the police, he wasn't meant to be there. He placed the pile of notes into the tool bag, quietly closed the cabinet drawer, picked up his tool bag and stepped back toward the cupboard door. He stopped and listened. There was the faint sound of movement in the direction of Fay's consulting room but otherwise it was quiet. He cracked open the cupboard door and checked the kitchen was all clear, switched off the light and stepped into the room.

The sound of movement and footsteps was getting louder. Someone was in the reception area, just behind the kitchen. Daniel closed the cupboard door behind him and tiptoed to the back door. He opened it and let himself into the yard, closing it behind him. He locked it, glancing back just as a figure stepped into the kitchen. He couldn't see who it was but they seemed to peer around the room as if they had heard a noise before stepping back into the reception area.

Daniel made a quick exit from the yard and into the back lane. It had been a narrow escape, whoever had been in there. Maybe the SOCOs or one of DS Harper's team? For now, Daniel needed to go through these notes and try to find something that could lead him to Fay. It was something he needed to do himself. He was getting frustrated waiting for the police investigation.

THIRTY-FOUR

Wednesday 21st August 2019

Daniel arrived home, grabbed the tool bag from the car and let himself into the house. The dogs had barely moved but leapt up to greet him. Daniel made a fuss of them and threw the tool bag onto the floor next to the sofa. He went into the kitchen to make himself a mug of instant coffee and found a few shortbread biscuits in the tin. He helped himself to four. The next couple of hours could make for interesting reading.

Daniel grabbed an A4 notepad and pen and was just pouring the coffee when there was a loud knock on the door. He grabbed his coffee and went into the hallway to see the shadows of two men through the frosted glass of the front door. He shut the dogs in the kitchen and opened it cautiously.

On Daniel's doorstep stood DS Harper and another police officer; a tall, thin man with a pale complexion and eyes that looked too big for his head. He looked like he'd eaten a bad curry.

"Dr Kendrick. I'm sure you'll remember me; DS Harper, and this is detective constable Clive Wilkins." Harper nodded toward the DC. "May we come in for a chat?"

Daniel assumed they had come to update him on the investigation. "Yes, of course." He opened the door and stood aside for them to enter. He could see a black unmarked Vauxhall Astra parked in the driveway behind his BMW.

Daniel closed the door and ushered them into the living room. "Please, sit down detectives. Can I offer you a coffee or tea? I've just made some fresh coffee." He was hoping they would have some good news; that they'd found Fay.

"No thank you," DS Harper said. He sat on the sofa and DC Wilkins sat next to him.

Daniel pushed Maisie off the chair and sat in the warm spot she'd left. He sipped his coffee. "Has there been a development?" he asked.

"You could say that," Harper said. He looked at Daniel, his expression serious. "I'm afraid we've had some new information."

"Oh?" Daniel's stomach lurched. It didn't sound as if it was going to be good news. He twisted the right side of his head toward the detective.

"We understand that you and your wife have been having some rather heated arguments recently." He took a notebook from his jacket pocket and flicked through a few pages, finding what he was looking for. "It seems that on the evening of last Sunday, you had a particularly aggressive interaction. Can you explain what this was about?" DS Harper fixed Daniel with a questioning gaze.

Daniel flushed with embarrassment. "What do you mean? How would you know about an argument we had?"

"I'm afraid I'm not at liberty to say, sir. Is it true that you had a row with your wife on Sunday evening which seemed to continue on into Monday morning?"

Those bloody nosey neighbours, Daniel thought. It had to be Jane Hopkins. That would explain the way she snubbed him on the driveway. She was always out to cause trouble – she was renowned for it in the street.

"I'm guessing you've been speaking to my neighbour, Jane Hopkins. Our local curtain twitcher." Daniel paused, trying to gather his thoughts. It would be pointless denying it.

The detectives didn't answer but sat, watching Daniel, waiting for his response.

"Yes, OK. We did have a row – a humdinger on Sunday evening – but I can't remember what it was about. Something and nothing probably." Daniel sat back in the chair, hoping that would be the end of the matter. He wasn't about to discuss their private business.

"You can't remember why you and your wife argued? Yet it was just a few days ago. Do you have frequent arguments? So frequent that you can't remember one in particular?" Harper's tone was hardening and he was staring at Daniel with an intensity that was meant to be intimidating.

"We've had a few rows but we get over it pretty quickly." Daniel sat forward in his chair, as if he was bracing himself for more awkward questions.

"Is it true that you are a heavy drinker, Dr Kendrick?" DS Harper asked.

"What are you implying? That I get drunk and hit my wife?" Daniel didn't like where this was going. He could feel the hair on the back of his neck prickling.

"We are just trying to piece together the events that led up to your wife's disappearance, sir."

"Look, detective. Couples have rows all the time. What's the problem? We're no different to many other married couples."

"Is it true that you are a heavy drinker?" DS Harper persisted.

"I like a drink in the evenings, sure, and so does Fay. There's nothing unusual about that."

"Would you say, sir, that you and your wife have been experiencing difficulties with your relationship since the death of your daughter?"

Daniel felt a sudden flush of anger. How dare Harper bring

Sophie into it. That was their private grief and out of bounds for discussion.

"I don't think that's anyone else's business," Daniel said, trying hard to maintain his composure.

"Sir, we are simply trying to understand the situation and respond to the complaints we've had about the rows you and your wife have been having recently. It could be important to our enquiry. Could it be that Dr Kendrick has left you following a heated row?" Harper's tone had softened. It seemed he had picked up on Daniel's irritation and was evidently trying to keep the situation calm.

"No, I don't think she's left me, detective and I'm not sure why you would believe that. Who have you been talking to?"

Daniel felt exposed and angry at being forced to discuss his difficulties with Fay. How the hell had the police got this information? Then he had a sudden flash of realisation.

"Just a minute, officer. Have you been talking to Melissa Davenport by any chance?" He glanced at the tool bag lying at the side of the sofa, next to DS Harper, knowing Fay's private notes on Melissa were in the bag.

Harper's eyebrows rose in surprise. "Why do you ask? What is your relationship with Ms Davenport?"

"That's just it, officer, there is no relationship between us. She is a venomous bitch who is trying to get back at me because I snubbed her advances. She warned me she would make my life hell and now I see what she means. She is also bosom pals with Jane Hopkins, my nosey neighbour. They've concocted this up between them to get back at me." Daniel's indignance at Melissa was turning to fury.

"And yet, you were seen with Ms Davenport at a charity function on Monday evening. By all accounts, you seemed quite intimate with her." Harper scribbled something on his notepad.

"I wouldn't say intimate. She was drunk and hanging on to me. That's not intimate."

"Yet you spend almost the whole evening with her. Isn't that correct?"

"I guess so but that doesn't mean there is anything more to our acquaintance. Look, I know her husband. He is a colleague of mine. He knows Melissa – she's well known to be flirtatious with a lot of men. Not just me."

"And yet she was here at your home just this afternoon."

Daniel felt exasperated as he explained to the two detectives what had happened with Melissa and her threat to make his life hell. Harper made notes as he spoke.

"I see. But you don't deny that you and your wife have been having heated arguments just before her disappearance? About Ms Davenport, perhaps?"

"No, absolutely not. There is nothing going on between Melissa and I – never has been – and Fay is well aware of that." Daniel sighed. He felt cornered and angry at Melissa – it had to be her that had gone to the police. Her and that bitch Jane Hopkins.

Daniel drained his coffee mug. He caught DS Harper trying to suppress a grin. The two police officers exchanged a look of amusement.

"But you did have an argument," Harper managed with a wistful smile.

"Yes, we did have an argument but, as I said, I honestly don't remember what it was all about. I do know it had nothing to do with Fay's disappearance, or Melissa bloody Davenport." Daniel looked at Harper, at PC Wilkins and back to Harper.

DS Harper stood and PC Wilkins followed suit.

"We'd like to take a look around your home if that's alright. It's a normal part of our investigation into a missing person." DS Harper said, his expression unreadable.

"Yes, of course," Daniel said, knowing it was inevitable.

"Please, help yourself."

"Thank you." DS Harper said.

He and PC Wilkins checked the living room, opening cupboard doors and drawers. They checked the kitchen and made their way upstairs, working their way through every room.

Daniel took his mug to the kitchen, unsure whether he should follow the police officers. He rinsed his mug under the tap and realised what the earlier source of amusement – at his expense – had been. On the underside of the mug was a slogan that read, 'I'm a twat', another thoughtful gift from his son Richard. Daniel rolled his eyes.

He decided to follow the two policemen upstairs. They were in the master bedroom.

"Is this your wife's hairbrush?" Harper asked, holding up a black plastic brush with Fay's hairs tangled among the bristles.

"Yes, it is," Daniel said, hanging back in the doorway.

"I'd like to take this to obtain another sample of Dr Kendrick's DNA."

"Yes, that's fine."

The DS took a forensics bag from his pocket and slipped the brush into it.

Daniel stood aside as the two detectives opened the door to Sophie's nursery.

"Please – be careful in there. Fay has kept everything as it was after we lost our baby. She wouldn't want anything to be disturbed." Daniel could see into the room but couldn't bring himself to go in. It had become Fay's shrine to their child and seemed to bring her comfort. He hadn't yet been able to face those raw emotions.

"Yes, of course," DS Harper said. "I understand your baby was abducted."

"And murdered," Daniel said, coldly.

Harper gave him a sympathetic smile and looked around the nursery, opening a few cupboards, glancing at the photographs of Sophie – of them as a family – that Fay had arranged around the room. Heart-breaking reminders of what had happened.

"Alright. We'll leave it at that for now, Dr Kendrick, but we may need to speak to you again."

Daniel stood. "Am I under arrest?"

"No. But we would like you to help us eliminate you from our line of enquiry."

Daniel wasn't sure what that meant but it didn't sound good. He was obviously now a suspect in Fay's disappearance, thanks to that bitch, Melissa. Now he felt completely alone and out of his depth.

THIRTY-FIVE

Wednesday 21st August 2019

After DS Harper and DC Wilkins left the house, Daniel poured himself a large glass of shiraz and sat on the sofa in his living room, stunned at what had happened. Ella put her head on his lap, watching him closely. Her nut-brown eyes deep pools of concern. Chester went back to his sofa. Daniel absently played with Ella's soft ear. God knows what Melissa had told the police but now he was a suspect or at the very least, a person of interest. There would be no way DS Harper would keep him informed of any progress in the investigation. Unless, of course, they had found Fay unharmed and able to testify in his favour. Now, not only did he have to find Fay but he would also have to prove his innocence in her disappearance.

Shit!

What a bloody mess, he thought, as he took a large glug of wine. It wasn't the time to give up drinking and he'd gone past caring about it after the day he'd had. So, what if he liked a drink – he wasn't hurting anyone. He finished the glass and poured another. Ella grabbed her teddy bear, Eddie, in her mouth and went off to curl up on her rug. Maisie jumped up to fill the empty space on his warm lap. He let her stay there, stroking her head and rubbing under her chin. The animals had become a comfort and, seemingly, his only connection to Fay.

Daniel wondered what Fay was doing. Was she OK? Had she eaten something? Was she warm enough? Where the hell was she? Was there someone with her or was she alone and frightened. He had to find her – whatever it took…

Daniel's iPhone rang. It was Emily, Fay's mother. He let it ring. Right now, he had to concentrate on finding Fay. He would text Emily later – God knows what she knew now. How far did Melissa's resentment reach? Would she have sought out his family and his colleagues at work, spreading malicious gossip and blatant lies? All he knew was that he couldn't cope with explaining Melissa to Fay's mother, or the rows he and her daughter had been having.

Daniel reached down for his tool bag and the private notes about Fay's patients that it contained. Maisie settled down on the sofa next to him while he looked through, making notes of his own: when Fay last saw each person and where, was there any sign of an acrimonious relationship between them and whether Fay seemed intimidated by anyone. Somewhere in that pile of folders, there had to be a suspect – someone that might know what had happened to Fay and where she was. Someone who might even be responsible for her disappearance.

He checked Melissa's notes. Her selfishness bordered on narcissism and she could be manipulative in the extreme – as he was beginning to find out. He wasn't surprised to learn that she and Oliver were splitting up and Fay had mentioned as much in her notes. One sentence, though, jumped out at him.

'I just hope she keeps her hands off my husband! He might be useless sometimes but I don't think he'd be unfaithful – not with her.'

Was that what Fay thought – that he could be useless? He thought about the mess he often left in the kitchen and elsewhere around the house and his habitual lack of thought for her. He had to admit, he could see why she would make a comment like that. But what troubled him was the implication that he could be unfaithful – not with Melissa but with someone. That hurt. He had been a faithful husband and always intended to be. Perhaps his indifference to Fay had stirred up her insecurities. There was so much he needed to say to her. He wished she was there with him now so he could reassure her of his love and commitment.

He stroked Maisie again. It was if she had become an emotional bridge to Fay.

Daniel took the next folder from the pile. He'd seen and read enough about Melissa and although he'd now seen her for what she was; a shallow, egoistical bitch, he didn't think she was responsible for Fay's disappearance.

He picked up a folder marked Tracey Goodwin – another of Fay's recent patients. She had been having CBT treatment for anorexia, triggered, it was thought, by the suicide of her best friend. There was nothing in her notes to indicate any disagreements between them or any malice from Tracey. In fact, it looked like she may have been re-admitted to the psych unit recently having dropped, worryingly, to five stone in weight. She was not on Daniel's list of possible suspects.

He read through Justin McCartney's notes. He had suffered with psychotic episodes for several years and Fay seemed to have a great deal of sympathy for him. She'd been worried that she'd not been able to help him – hence the referral to Dr Maddison. Daniel was sure in his mind that Justin had nothing to do with Fay's disappearance, even though he must have been one of the last people to see her at her office.

Daniel thought again about Damon Wixx. He was a nasty piece of work; no doubt about that. What did Fay have to say about him, he wondered. He hadn't found any notes on him in the filing cabinet but maybe he'd picked them up with the pile from the second drawer after he'd been disturbed. He looked through the remaining pile of notes and there was nothing on Wixx. Perhaps the notes had been in Fay's briefcase or in her desk, he reasoned. There would be no way he'd be able to get his hands on them now.

One name stood out, Jaxon Sloan. He'd heard the name somewhere but couldn't recall where. He leafed through the pages and the reams of notes in Fay's handwriting. It seemed he'd suffered with depression and bouts of anger and had been jailed for GBH – grievous bodily harm. Fay had written that she was worried that she had testified against him in court as an expert witness, yet he had been allocated to her as a patient while serving his time at Gallow Hill. In fact, he had volunteered for therapy and had requested Fay as his psychiatrist. Somehow that had slipped the net – surely, she shouldn't have been treating him after effectively putting him behind bars. Either that or there was a shortage of qualified staff. Why had she gone along with this and not requested another psychiatrist? Her colleague Shelly Winters, for example, could have taken him on. They could have swapped patients to share the workload. Did Sloan have an axe to grind? Was he seeking revenge against her for testifying that he was fit to stand trial and that he was 'bad, not mad' and therefore responsible for his crimes? Thanks to her testimony, he had been handed a custodial sentence. Fay's notes ended with a therapy session inside Gallow Hill some eighteen months ago. He had been depressed and angry and referred elsewhere for more anger management sessions. Daniel had no idea what had happened since.

Daniel poured himself another large glass of wine, emptying the bottle. Maybe there was something going on with this Sloan character. He checked the front section of his notes for an address. There was no residential address, simply c/o HMP Gallow Hill.

It occurred to him that not only should he be looking at current patients – like the ones obtained from Fay's appointment book – but also past patients that might have an axe to grind. Patients that Fay had testified against in court as an expert witness. Criminals that had been sent to prison thanks to her testimony. He had no idea where he could find that information. Perhaps Meredith, Fay's receptionist, would have an appointment book for Fay's expert witness appearances in court. Would the court be willing to give him that information? Unlikely.

Daniel checked through all the files and found one other patient who had been sent to prison after Fay's expert witness testimony.

Robert Horton.

That name was familiar too but again he couldn't place him. From Fay's notes, he could see that Horton had been handed a life sentence for child murder. He had pleaded insanity but Fay's testimony had ruled that out. She had effectively sent him to prison for the rest of his life. The notes were old – the last entry was over fifteen years ago – but Fay had been adamant that he was in his right mind and was fully responsible for his crimes. Daniel had no idea what had happened after that but assumed if Horton had been given a life sentence he was still in prison. Probably at the category A prison, HMP Ravenwood, if he had remained in the local area. He placed Horton's notes in a separate pile along with Jaxon Sloan's.

Daniel looked at the clock. It was gone midnight. Too late to call Meredith Baily. He would call her first thing and try to glean further information about Horton and Sloan and if there was a record of all the patient's Fay had testified against.

He was tempted to pour himself a whisky. Instead, he settled Chester and Ella in the Dog House, stroked Maisie, fed her, then checked the doors were locked and went to bed. He would have a busy day tomorrow.

THIRTY-SIX

Damon Wixx was short of cash. He'd lost out on the drugs he'd jettisoned before the police visit, unnecessarily as it had turned out. He could have kept them and sold them on the estate for several thousand had he known the police were not intending to search his flat. Now he was back to square one with no money.

He had decided it was time to pay his uncle a visit.

His parasitic lifestyle frequently took him to the house of Wallace Frazer. An uncle by marriage – the brother of Damon's adoptive mother – he had moved down from Aberdeen in the mid-1980s to take up an administration position in a recruitment agency. Childless himself, he had, on occasion, taken Damon under his wing during his turbulent childhood. He had always been a soft touch. Always saw the good in people. Had tried his best to guide Damon toward a decent and productive life.

Damon had borrowed his mate's Ford Focus and driven to his uncle's house on the outskirts of Riverbeke – south of the river in a quiet, well-heeled rural area. He parked on the gravel drive and scrunched his way to the front door of the large detached stone-built bungalow. The bungalow had been well maintained and stood in immaculate gardens, bordered by tall leylandii hedges. Damon rapped on the door with his knuckles and waited. A carved wooden sign at the side of the door read 'Auchenblae' – 'Home' in Gaelic.

The door was opened by a stout, kindly-looking man in his mid-seventies. Balding with wisps of white hair and a short, neat white beard and moustache, he wore grey trousers, tartan slippers and a thin navy sweater over a dark green polo shirt. He smiled warily at Damon. He knew what was coming.

"Wally. How the hell are you?" Damon pushed past his uncle and entered the large square hallway that was groaning with highly polished antique clocks. The sound of Westminster chimes was resonating from the sitting room and there was a slightly musty smell mingled with lavender and a hint of floor cleaner.

Wallace Frazer shook his head, almost imperceptibly. He was well used to Damon's sense of grandiose entitlement and had long given up trying to influence him. He had finally accepted that his adoptive nephew was a lost cause and had come to dread his visits.

Frazer closed the door and followed Damon into the kitchen. He was shuffling and bent over due to an arthritic spine and hips.

Damon was sat, sprawled, in a display of arrogance, on a wooden chair at the kitchen table and was helping himself to biscuits from a tin. "How are things uncle Wally?" he asked around a mouthful of Scottish shortbread.

"I'm fine. Been gardening, ay. Have you heard from your mother?" Frazer had retained a trace of his Aberdeenshire Doric Dialect accent.

Damon shook his head, seemingly unconcerned. He had written to his biological mother on a whim over two months ago with the help of a tracing agency, who had tracked her down to an address in the north of England. The force driving him to make contact had nothing whatsoever to do with curiosity about his birth mother. Damon had nothing but contempt for the woman who had given birth to him, such was his inability to experience or understand the emotions that normal human beings feel. Giving in to his sense of superiority, peevish resentment and self-pity, he had wanted to hurt her and destroy her for abandoning him. Mostly, though, he felt entitled to her money and contacting his mother was simply another avenue to explore in his parasitic quest for financial gain. Of course, he hid, as usual, behind a mask of sanity and the pretence of motivations that would be acceptable to others and society.

"Maybe she nae want to make contact, no? Ye have to be prepared for that Damon," Frazer said gently.

Damon shrugged and pushed another shortbread finger into his mouth. "It is what it is, uncle."

"So, what brings ye here. I haven't seen ye in a little while, no?" Frazer said, braced for the request that inevitably came.

"Any chance of a sub?" Damon didn't even bother to oil the wheels with social niceties any more.

Frazer sighed and shook his head. "Not this time, Damon, no. I'm sorry, ay."

Damon looked at his uncle disdainfully. "What do you mean 'not this time' – I need some cash."

"I simply haven't got it. I haven't, no." Frazer was uncharacteristically holding his ground.

Damon felt a sudden surge of anger. He was incapable of feeling gratitude for the considerable help his uncle had given him over the years and felt entitled to take whatever he wanted from him – whenever he wanted it.

The two men glared at one another. Frazer unwilling to back down and Damon determined to get the cash he came for.

Still glaring at Frazer, Damon stood, pushing his chair noisily across the stone floor with the back of his legs. He strode over to his uncle, towered over him, and began jabbing his chest with a grubby index finger. "What's the matter with you Wally. Hand over the fucking money. I know you have it." His face was etched with utter contempt.

Frazer backed away, reaching behind for the kitchen counter in an effort to steady himself. "I... I don't have it, ay, Damon. Not this time, no. You've bled me dry. There's no more left."

"You're lying. I know you're loaded. Surely you can help your only nephew, you old bastard." Damon continued to prod and push Frazer as he backed away.

Frazer's eyes were suddenly wide and dark with terror as he clutched at his chest.

Becoming impatient, Damon shoved his uncle against the kitchen cupboards and turned away, pacing the room; ranting in self-righteous indignation. "You make me sick – you should be helping me. What about family loyalty, eh? I thought you cared about your precious bloody family, yet you don't give a shit do you. Not really. What do you think Mum would say if she was still alive? She'd be absolutely ashamed of you. Yeah – shame on you Wally. You could have given me a decent roof over my head instead of letting me rot in that hell hole on the estate. Why should you have all this...," he swept an arm around, indicating the house and garden, "and you give me bugger all? The least you could do is help me with some cash now and again. It wouldn't kill you..." Damon turned to face his uncle, expecting his taunts to have the desired effect.

Frazer was doubled over, clutching his chest with both hands; his face ashen and gnarled with pain. His eyes wide and staring, he was clearly terrified. His mouth gaped uselessly as he tried to speak.

Damon smirked. He'd hit the spot by the look of it. Frazer's legs were starting to give way from under him, weak and unable to support his weight. He was still clutching his chest with one hand, bent into the pain that was searing through his body, leaning on the kitchen counter for support. He was reaching his other arm toward Damon in a breathless plea for help. "Help me lad… heart… my heart… call an ambulance…"

Damon quickly realised his uncle was suffering a heart attack. He also knew he could help him. He could call an ambulance, perform cardiac resuscitation – he'd learned what to do in prison as part of an accredited qualification to impress the parole board. Yes, he knew exactly what to do to save Frazer's life.

In that moment, he had to make a choice.

Save him or let him die…

THIRTY-SEVEN

Thursday 22nd August 2019

Daniel woke early and without a hangover for once. Maisie had slept at the bottom of the bed all night and, unusually, Daniel had let her stay there. Normally he banned her from the bedroom, to the disappointment of Fay, but he was becoming very fond of her.

He let Chester and Ella out into the garden, showered and dressed then found some bread in the freezer, which he toasted and slathered with butter and jam, making an extra slice for the dogs. He ate whilst standing in the kitchen, leaning against one of the cabinets, slipping titbits to Chester. Ella was busy chewing a hide bone in the garden, watched by a blackbird in the cherry tree. Daniel made a mug of tea and wrote a list of groceries to pick up while he was out. He needed to eat, and if Fay did come home, she would need a decent meal as well. He added pet food to the list, some washing powder and more refuse bags. Daniel pocketed the list and loaded the dishwasher.

He checked the time. Just gone 8 am. He should text Emily before she tried to call him again. He wanted to avoid an awkward conversation. He unplugged his iPhone from the charger and texted:

Sorry Emily. Busy day yesterday. No sign of Fay yet but we're working on a few ideas. Will let you know if there are any developments. Try not to worry x

He glanced at the notes he had made last evening. Jaxon Sloan and Robert Horton were top of his list of Fay's patients to check out. He decided to call Meredith Baily, Fay's receptionist. Perhaps she would know something. He found her number and just as he was about to hit 'call', a text came through from Emily:

Alright but please let me know the minute you find out anything. I'm worried sick.

He texted back:

Yes, I will x

Daniel sighed with relief. From her reply, it didn't seem that Melissa or the police had got to Emily. He hoped they wouldn't but it seemed inevitable that the police would want to speak to her sooner or later since she was Fay's mother. There was nothing he could do about that now, he thought. He called Meredith's number. It rang several times before a sleepy voice answered.

"Hello?"

"Sorry Meredith. Did I wake you? It's Daniel Kendrick."

"It's OK – I should be up by now anyway. What's happening? Any news?" Meredith cleared her throat.

"No news of Fay but I was wondering if you might be able to help me with some more information?"

"Sure, if I can."

"Do you know of a patient called Robert Horton?"

There was a long pause. "No, but the name sounds familiar. I don't think he's been to the office though."

"What about a Jaxon Sloan?" Daniel sat at the kitchen table with his notepad.

"No, sorry. Don't know him either."

"Do you know whether any of Fay's colleagues might know them?" Daniel was tapping a pen on the pad.

"Not sure but I know she worked with Dr Shelly Winters quite a lot. She's based at Riverbeke General, in the psych department. She might be worth a try."

"Thanks." Daniel knew Shelly and scribbled her name on the pad.

"Just one last question. Would there be a list or a diary with the details of Fay's expert witness testimonies? Maybe at the clinic somewhere?"

"No. Not that I know of. She managed those herself in her personal diary. I just deal with the general appointments for patients. Sorry I can't be more helpful." Meredith sounded as if she was stifling a yawn.

"No problem. Thanks for your help."

They ended the call. Apart from a lead to Shelly, there was no new information from Meredith. She had heard of Robert Horton though, as he had. He just couldn't think where he'd heard the name. Fay's personal diary would have been in her handbag, which was being kept for forensic evidence.

Maybe he should speak to Shelly.

He looked up her number and called.

"Hi Daniel. Any news?" Her voice was a little distant. It sounded like she was in the car.

"Are you driving?"

"Hands free."

"Good. No news of Fay but I was wondering if we could have a chat sometime soon. I just wanted to ask you about a few of Fay's patients."

"Yes, of course. I'm due in court in fifteen minutes but should be free by about 10 am. Can we meet for coffee in town? I have to go shopping anyway. How about Tatiana's by the river at 10.15 am? It's usually quiet there during the week and it's easier to park."

"Great. I'm buying. See you there." Daniel was relieved they were meeting away from the hospital – another source of awkwardness.

They rang off. Daniel knew that Fay liked Tatiana's Coffee Shop as a place to meet friends and colleagues and she often took the dogs but he'd never been there with her. That was another thing they never seemed to do anymore – go for coffee, chat and hang out together.

There were quite a lot of things that had to change if Fay ever came home, he thought.

THIRTY-EIGHT

Thursday 22nd August 2019

Jaxon Sloan woke to the booming sound of EC145 police helicopter blades rotating overhead. His instinct was to dive for cover and in his panic, he glanced around and saw a large fallen oak just a few yards away. Still groggy from the rude awakening, he jumped up from where he had been leaning against a beech tree and made for the oak, rolling underneath it and moulding his body to fit its slightly curved trunk. In his haste he had stepped on a stone in his bare feet and his instep was throbbing. He winced but stayed quiet, lying motionless beneath the oak. His holdall was still beside the beech but it was well tucked in. His socks were draped over the trunk, drying from his river crossing that morning. He hoped they wouldn't be seen.

He dared not move, despite twigs and stones digging painfully into his back. He couldn't take any chances. With the surveillance equipment the police had at their disposal, any movement would be seen. By now, they would have had several hours to draft in additional equipment and personnel from other National Police Air Service units in England and Wales. The helicopter made two more passes, one almost directly overhead, before it flew south following the course of the river. Gradually the whirring of rotating blades receded into the distance and Sloan relaxed. With the thick tree canopy overhead, it was unlikely that he'd been spotted. He stuck his head out from beneath the oak and checked the sky. No drones, no aircraft. Only the distant humming of the helicopter and the smouldering glow of the sun shining directly overhead. He rolled out from his hiding place and limped back to the beech tree and his belongings. All he had in the world at that moment was packed into his holdall. He retrieved damp socks and pulled them on, rubbing his bruised insole until the pain diffused.

Sloan didn't remember doing so, but he'd obviously fallen asleep. He had been exhausted and restless at Mateo's and then on the run the rest of the night. Adrenaline had kept him alert until he'd found the safety of the woodland. He'd have to be more careful and plan rest times so that he could remain hidden. By day, he could probably hide from high-definition cameras in the thick forest but by night, he would have to be watchful of silent drones and thermal imaging cameras.

Sloan pulled on his soggy boots and tidied away the remains of his meal into the holdall. He finished drinking the tepid water from the bottle he'd started earlier and pushed the empty plastic container to the bottom of the bag, not wanting to leave the smallest trace of himself behind. He rubbed a rough hand over his face, aghast at how his life had come to this. One minute he was being released from prison, sentence served, his life ahead of him – now he was on the run for a double murder.

How long could he stay on the run, he wondered. He'd heard of others that had evaded capture for decades despite the tens of thousands in reward money that was on offer. He didn't relish the thought of living like a fugitive for years to come but what was the alternative? He sat for some minutes contemplating his next move. He might be safe here for a while. He was well hidden and had plenty of provisions but he would have to move on sometime. Perhaps he could find somewhere more sheltered for the night.

Sloan decided to make his way further west; deeper into the woodland. He tried to remember some of the survival skills he'd heard about. Making a simple shelter, staying safe, keeping warm – winter was only a matter of months away. And what about finding enough to eat? He couldn't imagine himself killing and eating an animal. Buying packaged meat was one thing but he couldn't contemplate looking a deer or a rabbit in the eye and killing it in cold blood.

And yet: he'd just shot his wife dead. Sloan had to marvel at the paradox.

He tried to focus on the here and now. He had to take each day – each hour – as it came. Jaxon peered up through the tree branches. The sun was past its highest point and was beginning to fall toward the west. He had become a little disoriented with the same dense woodland in all directions but he decided to follow the sun since it would lead him deeper into the countryside. He hoisted his holdall over his shoulder and began pushing his way through the undergrowth, stopping periodically to check the sun's position. His jeans were drying but still felt cold and damp in the shade of the forest. Discomfort was something he would have to get used to if he was going to stay on the run, he realised. But even this was preferable to the claustrophobic confines of a prison cell and the constant proximity of other people. He wasn't sure how he would cope with solitude for long periods, maybe months or years, but for the time being, he was better off alone.

The sound of a twig cracking and leaves rustling close by made Sloan stop dead in his tracks. He stood motionless for some moments. There it was again. There was definitely something moving to his left. He turned and scanned the area from where the sound had come but could see nothing; just trees and pools of light breaking through the thick canopy. Could it be tracker dogs or police on his trail? His heart lurched as he heard the sound again. Then to his relief, he saw three adult fallow deer strolling through the woodland, their brown spotted coats perfect camouflage amongst the foliage. He watched them as they ventured slightly closer, saw him and darted off into the woods.

Sloan kept a vigilant eye on the sky, checking for drones, helicopters, aircraft and the position of the sun. Without his phone to check the time, he was now reliant on nature for his cues. He guessed it was early-afternoon. Apart from the numerous contrails from jets high in the sky, there was no sign of any further aerial surveillance. Perhaps they were concentrating their efforts on the outskirts of the town? He was sure he must be at least ten miles out of Riverbeke by now and in the heart of the countryside. He knew the stately home was way off the beaten track and miles behind him on the other side of the river. In his mind, he pictured a map of the area and remembered a lake somewhere amongst the acres of ancient woodland. That could make a good place to spend the night and perhaps he could wash in the lake. He felt dirty and sweaty and could do with freshening his clothes.

Sloan battled his way deeper into dense forest for what he estimated to be a couple of hours, resting occasionally for a drink of water from the bottles he'd stolen from the tearoom. He would try to ration himself, only eating or drinking when he was really hungry or thirsty. He didn't know when he would get the chance to stock up again. He reached an old stone wall, thick with moss and collapsed in places. It obviously hadn't been maintained for many years but extended as far as he could see in both directions. He clambered over the stones and continued to travel west. In places, the woodland cleared and there were open patches of bare earth but deciduous trees continued into the far distance.

He walked for what seemed like twenty minutes then came to a clearing in the forest with a large lake. He guessed it must be at least three acres and well established, with an island toward one end. Beyond the island, he could see a wooden structure – a cabin of some sort. He carefully skirted around the lake, keeping within the shadows of the tree line, stepping slowly in the direction of the cabin.

Then he saw her.

A beautiful woman, slim with long blonde hair and delicate features. Her skin looked as smooth as porcelain and was glowing with exposure to the sun. Sloan stopped dead in his tracks. The woman was sitting on a hefty log at the side of the lake, her face turned to the sun as it tracked toward the western horizon. She was wearing a floral dress that was covered in mud splashes and he could see that her hair looked tangled and unkempt. She turned her head to watch a heron fly over the lake and he could see a dark patch of dried blood at the side of her forehead. Somehow, she looked familiar.

Sloan stood for several minutes watching the woman. What should he do? Slink away so that she would never know he'd been there? He decided to watch a while longer. Perhaps there was somebody else there with her. Maybe she had seen the news and would immediately call the police. He would have to be cautious. Intrigued by her, he placed his holdall carefully on the ground and crouched, hidden by undergrowth. She looked so familiar and yet he couldn't place her. He could only see the side of her face. Perhaps if she turned toward him, he could get a better look.

Suddenly, behind him in the tree, a couple of crows squawked as they squabbled over something and the woman glanced across. She kept looking even after the crows had flown off and Jaxon sensed she'd seen him. He stayed quiet and still.

The woman stood and walked slowly toward him.

THIRTY-NINE

Thursday 22nd August 2019

Daniel had time before his meeting with Shelly Winters to do a quick shop at the local supermarket. He'd lived on takeaways and party food for the past few days and it was turning his stomach sour. He had stocked up on healthy food but bought a box of Fay's favourite chocolates in anticipation of her getting home safe and well. He had put everything away and timed it perfectly for getting into town to meet Shelly, a forensic psychiatrist and Fay's colleague. He grabbed the dog's leads, loaded them into the back of the car and slipped into the driver's seat.

Daniel found an old packet of wine gums in the glove box and ate them as he drove through Riverbeke. He turned right toward the river, found Tatiana's Coffee Shop and found a parking space close to the entrance. The building was an old warehouse, one of several that had been recently converted into a smart riverside development of retail shops, restaurants and cafes.

Daniel let the dogs out, clipped on their leads and went into the seating area of Tatiana's via the open veranda. It overlooked a small lawned garden that led down to the river. There was no sign of Shelly.

He found a table for two and slipped the dogs a couple of mini bone-shaped biscuits he found in his pocket. Chester settled down beside his chair and Ella under the table. The building had been renovated in rustic brick and wood, reclaiming many of the original materials. Daniel liked the effect – a mix of traditional and contemporary. He sat and watched the river meandering past and the sunlight glinting off the water as it flowed downstream. A pair of mallards were floating with the current and there was a swan and three signets sitting on the far bank. Willow trees swayed in the breeze, their leaves dipping in and out of the water. The air was warm and tinged with the smell of fragrant roses and coffee. It was an idyllic spot.

"Can I take your order?" A young woman dressed in black leggings and a cobalt blue polo shirt emblazoned with the company logo stood next to Daniel, a pad and pen poised.

"Could I have five minutes? I'm waiting for someone."

"Sure, no problem. Just let me know when you're ready." The woman smiled, glanced at the cut on his cheek a moment too long and went off to serve another customer.

Daniel thought of Fay. He could imagine her here, with her friends and colleagues; chatting and laughing with them. She'd often spoken of the place, and he could see the attraction now. Yet he'd never brought her here. Had he really been so wrapped up in himself that he had neglected his wife and failed to put some effort into his marriage? To share some of the things she enjoyed too? He wished Fay was with him now – instead, he was trying to make sense of her disappearance.

Shelly burst through the door onto the veranda, she looked harried. "Daniel. Sorry, I'm running a bit late. Been waiting long?" She dumped a voluminous leather handbag on the floor next to her seat and extended her hand to Daniel.

Daniel stood and shook her hand. He could feel the warmth of her skin and the delicate bone structure of her petite frame as his hand engulfed hers. "Shelly. No problem, I've been enjoying watching the river. Thanks for coming." Despite Fay's close friendship with Shelly, Daniel had only met her once before, at a psychiatric conference he'd attended with Fay some four years ago.

Shelly greeted the dogs. She'd seen them with Fay many times at Tatiana's.

Daniel swept a hand over the scenery before them. "A beautiful setting, isn't it?"

"Yes, it's lovely. My favourite coffee shop – and Fay's, I think. We often come here to catch up with things." Shelly settled into her chair and slipped off her formal navy jacket to reveal a pretty floral dress. It reminded Daniel of the dress Fay was wearing when he'd last seen her.

"Coffee?" Daniel asked, summoning the waitress.

"Yes please, a decaf latte."

Daniel ordered Shelly's latte and a hot chocolate for himself. Shelly declined the offer of cake and Daniel followed suit, even though he craved a large slab of the scrumptious-looking fudge cake topped with thick butter cream that he could see on the counter through the doorway.

Shelly rubbed her hands together as if she was about to get to the point of their meeting. "So, what is it you want to know? Something about Fay's patients? I'll do whatever I can to help find her. She's been a very good friend to me over the years."

"Yes, I could do with your input," Daniel said, retrieving the note he'd put in his pocket earlier. He looked at it, placed it on the table in front of Shelly and read off the two names. "Robert Horton and Jaxon Sloan. Know anything about them?"

Shelly ran her index finger with its perfectly manicured nail along the first name. "Robert Horton. Yes, I know him. A notorious child murderer. He was given a life sentence around fifteen years ago at Ravenwood prison but he was released on parole recently having been given a new identity. There was a lot of controversy about it and complaints about the enormous cost to the taxpayer. It's been in the papers."

Daniel recalled where he'd heard the name. "Ah, yes. That's right. An eyewatering half a million, wasn't it? I remember the story now."

"You might also recall that he had his throat slit in his back garden a few weeks ago."

"I hadn't heard about that."

Shelly looked surprised.

"I have had other things on my mind and it seems there are murderers on the loose all over the place at the moment. Is he dead?"

"Yes, he died at the scene and there are no clues as to the perpetrator. The police think he could be a victim of the serial killer that's been at large around here recently." Shelly sipped her coffee.

Daniel felt relieved that Horton was no longer a threat to Fay but he could have had the opportunity to harm her before he died. "He was one of Fay's patients?"

"Yes, for a while before he was sentenced."

"And she was assessing him for the trial?"

"He'd put in a plea of insanity in an effort by his defence brief to reduce the charge but Fay proved he was completely sane and he was sentenced to life in prison."

"Until he was let out and given a new identity," Daniel said sarcastically.

Shelly nodded her agreement. Like him, she appeared to have little sympathy for him.

"Do you think Horton might have gone after Fay before he died – revenge for putting him in jail?"

Shelly thought for some moments before replying. "The testimony was a long time ago, Daniel. Over fifteen years. Of course, he probably did harbour considerable resentment toward Fay – she helped to put him behind bars – but don't forget, he was being watched very closely by parole officers after his release. One false move and he would have been straight back to prison. I don't think he would have risked that."

Daniel nodded reflectively, twisting the hot chocolate mug in his hands.

Shelly continued. "He just wouldn't have had the time or opportunity to get organised for an attack on Fay. Besides which, he had only been released a matter of days before he was murdered and that was weeks before Fay went missing. I just don't see how he could have been involved."

"It does seem unlikely – if only from the timing of his death and Fay's disappearance. I wonder who might have murdered him?"

"I don't think he was short of enemies," Shelly said.

"I can imagine," Daniel said. He glanced back at the note. "So, we can rule out Horton. What about Jaxon Sloan? Didn't Fay testify against him too?"

"Yes, she did a few years ago." Shelly put her coffee cup down and looked at Daniel. "You really don't watch the news much do you?"

"What do you mean?"

"Jaxon Sloan murdered his wife and her lover in their bed two days ago – at point-blank range with a sawn-off shotgun."

"Shit! That was Sloan?"

"Yes, it was him. He was released from Gallow Hill on Monday morning and murdered the two of them early the next morning. Now he's on the run." Shelly looked aghast that Daniel didn't know.

"I saw some of the story on TV but didn't realise he was one of Fay's patients."

Daniel looked across at Shelly, a flush of adrenaline knotting his stomach. "Fay went missing the same day as the murders. What if Sloan killed his wife and her lover, then went after Fay."

Shelly watched Daniel in silence.

"Let me get this straight," Daniel said, "Jaxon Sloan murdered his wife and their lover in the early hours of Tuesday morning, right?"

"Yes, that's right. Around 4 am, according to the news report," Shelly said, draining her coffee cup.

"Fay went missing around 1 pm on Monday. He was on the loose in this area and he had a motive – Fay effectively put him in jail with her expert witness testimony, didn't she?" Daniel felt a mix of fear for Fay's welfare and excitement that he could be on to something that could lead him to her.

"I guess so. You think he may have abducted her?" Shelly asked.

"It's a possibility. He had time to get to Fay's clinic and there are signs of a struggle with blood on her scarf, the floor and the door frames on the way out of the building."

"And the police were searching for Sloan in the woods around his home, not in the town."

"Nobody would have thought he would run to a densely populated area, especially with all the publicity – which I mostly missed." Daniel feigned embarrassment at his ignorance.

Shelly nodded her agreement. "I know, from what Fay has told me, that Sloan had serious anger management issues. He would fly into an uncontrollable rage and I'm guessing that's what happened when he killed his wife and her lover."

Daniel leaned forward. He was beginning to think Jaxon Sloan was a definite suspect. "Can you tell me any more about him, Shelly?"

"All I know is that he didn't settle at all well in prison. He wanted to get help and volunteered to have a few sessions with Fay."

"Why did he see her rather than another psychiatrist? Surely there would have been a conflict there since Fay testified against him."

"I guess. Fay didn't say anything to me about it but then she was very professional about keeping patient confidentiality."

Daniel knew that was true. She hadn't written anything derogatory about Sloan in her private notes either but that didn't mean he hadn't threatened her.

"Shelly – do you have any ideas as to where Sloan could be. If he has taken Fay, where would he have gone?"

Shelly thought for several seconds. "I have absolutely no idea. There's a lot of countryside around Riverbeke. Many abandoned farm buildings and thousands of acres of dense woodland. He could be anywhere by now."

"Could he have had help? Someone he knows who could be harbouring them both?"

"I really don't know, Daniel. I do know he had a mate in prison," Shelly thought for a few moments, trying to recall his name. "I think his name is Sully. Sully Rathmore. They shared a cell for quite a while. Goodness knows if he's still at Gallow Hill but he was serving a long sentence, so it's possible. Other than him, I can't think of anyone else."

"Would I be able to see Sully?" Daniel didn't relish the idea of going into a prison visiting room but it might be worth talking to him.

"I don't know. Perhaps the police should be following this up," Shelly said, her eyes flashing him a warning.

Daniel hesitated to tell Shelly the truth, that the police actually had him on their radar as a possible suspect. "I just need to follow this up myself. If I come up with any leads, I'll pass them on to the police."

Shelly nodded. "I guess I could pull a few strings. Leave it with me. Would you be free this afternoon?"

"Yes, the sooner the better."

FORTY

"Hello?" she called cautiously.

Sloan could see the woman's face clearly now and he recognised her. It was Fay Kendrick – the psychiatrist he'd seen months ago. It had only been a couple of sessions but she had been very kind to him. Very understanding. Instinctively, he had trusted her. He stood slowly and moved toward her.

"Dr Kendrick."

"Who are you?" she asked, a look of puzzlement etched into her face. She stood, some twenty feet away from him, apparently nervous about approaching any further.

"I'm one of your patients – or rather, former patients." Perhaps she didn't remember him. She did seem to have a heavy workload – too many people to remember them all, he guessed.

"Patients? What do you mean?"

"I came to see you at your clinic in Riverbeke. I guess you don't remember me."

"No... I'm not sure... I don't remember. Do you know who I am?"

Sloan could see Dr Kendrick was struggling with her memory. She wasn't reacting to him as if he was an armed murderer on the loose, so maybe she hadn't heard the news. "Yes, you're Dr Kendrick. Fay Kendrick. You're a forensic psychiatrist."

"Am I?" She looked puzzled; a deep frown furrowed into her forehead.

Sloan relaxed. He could see she'd suffered a bump to her head. It seemed as if she'd lost her memory. But what the hell was she doing here in the middle of nowhere?

"Yes, a doctor." He said, moving a little closer. She definitely looked bewildered, quite dishevelled and very vulnerable. He began to feel a surge of compassion, as if he'd found a stray dog.

"Are you alright, Dr Kendrick?" he asked gently.

"I'm not sure," she said, still puzzled. "Where is this?"

"It's an area of woodland outside Riverbeke. About fifteen miles at least. It's north west of the town. How did you get here, do you know? It's very remote." Sloan took a couple of steps toward her. She stayed where she was, gazing up at him as if she was completely mystified.

"No... I don't know how I got here. I can't remember..." She touched her temple as if she was showing him, she'd hit her head.

Sloan took a few more steps toward her. "Do you have a phone, to call for help?" Sloan asked.

Fay shook her head. "I don't have anything."

"No bag; no ID?"

Again, she shook her head. "Nothing." Her eyes were blank as she stared at Jaxon. She obviously didn't have a clue who she was or where she was – or who he was. Thankfully, she had no idea he had shot and killed two people just a few hours before.

Jaxon relaxed. He felt safe here with Dr Kendrick. She obviously needed help and would pose no threat to him. He stepped closer to her and looked gently into her eyes. "It's alright, I'll help you." He touched her arm lightly, trying to reassure her.

"Thank you." She held his gaze, searching for something in his eyes that she could make sense of.

"Are you hungry?" Sloan asked.

Fay simply nodded. She couldn't remember when she'd eaten last, apart from some fruit she'd collected from the trees in the orchard.

"Shall we go and sit over there?" He gestured toward the log that Fay had been sitting on when he stumbled across her.

She simply nodded.

"I'll just get my bag. I have some food in there. OK?"

"OK."

Sloan retrieved his holdall and gently ushered her toward the cabin and the seat. She sat down on one end, making room for him and he sat beside her, keeping a respectful distance between them. He placed the holdall on the ground next to him, unzipped it and took out some bread, cheese and a bottle of water. He rummaged for the paring knife and handed it, with the food to her. She took it, cutting off a chunk of the cheese and biting at it as if she was famished. He found some chocolate, which he shared between them. Sloan re-zipped the bag, careful to hide the shotgun. He sat quietly beside her while they ate, wondering what must have happened to her and whether she remembered anything at all about her circumstances or her life.

Sloan looked at the lake. It was beautiful; the water was still and glistening in the late afternoon sunlight. Mallards were gliding through the water near the island and there was a flock of Canada geese honking at the other end of the lake. He saw a couple of coots and a moorhen foraging among the reeds. It was a picture of peace and tranquillity and a world away from Riverbeke and the trauma he'd left behind. Next to them, the cabin stood solid and timeless. A welcoming retreat.

"Thank you," Fay said, as she finished the last bite of bread. She was looking at Sloan but there was still no recognition of him in her eyes.

"That's alright," he replied.

Fay looked at the lake. "Isn't this beautiful?" she said.

"Very peaceful. Have you been here before?"

"Yes, I think so," she said, "it feels like I know the place quite well but I can't remember much detail." She turned to him, "I'm sure I used to come here as a child. It was my little hideaway. My secret hideaway." She smiled.

"I guess we all need a place to hide sometimes," Sloan said wistfully. It was a gross understatement in his current circumstances.

"Are you hiding Mr…." Fay's voice trailed off.

"Jaxon. Jaxon Sloan. And yes, you could say I'm hiding." He smiled at her and she returned the gesture. "What about you? Are you hiding too?" He deflected the question back to her.

"I feel as if I am," she said, her gaze returning to the lake.

"Do you want to talk about it? Perhaps it will jolt your memory." Jaxon said. He felt sad for Fay and keen to help her if he could – if only to distract himself from his own self-created predicament.

She hesitated. "I'm not sure."

They sat in companionable silence for a few moments, watching the birds on the lake.

"I remember a man," Fay said, "he was in my office and he was upset. Very upset and then he ran off." She tilted her head, as if she was trying to remember. "He pushed against me as he ran and I fell – hit my head on the corner of the desk."

"Do you know who it was? One of your patients maybe?"

"I don't know." She looked at Sloan, a look of haunting sadness in her eyes.

FORTY-ONE

Daniel had gone home to wait for Shelly's call. He'd been feeling wired since his meeting with her. He really believed this Sloan character had motive. He probably harboured resentment toward Fay for her expert witness testimony that had helped to put him behind bars. He was also on the loose with a sawn-off shotgun after killing two people. He had nothing to lose by acting out his resentment toward Fay. He might even use her as a hostage to bargain with if the police finally caught up with him. If Daniel could only track him down, he might be able to rescue Fay and clear his name. He had to find Sloan and maybe his cell mate, Sully Rathmore, would be able to shed some light on his whereabouts. It was worth a try.

Daniel realised it wouldn't be as simple as walking in to the prison, asking Sully a few questions and getting the answers he needed. He'd called at the ATM and bundled up several £10 and £5 notes; £100 in total. He'd rolled them up together, secured with an elastic band ready to hand to Sully. All he needed was some information and a small bribe might just do the trick. Shelly had assured him she could get the screws to turn a blind eye, since she knew most of them at Gallow Hill. She was turning into a useful contact and willing to do all she could to help track down Fay.

Daniel's iPhone rang. It was Shelly.

"Any progress?"

"Can you get to Gallow Hill by 12.30?"

"Sure, no problem." Daniel glanced at his watch. It was already midday but that gave him enough time to get through town and up to Gallow Hill if he left straight away.

"Good. I'll meet you there. One of the prison officers, Jamie Rakes, is on duty. I know him quite well and he's agreed to let us in for a little chat with Sully. Wait at the entrance for me."

"That's brilliant. See you there."

They rang off.

Daniel pushed the roll of notes into his jacket pocket, put the dogs in the Dog House, and began the drive to HMP Gallow Hill. His mind was racing. What would he ask Sully? Would he be willing to answer? Would the bribe he'd brought with him be enough?

The traffic was slow through Riverbeke and Daniel managed to finish off the family pack of wine gums that he kept hidden in the glove box. Once he was clear of the town centre, he drove up Gallow Hill and parked easily in the prison car park. He saw Shelly as she arrived at the entrance and ran to catch up with her.

"Thanks for this," he said.

"Anything to help find Fay. I just hope Rathmore has some answers; although I'm not convinced that he'll be cooperative."

"Well, it's worth a try, I guess. I brought a little bribe to help him remember. Just some cash. Couldn't think what else to bring."

"That should do the trick. It's always good to have a bargaining tool in here." Shelly smiled wistfully at Daniel.

They walked into the prison together. The place was stark and dreary with bright overhead fluorescent lights.

"Normally, we'd need a booking reference to visit someone in prison but Jamie has waived this for us."

They arrived at the reception desk, to be greeted by a short, balding man in his fifties. He smiled at Shelly and shook both their hands in turn.

"Thanks for this, Jamie," Shelly said.

"A pleasure Dr Winters. I've told Rathmore he has a couple of visitors and that he'd better be nice to you." He smiled again. "Please, take a seat in the reception area." Jamie gestured to a row of green plastic chairs, a coffee vending machine in the far corner. "Put any belongings you might have into the lockers."

Shelly secured her handbag into one of the lockers and pocketed the key. Daniel placed his wallet in another but kept the roll of money in his jacket pocket, hoping he could pass it to Sully unnoticed. They sat and waited. A Passive Drugs Dog was led along the row of visitors and Daniel turned to Shelly, tapping his pocket.

"Cash," he mouthed.

She patted his arm as if to reassure him. "Don't worry. It's fine," she whispered back.

The dog walked past several people, then stopped and sniffed the leg of a young man in his twenties, who was backing into his seat. The dog sniffed for a few seconds then sat quietly next to him, indicating he was carrying a banned substance. The handler retrieved his dog and asked the man to accompany him. They walked off toward a small side room.

Within minutes, Jamie returned, smiling at Shelly. "Come with me. We just have to clear security."

Again, Daniel winced, anxious about the money in his pocket.

Shelly noticed Daniel's nervousness. "Normally, you would have to hand in cash at reception and they would pay it into the prisoners account but I'm sure Jamie will turn a blind eye," she said, trying to reassure him.

They saw Jamie have a word with one of the security officers and they were waved through to the visiting room.

The room was stark with around twenty tables and chairs set out. Each table was numbered. There were just six other tables occupied by waiting visitors.

Jamie pointed to a table in the far corner. "Go to twelve please."

They did as they were asked and sat for several minutes in silence.

"What's he in for?" Daniel whispered.

"Armed robbery."

Daniel watched as a tall, thin man with badass hair in his early thirties swaggered across the room toward their table. Sully Rathmore. He was wearing faded jeans, a crumpled, bottle green T-shirt and Nike trainers – obviously his own clothes. It was an indication that he was an established inmate and had managed to keep his privileges with no bad behaviour. Other inmates were filing into the room dressed in prison issue grey tracksuit bottoms and light blue T-shirts. They all took seats at their respective tables. Daniel was surprised they looked like ordinary human beings – not like the monsters he'd sort of expected.

As Sully approached their table, Daniel began to feel nervous. He'd never been inside a prison before, although he'd heard plenty of anecdotes about the inmates from Fay. Some of them hair-raising accounts of violence and attacks on prison officers as well as other inmates. He glanced around. Jamie, their friendly prison officer was stood in the corner, quietly surveying the room. He nodded toward Daniel.

Sully scraped his chair across the floor and sat opposite Daniel. He leaned back with his legs spread wide and arms crossed against his chest; his facial expression and body language deliberately intimidating and arrogant. He chewed gum noisily but said nothing.

Shelly spoke first. "Sully, do you remember me? Shelly Winters. I think we've met before."

Sully looked at the psychiatrist. "Yeah. So, what do you want? You weren't cleared for a visit."

"Sully, we'd like to ask you a few questions. It's important. We need to find Jaxon Sloan. Do you know where he might have gone after he was released."

"How the fuck would I know?" Sully maintained the scowl that seemed to be etched permanently into his pasty, hawk-like face.

"You two shared a cell. Perhaps he told you his plans?"

Sully simply shrugged and chomped his gum.

Daniel was afraid they were getting nowhere fast. "Sully. My wife has gone missing. She was Jaxon's doctor – his psychiatrist, Dr Fay Kendrick. It's vital that I find her. Did Jaxon mention her at all? Do you think he might have wanted to talk to her?" Daniel hoped he sounded diplomatic. No sense in provoking Sully.

Sully looked directly at Daniel, his dark grey eyes exuding hostility.

Daniel took a deep breath to calm his nerves. "Would some cash help you to remember?" Daniel took the wad of money from his pocket and surreptitiously flashed it at Sully.

Sully leaned forward in his chair, glanced at Prison Officer Rakes, who's attention had been diverted away from them, then unfolded his arms and reached a tattooed hand around the side of the table.

Daniel slipped him the roll of money.

Sully glanced at it briefly and satisfied with what he saw, he kept it tucked into his palm as he folded his arms across his chest once again. He resumed his hostile stare at Daniel.

"Sully, do you have any information on Jaxon's whereabouts?" Shelly asked gently.

Sully kept glaring at Daniel, his grey eyes darkening further.

"I heard on the news that he'd killed his wife and Kieran but I don't know where he went after that."

"Thanks, Sully. Is there anywhere he might go to hide away from the police search? Anywhere at all you can think of? I just need to find my wife."

"My guess he's somewhere in the woods, keeping under cover but I don't know. Never heard from him after he left." Despite the cash inducement, Sully either genuinely didn't know any more or he was deliberately keeping quiet.

"Was there somewhere he was headed to – a relative? Friend?" Daniel asked.

"Never said anything to me," Sully said, a slight smirk played over his lips.

"Did he ever mention Fay Kendrick?" Shelly asked. "Did he express any resentment toward her because she testified in his trial?"

"Never said anything if he did," Sully said.

They were getting nowhere, Daniel thought. It seemed like Sully was being deliberately obtuse. Perhaps it had been naïve of him to expect a prisoner to snitch on his cell-mate but he had been desperate for any information that could help find Fay.

"OK, Sully, thanks for the visit," Shelly said, as she stood to leave. "Come on Daniel, we're not getting anywhere here."

They walked away, thanking the prison officer as they left. They retrieved their belongings from the lockers and left the building.

Daniel had just paid a hundred quid for that. He felt robbed.

FORTY-TWO

Thursday 22nd August 2019

Damon stood and watched as his uncle begged him for help. Saw the abject terror in his watery eyes. Watched as he clung onto the kitchen counter and cried out in agony – over and over again. In the desolation of Damon's dark and shallow soul, he took the greatest of pleasure in watching his uncle's suffering.

Damon sneered, then sauntered over to the refrigerator, found what he was looking for and coolly cracked open a can of beer. He took a swig of the cold liquid, then another before placing the can on the table in front of him. He reached into his pocket and found a small tin box containing cannabis, filters, a pack of cigarette papers and a small box of matches.

Frazer was calling for help, his arm reaching out to Damon. Pleading for help. "Help me lad..." His voice was barely a whisper as a massive blood clot lodged further into his coronary artery.

Watching Frazer with cold, reptilian callousness, Damon leaned nonchalantly against the kitchen counter opposite and grinned as he casually rolled a splif. He took out his rolling paper, placed a filter at the end and filled the paper generously with cannabis shake; shaping it leisurely with his fingers. He glanced across at Frazer, still imploring him with agonising cries for help, then, with the finesse of a practiced expert, he slowly rolled the joint into shape, ran his tongue along the upper length of the paper and sealed it with a final roll. With a closing twist on the end, he struck a match and sparked up, drawing the smoke deeply into his lungs. He was grinning as he threw his head back and blew a thick cloud of smoke into the air.

"Please lad… help me…" Frazer could barely get the words out now. The horrific, crushing pain in his chest was becoming unbearable.

Damon took a large swig of his beer and drew again on the joint. He leaned across the kitchen table, watching with calm indifference as his uncle begged for help.

"Call… an ambulance… ay, lad… please…" Frazer's voice was barely audible. He was clutching his chest with both arms now, his face crumpled into a picture of agony and terror. His heart was weakening, the electrical impulses that traced across his heart muscle were faltering. His heart beat was slowing… becoming erratic.

Damon casually strolled over to his uncle. Frazer looked up at him, pleadingly; his eyes filled with the fear of someone who knew he was about to die. Damon smirked, enjoying the unexpected drama. "Well now, uncle Wally. Dear uncle Wally. Whether you like it or not, I'll have your money now – all of it. Just hurry up and die, you miserable, miserly old bastard…"

The expression in Frazer's eyes turned briefly to hatred, then defeat. Through crushing pain, his heart beat slowed. Forty beats a minute… thirty… twenty-five… palpitations from missed beats thudding against his chest…

Damon drew once more on his joint then bent to blow a rancid cloud of cannabis smoke into his uncle's face as a final act of defiance, before casually walking away.

Frazer coughed weakly. His heart muscle was beginning to die as the clot in his coronary artery cut off the blood supply. He was becoming dizzy, unable to concentrate as his heart struggled to pump blood around his body. His blood pressure plummeted. The crushing pain was excruciating.

Damon stood and watched, coolly sipping beer and smoking his joint. A warm sense of gratification was creeping over him. His mind was beginning to turn over the possibilities that this afternoon's unexpected events had opened up for him…

Frazer was losing consciousness fast as his blood pressure ebbed away.

Blackness closed in…

He slumped to the floor as his heart fluttered and finally stopped beating.

Damon grinned as Wallace Frazer's lifeless body lay on the kitchen floor, his eyes staring sightlessly at his nephew.

FORTY-THREE

Thursday 22nd August 2019

Daniel walked with Shelly across the prison car park toward her Audi. The visit with Sully had proved to be a complete waste of time. Daniel realised he'd been naïve in thinking he would glean any new information from Sloan's cell mate.

"What now?" Shelly asked.

"Not sure but I need to track down Sloan. He could be the key to finding Fay."

"Have you suggested this to the police?"

"No, I haven't." Daniel was still reluctant to come clean with Shelly.

"Maybe you should. They would have information on him and they are putting a lot of resources into searching for him. Just get in touch with the detective…"

"Harper. DS Ian Harper," Daniel said.

"Just talk to him Daniel."

Daniel looked at Shelly and nodded. Maybe he should just make the call.

"Look, I have to go. I have a couple of appointments with patients this afternoon but I'll keep an eye on the news – there seems to be regular updates on the Sloan case. Everyone around here is nervous with an armed murderer on the run."

"Thanks for your help, Shelly." Daniel shook her hand and left to find his car.

As he drove toward Riverbeke, he considered again calling the police. It might be an awkward conversation but at least it would put Sloan on their radar in their search for Fay. He pulled over into a layby, turned off the engine, searched for Harper's number and called.

"DS Harper." The detective sounded upbeat.

"Detective, it's Daniel Kendrick. Just wanted to know if there any further developments with finding my wife?"

"Not yet, Dr Kendrick. I'm afraid we have been extremely busy with urgent cases."

Daniel switched the phone to his right ear. "Jaxon Sloan?" Daniel asked.

"I'm afraid I can't discuss that with you."

"About Sloan. He was one of Fay's patients whilst he was an inmate at Gallow Hill. She also gave an expert witness testimony in court, which helped to have him imprisoned. I think he may have abducted her." Daniel waited as the line went silent for several seconds.

"What makes you think that?"

"Maybe he's trying to get revenge. He has a motive."

"I'll consider that, sir."

"Detective, am I still under suspicion? You know, I've done nothing wrong and I'm desperate to find my wife." Daniel could feel himself welling up with emotion – sadness and frustration at Fay's disappearance and anger at Melissa for her selfish behaviour.

"We would still like to be able to eliminate you from our enquiry, sir. We'll have another chat but right now, we are under pressure with other cases. I can assure you; we are doing all we can to find your wife."

Daniel knew he still wasn't off the hook. Until he had some evidence to present to DS Harper, either to incriminate Sloan or to vindicate himself, he wouldn't be taken seriously. "Alright, thank you. Please, would you keep me informed?"

"We will. Good day, Dr Kendrick." Harper rang off.

Daniel sat in his car for a few minutes. He felt downhearted. His attempt to glean information from Sully had been a waste of time and now the police seemed to be too busy to make their investigation into Fay's disappearance a priority. He realised there was a serial killer and an armed murderer on the loose but Sloan had a motive to harm Fay. He felt forced into taking matters into his own hands. He had to track down Sloan. At the moment, it was his only hope.

Daniel wondered how else he could get information about Sloan. Then he remembered Shelly talking about the news story. If he could track down a reporter, perhaps he could get some inside information. With renewed hope, Daniel started the car and drove into Riverbeke.

Daniel parked in one of the municipal car parks in the centre of town. He was starving and simply had to eat. He called into his favourite fish and chip shop near the river. He bought cod and chips, his favourite comfort food, called in to the newsagent, bought the Times, the Daily Express and the local Argus and took his lunch to a bench on the riverbank. He flicked through the papers as he ate and found a couple of articles on the Sloan murders. The local Argus seemed to give more information than the nationals. The reporter was Hayley Shepherd.

Daniel finished his lunch, threw the chip paper in a recycling bin and found the contacts page for the Argus. He dialled the number for the editor's desk.

"Argus. David Jenkins. How can I help." The man's voice sounded flat and distant, as if he was having a bad day.

"I'd like to speak to Hayley Shepherd please. She wrote a piece about the Jaxon Sloan murders."

"Who's calling?"

"Daniel Kendrick."

"Just a minute, I'll put you through." The line went silent, then there was a click followed by a ringing tone.

"Hayley Shepherd."

"Hello, Ms Shepherd. Daniel Kendrick. I'm a surgeon at Riverbeke General. I'm calling about the piece you wrote in the Argus about the Jaxon Sloan murders."

"Yes. How can I help you?" Hayley sounded friendly and approachable.

"Well. I was wondering if you had any further information. I desperately need to track him down."

"I think everyone and their dog wants him found and locked up. Why is it so urgent for you?"

Daniel waited a few moments for an elderly couple to walk past the bench where he was sitting before he spoke again. "I think he may have abducted my wife – but this is strictly off the record. I don't want this reported in the paper."

"I see. Yes, I can see why you want to find him."

"Do you have anything more?" Daniel asked.

"Well… not really but there was a robbery at the Riverbeke Falls tea room the night of the murder. It wasn't reported in the media at the request of the manager. He was afraid of losing business – you know with a murderer on the loose. But the kitchen was broken into and there were several items of food taken as well as a couple of knives. It could have been Sloan stocking up and getting ready to go on the run."

"Yes, that's interesting," Daniel said, trying to think where the tea rooms were in relation to Riverbeke. "Remind me where it is."

"It's very close to Hallbrook Manor. It's well signposted. A few miles north west of Riverbeke."

"And the manager's name?"

"Trevor Reeves." Daniel wrote the name down on a scrap of newspaper, tore it off and pocketed it.

"Thank you, Hayley."

"Let me know if you find out anything more."

They ended the call. Daniel was fired up again. Perhaps this was the direction Sloan had gone on the run; if he could get to the tea room, he might get a sense of where Sloan and possibly Fay might be.

Daniel gathered up the newspapers and headed back to the car.

FORTY-FOUR

Thursday 22nd August 2019

"You have a husband." Jaxon Sloan said.

Fay turned to him; her expression blank. "Do I?"

"Yes, Dr Daniel Kendrick. He's a surgeon at Riverbeke General. You told me about him once and he operated on my aunt a few months ago. Do you remember him?"

Fay looked away for some moments as if she was searching her mind. "I do remember something. He has a gentle, kind heart… Daniel. Yes, I remember him. Our wedding day, walking the dogs…" Her voice trailed off as if that was the sum of her recollection.

Jaxon nodded pensively. "We have to get you home to him." He began to feel protective of Fay, the way he used to feel about Lisa when they first met. That was until she betrayed him.

"Yes," was all she said.

In her state of confusion and the amnesia from her fall, Fay seemed unconcerned about who Sloan was or what he was doing there. He was relieved but also troubled and unsure what he should do. He was beginning to feel a sense of responsibility toward her and yet he had his own troubles to contend with.

Perhaps she would recall her memories and find her own way home but he couldn't simply leave her here in this wilderness.

"Why don't you stay a while, Mr Sloan. I'd like to take a walk around the lake – try to remember Daniel, if I can." Fay smiled, stood and strolled barefooted along the shore of the lake.

Sloan nodded. She had a home, a family to go to. Did they even know she was here?

Family. He'd had a wife but now she was dead – his anger had overwhelmed him because of what she'd done. It was a raw anger that had driven him to kill her and her lover, to take revenge for their betrayal.

Now, he realised, he had not only cut short their lives but he had ruined his own in the process. He would be nothing more than a fugitive; on the run for the rest of his life. It was either that or give himself up and spend the rest of his days behind bars. Life in prison without parole would be a living death. He wasn't sure he had the resources within himself to cope with that. Just a few months of being banged up at Gallow Hill had been torturous enough for him. He had known lifers that had committed suicide in prison and he could understand why they craved that release from their suffering, knowing they would never be eligible for parole.

If he was caught, he wasn't sure he would have the courage to kill himself but maybe if his life became unbearable…

Life on the run seemed by far the better option, even with the challenges it would present. At least he would be free and, in his own mind, he was no danger to society. It had been a personal vendetta that had driven him to kill. He believed now that it had been a crime of passion, although he could hear the arguments from his accusers that he had gone to the house armed with a sawn-off shotgun, knowing his wife and her lover would be there. They would say he killed in cold blood. He didn't have the stomach for a trial.

He watched as Fay wandered around the lake, stopping to smell flowers, watching the wildlife on the water. As idyllic as the lake and the cabin was, he knew he couldn't stay. He would push further west, then north into the countryside. Perhaps he could find a vehicle and get as far away from the vicinity of Riverbeke as he could. Maybe a remote area of Scotland? Find an abandoned croft and make a living for himself there. Sloan smiled – it sounded like a plan.

Sloan felt a shift in his inner being – a sense of peace and acceptance within himself. Whatever this day brought; he knew that all would be well. That it was meant to be. He had a plan and today was the first day of his new life.

He watched as Fay walked to a small orchard and picked a few apples and plums. Maybe she could travel with him and he could get her to a safe place? But she would slow him down, she would eventually recall her memory and he would have to explain why he was on the run – it would all be too complicated.

Fay started walking back along the edge of the woodland but she tripped and fell, the fruit rolling away from her. He hadn't seen exactly what had happened but he heard her cry out and ran across to her. She had rolled onto her side and was clutching her ankle.

"Are you alright?" Sloan called out.

"I... I think so." She tried to sit up.

He took her foot in his hand and moved it gently. It could be broken, or a bad strain, he couldn't tell but it was already starting to swell.

"Can you put any weight on it?" He helped her to her feet.

Fay tried to put her foot to the ground but retracted it sharply. "No... it's so painful."

"Let me carry you back to the cabin," Sloan said.

"Thank you. You're very kind."

Sloan lifted her easily into his arms and carried her back along the lake to the cabin. She seemed so vulnerable, so alone, like a stray puppy that had been abandoned at the side of the road.

He took her into the cabin, looked around the room and carried her over to a couch. He placed her there and put a pillow behind her head and another under her injured foot. He draped a colourful knitted blanket over her shoulders. She looked up at him, her eyes deep hollows of confusion and sadness.

"Do you think it's broken?" she asked.

"I don't know but we have to get you out of here and back where you belong."

Somehow, he would have to get a message to her husband. She was vulnerable here and it could take days or weeks for someone to find her in this dense woodland. If he moved directly north, he should come across a few houses or farms. Maybe he could leave a message for someone to alert the police and her husband of her whereabouts. He knew Daniel Kendrick worked at Riverbeke General Hospital. He would find a car that would get him away from the Riverbeke area and perhaps then on to Scotland.

Sloan went for his holdall and took out some food and a few bottles of water and placed them on the couch for her. He found some old papers and magazines and gave them to her to keep her mind occupied.

"I'll get help as quickly as I can and try to get a message to your husband."

Fay looked into his eyes. "Daniel. I'm remembering him now. He's a good man. I don't deserve him."

"I'm sure you do," Sloan said, "now, stay calm and rest. I'll be as fast as I can." Sloan smiled.

He noticed an oil lamp on the table and brought it over to her with some matches from the dresser. He placed it on a side table next to the couch.

"In case you're still here tonight," he said.

"Thank you, I'll be fine." Fay said.

Sloan grabbed his bag, walked toward the door and they said their goodbyes.

He decided it would be quicker to retrace his steps from the previous day, crossing the river once again as he was unsure what the terrain would be like if he kept going north – probably even more impenetrable woodland that would slow him down. If he kept close to the river on the eastern bank, the woodland would still offer some cover. For a while anyway.

Once across the river, he walked briskly in a northerly direction. Fay had said he was kind but she had no idea who he really was. What he was capable of. In some way, helping Fay eased his guilt just a little. She had tried to help him with his anger problems while he was in prison. Now he had the opportunity to repay the favour. It might put his cover at risk, he realised that, but he had to do what he could to help her.

He battled through woodland and shrub, climbing sheep fencing and stone walls, seemingly for hours before he saw an opening in the canopy. Ahead were gently rolling hills dotted with sheep. He stepped out from the tree cover slowly, glancing around like a nervous deer. In the distance he could see a white-washed farmhouse and beyond that, several other buildings. Maybe he could make for them and get a message to someone that Fay needed help. Surely, there would be a vehicle that he could 'borrow' to make his getaway.

Sloan walked toward the farmhouse. He had to help Fay. He would never forgive himself if he walked away now and left her to her fate.

As he walked across the open field, he failed to notice a police surveillance drone tracking him from 60 metres overhead.

FORTY-FIVE

Thursday 22nd August 2019

Sloan reached the farmhouse and carefully skirted around to the back, checking for people or dogs. The place was quiet. Maybe the occupiers were out tending to their animals. Across the yard, there was a fairly new-looking Land Rover with a trailer hitched to the tow bar at the back and also an old Vauxhall Astra that looked as if it was roadworthy but had seen better days with its peeling red paint and a dent in the front wing. Sloan crept toward the back door of the farmhouse and tried the handle. The door was unlocked. He opened it a crack and peered into the kitchen, a knot of apprehension gripping his gut. There was nobody there. The house was eerily quiet apart from the hum of a refrigerator.

He let himself into the room. It was large and crammed with gadgets. There was a Belfast sink full of dishes and a red Aga sitting in an alcove, draped with tea towels and oven gloves. Dominating the centre of the room was a long pine table with six mismatched chairs. Scattered along its length were newspapers, letters and bills along with the remains of a meal. Sloan crept toward it, found a pen and turned over an envelope, giving him a blank page. On it he wrote:

PLEASE HELP FAY KENDRICK. SHE MAY HAVE
BROKEN HER ANKLE AND IS STRANDED IN
WOODLAND SOUTH OF HERE. ABOUT A 2 HOUR
WALK. SHE IS IN A CABIN BY A LAKE. PLEASE LET
HER HUSBAND KNOW. HE IS Dr DANIEL KENDRICK,
A SURGEON AT RIVERBEKE GENERAL HOSPITAL.
PLEASE FIND HER URGENTLY.

Sloan left the note in a prominent place on the kitchen table, weighted down with a coffee mug, then looked around for some car keys. He was no car thief, but he could hotwire an old banger if he had to. Still, it would be easier and quicker if he had the keys. Sure enough, near the back door was a wooden bowl with several sets of keys. He grabbed them all and let himself out of the house. The only sound he could hear was a robin singing in the trees and his own footsteps. He walked over to the Land Rover but had second thoughts about it. The trailer was big and it would take time to unhitch it, even if he could manage the weight of it himself.

He turned to the old Astra, fumbled through the keys and found one that fitted. He unlocked the door, dropped the others on the ground and threw his holdall on the passenger seat before sliding into the driver's seat. He primed the ignition and the needle on the petrol gage rose to well over half full. Now was the moment of truth. He turned the key in the ignition and the engine roared into life. He jolted the gear lever into reverse and pulled away from its parking place behind the Land Rover. Then he nosed the Astra out into the long driveway that led to the road. He looked around. There was still no sign of anybody. So far so good. He reached the end of the driveway and looked right and left. He glanced up at the sun: it was dead ahead. He headed north.

Sloan drove for a mile or so along a winding single-track lane before he reached a T-junction. Again, he turned left onto

232

a 'B' road that was signposted for the village of Catsash. It was a little over four miles north. Once through there, Sloan reckoned he would pick up signs for the dual carriageway that would take him to the M5, M6 and then on to Scotland. He felt he'd done his duty. Hopefully, Fay should be safe now but there was nothing more he could do. He had to get as far away as possible and soon. Once they found Fay, he would be identified and the chase would be on to find him. He realised he'd just given up any advantage he'd gained by hiding in the woodland. If he drove all day, just stopping for short breaks, he could reach Scotland by late-afternoon and find shelter by nightfall. Somewhere along the way, he would have to abandon the Astra as it would surely be reported as stolen. But he would face that when he came to it. For now, all he could think of was getting to the motorway.

He reached the Catsash village sign and slowed to 30mph, not wanting to draw attention to himself. He followed the main road through the village. A group of children waiting for a school bus on his left were chatting and laughing and there was a man walking a black Labrador on the opposite side of the road. There were a few people putting bin bags out or getting into cars in their driveway but nobody paid him any attention. He began to feel more relaxed, the knot of anxiety easing its grip on his stomach.

Sloan left the village boundary and picked up speed again. The road widened out a little and it was easier to pass oncoming vehicles. He flicked the radio on and the news blasted out of the speakers. The Brexit debacle was still ongoing and the Prime Minister, Boris Johnson, had announced he was proroguing Parliament to the uproar of remain supporters. Sloan shook his head in disbelief. The newscaster announced that there was still no progress on the serial killer case but the police were doing all they could to catch the perpetrator. Then Sloan's blood ran cold as he heard his name.

"Jaxon Sloan, recently released from Gallow Hill prison is still at large after killing his wife Lisa Sloan and her lover, Kieran Hook with a sawn-off shotgun. Police are widening their search in an effort to seize and arrest him."

The weather forecast followed and Sloan turned the radio off. So, they still had no idea where he was. Maybe he would get to Scotland after all.

He still hadn't noticed the police surveillance drone tracking him from 90 metres above.

FORTY-SIX

Thursday 22nd August 2019

Daniel drove through Riverbeke and out onto the road that would take him to Hallbrook Manor and the Riverbeke Falls tea room. Once north of town, he joined the ring road and followed the brown tourist road signs to the stately home. He was soon out onto the country roads. The new out-of-town housing estates had petered out until he passed just the occasional farm. To the west, beyond the river, lay acres of dense woodland, left to nature by the conservancy council. To the east, lay flat farmland for miles, and to the north, the village of Catsash and the dual carriageway that led to the M5 and then M6 north.

Daniel took a left turn signposted for Hallbrook Manor and drove a mile and a half down a narrow tree-lined lane to the stately home. The tea room was signposted to his left; a corrugated metal building painted dark green. He turned off and parked on the gravel near the front entrance.

Daniel checked the name on his note as he walked into the tea room. The place was rustic styled, furnished with several wooden tables, mismatched chairs and bifold glass doors that afforded an open frontage to the garden. There was a smell of fresh baked scones and coffee with a faint whiff of burned toast. At the counter he asked to speak to Trevor Reeves, the manager. There was an array of various cakes on display beneath several glass-domed plates.

"Yes, that's me," a deep voice came from the side of the counter hatch. A slim man in his fifties with a mass of red, wiry hair and freckles appeared in front of Daniel.

"I'm Daniel Kendrick. I was wondering if I might have a word in private?" Daniel remembered the reporter saying the break-in should be kept quiet and there were several customers at tables within hearing range. He didn't want to be the one to spill the beans.

"Sure. Come through." Reeves wiped his hands on his apron and gestured to a door at the side of the counter.

Daniel thanked him and went through the doorway into the kitchen area. There were several kitchen staff busily preparing coffees and pots of tea for the visitors. He weaved his way through to the back, following the manager.

"What can I do for you. Is everything alright?" Reeves looked concerned – as if he was expecting a complaint.

"Mr Reeves, I understand from a reporter at the Argus, that you had a break in on Monday night. I was wondering if you'd be willing to tell me about it."

"Are you from the police?"

"No. But I am investigating the disappearance of my wife and I have a suspicion that the person who broke in here may have abducted her."

"Gosh. That sounds rather serious," the manager was obviously taken aback. He guided Daniel gently to the side to allow a waitress to pass with a tray full of dishes.

Daniel lowered his voice and leaned closer to the manager. "It could be, yes. I think the person who broke into your kitchen might have been the same man on the run for murder. Jaxon Sloan."

"It crossed my mind as well, Mr…"

"Kendrick. Daniel Kendrick." Daniel dodged another waitress with a tray as she hurried past.

"Follow me, Mr Kendrick." Reeves walked out toward the back door, away from the bustle of the main kitchen.

Reeves pointed to the boarded-up door. "This is where he broke in. I still haven't managed to get it fixed."

"Was there much taken?" Daniel asked.

"Quite a bit of food from the fridge and pantry, a torch, a few other bits and pieces and a couple of large knives. Nothing of any great value, which made me think it was someone who needed provisions."

"Yes, it sounds like it to me too. What have the police said?"

"They just made notes and said they would look into it but I've heard nothing since."

"Mr Reeves, do you know the area well?" Daniel was hoping he did.

"Yes, I've lived in this area all my life. Born and brought up in Catsash, just up the road." He smiled, proud to be a local.

"In your opinion – assuming it was Jaxon Sloan that broke in here – where would he have gone if he was on the run?"

"I'd say north, following the river. There's dense woodland all along there for cover and a few deserted farm buildings along the way. Just a second – I'll get a map." Reeves disappeared out into the tea room.

Daniel felt buoyed. At last, he had a lead on Sloan. It made sense for him to have broken in here for supplies before going on the run. He wondered if DS Harper had made the connection too. He would call him when he had more evidence.

Reeves returned with a tourist map of the area. The river was clearly marked, running north to south and the manager pointed out their location in relation to the town of Riverbeke and the village of Catsash. A few farms were also marked between here and the dual carriageway.

"In my opinion, Mr Kendrick, the killer is more likely to have gone north, away from the town and unless he actually crossed the river – which is quite deep in places – he might have followed the river upstream. If he kept to the river bank on this side, the topography is fairly flat and he would have had plenty of tree cover."

"I see," Daniel said, "I think it unlikely he crossed the river if he had my wife with him. I agree that this is the most likely route. May I keep this?" He tapped the map.

"Be my guest," the manager said. "I hope you find your wife."

They shook hands.

"Yes, I do too," Daniel said.

FORTY-SEVEN

Thursday 22nd August 2019

Daniel drove slowly north along a narrow 'B' road toward the village of Catsash. Whenever there was a gap in the hedgerow or open fencing, he was on the lookout for Sloan. He had murdered his wife and her lover in Riverbeke in the early hours of Tuesday, so he could easily have made it to Fay's clinic sometime after 1 pm, abducted her and gone on the run into the woodlands or along the river bank, as Trevor Reeves had suggested. The only thing that didn't make sense was that the tea room had been broken into during the night, or at least early on Tuesday morning before any of the staff were around. Sloan would have had to leave the murder scene, get to the tea rooms, several miles north, then go back into Riverbeke for Fay. Why didn't he just break into one of the many cafés, shops and restaurants in town? If he was on foot, as the news report suggested, it wouldn't make sense to double back on himself like that.

Daniel's mind was racing as he drove. Then he spotted a helicopter, seemingly following the course of the road he was on. He drove a few more miles. The helicopter was still ahead and slightly to his left above the outline of trees against the horizon. He slowed as he approached the village of Catsash. The helicopter was still there and another was a short distance behind.

FORTY-EIGHT

Thursday 22nd August 2019

Sloan drove past the village of Catsash, toward the short 'A' road that led to the dual carriageway. He reached a crossroads, checked the signage and turned left. Now the M5 was signposted. It couldn't be far. He picked up speed and began to relax. He was well away from the woodland and Fay and soon he would be cruising on the motorway. Perhaps he would stop for a short break soon. Helping Fay had not been part of his plan but he felt like he had no choice. It might have set him back but it was a decision he would have to live with.

Sloan thought he heard something ominous and wound down his window to listen. Sirens.

Shit.

In his rear-view mirror, he saw the sickening sight of blue lights flashing. They were coming up fast behind him. He was being signalled to pull over. Instantly, his instincts kicked in. There was no way he was going to stop. He dropped down into third gear and floored the accelerator, the force pushing him back in his seat. Adrenaline flooded his body as he drove at high speed along the road, taking the corners way too fast

241

and straddling the white line. Oncoming cars were forced into the side of the road but he kept driving, the engine roaring, tyres screeching on tarmac, the sound of sirens behind him resounding in his ears. He reached a 40mph area but kept accelerating, manoeuvring the Astra around the chicane of cars and vans that had pulled into the side of the road in response to the police sirens.

Sloan reached the roundabout that led to the dual carriageway, slowed briefly but pulled out into oncoming traffic. Cars screeched to a halt, and others pulled over, allowing the pursuing police vehicles to pass as Sloan slammed the car around the roundabout and onto the dual carriageway. He had to get away.

Just 200 yards onto the dual carriageway, three Volvo V90 police vehicles increased their speed and passed him; a blaze of strobing lights and sirens. One went ahead blocking him from the front, one cut across his offside and another flanked him from the driver's side. To his nearside, a stone wall was blocking him in. Sloan checked his mirror; he could see a police BMW X5 blocking him from behind. The Tactical Pursuit and Containment (TPAC) vehicles had surrounded him in a 'box and stop' manoeuvre and he had no choice but to brake hard and bring the Astra to a juddering halt. The wheels locked and skidded as the engine stalled.

He sat for a moment, unsure what to do. His mind was racing. He felt like a cornered animal but could he still escape capture? Surely, there had to be a way. Instinctively he reached for his holdall on the seat beside him, unzipped the bag and reached in for the loaded shotgun. He pulled it out of the bag and kept it low beneath the dashboard. Armed Police officers were getting out of the cars and taking up their positions with firearms aimed directly at him. One policewoman sat in the passenger seat of the Volvo and aimed a self-loading Glock 17 pistol through the open window at his chest. Behind, other police vehicles were arriving, their sirens adding to the din. Above, the deafening roar of rotating helicopter blades told him he was completely surrounded.

"Driver, get out of the car," an Authorised Firearms Officer shouted, a Heckler & Koch G36C carbine assault rifle trained on him.

Sloan could see a police officer behind trying to keep hold of a German Shepherd that was straining at the leash. He ran his hand along the butt of the shotgun and slipped the safety off. He carefully and deliberately cocked both hammers.

"Driver, get out of the car. We know it's you Sloan. You've got no chance of getting away. Get out of the car now." The woman's voice was calm but firm as she scrutinised his every move down the barrel of the rifle. A red dot glowed from the top of the ACOG sight.

Sloan felt a rush of adrenaline and the crushing grip of fear like his innards were plunging down a cliff face. He slowly reached across and opened the door with his left hand; his right holding the gun. He stepped out of the car and heard the police shouting further instructions to him to put the gun down, lie on the ground, face down with his hands behind his back and his ankles crossed. All around him was the sound of police radios crackling with voices.

He stood; the loaded gun cocked and ready to fire in his right hand. He was holding it against his right temple. The gesture was effectively a warning to the police that he was threatening to shoot himself. He turned slowly to see police vehicles in every direction and armed officers swathed in Kevlar marking him with rifles and pistols. One officer pointed a taser at him, a red dot played over his back.

"Hold your fire," he heard a police officer shout.

He was trapped on all sides as if he was boxed into a coffin. He stood, holding the gun against his temple, as he weighed his options. Give himself up or take his own life. That was all he could come up with. A life on the run was no longer possible. He would never have his freedom again. He thought of Dr Kendrick and pictured her beautiful face smiling at him. Had he sacrificed his freedom and maybe even his life to help her? Perhaps he would have been caught eventually whether he had helped her or not. He didn't regret it. What he did regret now – and it hit him like a tsunami – was murdering his wife and Hook. In that moment, he wasn't sure if he felt remorse for taking two lives or whether he was just sorry he'd got caught. If he could have controlled his rage; just filed for divorce like a normal person would do in those circumstances, he would be a free man now. Maybe his life was always going to end like this. The simmering anger and hatred he'd felt for most of his life culminating in a standoff with armed police.

How long could Sloan maintain the deadlock? What would be the point, he thought? Whichever way it ended; he was finished. Prison or death. That was the stark choice he was faced with. Whether society decided to imprison him for life or even execute him for his crime, in this moment, he had a brutal choice. Pull the trigger or put the gun down.

Prison or death?

His choice.

Sloan knelt onto the ground, the police still shouting instructions to him to lie on the floor, to drop the gun. It all became a blur; overwhelming his senses with the strobing police lights and the roar of the helicopter circling above, a police dog barking. Sloan could feel his heart hammering hard against his ribs and his right arm shaking with shock and the cocktail of adrenaline and cortisol that had drenched his body.

Prison.

Or death?

FORTY-NINE

Thursday 22nd August 2019

Daniel was driving through the pretty village of Catsash with its row of stone cottages, a country pub and a medieval church, when his iPhone rang. It was Shelly.

Daniel pulled over and answered. "Hi Shelly."

"Daniel, I've just heard on the news that the police have got Sloan." Shelly sounded excited.

"Blimey. Where?"

"On the slip road to the dual carriageway north of Catsash. Where are you now?"

"In Catsash," he said, aghast that he was so close.

"It looks like he was driving and heading for the motorway. They managed to stop him but apparently, there's some sort of standoff going on. He's still armed."

"Is Fay with him?"

"It looks like he's alone."

"I'm on my way."

Daniel rang off, checked his wing mirror and pulled out. He could see the helicopters, now circling a few miles ahead. He desperately wanted to speak to Sloan. Did he have Fay?

Somehow, he had to get to him. Maybe DS Harper would be there. Surely, he would listen now.

Daniel put his foot down. He was doing 45mph through the village, weaving around a line of parked cars. A man walking a dog waived a stick at him as he sped past but he was oblivious – all he could focus on was getting to Sloan. To Fay.

Daniel could see the deregulation signs up ahead and accelerated to 50-, then 65mph, struggling to steer around the tight bends without veering over to the other side of the road. There were three cyclists up ahead and he slowed briefly to overtake them. He shouted obscenities as one of the cyclists pulled out into the road, forcing him to swerve, narrowly missing an oncoming car.

He could hear a car horn in the distance as he increased his speed once again. Then he saw a tractor up ahead. He slowed then accelerated past it on a blind corner, adrenaline pumping through his veins. He had to get to Sloan. He drove up a steep hill, crested the top, then down the other side, negotiating a series of hairpin bends way too fast. An oncoming van was forced to swerve into the hedge but Daniel kept his speed up, changing down into third gear for the tight corners and accelerating dangerously as the road straightened up again.

Soon, he was approaching the short 'A' road that led to the dual carriageway. He reached a crossroads, slammed on the brakes as several cars sped past, then pulled out, turning left. He floored the accelerator, the tyres of his BMW squealing on the tarmac as he pulled away. He ignored the 40mph signs and speeded up to 67- then 74mph, banking on the corners. He overtook several cars, narrowly missing an oncoming lorry.

Daniel reached the roundabout that led to the dual carriageway. He could see the strobing lights of the stationary police vehicles up ahead. He pulled out in front of a van and took the roundabout too fast, mounting the curb but managing to steer back onto the road. As he entered the slipway, the road was blocked to traffic but he could see the back of a police BMW X5 and in front of that, three police Volvo V90s surrounding a red Astra that was jammed against a stone wall. Above, two helicopters circled the dramatic scene. A police dog handler was restraining a German Shepherd.

Daniel stopped the car and got out, leaving the door open. His eyes were darting around, searching for Fay. A crowd of onlookers had gathered, taking photos and video footage on their phones from behind the police roadblock. He took a few steps forward and could see several armed police officers, their firearms trained on a man who was kneeling on the road, red dots dancing over his torso.

Jaxon Sloan.

Daniel moved closer. He could hear police officers shouting at Sloan to put the gun down, lie on the ground, face down. To give himself up. He could see that Sloan was holding a sawn-off shot gun to his right temple. Daniel had to get to him – it was all he could think of. His mind was swimming with images of Fay trapped and abandoned in some filthy farm building, miles from anywhere. He was sure Sloan was involved in her disappearance but where was she now? Had he killed her? Was she harmed? He had to speak to Sloan; but how could he get to him through the barricade of armed police officers?

He looked around. There on the far side, he could see DS Harper. If he could get to him – plead with him to ask Sloan about Fay. A police officer was standing close by, controlling the gathering crowd of onlookers. He stepped up to him.

"Please, officer, I need to speak with DS Harper – urgently." Daniel had to shout above the noise of helicopter blades rotating overhead.

"I'm sorry, sir, please step back," the officer called back, holding up a restraining hand.

"But I need to speak to DS Harper. He's just over there." Daniel pointed to the detective.

"Step back, sir." The officer was adamant.

"Please, it's urgent. My wife's life is at risk."

The officer maintained his stance, struggling to control the gathering crown as they surged forward to get a better look.

Daniel could see the detective speaking into his personal radio. He looked over to see Sloan, still kneeling motionless on the road, marked by riffles and a taser trained on his torso.

Harper or Sloan?

Sloan was closer.

Daniel's heart was pounding against his ribcage. In a blinding split second, fuelled by adrenaline, he'd made the decision to get to Sloan. He was desperate to find his wife, oblivious to the danger.

Daniel broke through the police road block and ran toward Sloan.

"Don't shoot," he shouted repeatedly, arms held high in the air, "I need to speak to this man." He took a few steps sideways toward Sloan, twisting his body toward the police to show he was unarmed. Police officers bellowed at him to get down. To lie on the ground. He sensed several riffles now trained on him but he continued to step closer to Sloan.

Amid the noise of rotating helicopter blades, voices over police radios and armed officers barking instructions, he stepped slowly toward Sloan, approaching him from the front and right side, so he could be seen.

Sloan startled slightly and looked up at him; his head steady, the gun still aimed at his right temple. There was abject terror in his eyes and he was visibly shaking.

Daniel extended a hand, palm turned upward, toward Sloan, a gesture meant to show he was no threat and to hold his fire. His other arm was held high in the air and meant to assure the police. In the background, he could hear DS Harper shouting.

"Hold your fire. It's Daniel Kendrick. Hold your fire." The detective was moving closer but remained behind the armed officers.

Daniel moved closer to Sloan's face, bending to be heard above the din and looking straight into his eyes. "I'm Daniel, Fay Kendrick's husband. Please tell me if you have my wife." He had to raise his voice to be heard.

Sloan fixed Daniel's eyes with his; his pupils dilated with fear. "Fay?" he mouthed.

"Yes, my wife. Do you know where she is?" Daniel could see a flash of recognition on Sloan's face. He did know where she was.

"She's hurt... needs... help," Sloan croaked, barely audible above the noise.

Daniel could hear police officers barking instructions to him to lie on the ground. He held up an acknowledging hand in their direction, his focus still on Sloan. He slowly lowered himself to the road, kneeling next to Sloan, his face turned toward him, arms behind him as instructed. Red laser dots now dancing over both of them.

Sloan looked at Daniel, past the gun, still pointed at his own temple. His face was red and blotchy, his eyes wide and staring in terror. "I didn't... hurt her... just found her," Sloan was saying, tears now pouring freely down his face.

Daniel looked deeply into his anguished eyes and believed him. "Where is she? I have to find her." He pleaded with him.

Police officers were creeping in gradually, closing the space between them. They were still shouting to both of them to lie face down on the ground. The German Shepherd was barking incessantly.

Daniel was desperate now. "Please, tell me where she is."

FIFTY

Thursday 22nd August 2019

Sloan saw the red laser sight of the taser that was trained on his chest just moments before he felt the painful muscle contractions of 50,000 volts tearing through his whole body. He convulsed, falling face down on the ground. His right hand still clutching the shotgun.

Jaxon Sloan tried to speak, then all he knew was a hot searing pain then the cold, black, finality of death as the bullets from his own shotgun tore into his skull and ripped his brain apart.

FIFTY-ONE

Thursday 22nd August 2019

Daniel watched with horror as Sloan shuddered and convulsed before he fell to the ground.

"She's…"

That was the last thing Daniel heard before the deafening bang of gunshot.

He had been kneeling on the road next to Sloan, but had been pushed sideways from the pressure of the blast from the shotgun as it tore into Sloan's head. He instinctively rolled into a foetal ball, raised his arms and covered his ears with his hands, his eyes shut tight. His head was ringing from the discharge of Jaxon Sloan's shotgun just feet away. It had been unbelievably loud but now, all he could hear was silence caused by the temporary damage to his hearing. Daniel breathed in the pungent smell of gun smoke – a heady mix of fireworks and spice with a distinctive metallic zing.

For a moment, he thought he had been hit by shrapnel but as he slowly opened his eyes, he could see police officers rushing toward him, checking his body for injuries. He seemed to be unhurt, although the wound to his forearm from the scuffle with

251

Justin McCartney was sore after he hit the ground, the wound on his cheek felt numb. Two officers manoeuvred him so that he was lying face down on the road and one of them yanked his arms behind him. He felt the cold, hard metal of handcuffs encase his wrists.

"What the bloody hell do you think you were doing?" DS Harper shouted as he ran across to Daniel.

Daniel only saw the fuzzy outline of the detective's angry expression and his mouth moving. He could hear nothing but the silence inside his brain.

He twisted his head to see Sloan, the right side of his face on the road, eyes staring sightlessly in death. He could smell the man's singed hair and skin and see the ragged, irregular exit wound on the left side of his head from the discharge of close-range gunshot pellets. It was a bloodied mess, covered in soot, with pieces of skull and brain tissue spread over a wide area.

Daniel felt strong arms lift him up onto his feet from both sides and drag him toward a police Volvo. The rear door was opened and a police officer pushed him down into the seat. Daniel sat back, stunned at what had just happened.

He looked back to see police gathered around the body of Jaxon Sloan.

Shit.

Sloan had been on the verge of telling him where Fay was. His instincts had been right – that Sloan knew something about Fay. But he had not been responsible for her disappearance. Questions whirred in his mind but he struggled to focus on anything. He was in shock.

He was left to sit in the back of the police car for some time. Sloan's body had been loosely covered with black plastic. Police were milling about, radios crackling, officers in groups discussing what had happened and what their next moves would be. The K9 Dog Unit had left. The Major Incident Team were gathering to begin their investigation. More police constables had been drafted in to control the crowds of onlookers and the press were arriving in force. The India 99 police helicopters had gone. The dual carriageway was closed in both directions, with traffic tailbacks snaking their way into the distance.

Gradually, Daniel's hearing began to return. Faintly at first but he still had a loud buzzing in his head, which no amount of head shaking could shift. His left ear seemed to have gone completely deaf. In the distance, he heard more sirens – an ambulance for Sloan? Probably not. It was too late for him now. He felt the heavy drag of defeat as he realised Sloan had taken the information about Fay's whereabouts to his grave.

Then he heard the familiar voice of DS Harper. "Let's get him to the station," he said to a young police constable.

DS Harper bent to look Daniel in the eye. He didn't seem pleased. Then Daniel's blood ran ice cold as he was read his rights.

"Daniel Kendrick, I am arresting you for obstructing the police. You do not have to say anything. But it may harm your defence if you do not mention when questioned something which you later rely on in court. Anything you do say may be given in evidence."

Harper slammed the door of the Volvo and told the PC he would see him back at the station. A woman police constable slid into the passenger seat and they drove away from the devastating scene. The road would be closed for some time.

They drove in silence apart from the occasional comment between the two police officers and the background noise of the police radio and the officer's personal radios. Daniel was lost in thought, replaying the incident over and over in his mind. Had he caused Sloan's death by interfering – or obstructing the police, as Harper had said? Had Sloan shot himself deliberately or did he pull the trigger in reaction to muscle contractions caused by the taser? Perhaps he would never know but one thing was sure. Sloan had seen Fay and although he said she was injured – she was alive.

His wife was still alive.

FIFTY-TWO

Daniel was taken to Riverbeke police station and handed over to the custody officer, sergeant Bradley Morris; a tall, thirty-something man with a laid-back disposition and a shock of dark hair. He was taken to a room, asked to remove any possessions, including his shoes. He handed over his wallet and iPhone, took off his wrist watch, belt and shoes, handing them to the custody officer, who placed them in a plastic bag inside a locker.

He was then processed and booked in, his fingerprints taken, photographed for mug shots and DNA obtained using a mouth swab. Daniel felt numb through the whole process. He was a senior surgeon, yet now he'd been arrested and was in custody – for what? For trying to find his missing wife. For trying to talk to someone who knew where she was. How the hell had it come to this? What if he was held responsible for Sloan's death and sent to prison – what would become of Fay? He was in despair.

"Come with me, Mr Kendrick," the custody officed said.

He was led down a stark, grey-painted corridor to Interview Room 3. There was a sign on the door that said: Audio Video Recorded Room.

Inside the tiny room was a grey metal desk and three hard-backed chairs, illuminated by stark fluorescent light. Behind the desk sat DS Harper and a woman police officer.

"Sit down Dr Kendrick," Harper said. "I'm Detective Sergeant Ian Harper and this is Detective Inspector Emma Oakes." His voice echoed around the bare walls.

Daniel sat at the desk. It was a bleak environment.

"Let's start the recording," Harper said, switching on a tape recorder.

Daniel looked up to see a video camera pointed at them.

"Dr Kendrick. Before we start the interview, I must warn you that you are under caution. You do not have to say anything. But it may harm your defence if you do not mention when questioned something which you later rely on in court. Anything you do say may be given in evidence. Do you understand?"

Daniel nodded and turned the right side of his head slightly toward the detectives. "Yes, I understand." His ears were still ringing slightly from the gunshot. The hearing in his left ear was thankfully coming back and he was managing to block out most of the ringing sound. He had to get through this.

"You have certain rights. You are entitled to free legal advice. Do you want a solicitor present?"

"No – I'm fine, thanks." Daniel just wanted to get this over with, get out of there and try to find his wife. Finding a solicitor would just hold things up.

"Well, if you change your mind, please inform the custody officer. You also have the right to tell someone where you are. Is there anyone we should inform that you are in police custody?"

"No. Absolutely not." Daniel was horrified to think of his son, Fay's mother or any of his colleagues knowing he had been arrested. He particularly didn't want to give that bitch Melissa the satisfaction either.

DS Harper then informed Daniel about his right to medical treatment if he was ill and he showed him a written notice explaining about his rights to regular breaks for food and to use the toilet, or to have an interpreter present.

"I'm fine with all this," Daniel said, feeling nervous in anticipation of the interview starting but just wanting to get on with it.

"Please state for the benefit of the tape your full name, address and date of birth."

Daniel gave the information as Harper and Inspector Oakes waited. They were making notes. He was then given a form to sign to confirm that he understood his rights.

"Now, Dr Kendrick. Can you explain why you approached Jaxon Sloan during a tense police operation earlier today?" DS Harper leaned back in his chair expectantly waiting for an answer. Inspector Emma Oakes watched Daniel; her expression unreadable.

Daniel took a deep breath then leaned forward, looking directly at Harper. "Detective, I believed Jaxon Sloan might have been involved with my wife's disappearance – as I told you earlier – he was one of her patients. She gave an expert witness testimony in court that helped to have him jailed. I thought he might harbour a lot of resentment about that." Daniel took another deep breath, trying to calm the emotional turmoil that was threatening to overwhelm him. "I thought he might have abducted her after he murdered his wife. I just needed to speak to him."

"And you thought it would be perfectly in order to approach a man being marked by armed police while he was holding a gun to his head?" Harper looked across at Inspector Oakes and they exchanged a look of incredulity.

"I was desperate. I just want to find Fay." Daniel was choking back tears, desperate to stay in control.

"You realise you may have jeopardised our operation?" Inspector Oakes spoke now. Her voice was firm; her expression dour and serious.

Daniel stayed silent, looking down at his hands.

"Dr Kendrick. What did you say to Jaxon Sloan?"

Daniel looked up at Harper. "I asked him if he knew where Fay was. He said he that he did. He said that she was hurt and needed help."

"Had he abducted your wife or harmed her as you feared?"

"No. He said he hadn't hurt her – that he had just found her."

"And you believed him?" Inspector Oakes asked.

Yes, I believed him. I could see it in his eyes. He was telling the truth."

"And did he tell you where she is?" Harper said.

Daniel closed his eyes momentarily, trying to block out the awful truth. "He was about to tell me when the gun went off."

FIFTY-THREE

Thursday 22nd August 2019

Damon smirked as his uncle lay dead on the kitchen floor. He coolly finished smoking his splif and drained his beer from the can. No hurry. Uncle Wally was dead. He wasn't going anywhere.

Damon pushed the butt of his joint into the empty can and wandered around the kitchen, opening and shutting cupboard doors, examining the contents; searching for something else to eat. He wandered into the sitting room – a large square room filled with old-fashioned furniture and dominated by a large, lovingly polished rosewood table and six chairs. The fireplace had been blocked off years ago and a four-bar electric fire stood on the hearth. An old photograph of a smiling Frazer and his late wife sat on the oak mantlepiece. Frazer's Queen Anne style armchair stood next to it with its matching dark green leather footrest. An open copy of the local newspaper lay across it, as if he had been reading it when Damon had knocked the door. There was a piece about the local murders, the reporter writing that the police were still no further ahead in their investigation.

The sash windows afforded views to the garden, with its pretty flower boarders and the new wooden summerhouse that Frazer had installed last Spring. A rosewood bureau stood against one wall. Damon was drawn to it. He rummaged for the key in an adjacent vase, opened the lid and leafed through the piles of papers inside – mainly bills and letters from the council about the change in refuse collection days and recycling arrangements. There were a few leaflets for various takeaways in town and an advertisement leaflet for a miniature hearing aid.

Damon opened a drawer and found Frazer's worn brown leather wallet. He opened it and pocketed a wad of notes – some £200, he estimated. He took his uncle's debit and credit cards and smiled. He could have some fun with this, he thought. In another drawer, he found the details of Frazer's savings accounts and his work and State pensions. There was no will that he could find. He looked around the room. It was immaculately tidy and clean. His uncle had lived alone with no close relatives apart from himself – a nephew by marriage only. As far as he knew Frazer had few visitors and had become something of a recluse since his wife had died from an aortic aneurism over ten years ago.

Damon saw immediately the possibility of taking on his uncle's home and his assets. Of stealing his identity. Typically, he hadn't thought through the consequences or his likelihood of succeeding – he was driven by impulsivity, recklessness and his inability to resist temptation.

Yes, he could live here, he thought. Give up the grotty flat and move to the country. He would use Frazer's car, a very nice, X-Type Jaguar in gleaming black. He could spend his uncle's money to his heart's content and it would be a good place to bring Fay Kendrick since it was fairly isolated and private.

Now all he had to do was dispose of Frazer's body.

Damon had checked Frazer's pockets for anything that might identify him and struggling with the weight, dragged his uncle's dead body through the kitchen and onto the driveway. Thankfully there had been no mess to clean up.

He opened the boot of Frazer's Jaguar and hefted his body inside. Frazer's lifeless, half open eyes stared at him accusingly. He shut the boot lid. After dark, he would take it and dump it where it would never be found.

In the meantime, he was hungry. He rummaged in the kitchen for something to eat and found a frozen pepperoni pizza which he put in the oven. There were plenty of beers in the fridge and more in a second fridge in the garage. He went through the cupboards in the sitting room and study and found half a bottle of brandy and a large, unopened bottle of Jack Daniels. He opened the whiskey and poured himself a large one in a crystal tumbler – the ones Frazer kept for special visitors and Christmas.

Damon felt rather pleased with himself. It had been a good result today – an unexpected upward turn of events that could be a life changer for him.

Damon could barely wait to start spending his uncle's money and went into the study and fired up the old desktop computer. He sipped his drink while he waited for it to boot up, savouring the fine taste of the Tennessee whiskey. He had big plans now. He could be much more than a small-time drug dealer. Once he was settled at his uncle's place, he would turn his attention back to Fay. He still had the urge to possess her – to hold power over her. In this place, once he had disposed of her husband, he could easily isolate her from the rest of her family and anyone else she cared about. No one would know where the hell she was. He was looking forward to it. But first; he had some shopping to do.

The computer had loaded up Google Chrome and Damon typed in the web address of his favourite betting shop. He created an account in Frazer's name and tried to place a bet on the afternoon's horse race at Cheltenham. £250 to win on Dizzy Dora in the 4.30 pm race. The odds looked good.

The bet was declined.

Puzzled, Damon tried again but once more, it was declined. He shrugged. Maybe he would try to buy something on Frazer's credit card instead. He smelled the pizza he had cooking in the oven and went to retrieve it. He sliced it and carried it on a plate back to the study, topping up his whiskey on the way. As he ate, he found a menswear shop online – he could do with some new clothes and shoes.

He found several pairs of chinos, a few T-shirts, an expensive pair of trainers and an on-trend leather jacket, then went to the checkout. He punched the card details into the relevant fields and waited for the card payment to process. Again, it was declined.

What the hell was going on. Damon tried removing some of the more expensive items from the shopping cart and tried again. This time the payment went through. Frazer's card must be near the limit, Damon reasoned.

He tried a few more purchases with both the credit and debit cards with similar results. Finally, even small amounts were being declined.

Then he heard Frazer's mobile phone ping and went to investigate. It was a text message from his uncle's bank warning him of suspicious activity on his account and that they were freezing his cards until he called them.

Shit.

Damon finished eating his pizza and decided to do a thorough search of the house for cash and valuables.

He looked through Frazer's wallet once more then checked every drawer and cupboard in every room, under the bed, under the mattress, in the loft, the garage and finally behind the sofa. There was no sign of any cash, credit cards or any other liquid assets. He looked through every piece of paper in the bureau; more carefully this time. There were the papers to do with Frazer's modest company pension but his heart sank when he read a recent one from the mortgage company stating that they were threatening to re-possess the house if he failed to keep up with the payments. He had a month's grace.

It looked like uncle Wally was right – there was no more money. The old bastard was in the shit financially.

The only way he was going to get hold of any money was to go to the pension company and present himself as Frazer's only living relative. The snag was, he would need a death certificate and all the rest of the rigmarole he would need to prove who he was if he was to access any funds. He wasn't sure he could pull it off. Fraud was not his forte and he was out of his depth. Also, he wasn't sure what other living relatives Frazer had. He knew there was a sister somewhere and several cousins that would all come out of the woodwork if they knew Frazer was dead. They would be clamouring to be beneficiaries if there was any money to be had. And it looked like it was a big 'if'.

It was beginning to feel like old uncle Wally was having the last laugh…

FIFTY-FOUR

Thursday 22nd August 2019

Daniel had been given a cup of coffee and had been questioned for over two hours. Mainly going over and over the same questions. DS Harper had brought up the fact that he and Fay had been arguing recently but the thrust of the interview was about the fact that he had approached Sloan during a police operation. Daniel was exasperated. He couldn't change what he'd done and if he was honest, he didn't regret it. He had simply been desperate to find Fay and Sloan was his best lead. He hadn't thought about the danger to himself or others – he had just acted on impulse.

There was a knock at the door of the interview room and the custody sergeant stuck his head around the door.

"Can I have a word, detectives?" He said, waiting for both Harper and Oakes to speak to him outside.

They both stood and went out of the room. Just as the door was closing behind them, Daniel heard something that chilled him to the core. He heard the custody sergeant say that a woman's body had been found.

Oh God no. No. Not Fay. Please not Fay…

Daniel leapt from his chair and yanked open the door of the interview room. "My God – you've found Fay? Is she dead?" He was desperately searching the faces of the two detectives and the custody sergeant.

Inspector Oakes grabbed his arm. "Calm down, it's OK. It's not your wife."

"How do you know? It could be." Daniel was panic stricken.

"It is the body of a woman, Dr Kendrick, but she was washed up on the beach and has been dead a very long time. It's one of our cold cases. It can't possibly be your wife," the custody sergeant cut in, flashing DS Harper a look that said he had no choice but to tell him.

"Alright, Dr Kendrick. We'll leave it there for now," DS Harper said, turning to Daniel.

"Keep him in sergeant Morris," Oakes said to the custody sergeant as they left for a briefing.

"Shit," Daniel said.

Daniel was taken to a cell in the police station, given a blanket but no pillow and locked in, the sound of the metal door slamming echoed around the room. He had no idea how long he would be in there. The room was windowless and small with white-painted breeze block walls; dim, with just a bare lightbulb hanging from the ceiling. Along one wall ran a concrete bed base topped with a thin, plastic-covered mattress. In the corner there was a stainless-steel toilet bowl, one toilet roll and washbasin unit. High on one wall, a CCTV was recording constantly.

Daniel sat on the hard bed; his thin blanket still folded. He felt desperate. The adrenaline that had flooded his system when he thought Fay's body had been found was still making him feel panicky and jittery. He needed to exercise to work it off but there was no way he could in this small cell. He knew she was still alive this morning when he'd spoken to Sloan and he had to keep hoping she was alright. She was hurt, Sloan had said but he had no idea what could be wrong. She was normally in good health, although the stress of the last two years – after Sophie's death – must have taken its toll. Could it be to do with the blood stains found in her consulting room? Images of Fay and the injuries she could have sustained were swimming around his head. He had to get out of there. Had to find another lead and look for Fay.

Sergeant Morris had brought him a mug of tea. He appeared to be kind and understanding but Daniel knew he was bound by the law and the rules of policing. There was no way he was simply going to let him out, however sympathetic he was to his cause. He had no idea how long they would keep him there or whether they intended to charge him. He remembered being told that they could keep him in custody for 24 hours before either charging him, applying for further time or releasing him. It would be a long night.

Daniel sat and sipped the luke-warm tea, it was way too strong for his liking but he was grateful for something to quench his thirst. He hadn't eaten for hours but his stomach felt queasy and he couldn't face food. The whole day seemed surreal now. The dramatic incident with Sloan, his subsequent arrest and now being held in a police cell.

Daniel thought of Maisie, Chester and Ella back at home. Maisie was used to being left all day while they were at work but she would need to be fed. He would need to call Rosie to deal with the dogs if he was kept for much longer.

He felt lost without Fay. He missed her company. Missed her smile. She had done more for him than he had ever realised. She had given him a life after Susan, his first wife, had died. He just hoped that he could find her before something happened to her – that this injury that Sloan mentioned was nothing serious.

He couldn't bear the thought of losing the woman he loved – he wasn't equipped to go through the harrowing grief and sorrow again. He'd tried to stay numb emotionally after Sophie's death but losing Fay as well would be too much to bear. He stroked the thin white scars on his wrist. He was much stronger now but always fearful of the dark place he had found himself in.

Tears welled up in his eyes. In the dimly lit cell in Riverbeke police station, Daniel Kendrick sobbed for the first time in years.

FIFTY-FIVE

Thursday 22nd August 2019

Damon felt snookered. His glorious new future was rapidly sliding down the pan. Still, at least he had the use of the house and car and the £200 he'd pocketed in cash. There was also a house full of antiques – surely, they would have a cash value.

Damon reasoned that if he played his cards right, no one need know Frazer was dead – not yet. If ever. He looked out of the window. It was twilight.

He grabbed Frazer's car keys, a torch from the kitchen windowsill, locked the house and slid into the plush leather driver's seat of the Jaguar.

It was time to dispose of his uncle's body that lay in the boot of the car.

As the light faded, Damon drove his uncle's Jaguar further out into the countryside. Frazer's body was moving about unnervingly in the boot as he took the corners but after ten miles, he pulled up outside a disused quarry, situated on a scrubby brownfield site with layers of mountains off into the distance. A quick look around revealed that the security fencing surrounding the quarry was pretty old and broken and he easily found a gap large enough to enter.

There was no one around as he hauled Frazer's stiffening, lifeless body out of the boot. It landed on the ground with a resounding thud and Damon grabbed both arms by the wrists and dragged his uncle unceremoniously through the fence, placed it on the edge of the quarry and pushed the old man into the darkness with the toe of his boot. The body rolled down into the depths of the pit, slipping on the gravel and sending up clouds of limestone dust. Damon looked down into the shadowy depths. He was certain it was lost for good.

"Good riddance, you old bastard," Damon said without a trace of remorse.

He closed the boot of the Jaguar and drove back to his uncle's house. Damon, with his grandiose sense of entitlement, didn't question for a moment the morality of what he had done, or what he was planning to do. He considered Frazer's house to be his now, at least until the family came sniffing around, wondering where the old bugger was. The house was old fashioned and in need of a makeover but it would do for the time being. It was certainly better than his cramped, grimy flat at Bridgeman Towers.

Damon arrived back at the house, parked on the gravel drive and let himself back in. He poured himself another large Jack Daniels, grabbed a family-sized bag of salt and vinegar crisps and sat in the living room in his uncle's armchair.

He began to feel frustrated that the bank had frozen Frazer's accounts. Maybe Frazer had been telling the truth – that there was no more money. Damon felt the drag of disappointment. Already he wanted more. And as he often did, he imagined himself with a cool couple of million to do as he pleased with – wild parties, drugs, women – whatever he wanted.

There had to be a way to get it.

FIFTY-SIX

Thursday 22nd August 2019

Detective Sergeant Ian Harper and Detective Inspector Emma Oakes sat in one of the offices of the MIT – Major Incident Team – at Riverbeke Police Headquarters. Also present were Detective Superintendent, Edward Henderson, who's office they were in, Detective Inspector Ray Knight, who was leading the serial killer investigation, Detective Sergeant Laura Miller and Detective Constable Jeff Blackburn.

The Detective Superintendent cleared his throat, capturing everyone's attention. "You are aware that a dog walker found the badly decomposed body of a woman early this morning?" Several of the officers nodded their heads. "The cold case team are investigating, led by DI Phil Jameson." His voice was sombre.

The Superintendent cleared his throat and went on. "We will be liaising closely with Phil's team, should there be a link to the Riverbeke serial killer, codenamed Operation Viper."

DC Blackburn, a cocky young copper recently down from the Met, addressed Henderson. "Any further developments on the serial killer?"

Henderson differed to Detective Inspector Ray Knight.

"No, nothing more at this stage," the DI said.

DC Blackburn leaned back in his chair. "So, basically, we're completely in the dark. Don't you just love failure – so easy to achieve." He glanced around the room looking for approval.

There was a murmur of voices and Detective Sergeant Laura Miller shot him a disapproving look.

"Alright, people," DS Henderson cut in, "I've called this meeting to discuss the incident with Jaxon Sloan this morning."

DS Harper squirmed in his chair, anticipating what was coming.

"Let's try and unravel the absolute dog's bollocks of an operation that went on this morning." Henderson glanced at his notes.

Harper glanced at Emma Oakes, who was looking decidedly sheepish.

"I am aware that a Daniel Kendrick somehow broke through the police cordon and managed to approach the suspect – he was lucky he didn't get himself killed. I am also aware that his wife has gone missing and DS Harper is the lead on the missing persons enquiry." He looked at Harper.

"Yes, sir," Harper said.

"Now, the question is this. Did Jaxon Sloan shoot himself in an act of suicide, was he shot by an armed police officer or was it the taser that caused Sloan to discharge the gun that he had pointed at his head?" He sat back in his chair, waiting for some input from the room.

"We don't know yet, sir," DI Oakes said. "There will be a Home Office Post Mortem later today. We might know more after that. We are certain that the gun he was holding to his right temple was discharged, causing fatal wounding. There were no other firearms discharged."

"That still leaves the question of whether the taser caused the suspect to discharge the gun or whether it was a deliberate suicide."

DS Laura Miller spoke up. "There is one witness that was right next to him – Daniel Kendrick." She glanced at Harper, knowing he had been right there at the scene.

"And it all happened in front of the general public," DC Blackburn chipped in.

"As well as the bloody media – in the full glare of TV cameras," DI Roy Knight said. "We're not short of witnesses."

"There will be an inquest into this, of course," Detective Superintendent Henderson said. "Has the marksman that tasered Sloan been interviewed?"

"I'll look into it, sir, but as far as I am aware, he believed Sloan was about to kill himself," Emma Oakes said.

"Well, an Independent Police Complaints Commission report will have to rule out misconduct by officers," Henderson said. "What about Kendrick? Is there any evidence he was to blame?"

"No sir. Kendrick was desperate to find his wife and he did have reason to believe that Sloan might know where she was."

"And was that being investigated in the missing person's case?" Henderson asked Harper.

Everyone in the room turned to look at DS Harper.

"We were very busy with the Sloan case, sir. We hadn't had time to hold a briefing."

"Do you not think it might have diffused the situation if Dr Kendrick had been allowed to speak to Sloan under more controlled conditions?"

"Possibly, if we'd had the opportunity. Kendrick broke through the police cordon and took it upon himself to approach Sloan, although he says he did ask a PC if he could speak to me, sir." Harper said.

"Are you going to charge Kendrick?" Henderson asked.

"His presence there was an unfortunate complication but he wasn't to blame in my opinion," Harper said. He looked at Emma Oakes.

"Nor in mine, sir." Oakes said.

"Well, you'd better release him, then."

"Yes sir," Harper said.

FIFTY-SEVEN

Thursday 22nd August 2019

Damon was getting bored. He got bored easily and was in need of some stimulation. The house, Auchenblae, was quiet – too quiet – and the Red Lion was too far away to call in for a quick pint. There was nothing that interested him on the TV and Frazer's computer was frustratingly slow. On top of that, his phone needed charging.

It was an old man's house and he wanted more. Much more. Still, on the bright side, it was comfortable for the time being and at least it would enable him to get out of his grotty flat. He'd found a few antiques that might fetch a good price.

"Thanks Wally!" Damon raised a glass of Jack Daniels to his dead uncle and all that he could steal from him.

He would fetch his laptop in the morning, along with the rest of his stuff. He would move in to Auchenblae and make it his home. Maybe his old mate Jason would help him with the identity theft side of things – he was good at that sort of thing. He would have to keep up the mortgage payments for his plan to work but it would be worth it. Maybe he could hide behind the pretence that he was house-sitting for his uncle while he was away on a world cruise or something. That could work. It would be months before anyone questioned it.

He looked at the breaking news on his phone and scoffed at the photographs and the writeup on Daniel Kendrick. What an idiot, Damon thought. Still, he'd admired Jaxon Sloan. He imagined what it must have felt like to shoot your misses and her lover in cold blood and at such close range. That must have been dead cool, Damon thought. Yes, he admired that. Wished he could have done that himself. Maybe it would be fun to shoot Daniel Kendrick. He'd been toying with which method to use to take his life – and there was plenty of choice.

He squeezed an imaginary trigger, acting out the murder.

He turned his attention back to the newspaper and the piece about the serial killer that was on the loose around Riverbeke. He was certainly giving the police the slip. Good for him. He'd always admired murderers – been fascinated with them since he was a kid. He'd especially admired Peter Sutcliffe; the Yorkshire Ripper, who had raped and killed at least thirteen women; Fred and Rosemary West who raped and murdered at least twelve victims in their own home, including Fred's daughter. They got away with that for twenty years. Then there was Harold Shipman – Dr Death – who was thought to have been responsible for the deaths of more than two hundred and fifty of his patients. That was some record to beat. And, of course, Dennis Nilsen who killed fifteen men in his own London apartment, clogging up the drains with their putrid remains. That was a stupid mistake that got him caught, Damon thought. One he would learn from. Don't crap on your own doorstep.

Damon smiled, imagining how gratifying it must have been to take the lives of so many. These particular killers got caught eventually; probably because of their own stupid mistakes but Damon knew many others were still at large – just like their own local serial killer. There was no reason why – if he was careful – he couldn't get away with murder too. He had already, after all. Nobody even seemed to have missed the girl he killed – at least it never did make the news. It was as if she'd vanished in a puff of smoke.

Magic.

Pure genius.

Damon topped up his whiskey and settled back into Frazer's armchair. He began recalling killers like 'The Long Island Killer' who eluded capture since the mid-1990s and killed at least ten victims over the years; the 'Jeff Davis 8 Killers' – the bodies of eight women found in the swamps of Jefferson Davis Parish, Louisiana. The killer or killers have never been found to this day.

Damon thought of uncle Wally's body in the depths of the quarry. That would be another unsolved case if he was ever found and anyway, a post mortem would show he died of a heart attack. Natural causes. But there would always be the question, 'how did he get in the quarry?' He clearly hadn't been out walking in his tartan slippers and Damon had stripped the body of any identifying evidence. Damon smiled at the thought of the police scratching their heads over that one.

'The Daytona Beach Killer' had got away with killing several prostitutes, Damon recalled; vanishing as mysteriously as he'd appeared with no serious suspects ever identified by the police. Damon was starting to feel confident and assured. There were plenty of killers that had got away with murder and he could easily be one of them. 'The B1 Butcher' in Namibia, 'The Maryvale Shooter' in Arizona, 'The West Mesa Bone Collector' in Albuquerque, New Mexico, 'The Rainbow Maniac' in Brazil, 'The Johannesburg Killer', 'The Highway Serial Killers' in the US and Canada, thought to be long-haul truckers with more than five hundred cases unsolved. All still on the run. He briefly wondered what his own handle would be.

Yes, Damon thought, there were plenty of unsolved murders and killers free to kill again, whenever they felt the urge. He felt that urge. He wanted to be one of them. He wondered if he was late to start a career as a serial killer. Most begin their killing spree in their twenties and he had killed that girl when he was twenty-six, and the child at thirty-two but plenty began their serious work in their thirties and beyond. Shipman, Sutcliffe and Bundy, for instance, who began close to thirty. He was in good company. His thirty fourth birthday was looming. It was time he got into it, Damon thought. Wally's death had spurred him on. It was time to murder Daniel Kendrick.

Damon had little ambition in life but he desperately aspired to join the ranks of the serial killers he admired. He needed to feel that level of power and control over another human being for his own life to feel as if it were worth living. It had felt good to watch old uncle Wally die. It had been fun and entertaining. But it didn't come close to killing someone. The planning, the anticipation. To be the one to pull the trigger or stick a knife into someone's belly or throttle them with your bare hands. That's what he needed in his life.

He thought about the yearnings he'd had through his childhood. The necessity to kill. He had pacified his urges by killing and torturing animals – mice, rats, rabbits, foxes and even deer when he could catch them, or maim them with a carefully aimed shot. He had enjoyed shooting squirrels and dissecting their bodies and a few times he had even shot and killed his neighbour's cats and a dog once. But since he'd killed that girl, his urges had become different; he had moved on from killing animals.

He remembered how it felt to overpower his first murder victim, the sensation of her struggling desperately against his strong, powerful hands as they crushed her throat. The look of terror in her eyes. The feeling of control. He, and he alone – Damon Wixx – decided whether she lived or died.

As he sipped his uncle's whiskey, he knew he had to feed this insatiable appetite for harm and destruction. He desperately needed to possess and destroy others – body and soul. The emotional vacuum in his psyche demanded to be filled and the only way it could be satisfied was by sucking the life from others. Fay had called him an emotional vampire. Damon realised it went much deeper than that. Not only was he an emotional predator – he felt a growing and intoxicating need to take the life of another human being.

Fay Kendrick…

Had she returned home? He had been wanting to see her – to progress his plans. Maybe he should call her clinic and find out if she was back. He was due an appointment, after all.

Damon found the number on his Samsung Galaxy and hit 'call'.

There was a recorded message telling him all appointments had been cancelled until further notice.

Sounds like she's still missing, Damon thought.

His infatuation with Fay had been escalating for some months, fuelled, in part, by her emotional distance from him – the professional barrier she'd erected between them. That and the fact that she was married to another man – a man he was beginning to despise. He had found it frustrating yet alluring in equal measure and it had sparked his competitive drive. She presented him with an exciting challenge. He had targeted her – like a predator stalking his prey. She was on his mind more and more of late and he sensed he was becoming more obsessed with her. He knew it would be short-lived, as it had with other women. His obsession would dissipate as soon as he had what he wanted from her.

Idealize, devalue, abuse and discard. That was the process of the psychopathic bond he had with all his victims.

He would conquer her, control her, abuse her and when she no longer served a purpose for him, he would discard her. Kill her, if it pleased him.

Damon felt a sudden flash of anger. If Fay had disappeared – intentionally or otherwise – she had effectively escaped from him. She had dared to leave him. She had taken away his control; his power. It was time to claim it back.

Wixx stood, paced the room as his irritation simmered, then, abruptly, decided to drive to the Red Lion. He was becoming bored and restless with his own company.

FIFTY-EIGHT

Thursday 22nd August 2019

At Riverbeke General, an elderly woman walked into main reception carrying a note for Mr Daniel Kendrick. She had carefully placed it in a brown envelope, so it wouldn't get damaged and written his name on it with her own name and address. It seemed to contain important information.

She'd found it on the kitchen table at her farmhouse when she'd got home that afternoon. She didn't know who it was from or how they got in to her house to leave it there but it seemed urgent and she felt she had to act on it. A woman could be in danger.

She had called her son straight away to drive her into town to the hospital so she could hand it over to Mr Kendrick in person. The kind lady in reception had assured her that a porter would take it to the ward immediately.

True to her word, the porter took the note and hurried to the surgical ward. He handed it to the ward clerk, saying it was an important letter for Mr Kendrick.

The clerk took it to Daniel's office and placed it on his desk, certain he would find it. Then, having finished her last shift before her holiday to the Italian lakes, she grabbed her bag and went home.

A nurse called into Daniel's office moments later with some old patient's notes for Daniel to review. She placed them on his desk and went back to her theatre shift.

The urgent note that Sloan had left giving Fay's location sat on Daniel's desk unopened beneath a pile of paperwork…

FIFTY-NINE

Daniel had sobbed himself into a fitful sleep in his police cell. He had no idea how long he had been there when the custody sergeant opened the door to his cell.

"OK, Mr Kendrick. You're free to go." Sergeant Morris smiled at Daniel.

"Am I being charged?"

"No, no charge. There'll be no further action but DS Harper is asking that you let them get on with the investigation into your wife's disappearance. We don't want to see you in here again…"

"Thank you, officer." Daniel rubbed his face, careful to avoid the cut on his cheek, trying to shake the last of his drowsiness away. He followed the custody officer back to the room he'd been processed in, was given his belongings back, along with the bunch of keys the officer had retrieved from his car and was asked to sign his release form. He was told that his car had been taken by recovery operatives and was at Williams' Garage in Riverbeke. It was around three miles away but since it was gone 6 pm, he would have to wait until the morning to retrieve it. The garage would be closed for the day.

Daniel checked his iPhone. There were four missed calls from Shelly. He checked his voicemail. It was Shelly, desperate to know what had been going on. She'd been glued to the news.

Daniel was ushered out of the building and he shook the policeman's hand as he was let out of the gate. It just seemed appropriate to Daniel. Then he called Shelly. He owed her an explanation.

"Where are you?" Shelly asked.

"Outside the police station. I've just been released."

"Stay there. I'll come and get you. Give me ten minutes."

"I'll start walking into town."

Daniel wanted to get as far away from the station as he could. That was one experience he'd rather forget. He began walking toward the town centre, grateful for the fresh air. It was still warm and the evening sun was bright. He turned his face toward the light. It felt good to be free.

The second call he made was to Rosie, asking her to take care of Chester and Ella. He wasn't sure what time he would be home.

Daniel was just turning into the main shopping street when Shelly pulled up in her Audi. Daniel climbed into the passenger seat.

"Bloody hell Daniel – are you alright? It's been all over the news." Shelly looked him over. "You look like shit."

"Thanks!" Daniel managed a thin smile. "I'm OK. Just glad to get out of there."

"So, they haven't charged you?"

"Nope. No further action, they said."

"I guess that's something." Shelly twisted in her seat, fixing him with soft blue eyes. "What the hell were you thinking, Daniel? That was reckless. You could have got yourself killed."

Daniel shrugged. "I just want to find Fay. At least now I know Sloan hadn't abducted her or meant her any harm."

"Do you want to tell me about it?" Shelly asked gently.

"I know what I do want…" Daniel said.

"What?"

"A drink."

"Sounds good to me. How about the Red Lion – it's just down the road. You can tell me the whole story." Shelly pulled out and they drove in pensive silence to the pub.

When they got to the Red Lion, Daniel ordered a chardonnay for Shelly and a double whiskey for himself. They found a quiet table in the corner of the pub and Daniel told her the whole story about the dramatic incident with Sloan that morning. He was glad to retell it – to someone who wasn't judging him. For him to make sense of it all.

Shelly had listened patiently, seeming to understand his motives for confronting Sloan. After a few more drinks, Daniel had even confessed that DS Harper had considered him as a suspect in her disappearance because of the rows he and Fay had been having. He still wasn't sure he was off the hook with the detective – especially after the disaster with Sloan this morning.

"So how have things been between you and Fay?" Shelly asked.

Daniel tilted his head toward Shelly, trying to hear clearly above the background din in the pub.

"She did mention that you were having your ups and downs and she was actually aware of Melissa and her manipulative behaviour."

Daniel slugged another whiskey down; the fiery liquid warm and comforting, easing the slight residual ringing in his ears from the gunshot. "Yeah… we have been arguing a lot lately. We just seem to be on different wavelengths." Daniel stared across the room, not knowing how to explain it when he could barely understand what was going on himself. All he knew was that things hadn't been good between them for a while.

"You know, grief can affect people profoundly," Shelly said. "Especially when you've lost a child."

Daniel looked at her, taken aback by her insight. "Sophie," he said simply.

Shelly nodded. "I think you have both been dealing with her death differently and it seems, from what Fay has told me, that you've been in denial for a long time. You've been shutting her out. Shutting your grief out."

Daniel realised it was probably true. The way he'd avoided the subject with Fay, avoiding his old friends, preferring to hang out with the likes of Melissa and Oliver Davenport – shallow and self-centred as they were. They never asked how he or Fay were coping. They never cared and it was easier for him that way. He'd shut down his emotions so he didn't have to confront them.

Daniel looked at Shelly. "And how about Fay? How do you think she's coping?"

"I sometimes think she's stuck too." Shelly said reflectively.

"What do you mean?"

Shelly twirled the stem of her wine glass between her fingers. "You know there are several stages of grief. The five stages described by Elizabeth Kübler-Ross are the most widely known but there are others. It's not neat or linear. Grief is very personal and can be very complex. It doesn't follow any timelines or tick lists. Everyone copes with loss differently."

"So, what are the stages of grief?"

"Well, the five main ones are denial, anger, bargaining, depression and finally, acceptance. Not everyone experiences all five stages and not always in that order. As I said, everyone experiences grief differently."

"And you think people can get stuck in certain stages?"

"Yes. Some people stay in one stage for months or even years and others can jump around between different stages as they try to cope with their grief. It's not a straightforward progression from one stage to the next."

"Do you think Fay is stuck in one of the stages?" Daniel leaned forward, twisting his empty glass between his hands, subconsciously mirroring Shelly.

"I think she's still pretty angry. It's so difficult to process the sort of loss you've experienced. How many people have to come to terms with the murder of their six-month-old baby? There's no protocol for dealing with something like that."

"Yes, Fay does seem angry and bitter a lot of the time. Maybe I should have been there for her more; tried to understand instead of letting things escalate into an argument all the time. I've just been in my own selfish world."

"Daniel, you mustn't blame yourself. You've both been struggling to cope. Perhaps when Fay returns you could get some professional help? I think you need it."

Daniel nodded pensively. "We should have gone for help before." He looked at Shelly. "Would you take us on as clients? I know Fay trusts you – and so do I."

Shelly touched Daniel's arm. "Yes, of course. I'll do anything to help you both."

SIXTY

Daniel and Shelly sat in the corner of The Red Lion. It was filling up with regulars; mostly young people having a couple of drinks before moving on to the nightclubs in town. David Jones was sat in his usual seat, keeping a watchful eye on everyone. Lady, his ancient collie dog was lying under the table. David raised his pint glass to acknowledge Daniel and he returned the gesture.

Then Daniel glanced across at the bar to see a familiar face. A man in his thirties that had just come into the pub and was ordering a drink. He'd seen him at Fay's clinic the other day. It was that nasty piece of work, Damon Wixx, with the jailbird haircut and the bad attitude.

"Isn't that one of Fay's patients?" Daniel asked Shelly, tilting his head in the direction of the bar.

Shelly turned surreptitiously to get a good look. "Yes, I think it is. What's his name now…"

"Wixx. Damon Wixx?"

"Yes, that's it. Not exactly one of Fay's favourite patients."

"You know him?" Daniel asked.

"Not really but he has a reputation for being aggressive and remorseless. A psychopath, I believe. Fay has been struggling with him for a while. A no-hoper by the sound of it."

"He looks it," Daniel said, looking into his empty glass. "Do you know where he lives?"

"No idea, Daniel. I guess somewhere in Riverbeke. He's not someone I've come across myself. I just hear bits and pieces about him from Fay. All I know is that he's bad news."

Shelly's mobile rang. It was her husband, Doug, a professor of psychiatry.

"Hi love," she said, "yes, Daniel's OK now. I'll be home soon." She turned to Daniel. "Better go. Can I drop you home?"

"No, you go on. I'll just have one more and get a cab. Could do with some time to wind down after the day I've had." He gave her a wry smile.

"Well, let me know how things go. If I can do anything to help – just say."

Shelly left and Daniel ordered another pint of craft beer. He eyed Damon Wixx, sprawling over the far end of the bar, chatting up the barmaid. He looked a right thug, Daniel thought. Wouldn't like to meet him in a dark alleyway.

Daniel took his pint and went back to his corner table. He was trying to think through the things Shelly had been telling him about grief and how it might have affected his relationship with Fay but his attention was constantly being drawn to Wixx. He watched the way he was letching at the young women in the pub and there was a minor skirmish with a man that had been trying to get served before him.

Despite his apparent innocence – he had turned up twice for appointments at the clinic after Fay had gone missing – Daniel couldn't shake off a nagging doubt.

Could Wixx have had something to do with Fay's disappearance?

SIXTY-ONE

It was late and the Red Lion was quietening down after many of the youngsters had moved on. Daniel had been sat nursing a pint of beer for over an hour. He'd ordered a hot steak and onion pie and some packets of crisps and nuts when his appetite had finally returned. He hadn't eaten since early that morning.

He was quietly watching Damon Wixx and popping dry roasted peanuts absently into his mouth. He was sat at a corner table, which was partially obscured by a low decorative screen woven with trailing plants. Wixx was getting drunk and increasingly loud and aggressive. He was a slob and a bully, thought Daniel. No wonder Fay was having trouble with him. He wished there had been some notes on him in Fay's filing cabinet but he'd taken all the notes he could find and there was nothing on Wixx. Shelly obviously didn't have any dealings with him but Daniel was beginning to think he might have a little word with him.

Daniel felt a tap on his shoulder and turned to see David Jones and his pooch, Lady. He had crisp crumbs in his long, wiry beard but Daniel ignored it.

"Hello Mr Jones. Had a nice evening?"

"Fine, thank you doctor. I'm just getting off back to the home. Just saying goodnight. Nice to see you, by the way – you're not normally in here." He was wearing his thick donkey jacket despite the warm evening.

"Thought I'd have a change of scenery," Daniel lied.

"Yes, of course. Why not. Goodnight," David said. He left with a wave of his walking stick.

"Night Mr Jones."

Daniel watched as David Jones limped out of the pub. His old dog trotting dutifully behind him.

He turned his attention back to Damon Wixx. Wixx was leaning on the end of the bar but he saw him turn and watch the old man as he left the pub. Wixx finished up his pint in one gulp, went to the men's toilet and when he came out, he glanced at Daniel and left the pub. Daniel waited thirty seconds and followed him, placing his empty glass on the bar on his way out.

Once outside, Daniel looked around and could see Damon staggering up ahead. He was heading toward the tow path, which ran alongside the canal. If he could follow him home and get an address for him, he could plan his next move – if only to alert DS Harper of his concerns, if he would listen. Wixx might even lead him to Fay. Spirits buoyed, he stayed well back in the shadows but kept Damon firmly in his sights.

He followed Wixx for half a mile along the side of the canal. It was a quiet, empty stretch, although he knew there were a few residential narrowboats about a mile ahead on the other bank. It was dark; the waxing moon was obscured by clouds. There were only a few street lights along this stretch, since several had been vandalised and not replaced. In a dark patch ahead, he heard a shout. It sounded like an old man – it was David Jones. There was a bark, then another. Daniel ran ahead and stopped dead in his tracks as he saw Wixx prodding David forcefully with his index finger; his face inches from the old man's. He was taunting him and poking his chest. Wixx's pasty face a picture of loathing and hatred. He kept prodding, shouting obscenities at the old man, who was backtracking away from him. Lady barked again and Wixx grabbed David's walking stick and hit her across the flank with it. Lady yelped then continued barking and growling, trying to snap at Wixx's ankles. She got another swipe with the stick and backed off a little.

Wixx continued to prod and push David, propelling him backward, step by faltering step toward the edge of the canal. Lady was barking and turning in circles, beside herself with agitation. Faithfully trying to save her master.

Daniel ran forward to help David. He shouted at Wixx to leave him alone but the thug ignored the warning. He shouted again but there was still no response.

Wixx sustained his attack on David, pushing and prodding him with his finger, hissing obscenities at the old man. He was propelling his victim backwards and perilously close to the water's edge.

Daniel was sprinting now. He called out again for Wixx to stop but he ignored him. Lady took a bite at Wixx's shin but he kicked her away. She yelped in pain but bravely came back to try again.

Then David Jones lost his footing at the side of the canal, stumbled and fell backwards into the black water. David called out – a terrified shriek. There was a loud splash.

Then silence.

Daniel arrived on the scene, shouted at Wixx but he laughed and ran off into the darkness of the night. Daniel looked into the canal and saw the splashing water in the shadows. The eighty-nine-year-old David struggling to keep his head above water, the weight of his wet jacket dragging him down.

Without a moment's hesitation, Daniel dived into the icy black water of the canal. He swam out to the centre, where David was flailing his arms wildly and spluttering.

He grabbed the back of the old man's jacket. "It's OK, I've got you. Just relax. Breathe."

Daniel flipped David over so he was floating on his back, wrapped his right arm around his neck, with the crook of his elbow under his chin to support his head above the water. Then, swimming gawkily on his side, he dragged him back to the bank of the canal.

The old collie was waiting for them, panting now and wining. Daniel looked for a way out of the water. The sides of the canal were not high but it would be difficult to hoist the old man from the water. He propelled them both a short way along the bank and found a metal mooring ring. He grabbed it with his free hand and told David to reach up for it. The old man tried several times, but he couldn't reach and was becoming breathless. Then Daniel repositioned his arm around the man's thick waist and heaved him up toward the ring. After two attempts, David managed to grab the ring with both hands.

"Hold on tight. I'm going to push you out onto the path."

Holding on to the mooring ring, Daniel grabbed David around the hips with his right arm and with an almighty effort, pushed him upward. He took his full weight as David left the water but managed to get his body onto the bank – one of his legs was still dangling in the water.

"Stay put, Mr Jones. I'll get out and pull you up." Daniel said breathlessly.

Daniel heaved himself up out of the water, stood and helped David Jones out of the canal and onto the tow path.

David lay, panting, for several minutes while he recovered from the effort, Lady was at her master's side, tail wagging and licking his hand. Daniel checked the old man for injuries. Remarkably, he seemed unhurt.

"Thank you, lad," David said, relieved the ordeal was over.

"Are you alright?" Daniel asked. "I'll call an ambulance."

"No, please don't. I'm fine, thanks to you."

They both sat on the tow path while David recovered from the shock of his unexpected dip.

"So, what was all that about, Mr Jones?" Daniel asked.

"No idea, but he's a bad 'un. He'd kill anyone that got in his way."

Daniel retrieved David Jones' walking stick and helped him to his feet in the darkness of the tow path. They were both sopping wet. David squeezed the water from his long beard and took his jacket off since it was completely drenched with water. It was surprisingly heavy. Daniel wrung out the thick material as best he could and carried it for him as they slowly made their way to Willow Lodge, the residential home where David lived, which was a few streets away toward the town. Lady was trotting at her master's side. David had declined Daniel's offer to call an ambulance or even a taxi. He was characteristically stoic – even in the face of yobbish torments from Damon Wixx.

"Why were you down here on your own?" Daniel asked.

"I just enjoy a stroll along the canal before going back to that awful home. I like to look at the moon and think of Blodwen. We used to come here walking the dogs," David said, his feet slopping in wet shoes.

The canal ran through the edge of town and was an area of tranquil beauty that belied its original purpose as an industrial corridor for coal and iron. It was now a haven for wildlife and Daniel could see the attraction.

"You must be lonely without your wife," Daniel said. His heart going out to him.

"I don't like it at the home, doctor. I miss Blodwen." He sighed and looked down at his old collie. "She's all I have left now."

"Oh dear. I'm sorry. When did Blodwen die?"

"A couple of years ago. I haven't even been able to get a headstone for her." David shook his head and blinked hard, as if he was trying to gain control of his emotions.

"It's hard when you lose someone you love." Daniel was well aware of the sorrow and sense of loss.

David nodded pensively. "Doesn't make it any easier with the likes of that ruffian around."

They walked slowly along the tow path, retracing their earlier route. Despite the warm summer evening, they were cold and drenched from their unexpected dip in the canal.

"Do you know anything about him? That Wixx character," Daniel asked.

David coughed and stroked his beard as they walked, David hobbling and leaning on his stick. "I know he's a bully and a hooligan – doesn't care about anyone or anything. No morals that one. I've seen him pick a fight in that pub over nothing. Nothing at all. He should be in jail. In fact, I think he did do a spell behind bars. They should've thrown away the key." David was shaking his head in disgust at the very thought of the man.

"Do you know where he lives?" Daniel asked.

"Somewhere on that council estate. The big tower block – I'm not sure which one – maybe Bridgeman Tower. Never did a day's work in his life that one – wouldn't last five minutes in a proper job."

Daniel tuned out as David continued his rampage about the jobless, feckless youth in the area.

Bridgeman Tower. It was a start.

SIXTY-TWO

42 days ago

The killer moved through the building with the stealth of a leopard stalking its prey. Walked unseen; concealed by the shadows of the night. Entered the locked hospital ward with ease and sought out the carefully chosen victim, Kenneth Shaw. The door to Shaw's small room closed silently and he barely stirred from his slumber as the killer took a syringe, with gloved hands, that had been prepared for the purpose, and injected a massive overdose of insulin into the intravenous infusion that had served to hydrate him as he recovered from a serious bout of gastroenteritis. The killer watched as the clear liquid surged into Shaw's veins and waited broodingly while his heart pumped the drug around his body, slowly but efficiently taking his life from him. Soon he would succumb to hypoglycaemic convulsions, coma and death. The killer stayed to witness Shaw rouse from sleep and struggle briefly, his eyes bulging with terror as a deeply seated primal instinct told him that he was about to die.

He looked pleadingly into the eyes of the killer but saw no mercy, no compassion, just hatred, loathing and a steely determination to see him dead. He recognised that same impulse to destroy life in himself. The killer knew of the mindless pleasure Kenneth Shaw had enjoyed as he'd hunted his quarry; had glimpsed the darkness in his soul and the boundless aggression from which his primitive urge to kill had arisen. Shaw had taken innocent lives, slaughtered decent people. Now his own life would be extinguished.

Shaw knew his killer but never suspected they were capable of this. Violence, he reasoned, as he waited for death to take him, is part of our human nature; anyone could become a killer in the heat of passion. A wife murders her husband in a fit of jealously; a man kills his employer when he is fired unjustly. But this – a chillingly calculated murder is quite another thing. Shaw knew that justice for his death would never come, just as justice for his own murder victims had not been done. He felt the terrifying fear of knowing he was dying, then the peace of acceptance as his inevitable demise finally beckoned.

The killer watched as Shaw's lifeforce ebbed away; as his lifeless eyes stared unseeing into the gloom. The killer, satisfied with their work, staged the scene to look like a suicide, then crept away unnoticed.

The killer's mission had been accomplished.

SIXTY-THREE

Thursday 22nd August 2019

Daniel was walking David Jones back to the Willow Lodge residential home. "I'll call the police and they can sort out Damon Wixx. He should be arrested for attacking you like that," Daniel said, reaching for his iPhone.

David stopped in his tracks and turned to face the doctor. "No, please don't. I just want to forget about it now." There was a determination in his eyes that warned Daniel not to go against his wishes.

"But he can't be allowed to get away with it."

David grabbed Daniels forearm as if to reinforce his message. "No. Please, just leave it alone. I've had dealings with him before and he'll just make my life a misery. I want to be able to sit in the pub and have a quiet drink – believe me – it's better for me to just let it go."

"But he pushed you in the canal," Daniel said as graciously as he could.

David fixed Daniel with a glare. He meant what he said. "No. Please doctor; leave it alone."

"Alright. If that's what you want. I won't call them." Daniel shrugged. David obviously had his reasons and it was his prerogative.

Just as they arrived at the main entrance, Daniel reached for his wallet and took out a wad of soggy £20 notes. He didn't count them but he guessed there was around £180. He folded the cash and handed it to David.

"Put it toward a headstone for Blodwen," he said, smiling at the old man.

"Oh, doctor, you can't do that." David tried to resist taking the money but Daniel was insistent.

"Please – I want you to have it." He pushed the money into David's hand.

David returned the smile but was choking back tears, his voice cracking with emotion. "Thank you. That means a lot to me."

"It's a pleasure. Now let's get you in and warmed up."

Daniel explained what had happened and handed him over to the care of the staff who made a huge fuss of him and Lady. David was smothering in big busts, bingo wings and sloppy lipstick kisses but he was home safely; if shaken up by the experience with Wixx at the canal.

Daniel called a taxi – amazingly, his iPhone had survived a dunking in the icy water. He was still wet through and the driver had found a plastic bag for him to sit on for the ten-minute drive back to Daniel's house.

Maisie had been meowing plaintively to be fed and he topped up her biscuits and gave her a double helping of fish-flavoured Felix before checking on the dogs. Rosie had left him a note saying that she'd returned and fed them at 9 pm.

Daniel stripped off his wet clothes and took a shower. All he wanted was to get back out there – track down Damon Wixx and do something to find Fay but he was exhausted and stuck with no car until the morning. His mind had been swimming with thoughts about Fay and whether Damon Wixx could be responsible for her disappearance. After his behaviour that evening, he wouldn't put anything past Wixx. It was a shame that David had resisted police involvement. It would have been a chance for them to question him about Fay as well.

Daniel decided to get a few hours' sleep and go looking for Wixx in daylight.

SIXTY-FOUR

Friday 23rd August 2019

It was 8 am. Daniel ate a quick breakfast of a banana chopped over granola and milk, washed down with a mug of tea. Maisie had brought a mouse in from the garden. It was still alive and Daniel managed to catch it and return it safely to the wild. Chester and Ella had a run in the garden, their morning feed and a dental chew each before Rosie came to fetch them.

He also called Fay's mother, Emily, for a brief chat on the phone. She was out of her mind with worry but Daniel did his best to reassure her and was grateful the incident with Sloan seemed to have escaped her attention. He couldn't imagine how he would begin to explain that.

His mission for the morning was to retrieve his car from Williams' Garage in town, then track down Damon Wixx and have a word with him about Fay's disappearance. He would also warn him to stay away from David Jones. He'd called a cab and was pacing back and forth to the living room window to check if it had arrived.

Daniel was determined to find Wixx, despite the warning from DS Harper to leave it to the police to investigate. He felt as if he would go crazy just waiting – he simply had to be proactive and take some sort of action. He heard a car horn outside – the taxi had arrived. He gulped down the rest of his tea, put Chester and Ella in the Dog House, picking up Ella's soggy bear and giving it to her. He checked once again that the doors were locked and headed for the garage in town.

Once Daniel had signed the release forms and got his car back, he set off to the north end of town and the tower blocks.

Daniel drove through the warren-like estate toward the central shopping precinct that served all four blocks of flats. He parked and walked into the main pedestrianized zone, passing a group of school children working on a wildlife pond they had created in a grassy area. He could hear their animated conversations and the glee at finding frogs.

While the tower blocks were over five decades old, the shops were surprisingly contemporary with a row of glass-fronted commercial buildings and a landscaped area with raised flower beds and new wooden benches. A recent addition to the community and a definite improvement.

A group of teenagers in ripped jeans and hoodies were gathered around one of the benches, laughing at a You Tube video on somebody's phone.

Daniel found a fingerpost sign pointing to the four tower blocks. Bridgeman Tower was to the far right. He would start there since David Jones seemed to think that was where Wixx lived.

Daniel hurried through the precinct, passing an elderly couple walking a Yorkshire terrier. They smiled and commented on the welcome sunshine.

He reached Bridgeman Tower, with its eight stories of flats, accessed by long communal landings. The tower blocks were grey and drab as they stood overbearingly at the edge of the modern precinct. They badly needed a facelift.

Daniel looked up at the ageing concrete tower blocks. Where the hell to start was the question. Should he do a methodical sweep of the flats or just wander around randomly, knock on a few doors and speak to the residents? He decided to take a walk along the landing of the second floor. He could see a huddle of older people chatting – perhaps they could point him in the right direction.

He climbed the concrete stairs, passing a sullen-looking hooded teenager, who, engrossed in his iPhone, blanked him completely. Then he was on the landing passing a long line of flats. A small child was riding a three-wheeled trike up and down the landing. The group Daniel had seen were still chatting. As he approached them, they stopped talking and turned to look at him. One of the men smiled warily.

"Alright mate?" He asked.

"Thanks, yes. I was wondering if any of you know Damon Wixx? Do you know which flat he lives in?"

They looked at one another, shaking their heads. One of them shrugged, looked at Daniel and said, "no idea, sorry."

"Sorry mate," another said.

They resumed their chat as Daniel passed them, thanking them for their help. He decided to try around the other side of the block, still on the second floor.

He passed a woman watering the flowers in her window box.

"Excuse me, do you know a man called Damon Wixx?" he asked.

She thought for a moment, then replied. "No, sorry." She smiled as Daniel thanked her.

Daniel wandered further along the landing, passing a couple of mobile phone 'zombies' and asked several others if they knew Wixx but nobody seemed to have heard of him. He decided to try the next landing then work methodically up the stories to the eighth floor. Surely someone knew Wixx. He glanced across at the three other towers. It would be a monumental task to comb through all of them. Maybe there was an easier way to track him down? He decided to stick with it for now.

Daniel took the concrete stairs to the third-floor landing. There he turned left. The landing looked deserted. He passed a flat around halfway along and heard a dog yapping. A woman was shouting to it to 'shut up'. At least someone was at home. Daniel knocked the door.

Through frosted glass, the wavy outline of a rather rotund woman came to answer the door, still shouting at the dog. She opened the door, a shapeless, sleeveless dress revealing mottled flabby arms, the right tattooed with serpents, the left, skull and crossbones. She looked at Daniel, wary and scowling, puffing on a vape pen.

"Sorry to bother you," Daniel said as a filthy white bichon fris bounded onto the landing, still yapping.

"Shut it, Gismo," the woman bellowed, blowing out a cloud of vapour. "What do you want?" She turned her attention to Daniel.

"Yes, sorry, I was wondering if you knew a Damon Wixx. Does he live around here?" Daniel had to raise his voice to be heard as Gismo continued to yap and leap up and down.

The woman picked the dog up and he licked her face. "You from the social?" She asked.

"No, I just need to have a chat with Damon." Daniel tried to sound amicable.

"The police?"

"No, not the police either." Daniel smiled at the woman.

She looked him up and down. Then pointed further along the landing with a chubby, gold-encased finger. "Next door. The flat with the red paint and broken glass door. Might be away though – haven't seen him for days."

Daniel was taken aback but relieved to have found Wixx's address so quickly. "Thanks, that's great." Daniel gave the woman another friendly smile as she shut the door; her wavy image retreating into the flat.

He could hear more yapping and shouting coming from

inside as he moved along the landing to the next flat. As the woman had said, the door was red, the paint peeling, and there was a strip of duct tape holding the glass pane together. He tried to peer in through the frosted glass but could see no movement. He suddenly felt nervous at confronting Wixx. Maybe he should have just told DS Harper about his suspicions. But Daniel was there, right outside Wixx's front door.

He hesitated, then knocked on the glass.

He knocked several times but there was no answer and no sound or movement from inside the flat. Perhaps he had gone away, as the woman next door had said, but he was very much at large last evening, in the Red Lion and later when he callously shoved David Jones into the canal.

Daniel took a note of the number of the flat and decided to try again later. He slowly made his way back through the precinct to his car. Would Wixx give him any information, he wondered? He was never going to admit that he'd abducted Fay. Daniel realised he'd been naïve. He wasn't going to get anywhere speaking to Wixx. He'd have to find another way.

Time was against him. Fay had been missing for four days and every hour was precious. There was no time for faffing about. What could he do? Call DS Harper and get them to search Wixx's flat? They would need a warrant for that and what grounds did they have? It would take too long and Daniel needed answers now. Jaxon Sloan had said Fay needed help. He had to find her and quickly.

SIXTY-FIVE

Friday 23rd August 2019

Damon had driven back to Auchenblae. He felt his luck was turning. He'd been surprised to find Daniel Kendrick in the Red Lion with Fay's colleague, Shelly Winters. He knew her by sight from his time in prison. He guessed that Daniel had been released with no further charges after the incident with Sloan.

He'd been looking for an opportunity to demonstrate to Daniel that he was in charge. That he had the power. And there – right there – was the perfect opportunity. It had come earlier than he could have hoped for. David Jones was obviously well acquainted with Daniel and he hated the old man. It was a chance to have a go at Jones.

It had been easy. Just a glance in Daniel's direction followed by a move that indicated he was following David was all it took to set the wheels in motion. Once he knew Daniel Kendrick was following him, it hadn't taken much to intimidate the old man and show the doctor who was in charge. He'd sensed his wariness of him when they met in the reception of Fay's clinic the other day. Just a simple show of strength and power was all it needed to make the doctor realise he meant business.

He tried to sleep but Wixx had brooded on Fay's disappearance for hours, fuelling his rage. He had bought more whiskey with the cash from Frazer's wallet, smoked joints, ate Frazer's food and drank until the early hours, while sat in Frazer's armchair. Thoughts were rattling around his brain like steel balls in a pinball machine.

One thing he knew – and it was really getting to him now – was that he had to see Fay. He had plans to carry out and his urges were becoming undeniable. She couldn't be allowed to get away from him.

He thought of her husband and family – frantic to find her. The police starting a search. A movie he'd seen recently.

Then he had a brainwave…

He needed money. Daniel Kendrick wanted his wife back. He could demand a ransom for her safe return. Problem solved. Daniel was loaded and once he had his cash, he could dispose of him. No sense in letting all that money go to waste. It would be enough to sustain his new life as a serial killer. The career he'd always wanted and he'd treat himself to all the things he'd dreamed of – a luxury house, cars, drugs, women. He deserved it.

Uncle Wally's house was fine for now but he knew he would be found out eventually and be forced to move on. But this was a plan that could work. He would demand a million pounds in cash. He could ask for more but he estimated Kendrick would be able to get his hand on a million quickly and without drawing too much attention. And no police. Absolutely no police. That would be part of the ransom demand. He knew he could pull it off. Daniel Kendrick was an easy target and he was desperate to get his wife back. It was a simple transaction – a million pounds for your wife.

There was one small hitch – he didn't have Fay.

SIXTY-SIX

Friday 23rd August 2019

Daniel didn't get into his car – instead he turned around and retraced his steps back to Wixx's flat. He climbed the stairs to the second-floor landing. There was nobody around. The dog next door to Wixx's flat was still yapping and the woman shouting to him to 'shut up'. It seemed incessant. Daniel stood outside Wixx's front door. There was still no movement inside. He checked the landing. It was all clear.

With his gut trembling with nerves, Daniel pulled the strip of duct tape off the broken window pane of the door and pocketed it. He looked around again. Still clear. Then, he pulled his shirt sleeve over his hand and pushed the broken pane. A large shard of glass broke off in his hand and came away from the frame. He froze, hoping he hadn't been heard but the racket from next door continued unabated, now enhanced by the sound of a raucous TV gameshow.

Daniel passed the shard to his other hand and reached in through the gap in the broken glass. He felt for the door latch, depressed it and the door clicked open easily. He looked around again. All clear. He let himself into Wixx's flat and closed the door behind him, replacing the broken shard of glass.

Daniel listened out for movement inside the flat but it seemed empty. He tiptoed from the narrow passage into Wixx's living room. It stank of stale food and beer with an overriding reek of cannabis. The room was a mess, with empty beer cans lined up along the window sill like targets in a rifle range; a low coffee table held an ashtray overflowing with the dog ends of splifs. There was a pile of porn magazines and papers strewn over the floor. Daniel flinched and turned away. There was no way he was touching that lot.

He wandered into the tiny kitchen. It was cluttered and greasy, with plates piled into the sink. They were covered in revolting dried-on food that looked days old. The smell made him gag.

Daniel went into the bedroom. It was a dismal room, sparsely furnished with a small wardrobe, queen-sized bed with stained grey sheets and a tatty duvet thrown over it. There was a makeshift bedside table that held another overflowing ashtray.

As Daniel turned to leave, he noticed a piece of paper sticking out from under the unmade bed. He bent to get a close look and froze when he saw it was a photograph of Fay. Daniel recognised it as one of the photographs that had been published in a magazine a few years ago when she had given an interview about psychiatric patients in the prison system and how not enough was being done to rehabilitate serious offenders.

What the hell was it doing in Wixx's flat?

It was just one flimsy piece of evidence but he was convinced that Wixx was responsible for Fay's disappearance.

But where was she? Where was he? He obviously hadn't been here for some days by the look of the place and from what his neighbour had said.

Daniel searched the other bedroom and the bathroom for signs that Fay had been there but there were none. Just her photograph, which he had pushed into his pocket. DS Harper would be interested to see that. He still felt angry and invaded.

What the hell was Damon Wixx doing with a photograph of his wife in his bedroom.

Daniel wandered out into the kitchen and saw a calendar on the wall. It had the two appointments with Fay scribbled in but nothing since. There were other appointments for Fay in July and back in June but that was it apart from a birthday for someone called Jade and a few scrawls that Daniel couldn't decipher. He took photographs of the relevant entries, deciding it would be best to leave the calendar on the wall.

Daniel needed to speak to DS Harper and explain his suspicions. Surely, they would want to question Wixx. He opened the front door and peered out. The landing was clear and the shouting and yapping coming from next door had finally abated. Either that or it had been drowned out by the noise from the TV. He let himself out and quietly closed the door behind him, replacing the duct tape over the broken glass.

Daniel retraced his steps through the precinct and back to his car. A couple of lanky lads dressed in grey tracksuits and hoodies were peering in through the rear windows of his BMW but sloped off as he approached. Daniel slid into the driver's seat, pulled his iPhone from his pocket and looked up DS Harpers number. He was about to tap 'call' but hesitated. He'd just been arrested; effectively for interfering in the police investigation. How would it go down if he was to admit he'd just broken into a suspect's home and taken away evidence? He knew the detective's patience was wearing thin.

Daniel pocketed his phone. Perhaps he should find out more before he went to Harper. Something more useful to add to the investigation. He started the engine and drove away from the estate. Maybe Shelly would have found out more on Wixx. It was worth a try.

He pulled over at a layby and called Shelly's number. It was about to go to voicemail when she answered.

"Shelly, it's Daniel. Have you got time for a chat?

"Sure. I'm with a patient at the moment at the hospital but I could meet you in the concourse for coffee in thirty minutes."

"Perfect. See you there."

Daniel ended the call and drove to the psychiatric wing of the hospital on the edge of town. He was tempted to call up to his own surgical ward and check on things; maybe pick up his mail and chat with Matt, his registrar but decided against it. He was supposed to be on leave and there was the pending investigation into Malcolm Phelps' death. Colin Mathias wouldn't thank him for showing up now.

He found a parking place easily and walked into the busy concourse of the hospital. A bright, spacious area, it was lined with cafes and shops – a newsagent, a pharmacy and a small gift shop. There were large terracotta pots displaying exotic ferns interwoven with tables and chairs for patients, visitors and hospital staff. Daniel scanned the room but didn't see Shelly. He found a table and sat down to wait for her.

Shelly appeared within five minutes holding two coffees.

"Hello Daniel. I guessed you'd be okay with a latte?" She handed him one of the cardboard cups.

"Thanks, Shelly." Daniel took the coffee and stood briefly to greet her with a light kiss on the cheek. It seemed too formal now to shake hands.

They sat and Shelly shot him a mischievous look. "So, what have you been up to now? Any news on Fay."

"You're so perceptive," Daniel said, realising that she could sense he had a confession to make. He had nothing to lose by telling her – she already knew about his arrest the day before for his intrusion into the Sloan case.

"I'm afraid I've just broken into Damon Wixx's flat."

Shelly rolled her eyes. "Bloody hell, Daniel. Whatever possessed you to do that?"

Daniel explained about Wixx's attack on David Jones and his suspicion that Wixx could be responsible for Fay's disappearance. He reached into his pocket for the photograph of Fay he'd found in the bedroom of the flat.

He showed it to Shelly. "So why the hell would he have a photograph of my wife in his bedroom if he's not involved somehow?"

Shelly looked at the photograph and then at Daniel. "I don't know but I'm pretty sure he had a crush on her," she hesitated, "…maybe even something more sinister."

"What do you mean? Do you know something?"

Shelly sipped her coffee. "Well, after our conversation yesterday, I did some digging around on Damon Wixx. He is most certainly a psychopath and although he's been in therapy with Fay, there is likely nothing she can do to help him or treat him. There is no cure for psychopathy and especially not for him."

"Yes, Meredith, Fay's receptionist said he was a no-hoper. Do you think he's dangerous? I mean really dangerous?"

Shelly leaned forward, contemplated her coffee cup for a moment, then looked at Daniel. If you want my honest opinion – yes, I do think he could be a very dangerous individual. He's been in prison for GBH and has shown no signs of remorse for what he did. And from what Fay has told me in confidence, she believes he is capable of anything and has probably already killed someone in the past from cryptic things he has told her."

"Shit." Daniel took a mouthful of coffee, swallowing it down hard. "Do you think he would harm her if he has taken her?"

"Possibly, yes. He's been assessed using the Hervey Cleckley's list of psychopathy symptoms and he shows considerable callousness, shallowness of emotion and the incapacity to love. He won't show the world that he's a heartless predator though. Psychopaths hide behind a mask of sanity and Damon Wixx comes across as charming, intelligent, romantic and kind. He lures his victims in with this believable persona."

"He was pretty heartless when he attacked Mr Jones last night," Daniel said.

"Yes, he let his mask slip and it may well have been for your benefit."

"What do you mean?"

"He could have been showing you what he was capable of. It's a show of power and control – the very thing he craves."

"If that's true, it makes me even more certain he has Fay." Daniel combed his fingers through his hair. "What else do you know about him?"

"I don't know Damon personally but from what Fay has said and from what I know about psychopaths generally, he's likely to be a pretty nasty character. He will be antisocial, impulsive and completely self-centred. In other words, incapable of forming meaningful relationships. It's a general poverty of deep or lasting emotions. He likely has a grossly inflated view of his own self-worth. He will be arrogant and believe he's superior to the rest of us."

Daniel stroked the photograph of Fay that lay on the table between them. "If he has her, what do you think he plans to do with Fay?"

"If he has her – and we don't know that he does – he is likely to be looking for something to relieve his boredom with life. For something challenging and stimulating. He'll be playing games with her, Daniel. Callous, ruthless games for his own entertainment."

"Shit. He's going to hurt her, isn't he?" Daniel touched the cut on his cheek. It was beginning to throb again.

Shelly shook her head. "Maybe not if he is obsessed with her at this stage."

"Obsessed? You mean he's stalking her?"

"Yes, quite possibly. Psychopaths like to lure women in with their superficial charm, with the aim of possessing them and isolating them from their family and friends. They're emotional vampires, Daniel. Predators feeding on the real, deep emotions of others."

"My God, Shelly. Sounds like she could be in serious danger." Daniel was nervously shredding a paper napkin he'd found on the table.

"Yes, she could. But don't forget, Fay knows how to handle him. She's known him for several years and has had a lot of experience with psychopaths. She will know how to keep him calm and how to communicate with him. Damon Wixx, like every other psychopath needs love. They regard the emotional lives of people with contempt but he can't tolerate loneliness. Just as we can't survive without food and water, he can't survive without his victims to fill the void – to try to alleviate the emotional poverty he's feeling."

"God, Shelly. This is awful."

"There are stages to the bond a psychopath has with his victim. They idealise, devalue – often abuse – and finally discard them when they become bored. If he stays in the first stages, Fay will be alright. We have to find her before he does – before he starts to abuse her or physically harm her."

"Where the hell could he have taken her?"

"I don't know, Daniel. I know nothing about his personal details; family, his associations with others – only what Fay has told me. It would be too risky for him to take her to the flat. I don't think you'll find her there."

"I need to find him first and get Fay back." Daniel drained his coffee, ready to go in search for Fay.

"No, Daniel, you need to tell the police and let them do their job. They know what they're doing."

"I'm just helping." Daniel gave Shelly a watery smile.

"I know but call them, please. He's dangerous."

"I'll let you know if I find out anything." Daniel kissed Shelly's cheek again and left her to finish her coffee.

SIXTY-SEVEN

Friday 23rd August 2019

Daniel sat in his car and called the number DS Harper had given him. He needed to know what a dangerous individual Wixx was and that he was capable of anything – maybe even murder.

"Harper," the detective sounded harassed and overworked once again.

"Detective, it's Daniel Kendrick. I just wanted to let you know that I believe one of my wife's patients, Damon Wixx, may be responsible for her disappearance. He was one of the last patients to see her." He hesitated to admit he'd been in Damon's flat.

"What makes you say that, Dr Kendrick." Harper sounded riled.

Daniel hesitated but reasoned he had nothing to lose by telling Harper about the photograph. It would be worth the fallout if it helped rescue Fay. "I found a photograph of my wife in his flat… in his bedroom." Daniel waited while there was a delay the other end.

"Are you telling me you spoke to Mr Wixx or that you broke into his flat?"

Daniel cringed but he had to own up to what he'd done, "I'm afraid I broke in. He wasn't home." Again, he waited while there was a momentary silence from Harper. He could sense his exasperation.

"You realise that is a criminal offense." Harper said flatly.

"Yes, I do detective but I desperately need to find my wife. He had a photograph of her. He's obsessed with her and I'm worried that he's abducted her. He's a psychopath. A very dangerous psychopath."

"Well, Dr Kendrick. It's not a criminal offense to have a photograph of someone and we have already spoken with Mr Wixx as part of our enquiry. He has a confirmed alibi for his whereabouts on the afternoon your wife went missing. Actually, he spent the afternoon at the Red Lion with around twenty witnesses who can testify to that effect, so I'm afraid your hunch is incorrect. I am advising you to let us do our jobs. We don't want a repetition of yesterday, now do we."

Daniel realised he wasn't getting anywhere but despite Wixx's alibi, he still believed he was responsible. "Alright detective Harper. I'll be in touch and do please let me know of any progress you make – my wife's life is in danger."

"We are doing our best, Dr Kendrick."

They ended the call and Daniel felt the heaviness of disappointment. The police didn't even have Damon Wixx down as a suspect but Daniel was convinced, he was involved up to his ears. He needed solid evidence.

If he could find Wixx, he could find Fay. It was all he had.

SIXTY-EIGHT

Friday 23rd August 2019

Wixx was up earlier than usual the next morning and dressed in black jeans with a black T-shirt, black leather jacket and his favourite greasy black leather Dr Martens.

His cunning plan to demand a million-pound ransom from Daniel Kendrick was missing one thing – Fay. But there again – as far as he knew – nobody else had her either. The fact that he didn't have a hostage needn't be a problem. Not with his charisma, charm and skill at manipulation. Daniel Kendrick would be a pushover. He could bluff his way through this, get his money then kill Daniel.

Wixx had rummaged in his uncle's garage for a few things he needed; gardening gloves, a crowbar, chisel, screwdriver, a hammer and his own heavy duty Lifeaxe, and placed them in a canvas tool bag. He grabbed some paper and a pen, wrote a note and pushed it into his jacket pocket. He left the house and called into a drive-through McDonalds for a breakfast muffin and a strong coffee. Then he called to the local supermarket and bought a pay-as-you-go mobile phone. He set it up within minutes once he got back to the car.

He set the sat nav on his Samsung phone and drove the Jaguar north, across the river and skirted around the centre of Riverbeke to Daniel and Fay Kendrick's house. He knew the address by heart but had not been there before. He followed the directions he was being given and eventually the flag appeared on the sat nav and the voice announced that he had reached his destination.

The street was very up-market with a row of architecturally diverse detached houses set in large, mature gardens. The road was a dead end with a kissing gate that led to a wooded path. He could see Daniel's house on his left and turned the car before he parked to enable a quick getaway. There was no car in the driveway and no lights on in the front or upstairs of the house. He sat for a few minutes to check for movements. The house seemed deserted, as was the street.

Damon decided it was all clear. He retrieved the tool bag from the boot of the Jaguar and walked nonchalantly toward the house, eyes darting everywhere to check he hadn't been seen. The coast was clear.

He walked up the side of the house, past a small orchard of fruit trees and around to the back, that was laid mainly to lawn with large flower boarders and winding stone paths. There were a few dog toys and a football scattered on the lawn. He peered through the windows. No lights on. No sign of life. He fished in the tool bag for the chisel and hammer and snapped on a pair of latex gloves beneath the thicker gardening gloves. He began to prise the double-glazed window from its frame in the kitchen door. It was proving difficult. The windows looked fairly new. Damon tried again with the crowbar but he was losing patience. He hated having to break a window – the noise could attract the attention of the neighbours. But he reasoned he would be in and out fast. He would have to take a chance.

Damon replaced the tools and brought out his Lifeaxe – an emergency window breaker designed to let people escape from difficult to break modern window units. He positioned the sharp point of the axe in the lower corner of the window pane of the kitchen door, then brought it back and hit it hard. The steel point broke a hole in the first pane. He swung at the second pane. It broke through easily and Damon leapt back as the whole window shattered into tiny pieces. He cringed at the sound of breaking glass and waited, holding his breath for the sound of voices. Silence.

Damon was surprised but delighted that a house alarm had not been triggered. He took off the gardening gloves but kept the latex ones on to avoid leaving fingerprints. He quickly put his arm through the gap, unlocked the door and let himself in; his Dr Martens crunching over the broken glass. He casually wandered around the downstairs of the house, the kitchen, living room, study, hallway. All very minimalist. It was interesting to be in Fay Kendrick's house. He could imagine her here, cooking dinner in the kitchen; lounging on the sofa. He envied the Kendrick's wealth, their luxurious home, but also felt contempt for what they had achieved in life. These opposing emotions co-existed easily in Damon's psyche. He wanted what others had – success, love, respect – but at the same time, distained it. It was a pendulum that sprung from the narcissism that underlined his psychopathic state of being.

Damon opened a couple of drawers in the sideboard in the hallway and saw in one of them what must have been one of Fay's many scarves. He'd seen her wear it once. It smelled of her perfume. He stuffed it in the pocket of his jacket as a little souvenir. Then a gold-coloured sculpture on the top of the sideboard caught his eye. It was of two cats sitting together, one licking the other's face. He picked it up. It was heavy. He turned it over to see a hallmark of some sort, although he wasn't sure what it was. It could be solid gold. He took it – maybe it was worth something.

He contemplated going upstairs to look for more but decided against it. The noise of shattering glass could have alerted the neighbours and it was time to get out. Once Daniel was out of the picture, he would be back to ransack the place.

Damon went back into the kitchen. Retrieved the note from his pocket and placed it on the island in the middle of the kitchen. He placed the pay-as-you-go phone – a burner that couldn't be traced – in its box on top of the note. Then, he walked over to the refrigerator, found a couple of bottles of craft beer and took them, along with a chocolate bar, then smiled at a fridge magnet that read, 'Lead us not into temptation; just tell us where it is and we'll find it.' He collected up his tools and gloves then placed them in the tool bag, along with the gold-coloured cat ornament. He closed the broken back door behind him – out of habit – and retraced his steps back to the car.

The street was still quiet as he drove away, swigging Daniel's beer.

SIXTY-NINE

Friday 22nd August 2019

The Red Lion. That was where DS Harper had said Damon Wixx had spent the afternoon of Fay's disappearance. He appeared to be a regular in there. It would be a good starting point since Daniel had little else to go on.

Daniel left the psychiatric wing of the hospital and drove across town to the pub. He parked near the canal and walked back up the hill to the Red Lion.

The pub was fairly busy with lunchtime clientele. He politely took his turn at the bar and spoke to a young barmaid – an anorexic-looking young woman with pale skin, purple lipstick and green streaks through bleached hair. She looked like she belonged in a zombie movie.

"Excuse me, do you know a Damon Wixx. He was here last evening and all afternoon on Monday." Daniel had to raise his voice above the hubbub in the pub.

"Yes, I know him. He's one of our regulars."

"Do you know where I might find him?" Daniel asked.

"He lives in the council estate – Bridgeman I think."

"Yes, I've tried there but he's not about. Anywhere else you know of?"

"I think he has an uncle somewhere out of town that he's always scrounging money off but other than that I can't help you. Hang on I'll ask the boss."

The barmaid – Janice – turned and spoke to the landlord. He shouted across to Daniel. "Sorry mate, can't help you. Try in here this evening."

Daniel thanked them and wondered briefly if he should get himself a pub lunch. The cooking smells made him realise he was starving. It wasn't like him to go so long without a decent meal. He decided it would be quicker to get home, grab a quick lunch and work out how to find Damon or this uncle he had out of town.

On the drive home, Daniel reflected on what Shelly had told him about psychopaths. There was no cure, she had said. Damon was callous and had shown no remorse for hurting others. He was the type that could murder in cold blood and not give a damn. What if he was the serial killer that had murdered four people in the last few months? It seemed he was capable of it. Now he could be planning to murder Fay. Daniel's stomach lurched at the thought.

He realised that Fay meant everything to him – he couldn't bear to lose her. In a sudden surge of emotion, he just wanted to hold her and love her and never let go. He wanted to tell her he was sorry for the rows, for not doing more to keep their marriage solid when their innocent baby had been murdered. He couldn't bear it if he never got to see his wife again.

Daniel blinked hard, shaking off the tears that were pricking his eyes. He had to stay focused. Had to be strong for both of them.

He arrived home, parked in his driveway and let himself into the house. Maisie was nowhere to be seen. There was a strange smell in the hallway – a faint whiff of something that was vaguely familiar. He went into the living room and there it was again. Then into the kitchen and it was stronger there.

Then he stopped dead in his tracks, goose bumps prickling all the way up his arms and across his chest. He had noticed a note and a small package on the kitchen table. Could it be from Fay? Had she come home?

He stepped closer, anticipating a note from his wife but stopped abruptly when he remembered with disgust what that smell was. He looked up to see the window in the kitchen door had been smashed. There was a trail of blood right through the shattered glass on the kitchen floor.

The reek of cannabis mixed with tobacco and the scribbled note on the table…

With a sickening realisation, Daniel knew that Damon Wixx had been in his house.

Daniel's stomach twisted with trepidation. What had that evil bastard done to Fay? To his beautiful, intelligent, wonderful wife.

Daniel scanned the note. It wasn't signed but he knew in his gut it was Wixx. He opened the parcel. It was a burner. A pay-as-you-go mobile phone that couldn't be traced. He read the note.

Daniel Kendrick,

I have your wife. She is unharmed but that could all change in an instant if you don't follow my instructions very carefully.

You'd better get some money together if you want to see your wife alive again.

DO NOT contact the police or I will hurt Fay.

I am watching you…

I will call you with further instructions.

Daniel put the note down. So, Fay *had* been kidnapped. His instincts had been correct. Was she alright? His mind was swimming with images of Fay being tortured at the hands of Damon Wixx. He felt sick to the pit of his stomach.

It had to be Wixx. Had to be. What the hell could he do now. Wixx had the upper hand. That bastard was in control now – exactly what Shelly had said he craved. Power and control. Should he ignore what Wixx had said and contact DS Harper? It was risky. Very risky. Wixx was capable of anything – even murder and Daniel was convinced he wouldn't think twice about murdering Fay if he felt so inclined.

Also, DS Harper wasn't exactly on his side at the moment after the incident with Jaxon Sloan. Would he believe him? Surely, he would have to with the evidence of the break in, the note and the burner. But involving the police could risk Wixx carrying out his threat to hurt Fay. On balance, he decided to wait and see what Wixx had to say.

What about Shelly. She would want to know what had happened. But what if Wixx really was watching him? Shelly would be put at risk if he knew she was involved. He decided to say nothing for the time being. Emily, Fay's mother would be frantic too if she knew. He decided to shield her from this for as long as he could.

Daniel looked at the broken window and the blood on the floor and felt invaded. He had been obsessive about locking doors and checking windows ever since Sophie had been abducted, and yet this vile thug had calmly broken into their home and made malicious threats. He wondered why the house alarm hadn't gone off, then remembered it was faulty and he had been intending to get it repaired – another item on the ever-lengthening list of jobs he never got around to.

Daniel wondered where else Wixx had been in the house. He ran upstairs and checked the bedrooms and bathroom. There was no sign of anything having been disturbed and the faint whiff of cannabis wasn't there. He walked past Sophie's nursery, hesitant to go in. But what if Wixx had been in there? He stepped back and stood for long moments outside the door, forcing himself to go inside. He had to go in – Wixx could even be in there, violating their grief. Daniel slowly turned the handle and opened the door. From the doorway, he could see that nothing had been disturbed. Sophie's things, her cot with her favourite teddy, her changing mat, her wardrobe, her toys were all just as Fay had left them – undisturbed since the day their six-month-old daughter had been taken from them. Daniel gently closed the door. It had been too painful for him to go in there – to re-live the nightmare they had both been through. Fay had found some comfort in that room. It was her last connection to her baby and she had spent hours shut away from the world with the memory of Sophie. But Daniel wasn't ready to face the raw and anguished pain of grief – let alone deal with it.

Daniel returned to the kitchen. Maisie had come in from the garden through her cat flap and was unusually subdued. She must have been frightened and scarpered when Wixx had broken in. He could see she was limping. She had left bloodied paw marks on the floor. She must have run through the broken glass. Daniel scooped her up in his arms, grabbed some kitchen paper from the roll, wet it and began gently cleaning the blood. She stayed still, quietly trusting him as he pulled out a small shard of glass from the soft pad of her paw and wiped it with clean wet kitchen paper, checking all the glass had gone. He cradled her in his arms, talking softly to her and stroking her head until the bleeding stopped, then gently wrapped her paw in a bandage he found in their first aid kit. He carried her through to the living room and placed her on a towel on the armchair. She settled down to groom her fur.

Had Damon really abducted Fay or was this some monstrous game to manipulate them both for his own gratification? For the first time in many years, Daniel said a silent prayer.

SEVENTY

Friday 23rd August 2019

Daniel had waited for two anxious hours for the call from the burner that Wixx had left. He'd boarded up the broken kitchen window with planks of wood he'd found in the garage and arranged an urgent call out from a local glazier to get it fixed. He had checked all around the house and garden and there was no sign that Wixx was watching him that he could detect. He must have broken in, wandered around downstairs and let himself out through the back door. He was glad the dogs were safely out of the way with Rosie at the dog creche.

He was pacing now, unsure what more he could do. He'd re-read the note umpteen times. Should he get some cash together as Wixx had demanded? He wasn't sure how much he would be able to get hold of at short notice. He wanted to hear Fay's voice – to know that she was safe and well. Surely, if it was money that Wixx was after, he wouldn't harm her until he had what he wanted. It could take several days, or even weeks, to get a large amount of cash together.

Daniel paced the kitchen; his appetite had vanished. All he wanted was to find out where Fay was and get her back home where she belonged. He paced the empty living room, his mind conjuring up memories and images of Fay. She was everywhere in this house – and so was Sophie. Now all he had were the ghostly memories of the people he loved most in the world. Only one of them could ever return to him alive and he was determined to do all he could to find his wife.

Daniel startled when his iPhone rang. Could it be Wixx trying to get through? He fumbled to answer before it rang off.

"Dr Kendrick, it's Hayley Shepherd from the Argus. I just wanted to have a chat to you about the incident with Jaxon Sloan yesterday. I heard you had been arrested and I understand they let you go without charge. Would you be willing to give me an interview?"

Daniel's heart sunk. He could do without this right now. "I'm sorry, not at the moment." Unusually brusque, he ended the call abruptly.

He looked at the burner, checking for missed calls for the umpteenth time. There were none. Wixx was playing a sadistic game, he thought. Perhaps he should do something to prepare for the inevitable – a ransom demand. He was certain Wixx wouldn't just hand Fay over without a substantial sum of money.

Daniel logged onto his Internet banking account and rounded up as much cash from various savings accounts as he could find. It amounted to a little over £60,000. Much of his money was tied up in pension funds, which he had no access to, but he did have some Premium Bonds he could cash in – an account of his own and one for his grandson that he had been paying into. That would bring the total to £110,000. Would that be enough to satisfy Wixx?

SEVENTY-ONE

Friday 23rd August 2019

Daniel jumped when he heard the unfamiliar ring tone of the burner phone that had been left in his kitchen just hours ago. His felt the crushing grip of apprehension as he answered it.

"Who is this?" Daniel asked, low and firm, desperate to hide the tremble in his voice.

"Come now Dr Kendrick, that's not a nice way to greet a caller now, is it?" A man's voice sounded sarcastic. Sneering.

"Where is my wife? Is she safe?"

"Your wife is safe... for now."

"What do you mean. What have you done to Fay?" Daniel paced the living room, trying to stay calm.

"Your wife will be safe if – and only if – you follow my instructions."

"What is it you want? No, let me guess. Money. Am I right? You're looking for a ransom." Daniel felt a growing resentment for this vile creature that had invaded his home and his life and taken his wife.

"How very perceptive, Dr Kendrick. Now that you mention it, a large sum of cash would be very acceptable. Thank you." The voice was sneering once again.

"So how much are you looking for?" Daniel just wanted to get this over with and get his precious Fay home.

"A cool million would be enough, I think, for me to release your wife. In cash, of course, and by tomorrow." The man's voice was contemptuous. "Are you with me Daniel?"

Daniel stopped pacing. He didn't have a million pounds and even if he did, he couldn't just conjure it up like a rabbit out of a magician's hat. He felt angry and affronted. "Who is this? Damon Wixx? How dare you threaten me and my wife. I don't have that sort of money and even if I did, why should I hand it over to you?"

"Because your wife will die if you don't. Good day Dr Kendrick."

The line went dead.

Daniel tried to call the number back but it had been blocked. Shit. Wixx was in control and was enjoying his sick game.

Daniel threw the phone onto the sofa. His mind was racing. What the hell should he do? He was pretty sure the man was Wixx. He hadn't denied it and the voice sounded familiar. Just like the arrogant shit that had turned up in Fay's clinic. Perhaps he should contact the police and take the risk. They would have experts that could help him deal with it. Undercover detectives that would talk him through. He felt out of his depth – wholly unequipped to handle a ransom situation. Look at the mess he'd made of dealing with Sloan. Maybe it was time to call DS Harper. Surely, he would believe him now and take action against Wixx.

Daniel was fumbling for his iPhone when the burner rang again. Daniel answered it.

"Don't do that, Dr Kendrick. If you call the police, your pretty little wife will die." Wixx's voice sounded dark and menacing.

Was Wixx watching him? How did he know he was about to call the police? All Daniel wanted was to know Fay was safe. "Let me talk to Fay. I need to hear her voice."

"Just get the money together – a million pounds in cash – and I will release your wife. A simple transaction. Unless, of course, you don't think your wife is worth a million. I want it by tomorrow. I will let you know where to bring it."

"Look Mr Wixx; Damon Wixx, I don't have that sort of cash lying around. I just don't have that sort of money." Daniel knew he must have sounded desperate. If only he had a police negotiator to deal with this.

"Tick tock, doctor. For every day you delay, the ransom will increase by £10,000. Remember, no police or your wife will die."

Click. The phone went dead.

Daniel placed the phone on the kitchen table and ran a hand along his stubbled face. He was out of his depth. He badly needed the help of the police but it was too risky. Wixx was capable of murder and he believed he would kill Fay if he didn't comply. His only recourse was to get the money together – but how? He didn't have a million in liquid assets. Maybe he could borrow it somehow on assets – the house, his car. Maybe. But could he raise an additional £880,000? It seemed impossible.

The only person he knew with that sort of money readily available was Oliver Davenport. He had cash put aside ready for his cosmetic surgery business investment.

The snag? How the hell was he going to ask Oliver for a loan after the disaster with his wife Melissa?

SEVENTY-TWO

Friday 23rd August 2019

There was no way Daniel could ask Oliver Davenport for a loan to make up the ransom money that would pay for Fay's release. No way. He had wracked his brains to think of someone else that might have that sort of money that he could possibly ask. Colin Mathias – definitely not. One of the other consultants? Not a chance. Shelly? A faint possibility but he didn't think she had that sort of money either.

Should he call Shelly? Would it be risky for her to be involved? Daniel paced the room, pondering whether to tell Shelly about the latest development. She always had good advice and it was a possibility – however small – that she could help him out with raising the ransom, or at least some advice on dealing with a psychopath.

Daniel was out of his depth. He badly needed a drink but he knew he had to keep a clear head. Fay's life was on the line.

Then he remembered the savings plan he'd come across in Fay's bedside drawer when he was searching for her passport. Maybe there was a way to use that.

He bounded up the stairs and took out the papers from the drawer. Fay had a savings account with Scottish Widows worth £62,240. It would be enough to make up the ransom if he borrowed on the house and the car as well.

There was only one problem. Scottish Widows were never going to release the money to him without Fay's permission or a death certificate and her will.

Then he realised he could use this as a bargaining chip with Wixx. He would have to speak to Fay to get her to access the money. Then he would know she was safe.

Now, he was looking forward to the next phone call.

SEVENTY-THREE

Friday 23rd August 2019

Daniel had called the bank before they closed for the afternoon and arranged, in principle, that he could borrow on the house and the car. He had to give twenty-four hours' notice to get the money in cash and they were willing to rush it though – for a hefty fee. With Fay's secret savings, he could just about make the million pounds ransom that Wixx was demanding.

He'd been anxiously waiting for a call on the burner but for over two hours there had been nothing. Daniel was still debating whether to call Shelly for some advice on how to handle Wixx. After all, she had experience with psychopaths, as Fay had. He could do with her words of wisdom right now.

Before he could decide, his iPhone rang. It was Shelly.

"Hi Shelly."

"Any news? Did you call the police?"

"Yes, I did, but apparently, Wixx has an alibi. He was in the Red Lion all afternoon the day Fay went missing." Daniel paused for a moment before continuing. "There's been a development…"

"What's happened? Is Fay alright?" Shelly's voice was anxious and shaky.

"I think… hope she is. Wixx broke into the house and left me a little present. A ransom note and a mobile phone. He's been in touch and says he has Fay. He'll release her for a million in cash by tomorrow."

"Bloody hell. Have you told the police? What did they say?"

"Wixx was emphatic. No police or he'll kill Fay. I believe him."

"Yes, I'm afraid I do too. Shit, Daniel, what are we going to do?"

"I don't know. I can just about raise the ransom money – part of it is in a savings account of Fay's. I could use that as a bargaining tool to get to speak to Fay."

"You mean you haven't spoken to her? You haven't verified that she is there and still alive?"

"No."

"Daniel, you need to insist he gives you proof he has her and that she's alright. He's a manipulator and a liar. He may not even have abducted her at all."

Daniel hadn't thought of that.

The burner rang on the kitchen table.

"It's Wixx. I'll call you back." Daniel rang off and reached for the burner.

"Wixx?"

"Dr Kendrick. Have you got the cash I asked for?"

"Yes, but I have to be sure that Fay is alright before you see a penny of it. Let me speak to her now." Daniel felt more in control, knowing he had something to use as a lever with Wixx.

"Well, that's excellent. I'll tell you where to bring the money – in cash – and come alone…"

Daniel interrupted, "not until I speak to Fay. In fact, a large chunk of the money cannot be released without her say so." His voice sounded more resolute than he felt.

"Come now, doctor, you will see your wife soon enough. Bring me the cash and I will hand her over to you – it's simple.

In less than an hour, you will be reunited and your nightmare will be over."

Daniel interrupted again, Shelly's warning still hanging in his mind. "No, Mr Wixx. Let me speak to my wife now or there will be no ransom – now that's simple."

The phone went dead.

Daniel now knew deep in his belly that Wixx didn't have Fay. He was bluffing. Manipulating him to gain money as Shelly had suggested. Perhaps DS Harper was right – Wixx did have an alibi and was innocent of abducting her.

On the one hand, it was a relief that Fay wasn't being tortured by a cold-blooded psychopath but on the other hand, they were back to square one. Where was Fay?

He called Shelly back.

"Shelly?"

"Daniel. What happened?"

"He doesn't have Fay; I'm convinced of it. He couldn't let me speak to her, even when I told him I had a million pounds in cash ready for him. He's bluffing."

"Yes, sounds like. But we still don't know where she is."

"Exactly. Where do we start?"

"I don't know but we have to consider one thing. Damon Wixx knows there is a million pounds waiting for him if he can find Fay. We have to get to her before he does, Daniel."

An icy shiver ran through Daniel's veins.

Now he had to find Fay before Wixx did.

SEVENTY-FOUR

Friday 23rd August 2019

Damon had killed the call. His plan had backfired. He didn't have Fay and now Daniel knew it too.

Shit! There was a million pounds at stake.

Wixx sat in the kitchen brooding. He felt the rage inside him bubble up as if a pressure cooker was coming to the boil. It simmered, then gurgled and spat like a boiling geyser. Finally, in a supernova explosion of fury, his temper blew.

He stood, kicked the chair across the room and began rampaging around his uncle's bungalow like a thing possessed. His fist crashed down on the kitchen table, sending a plate clattering to the floor. He kicked the cupboard doors, knocking one away from its hinges. He strode around the room, grabbed a glass vase and smashed it into the wall, bellowing expletives like a spoiled brat. Then he stomped along the length of the passage, banging the walls with his fists as he went, then punched a hole in the spare bedroom door. The door flung open against the wall and he tore into the room searching for something else to vent his anger on.

He grabbed one of his uncle Wally's treasured Niike Katana Samurai swords from its stand on the table. He wrenched it from its sheath; the curved, carbon steel blade glinting in the light. He admired it for a few seconds then began vehemently slashing at the bed, slicing the duvet and stabbing at the pillows as if he were attacking a ferocious opponent in battle. He was completely berserk as he worked off his frustration.

Finally, his rage began to abate and he stopped, breathless and clammy from the exertion. The bedsheets lay in tatters. A white snowstorm of feathers from the pillows was floating around the room. The huge sword was heavy and his arm ached. He threw it on the bed among the mayhem and stomped back to the kitchen.

He put his palms on the kitchen table, leaning for support. He was breathing deeply in an attempt to calm his temper. He could see his fist was raw and painful from punching the door. Slowly, his head began to clear and he regained control of his emotions. The cold, sudden display of anger was over. Perversely, he had enjoyed it.

But now, he needed to think. He grabbed his tin of paraphernalia, rolled himself a chunky joint, grabbed a beer from the fridge and sunk into his uncle's armchair, exhausted from his own rage. He stared at the wall as his fingers tapped manically on the arm of the chair; ash from his splif tumbling onto the floor.

As the cannabis began to calm his fury, he realised he had three choices. He could come up with some crafty scheme to manipulate Daniel into handing over the money, although he conceded, if he was honest, that the doctor would be unlikely to fall for it. He could just break in to the house and steal the money. Too crude; Daniel would immediately know it was him. He could kill Daniel as planned then take the money. Problem was, he wasn't convinced Daniel actually had the ransom in cash.

Wixx thought for several minutes, the cannabis soothing his broken, deluded mind. Then he realised, there was another way that allowed him to have everything he wanted. He could get his ransom money, kill Daniel and isolate the woman he was so obsessed with.

But first, he would have to find Fay.

SEVENTY-FIVE

Friday 23rd August 2019

"Why don't we meet up and try to work something out? We need to come up with a plan." Shelly said.

"We have to get to Fay before Wixx does." Daniel felt a renewed urgency to find his wife – especially now that Damon Wixx knew there was a million pounds ransom on offer. He might not have her now but he had more than enough motive to find her.

"Look, come to my office. I only have one patient left to see on the ward and I can easily postpone that."

"Good. I'll be there in thirty minutes."

Daniel rang off. If anyone could help him to understand the mind of a killer and now, as a potential abductor, Shelly could with her training in forensic psychiatry. If he couldn't turn to the police for help, he could rely on Shelly. She had been a good friend to Fay over the years and now she was becoming his friend too.

Daniel checked on Maisie. She seemed comfortable with her cut paw, although she was still limping slightly. Thankfully the bandage hadn't troubled her so the wound had stayed clean.

He would keep her in the house for a few days. Rosie had the dogs at the creche and would be back at 5 pm but they would be fine for an hour or two until he got back. He grabbed a few chocolate digestives from the tin in the kitchen cupboard to keep his growing hunger at bay, pocketed his iPhone and the burner and left for the hospital.

Daniel eased the BMW through the late afternoon rush hour traffic. It was a frustrating stop-start drive through the town of Riverbeke but he got to the hospital and parked easily outside the psychiatric unit. Most of the office staff had gone home for the day.

He walked the length of the main corridor, brightly lit from the huge expanses of glass and, on the wall opposite, artworks from local artists as part of an art therapy project. He skirted past the acute psychiatric ward to Shelly's office at the end of the corridor. The door was ajar. He knocked and went in to find Shelly sat at her desk going through a pile of notes. The room was stuffy, hot and smelled of musty paper and coffee.

She looked up and smiled. "Come in Daniel. Take a seat." Shelly gestured to a high-backed wooden chair on the opposite side of her desk.

Daniel sat. Across the span of polished oak, he took in his surroundings. Shelly's office was part of a recently built wing of the old general hospital, where his surgical ward was situated. The building was clean and modern with glossy floors and wide expanses of glass. There were piles of notes stacked on every surface with pens scattered everywhere and papers left lying around. It felt chaotic. Another desk, equally messy, was placed near the window. A row of neatly lined-up pens on one side of the desk seemed to be the only orderly fragment of the room.

"That's Doug's desk. He works at the hospital two days a week. Often the only time we get to see one another." Doug Winters was Shelly's husband and a professor of psychiatry at the nearby university.

338

Daniel looked at Shelly, desperation in his eyes. "What the hell are we going to do?"

Shelly put her papers down and slid a comforting hand across the desk toward Daniel. He took it and they shared a brief touch. "We have to find Fay, Daniel, before Wixx does. He's a dangerous criminal. If he gets to her first…"

"I know," Daniel cut in, "it doesn't bear thinking about." He felt cold despite the oppressive heat in the room.

"Any ideas at all about where she could be? If Wixx didn't abduct her, why did she disappear?"

"With no phone, no money, no passport," Daniel said, shaking his head. He checked the burner. There had been no further contact from Wixx.

Shelly stood and walked across the room, grabbed two heavy crystal tumblers and a bottle of Portwood-finish Penderyn whiskey. She placed them on the desk in front of Daniel and poured an inch in each. "I don't know about you but I need a drink". Shelly smiled and handed Daniel a glass.

Daniel thanked her, swirled the amber liquid and brought it to his nose. He could smell the rich aromas of dark chocolate and fruit with a hint of oak and nuts. He took a sip, the smooth creaminess slipped down easily and left warm notes of spice and sweet honey. "Very nice," Daniel said as he sipped some more.

Shelly glanced at Daniel's wrist – at the old scars etched into the skin. She looked away and took her seat behind the desk. "Ought to be at sixty-three quid a bottle." She took a sip and briefly closed her eyes in appreciation, then looked across at Daniel. "A present from Doug when he did a tour of the distillery in Wales."

"It was a good choice." Daniel was anxious to get back to the task of finding his wife. "Fay's been gone four days now. It's not like her. She's come home in the middle of the night a few times lately but never stayed away this long."

Shelly seemed to sense his urgency and sat upright, clasping her hands together. "We need to brainstorm." She opened a drawer in her desk and pulled out a notepad and a biro. "You've gone through all her friends and family and exhausted any possibilities there?"

"Yes," Daniel said. He sipped his whiskey, appreciating the soothing warmth in his throat.

"Someone, surely, must know something," Shelly said.

"I'm worried sick that this serial killer has her. What if she's being held somewhere? Being tortured. God, Shelly, she could even be dead." Daniel tried to stop the alarming images forming in his mind.

Shelly reached out and touched his arm again. It did little to reassure him. He looked into his glass and swirled the whiskey before taking another sip.

"You can't think like that, Daniel. We have to stay positive and believe she's still alive. We'll find her – we will." Shelly gave his arm a little rub before withdrawing her hand.

Daniel nodded his agreement but it was impossible not to consider the possibility that Fay was already dead. Why hadn't she come home for four days? He refused to believe she'd left him without a word. Without telling him it really was over. Something dreadful must have happened to her. His fingers traced the patterns in the glass of the crystal tumbler.

He took a deep breath and tried to gather his thoughts. "What about her patients? If one of them has had a mental breakdown, it's possible that they could have abducted her. I'm not saying someone would harm her but we have to rule out the possibility."

"I think we can rule out Justin McCartney," Shelly said.

"Any idea how he's doing?"

"As far as I know Dr Maddison is trying to stabilise him with medication and he's safely sectioned for the time being. Hopefully he'll be alight."

"That's good." Daniel said. "Do you know any of her other patients?"

"A few but she had quite a big list – there's no way I could find out about them all."

"What about the most recent ones?"

Shelly reached for a sheaf of papers at the side of the desk, pulling out one near the middle. "Let's see. I did make a few notes this morning but got side-tracked." She rifled through the papers.

Daniel looked across at the window. A wasp was crawling up the glass, dropping to the sill and repeating in an endless cycle of triumph and defeat. He sympathised.

Shelly ran her index finger down a handwritten list, stopping halfway down. "Jaxon Sloan was a patient, briefly, while he was in prison but we've ruled him out."

"Yes, Sloan. He could be the only person that knows where she is and now, he's dead."

Shelly gave Daniel a watery smile and looked back at her list.

He took another sip of his whiskey. "Damn, this is good stuff," he said, draining his glass.

"Help yourself," Shelly said pointing to the bottle with the end of her pen.

Daniel poured himself another splash and freshened up Shelly's glass. "We also ruled out that Horton character, didn't we?"

"Yes, Robert Horton. Fay testified against him but he's been under tight security with all this business of a new identity. I can't imagine he would have abducted her."

"He's also dead," Daniel said wryly.

"Quite."

Shelly looked at her notes again. "There are a few other patients of Fay's I know but I wouldn't put them high on my list of suspects."

Daniel nodded pensively. "Any other ideas?"

"She did run group therapy sessions for some of the serious offenders. I could look into that and let you know if I find anything interesting."

At that point, a tall, wiry man of about six-foot-five strode into the room. His hairy arms and huge hands dangled from the sleeves of his jacket, reminding Daniel of Frankenstein's monster. The hem of his trousers skimmed the top of his socks and were a good three inches too short. He looked badly in need of some fashion advice and a decent haircut. The man walked over to the desk near the window in three strides, placed a pile of textbooks on the desk and turned to face them.

"Hello sweetheart," Shelly said. "Daniel, this is my husband, Doug. Doug, this is Daniel Kendrick, Fay's husband."

The man smiled and studied Daniel over half-rimmed tortoiseshell spectacles. Then stepped forward, proffered a hand and engulfed Daniel's with his own. "Nice to meet you."

"Likewise," Daniel said. The man seemed pleasant enough but was nothing like he'd imagined Shelly's husband to be.

They exchanged a few social pleasantries then Daniel excused himself, saying he had to get home for the dogs.

He'd had an idea and he needed to call into the bookshop on the way home.

SEVENTY-SIX

10 days ago

Paula Bishop was handcuffed to her hospital bed. The prison officer that was guarding her had relented and allowed her the dignity to give birth when her midwife had declared that she was fully dilated and ready to push. Paula had tried pushing, she really had, but it had been difficult when the epidural that the anaesthetist had injected into her spine meant she had no feeling from the waist down. The midwife had shouted at her to push with each contraction and she'd tried her best, but it was nowhere near good enough and she got out of breath with all the weight she was carrying; not so much the baby weight but her own immense body fat accumulated from years of consuming a diet comprising solely of pizzas, burgers and chips with the odd chicken kebab; washed down with fizzy drinks and strong cider.

When her unborn baby became distressed, they had wheeled her into theatre for an emergency caesarean section under the epidural. At least she was able to lie back and let the obstetrician do the work of getting her baby out. It reminded her of those upper crust types branded 'too posh to push' and she fantasised that she was part of the jet setting scene with a rich, successful husband. The truth was, she had never managed to keep a man interested for more than a few weeks, even in their ignorance of the malevolency of her true nature. The baby's feckless father had been no exception; disappearing off the scene the minute he realised that she was pregnant. But the reality was that she didn't see why she had to make the supreme physical effort of pushing a baby out naturally when immediately after birth, social services had told her they would take it away from her and put it into foster care. It was the third child they'd taken from her but only the first she'd had while actually serving a prison sentence.

They'd let her out just to have the baby, then it would be straight back into jail with not even the privilege and respective comfort of being able to stay in the mother and baby unit like other prisoners that had become new mothers. She was far too dangerous to be allowed to be around children, they'd said; even tiny babies. She would be treated just like any other prisoner. No baby and no prospect of an early release. Prison had finally put a stop to Paula's monstrous crimes and she was looking at a very long stretch. Still, she reasoned sardonically, she had plenty of memories to keep her amused – it was all there in her head playing around on a loop like her favourite video clips on the dark web. Sickening and abhorrent to the normal mind, Paula Bishop revelled in her treasured mental images of the innocent children she'd abused: boys and girls.

The midwife was very nice, considering she didn't have to be. She'd told Paula that her baby was a girl and that she was very sorry but she wasn't permitted to see her. She was a sweet little babe, just 6 lb 2 oz, and had a crop of dark hair, like her mother. Paula was grateful for those crumbs of information but detested the way everyone looked down on her; judging her, even when they tried not to. Even her fellow prisoners were the same. It was OK for them to murder unfaithful husbands, steal tens of thousands from their boss or even hack their parents to death with a meat cleaver, as Jackie Lyndhurst had done, but because she'd shown a little love to those children, she was branded a paedophile and the scum of the Earth. She didn't see the problem. She'd never killed anyone or even harmed them in a bad way really, she reasoned in her psychopathically disturbed mind. She'd had therapy in prison in a futile attempt to 'cure' her but none of it had made one iota of difference. Her aberrant behaviour was deemed incurable.

As Paula lay in her hospital bed, glad of the break from her oppressive prison life, she tried to sleep and forget that her child had been taken from her. She felt colostrum leak from her nipples and pain from the constriction of her empty uterus – reminders that she had created and given birth to a new life. But her mind and her reasoning were so deranged, Paula Bishop couldn't feel the sentiments that new motherhood stirred in other women – nor sadness that the experience had been denied her. She knew she could never or would never deny the monstrous urges that drove her to sexually abuse children.

It was 2.30 am and her prison guard had fallen asleep, snoring, in the reclining armchair on the other side of the room. Paula's mind was a jumble of thoughts and emotions and she fidgeted, unable to sleep on her back with both her wrists handcuffed to the sides of the bed.

The killer crept into Paula's room. She could see the victim was still awake but approached the bed anyway. Paula looked up into her killer's eyes and nodded once in recognition. She knew this person and trusted them. The killer whispered, "can't sleep Paula?"

Paula whispered back that she couldn't and would be glad of something to help her get some much-needed shut eye and some help with the pain.

"I have just the thing. This will put you to sleep." The killer smiled, amused at the intended pun and administered an intravenous injection via the canula in the back of one of Paula's cuffed hands. The syringe contained warfarin, the anticoagulant in rat poison, along with twenty times the standard dose of pancuronium bromide, a potent paralysing agent often used alongside an anaesthetic when a patient is ventilated. It is also used in euthanasia and lethal injection, the killer mused poignantly, as the cocktail of deadly drugs surged into Paula's vein. In less than three minutes, the concoction would reach their full lethal effect.

Paula was acutely aware of everything going on around her, the pancuronium having no effect on her level of consciousness. She saw the killer's smile twist into a self-satisfied sneer, felt her heart beat urgently against her ribs, while hot flashes ravaged her body. She tried to call out, to alert the prison officer but her voice had already been silenced forever and her mouth gaped uselessly. She could feel warm viscous liquid soaking the sheets beneath her as blood gushed from between her legs; the warfarin doing its work. Yet she was powerless to move.

Paula was unaware that the pressure inside her arteries was rising dangerously and, mixed for good measure with warfarin, the sutures holding her uterus and abdominal wall together were unable to stem the flow of thinning blood that was rapidly filling her abdomen. Her heart began to flutter and fail, lacking the arterial pressure needed to keep it pumping.

Paula felt a terrorising panic engulf her senses as her breathing slowed and stopped. She was fully aware but alarmingly unable to take a breath. She was suffocating from the inside.

Nobody but the killer saw the violent body spasm that Paula Bishop suffered just before she gasped; desperately trying to take a final breath.

SEVENTY-SEVEN

Friday 23rd August 2019

Daniel called into WHSmith's on the way home and bought an OS Landranger Map of the local area. He was looking for inspiration as to where Fay could possibly be. There were thousands of acres of countryside around Riverbeke – the search would have to be narrowed down.

Daniel had been thinking that if Jaxon Sloan had been with Fay before he got caught, surely, she couldn't be a million miles away. It was worth investigating. Sloan had been on the run, on foot, just before the shooting and given the extensive media coverage, the most likely place to hide was in the countryside, away from crowded towns and cities where he would likely be recognised. A detailed map might give him a better sense of the area.

When Daniel arrived home, he could hear Chester and Ella barking in The Dog House. They sounded ferocious and were probably a deterrent to burglars but he was glad they had been at the dog creche all day – Wixx wouldn't have hesitated to hurt them and they were both far too trusting. He looked at the boarded-up kitchen door. The house may have been broken into but at least the animals were safe.

He let himself into the house and opened the door for the dogs. They bounded into the kitchen, greeting him excitedly. Chester was panting with exuberance and pushing his head under Daniel's hand to be stroked. Ella went straight to Maisie's dish and polished off her food before going back to Daniel for a fuss. Maisie sat on the kitchen worktop watching them all disdainfully with cold green eyes.

Finally, the greeting ritual over, they settled down in the living room, the sound of their claws clicking over the tiled kitchen floor stopped when they stepped onto the carpet. Chester stretched out on his blanket on the sofa and Ella curled up on the rug. Maisie sat on the coffee table washing herself awkwardly with the bandage on her paw coming loose but just about staying in place.

Daniel placed his iPhone and the burner on the kitchen counter to charge and flicked on the TV to catch the BBC news headlines. There was no more on the serial killer and the Sloan murders had already been superseded by the story of another attack on a London Mosque. There was more on Brexit and Boris Johnson, the new PM, was exasperated with rebel backbenchers in the House of Commons. Daniel had every sympathy with him and his predecessor, Teresa May. He switched the TV off, wandered into the kitchen, poured a large glass of shiraz and made himself a cheese, lettuce and tomato doorstop of a sandwich, thick with butter and a dollop of mayonnaise. He wasn't in the mood for cooking dinner.

He picked up the OS map and spread it open on the island in the kitchen. It covered Riverbeke and the surrounding countryside and at 1: 50 000 scale it was a detailed depiction of the area. He studied the map while he ate and found the tea rooms that Sloan had broken into. He'd been on foot at that point, so couldn't have travelled far. He knew where Fay was – surely, she must be reasonably close. Using the tea rooms as a central point, he radiated outward, scouring the topography for barns, outbuildings, derelict houses, caves – anywhere that Fay could have been taken if she'd been abducted. He followed the river and found various footpaths and bridleways, railway lines and restricted byways. The area was mainly flat and covered with mixed woodland, some privately owned but mostly, it was Forestry Commission land. Much of it had been left relatively unmanaged in a bid to encourage biodiversity. There were thousands of acres of woodland, much of it inaccessible. It would be impossible to pinpoint where she could be without further information.

Daniel finished his sandwich and delved in the cat-themed biscuit tin for a soggy chocolate biscuit and a couple of custard creams. How could he narrow down his search of the area, short of hiring a helicopter and conducting his own aerial search?

Wait. He realised the police helicopters had already searched the area with high-tech equipment like thermal imaging cameras. Maybe they had picked up on something. They were primarily hunting for Sloan but there was a chance.

Daniel grabbed his iPhone and called DS Harper.

"Harper." The detective sounded irritated.

"Hello Detective. Daniel Kendrick here."

"Yes, Dr Kendrick. What can I do for you?"

Daniel was tempted to tell Harper the whole story about Wixx and his demand for a ransom but thought better of it. He decided to keep it simple for now. The most important thing was to find Fay. "I'm looking at a map of Riverbeke and the surrounding countryside and I'm convinced Fay is somewhere in this area. I wondered if the police helicopter picked up anything during their search for Jaxon Sloan? It might help us to pinpoint where my wife could be."

There was an awkward silence for a few moments, then the detective sighed before he spoke. "Nothing has been reported to me, but I could get the team to go over the footage again."

"Have you made any further progress on the case?"

"Not yet, Dr Kendrick. We are doing our best." The irritation in Harper's voice was evident.

Daniel decided he wasn't getting anywhere. "Thank you, detective. You will let me know if anything is found on the aerial footage?"

"If we find anything, we will certainly look into it. Good evening, Dr Kendrick. I suggest you get a good night's sleep."

"Thank you, detective." Daniel sensed the police were not intending to share any information with him, even if they had something. Was he still under suspicion? It was a ludicrous idea that he could harm Fay in any way but he knew that most murder victims, over eighty percent, are killed by people they know. It was a logical line of enquiry for the police to check out the husband – he didn't blame them. He did get the sense, though, that Harper was tired of his interfering with the investigation. Yet he had to be proactive – it was his wife that was missing.

Then, thinking laterally of investigations, he remembered Hayley Shepherd, the keen young reporter from the Argus. She would, no doubt, have contacts – maybe on the force – that might even be willing to bend the rules, if necessary, for her to get the story she was after. Daniel retraced her number in his iPhone and called.

"Dr Kendrick. Hello. Have you changed your mind about giving me an interview?"

"Maybe," Daniel said. "But first, I need some information."

"Go on."

"Do you have any contacts in the police force that could get access to some footage from an aerial search done yesterday during the hunt for Jaxon Sloan? I'm thinking it could be useful in helping me finding my wife. Especially images from thermal cameras. I would be able to ID her from something like that."

"Ah yes. It was her disappearance that led you to Sloan. I understand she's a forensic psychiatrist and that Jaxon Sloan and the murdered local woman, Paula Bishop, were both patients of hers," Hayley said.

Paula Bishop? Daniel was struggling to recall who that was. He sort-of recognised the name from somewhere but couldn't place her. He certainly didn't want to get side-tracked into a discussion about Fay's patients. He just wanted to find his wife.

"No comment on that, sorry." Daniel said flatly. He began to feel irritated by the reporter but mindful that she might be able to help him.

"Have the police made any further progress finding your wife?" Hayley asked.

"No, not yet." Neither was he about to tell her about the developments with Wixx, or the inside story on Sloan – unless she'd earned it. "Do you think you can find out anything about the aerial search?"

"Let me think," she said. The phone went quiet apart from the sound of rustling paper in the background. A few moments later, she came back on the line. "I have a reliable contact that could probably get that information for you but not until at least tomorrow."

"Excellent. Who is it? Someone in the police?"

"Sorry, I can't tell you that but I will do my best for you. And you would be willing to do an interview if I can help you?"

"Of course. Let's see what happens."

"Fair enough. I hope your wife is found soon."

"So do I. Thanks Hayley."

They ended the call. He knew it was a long shot, but it was all he had. The aerial footage could turn up something – however small – that could lead to Fay.

SEVENTY-EIGHT

Friday 23rd August 2019

Damon Wixx had finally calmed down after his rampage. Daniel knew he didn't have Fay but he would find her, take her hostage and claim his million-pound ransom. Then he would kill Daniel – preferably slowly, and inflict as much pain and suffering as he could – with his bare hands. He smirked at the image forming in his deluded mind.

He'd been going around in circles trying to think of places she could be. He didn't know – and didn't particularly care – about Fay's family or friends or her social life but he'd heard gossip in the Red Lion about Jaxon Sloan and the speculation from onlookers who had been at Sloan's capture, that he had been with her before he was caught. Maybe in the countryside north of the river.

Then he remembered the manuscript of the book she had been writing. He'd retrieved it from his mate's car and left it in the flat. There had been a lot of annotations and scribbling in the margins. Something about a lake. Perhaps that would give some clue as to where she'd gone. It was thin but all he had. Daniel had obviously been trying to find her along with the police but he had the smug feeling he now had the upper hand.

Wixx grabbed the keys to the flat and drove his uncle's Jaguar back to Riverbeke and Bridgeman Tower. He walked through the litter-strewn precinct as the light was beginning to fade. The local louts were gathering outside the off licence dressed in drooping jeans, fake Nike trainers, baseball caps and hoodies. He recognised the distinct smell of cannabis and guessed there were some serious drug deals going down by the way the youths closed ranks and eyed him suspiciously as he passed.

He ignored them and rode the creaking lift to the third floor of his block. On the landing, Gizmo, the grubby Bison Frise, was taking a dump outside the door of his flat but scarpered as he approached. He muttered under his breath, went into the flat and grabbed a wad of old newspaper. He went back onto the landing, picked up the warm, stinking turd with the paper and posted it through next door's letter box. It wasn't the first time he'd been compelled to do that, but the fat bitch still hadn't got the message. If he could get hold of the stupid mutt, he would kill him this time.

Wixx went back into his flat, slamming the front door behind him. The loose glass rattled in the frame. He washed his hands over the dirty dishes in the kitchen sink and picked up a letter that had been posted through his own letterbox. He tore it open. The letterhead showed it was from the tracing agency that was attempting to find his birth mother. The letter explained that they had indeed found her but that she emphatically did not want to see him or have any further contact from him. He realised his goal of making some sort of financial gain from her had failed. Worse now, for him, was his lost opportunity to hurt her and destroy her for abandoning him.

With callous contempt for his mother, he ripped up the letter and pushed it into the overflowing kitchen bin. His mind quickly re-focused on the task in hand.

Wixx went in search of Fay's manuscript. He checked the bedroom, then the pile of magazines littering the floor in the living room. There, he found it. A draft of a book; Biophilia and the Healing Power of Nature. He flicked through the pages and stopped when he found a chapter entitled, Mental Health and Nature. In the margins were numerous scribbles, many of them indecipherable, but then he saw a passage that read:

'Otterbrook Lake; my sanctuary from the crazy world'.

Could Fay have gone there? If it was anywhere near the place where Sloan had seen her – if the gossip was true – then it was worth a try. He didn't have anything else to go on. He remembered Fay had told him once that it was important that we all had somewhere where we felt safe – a hiding place from the world when we felt stressed or overwhelmed. She had encouraged him to find his own safe place to calm his mind.

Yes, he felt confident. It was a distinct possibility she could be there – unless some maniac had already abducted her. The serial killer that was still at large? Wixx could take him on if he had to. No problem.

He began to feel excited. There was a lightness in his chest and a feeling of exhilaration. He had a new purpose, the prospect of a million pounds and the chance to kill Daniel Kendrick. That would be more fun than the money, although a million would be enough to support his lifestyle as a serial killer. His greatest aspiration.

When he found Fay, and he would, he would isolate her from all that was dear to her. Then, she would belong to him – and he could do whatever the hell he wanted.

Isolate, devalue, abuse and discard. The psychopath's bond with his victim.

Now, all he had to do was find Otterbrook Lake.

SEVENTY-NINE

Friday 23rd August 2019

Daniel felt restless. He'd drawn a blank with the map and had to wait for Hayley Shepherd to get back to him with information on the police helicopter search. It would be a long evening and another night that Fay would be spending – goodness knows where. He was worried. Was she eating, sleeping? Was she warm enough? Did she miss him?

He missed her, despite the arguments and the accusations. Had she really left him without a word? She had been pretty upset that morning. He glanced over at the broken table lamp and his dented saxophone. She had been angry and troubled. Where would she go if she was so distressed? She'd gone to work – he'd seen her car parked near her clinic. Yet she had disappeared by the time her receptionist had arrived for work at 1 pm.

Where could she have gone? She hadn't contacted any of her friends – not even Shelly. She wouldn't have gone to Richard and Ginny's. Not with the indifference that hung between them. She obviously hadn't gone to her mother's either. Sloan had seen her somewhere near the tea rooms, he was convinced. She may well have gone there on her own. But why there? Daniel knew of nothing in that area that would interest Fay – unless it was something to do with research for her book on Biophilia. She'd not said much about it lately but it was a possibility. Her PC was still with the police Technical Support Team being investigated, so he couldn't access it from there. There was no sign of a printed copy in the house. Maybe he would mention it to DS Harper.

Where would she go if she felt upset?

Daniel remembered the hours that Fay spent in Sophie's nursery. What did she do in there? How could it possibly help her deal with the grief of losing a baby? He'd effectively shut down his emotions, unable to deal with any of it. The pain. The grief. It had been an unbearable loss. How can anyone get over or even begin to deal with the murder of your child?

Then there was Susan, his first wife, whom he'd adored. She had died so young, when she was full of life and had plans for the future – their future. He'd slipped into denial after her death too, he realised. He'd put so much love into caring for her through her cancer. When she died, he was left bereft and at the lowest point in his life. Richard had only been twelve-years-old when his mother had died. Daniel had forced himself to be a strong father for him. Yet, even a year after Susan's death, he couldn't reconcile the painful feelings he'd tried to bury. He had uprooted his son and moved to Riverbeke to try to escape from painful memories and make a new life for them both. Richard had adjusted, made new friends, done well at school but never forgave his father for the disruption he put him through. The grief of Susan's death had followed them both like a ghost wherever they went.

Fay had helped him to live again, even though Richard resented her. Now, Fay was gone too. Except she was alive.

Daniel poured himself a large glass of shiraz and wandered into the hall to look at a framed photograph of Fay with little

Sophie; just three months old when that picture had been taken. They had been to the park and she was wrapped up in a snuggly, fur fabric suit against the November chill. Fay was a beaming, happy mother; finally holding in her arms, the baby she had longed for. They didn't know it then, but little Sophie had already lived half of her tragically short life.

Daniel looked at the photograph for several minutes. What was it that Fay felt when she sat in Sophie's nursery? Could it give him some clue as to where she was? A sort of spiritual connection that would help him to understand her?

EIGHTY

Friday 23rd August 2019

Daniel knew it would open the floodgates to his grief if he went into Sophie's nursery. No more hiding behind his shallow friends, enjoying the attention of Melissa, taking the easy route by going into cosmetic surgery with Oliver Davenport. Yet, he wanted to understand Fay. To know what she was feeling and where her grief had taken her.

He had to face it.

He had to.

He walked back into the kitchen and poured another glass of wine, took the rest of the bottle with him and started up the stairs. Fay was right. He had barely looked into Sophie's nursery since she had been murdered. But now, the time felt right. He had to know.

He hesitated for several moments at the door, looking at the sign that read in swirly pink letters, 'Sophie's Room'. He felt his heart thumping and there was an emptiness in the pit of his stomach.

He cleared his throat and took several quick breaths. He had to do this.

He slowly turned the handle and opened the door. He flicked a switch that lit up the little lamps that Fay loved so much – one decorated with unicorns, a pink, glittery lamp and one with teddy bears. There was a fairy solar jar on the windowsill. The soft light gave the room a calming atmosphere and an innocent, child-like feel that he hadn't felt since before Sophie's death. He put the wine bottle down on a side-table and wandered around the room. He felt the soft, plush fabric of her little pink rabbit, trailed his fingers over the wardrobe that he had installed for her. Images of Fay's happy smile filled his mind along with the sound of Sophie's giggles when she was being tickled. He wasn't sure he could stay in there. He felt the weight of sorrow and a tightness in his chest that he couldn't shift.

Then he saw Sophie's changing mat. It triggered memories of he and Fay in fits of laughter when he changed Sophie's nappy for the first time and made a complete hash of it. On the table, he opened the music box that Shelly had given her as a present when she was born. The joyful sound of 'Twinkle Twinkle, Little Star' filled the room. He closed the lid, the sound stopped and a sad silence prevailed once more. He opened a drawer and his fingers squeezed the soft, delicately lacy pink cardigan that Emily had knitted for her.

Then he turned and looked at Sophie's cot, still made up with white flannelette cot sheets and a pink and white patchwork blanket. It felt almost as if Fay would soon be putting her to bed after her bath. The large, golden-brown teddy bear that he had bought for her lay with its head on the pillow. Its big shiny-black button eyes now looked up at the ceiling, sad and forlorn, as if he missed her too. He trailed a hand over the bars of the cot, delicately touched the fish-themed metallic mobile that hung above it, the light glinting on the sides of the silver fish as they twirled.

Daniel sat heavily on the rocking chair next to it. He could sense her in this room, remember the smell of her hair, the sweet fragrance of her baby-soft skin. He looked around the room, the gentle, soothing light casting shadows and highlighting her things with soft pools of light. He could almost hear Fay humming a lullaby and the sound of snuffles as their baby settled to sleep.

Sophie.

His beautiful baby daughter. He could deny her death no longer. He felt her presence here. She had been alive on this Earth and was part of him, of them. He glimpsed the connection that Fay had found in this room. The precious bond with their daughter that had been shattered forever by an act of pure, unadulterated violence. Anger started to simmer inside him at the brutal maniac that had killed their beautiful girl but Daniel fought it, as he had done so proficiently, for so long. He took a deep breath. He wanted to hold on to that new-found and sacred bond with their child.

He started rocking in the chair. Trying to soothe the guilt he felt for being alive when his baby was dead. To ease the painful longing that dragged at his heart, to hold his little girl again, to hear her laughter and loose himself in those innocent clear blue eyes. Sophie's eyes had seemed to shine with the wisdom of ages, masked behind a child-like wonder of the world around her. He sat and gently rocked in the chair that Fay had always used to nurse Sophie. He closed his eyes and fleetingly felt her presence there with him. Her soul had touched his and he felt a momentary peace.

Daniel had opened his heart and found a renewed connection to them both. To his family. To the two people that meant more to him than anything in the world. To the love that had kept them together.

He had to find Fay.

Suddenly the spell was broken as images of Fay, cold, alone, frightened and hungry filled his mind once more. He reached across to the cot and gently lifted the teddy bear from the pillow and held it tight to his chest, as if he was trying to hold onto Sophie's presence. But reality overwhelmed him. He began to feel the raw grief of her death, the barren emptiness of her not being there. He missed his baby daughter. How could he ever move beyond this? Sophie, his baby, was his life. Fay was his life. He couldn't bear to live without them.

Through a veil of tears, he looked at the three fine scars on his wrists. He hadn't been able to bear to live without Susan either. He took a big slug of wine. He couldn't sink that low again. He had to be strong as he'd been forced to be strong for his son. Fay was alive – he knew it. He felt it in his gut. He would find her and bring her home and they would talk it all through. They would accept Shelly's help of counselling and work to get their marriage back. He wouldn't let Sophie's death break them apart. Their lives had been full of love and laughter once and they would be again, if only she would come home.

EIGHTY-ONE

Friday 23rd August 2019

Daniel looked into Sophie's cot. He noticed something beneath the pillow. He reached in and pulled it out. It was a tattered and well-used A4 spiral notebook. He opened the cover and saw Fay's handwriting. He flicked through the rest of the book and it was filled with pages and pages of her handwriting. He closed it. He felt like an intruder. This was Fay's personal journal. She hadn't intended for him to see it. It would be wrong to read her personal notes. Wouldn't it? He placed it on his lap with a hand on top of it, as if he was stopping himself from opening it. He sat, rocking in the chair for several minutes. Yes. It would be wrong to read her journal.

And yet... it could give him valuable insights into Fay's state of mind, as the notes on her patients had helped his understanding. Perhaps it could even let him work out where she was. He sat for several minutes. Should he open Fay's journal? It would take him inside her mind – her deepest thoughts and feelings. It could lead him to her.

Like a drug taking control of his brain, he had to know.

He grabbed his wine, poured himself a large glass and began to read.

With every page he read, Daniel felt as if he was glimpsing into Fay's soul. The beginning pages were a harrowing insight to the rawness of her grief just days after Sophie's body was found.

23rd January 2018

My baby. My sweet, precious, wonderful Sophie.

How can you be gone? How can you not be in this world with me? I love you more than anything. More than life itself. Your daddy and I both love you so much.

God, this hurts! Please, God, please stop the pain – I can't bear it.

I can't put into words the empty feeling I have in the pit of my stomach, my darling, beautiful girl. The policewoman said they had found your body but it can't be true. It can't be. We're not allowed to see you but I want more than anything to be with you. I want to hold you in my arms and never let you go. My precious, precious girl. Will I never see your gorgeous smile again or rock you in this chair and sing to you until you fall asleep? Will I never again be able to feed you? My breasts hurt so much and are full of milk for you, my darling. You need to be here with us.

How can this be happening?

I can't believe that you've gone or that you will never wake up... ever.

My beautiful, innocent little baby, it's too much to take. Your daddy and me are heartbroken, my precious, precious girl. I love you – we love you so very much – and I can't believe we'll never see you again.

Daniel trailed a finger over the page. The blue ink was smudged from the tears Fay had cried over their dead baby. He felt the rawness of grief well up from deep inside. From a cold, desolate corner of his heart that he had locked away for so long.

Fay's words and being in Sophie's room, with all the memories of their little girl had brought back all those raw emotions in a flood of dreadful sorrow. He tasted the saltiness of his own tears on his face. Tears that drenched the cut on his cheek. A wound that had become a mark of the pain they had both gone through.

He wiped his tears with his sleeve and turned the page. Fay's journal entry was dated a week after Sophie's death.

28th January 2018

My darling Sophie,

We miss you so much my darling girl. All we want is to have you back with us. For us to have the life we were meant to have before that evil, depraved monster took you away from us.

I can't believe you have gone. I would do anything to have you back in my arms. I feel so empty but I can feel you in this room. I can never let that go. Your daddy won't come in here. He can't believe that you're never coming back. We miss you so much.

I'd do anything to have you home. I miss your smile and having you in my arms. My heart feels cold and empty without you here. Daddy is trying his best to comfort me and make things better for us both but nothing can get rid of the desolation I feel without you. I would give away everything I have – everything – to have you here with us again.

I'm so sad that you'll never get to live your life. That you'll never go to school, make friends, have a career or get married and have children of your own. Some evil, sadistic monster has deprived you of that. Of your life. The police are looking for the evil bastard that did this to you, my darling. I hope they find him and lock him up forever to rot in jail.

Dear God, please make this pain go away...

Daniel was sobbing as he read the harrowing words that Fay had written. She had poured out her heart and yet he had been oblivious to it. How could he have let her feel so desolate and alone. Why had he closed his heart to her – and to his own grief?

Daniel put the journal down. His body was wracked with sobs now, his head buried in the crook of his arm. He howled as a wave of raw grief overwhelmed him. He felt the full despair and the agony of Sophie's death as he had in the days after she had been murdered. In the days before he had locked his heart in cold denial.

Daniel looked up to see Ella sitting next to him, her big brown eyes brimming with sadness for him. He put his arms around her neck and sobbed into her soft fur. She sat patiently while he cried out his anguish. She placed a paw on his knee as if to comfort him.

"Ella, I've been such a damned fool. Why didn't I see Fay's pain?" He lifted his head up and looked into the dog's kind, loving eyes and kissed the top of her head. His lips lingered on her silky warm fur, drawing comfort from her. She put her chin on his lap and he smoothed her ears.

EIGHTY-TWO

Friday 23rd August 2019

Daniel picked up Fay's journal once more. He felt compelled to read on. The next entry was dated nearly a month after Sophie's death, 26th February 2018.

> *My darling Sophie,*
>
> *I'm so lost and unhappy without you. I still can't believe you're gone. The police still haven't found the monster that did this to you. The evil, depraved excuse for a human being that took your life. I ache to hold you in my arms. I need to see your beautiful eyes.*
>
> *To see the life in them.*
>
> *The throbbing loneliness is unbearable.*
>
> *God, please make it stop.*

Daniel read further entries – Fay pouring out the desperate emptiness she was feeling. He could sense that her heart was turning to anger. He remembered Shelly's words about the stages of grief and he could see a record before him of how Fay had worked through denial, bargaining, depression. Now anger was beginning to be the predominant emotion she was feeling. There was no acceptance. She was angry at the depraved murderer that had taken the life of their innocent little girl. He also saw in her entries, the increasing isolation she felt in their marriage. He felt the heat of shame as he realised, he hadn't been there for her. He had become stuck in denial and left the woman he loved in a desperate and lonely rage.

One entry, almost year after Sophie's death read:

Sophie, my sweet little girl,

I still miss you more than anything in the world. I wish you were still here in my arms.

I know your daddy misses you too but he has moved on. I miss him too. I miss the love we once had but he has closed his heart. The pain is too much for him to bear but I need him. I don't know what to do. I feel so empty and lonely and angry. There is no room for anything but rage at the monster that took you away from us and broke our hearts.

I know you are with the angels now.

I wish I was there with you...

Daniel felt a surge of guilt. Fay had been trying to reach out to him and he had hidden behind a barricade of fear and denial. How could he have been so closed off. He smoothed Ella's soft head and turned the page.

Darling Sophie,

I miss you, my sweetheart. I look at your photograph and remember the lovely times we spent together. I'm so sad that you're not here. That you had your life stolen from you. The police still haven't found the evil bastard that did this to you and I'm going out of my mind with rage. Justice must be done.

I hope they find him soon or I will go mad...

Daniel noticed Fay's writing had become more angular, larger and less structured. Her anger was visible in her handwriting. He remembered the anguish they had both felt at the lack of progress on the case. There were no suspects, yet they knew someone out there was guilty of murder. Surely someone knew something. Someone could have been harbouring a killer or at least suspected someone of the murder. Why hadn't they come forward?

They had been offered counselling but had turned it down. Daniel had wanted to hide away from it and get on with his life. Fay had become increasingly angry and distant. Her training as a psychiatrist could never have prepared her for the murder of her own child.

EIGHTY-THREE

Friday 23rd August 2019

There were more letters to Sophie in Fay's journal. All increasingly angry at the murderer that had taken their baby away. There was little now about anything else. He read an entry from over a month ago.

8th July 2019

Sophie, my darling girl,

I'm going out of my mind with rage and hatred for the monster that did this to you. I have to have justice for you – for us all. The police still can't find the murderer but he or she is out there somewhere. There are so many evil people in the world – people that are capable of taking the life of an innocent child

None of them deserve to live.

Daniel was beginning to feel distinctly uncomfortable. Fay's feelings of anger were unfamiliar to him. He grabbed his glass of wine and topped it up from the bottle. Ella had settled down to sleep on the carpet at his feet, unwilling to leave him. He remembered Fay becoming angrier over the past few months. It was difficult to have a conversation with her – even about mundane, everyday things – without her flying off in a temper.

10th July 2019

Beautiful Sophie,

I'm sure the person that took your life is out there and I am determined to find them. I can think of nothing else. I have to rid this world of the scum that infests it. I see them every day in my clinic. The evil, debauched excuses for human beings that take pleasure in hurting others. I can stand it no longer. If I perish in the process – so be it. We will be together again my darling.

But I must do this.

I must...

Daniel was almost afraid to read the next entry. A sense of foreboding washed over him.

13th July 2019

My sweet, innocent Sophie,

I have done it!

Last night I killed one of the evil monsters that might well have taken your life. He was a wretched, malicious criminal and didn't deserve to live.

I don't think anyone saw me. I made it look like suicide from an insulin overdose. It was easier that I thought to take the life of this miserable wretch.

It actually felt good.

He deserved everything he got. He was a heartless killer who had slaughtered several people. Kenneth Shaw did not deserve to live and now he can't hurt anyone else.

There are others out there, my darling.

One of them must surely be the one that took you from me...

Daniel felt the sickening realisation that Fay had murdered Kenneth Shaw. He looked around Sophie's room. The innocence, the normality of a child's bedroom was belying this brutal act of murder. First, their daughter – and now a ravaged act of revenge by his own wife. He rubbed his palm along the material of his trousers as if to rid himself of the horror of what he had just read.

He turned the page, his hand shaking with trepidation.

27th July 2019

Darling Sophie,

I am making progress in ridding the world of murderers and rapists and evil paedophiles. This evening I killed Robert Horton. I thought I had helped to put him behind bars for life but he has been released with a new identity – a privilege we are all paying for and which he doesn't deserve. He will kill again, I know he will. I can't let another mother suffer the harrowing torment of losing her baby to a vicious murderer.

It was harder this time. I crept up behind him and slashed his throat with a knife.

I think I will use drugs again in future...

Daniel was feeling sick. He could feel the burn of bile in the back of his throat. An uncomfortable shudder swept through his entire body, ending with a hard thudding in his chest from his increased heart rate. Fay Kendrick – his beautiful wife – was capable of murder.

Like a gruesome spectator at the scene of a car crash, he had to read on...

Sweet, innocent Sophie,

I have rid the world of another evil monster. Jack Butler. He raped and killed too many women and he could have killed you too, my darling. I can't bear to think of it.

At least now there is some justice being done. The police still haven't made any progress in finding the evil bastard that took you from me. But I will find him and kill him, if I have to kill all the murderers in the world.

I love you my darling…

Daniel was horrified. He took a deep breath in an effort to control the shocking turmoil of emotions he was feeling. He drained his wine glass, trying to steady his fluttering heartbeat.

He could see that Fay had widened her scope to kill people on behalf of other mothers. Where would it end? She had been possessed of a madness, driven by revenge. Why hadn't he seen it. He thought all her anger had been directed at him but now he could see their rows were just a symptom of a much more harrowing reality.

A cold chill shivered through him as he turned the page. It was the last entry.

13th August 2019

Sweet, innocent Sophie,

I have killed again. I looked into Paula Bishop's black eyes and killed her. She was evil and depraved – a convicted paedophile.

She didn't deserve to live a moment longer.

She would have hurt and killed another child in time, including her own. The baby she had just given birth to.

What sort of evil monster would do such a thing?

It was easy, my darling – so simple to steel drugs from the hospital and use them to rid the world of evil.

There are more murderers out there, my beautiful girl.

I have to find and kill the one that took you from us. I can never rest until that is done...

Daniel was stunned. His breathing was fast and he could feel his heart thudding in his chest. His eyes recoiled from the page – from Fay's handwriting.

From her confession of murder.

His head shook slowly back and forth in a sweep of denial. His wife – a killer?

He looked back at Fay's journal. Reread the words to confirm it was true.

His blood had turned icy-cold. It was undeniably true. She had written those words. He knew those people were dead. Had heard their names on the news. Had heard Shelly tell him they were dead.

He closed the journal and placed it on the floor.

What the hell was he supposed to do with this? How could he ever come to terms with the fact that his wife was a killer. She had become a vigilante that had taken it upon herself, in her grief, to kill.

Fay was the serial killer that the police were looking for.

What the bloody hell was he supposed to do now?

EIGHTY-FOUR

Friday 23rd August 2019

Damon Wixx drove back to his uncle's bungalow with Fay's manuscript and fired up his laptop. He did a Google search for 'Otterbrook Lake, Riverbeke'. Nothing relevant came up. He tried a more general search, 'Lakes around Riverbeke'. A few lakes came up but none named Otterbrook. It would be an impossible wild goose chase trying to find them all on the off-chance Fay was there. And a waste of his time. He slammed the lid of his laptop.

He'd drawn a blank.

Then he remembered he'd seen some maps tucked into the book case in the hall. He rummaged among the books – mainly war memoirs, Agatha Christie novels and antique guides – and found an OS Landranger map of Riverbeke and the surrounding countryside. It was worth a look at least.

He spread the map out on the kitchen table, flicked on the overhead fluorescent light and found his uncle's magnifying glass, which he used to hunt out 'Otterbrook Lake'. After an hour of searching, he gave up. He'd covered practically the whole map but there was no lake called Otterbrook. There were several large lakes, a reservoir and plenty of rivers and streams but he couldn't find what he was looking for. He hurled the magnifying glass across the room in a flash of temper and it hit the floor, shattering in three places.

What now?

Wixx went to the fridge and cracked open a beer. He took a gulp, then another and belched loudly. He grabbed a half-eaten Cornish pasty and wandered out into the garden trying to calm his rambling, restless mind. He looked up at the stars that were beginning to reveal themselves as evening turned to night. He sensed the immensity of the sky above him but felt nothing of the spiritual human connection to the universe or of any deeper meaning to life. His soul, like much of the vastness of the cosmos, was occupied by a dark void.

Wixx sat on his uncle's bench, next to a raised bed filled with old fashioned fragrant roses. The warm evening breeze played over his skin. He finished his pasty and rolled a joint, blowing smoke into the evening air and watching it swirl upwards as it caught the diffused light coming from the living room window.

He glanced at the roses and remembered Fay's delicate features, the kindness of her words. She had been the only person in his life that had shown him any compassion. Even his mother – his own flesh and blood – had abandoned him. Why, he pondered, with emotionless logic, would a mother abandon her new-born baby? Now she had rejected him for a second time. So be it. He would find solace elsewhere. Fay was now the object of his attention. Soon, he would be solvent and in possession of a bright, attractive woman. She would entertain him until he had no further use for her.

He thought of Daniel and felt a surge of resentment and contempt for the man that had all that he wanted. Fay. The surgeon had to die. He stroked the two death-head moth tattoos on his wrist. Soon, there would be another.

But first he needed to find Fay. All he had to go on was her manuscript and a mention of Otterbrook Lake, but in reality, that was a shot in the dark. He was deluding himself.

Maybe he should reconsider his other options. Manipulate Daniel into handing over the cash and forget about finding Fay? Despite his obsession with her, he knew she would be a temporary amusement and dispensable.

Kill Daniel for the hell of it and just take the money? Risky, since he wasn't even sure Daniel had gathered the money together in cash yet. He had said something about needing Fay's permission to cash in a chunk of it. Maybe it would be worth settling for less to have the pleasure of getting his hands around Daniel Kendrick's throat and crushing the life out of him.

But Wixx wanted it all and was loathed to compromise. Compromise wasn't part of his psyche. He truly believed he was a superior being to the rest of humanity and he deserved to get all that he wanted. Whatever it was – money, another man's wife or the satisfaction of killing.

Wixx watched the smoke from his joint swirl into the air and decided that, on reflection, manipulating Daniel to get the money could be the answer. He would insist on speaking to Fay but if he showed him who was boss, he could get around that.

The incident with the old man, David Jones, had been fun and it had put him in control. All he had to do was find someone else the doctor cared about and threaten them – or better still, actually hurt them. That would send a powerful message to Daniel – don't mess with me or your wife will get the same treatment.

Yes, that's what he'd do. But who did Daniel care about enough to make his plan work? He knew Daniel had a son but he had no idea where he lived. It would be far too much trouble trying to track him down. He may as well keep looking for Fay. Fay's mother? He didn't know where he could find her either and to be honest, where was the challenge in taking down an old lady?

Then he came up with the solution. Shelly Winters. Dr Shelly Winters – colleague of Fay's and, by the look of their cosy meeting the other night in the Red Lion, she was a good friend of Daniel's too. Maybe more than a friend.

Shelly.

He might also be able to score some bonus points. If he ever did find Fay, he could use the attack on Shelly to manipulate her too.

Where would he find Shelly Winters? If he remembered correctly, from what Fay had said, she ran a group therapy session at her clinic on a Saturday morning. She had encouraged him to join but there was no way he was going to sit there listening to all those crazy psychos bleating on about their miserable, good for nothing lives.

Tomorrow morning.

Wixx smiled, drained his beer and cracked open another. He was looking forward to his Saturday morning for a change.

EIGHTY-FIVE

Saturday 24th August 2019

Daniel had stayed up late into the night, unable to reconcile the alarming realisation that Fay had killed four people. He had finally drunk enough whisky to knock him out and had let the dogs and Maisie sleep on the bed. It had been more for his benefit than theirs. He needed their company.

But already he was beginning to regret it. He had woken trapped under the duvet, with Chester spread out beside him, his head on the pillow, legs outstretched with paws hanging over the edge, yet still taking up half the bed. He couldn't feel his feet and craned his neck to see Ella lying across his legs, cutting off the circulation in his feet. He looked behind him to see Maisie sat on the bedside table coldly observing them all, her paws neatly placed together beneath her coiled tail, the bandage abandoned somewhere around the house. She mouthed a silent meow as if to tell him it was high time she was served her breakfast.

Daniel groaned, pulled his legs from beneath Ella's considerable weight and flopped back onto the pillow. His head hurt, his mouth was as parched as the dust of the Kalahari

Desert and pins and needles were starting to stab in his feet. He glanced at the time on his novelty alarm clock. It was shaped like a stick of dynamite with an attached bomb, that showed the clock face. It told him it was 9 am. He'd slept late.

"Come on you lot, let me get up," Daniel said to no response.

Chester was snoring, oblivious to the world and Ella simply opened one eye and watched him intently from where she lay. He manoeuvred himself from beneath Ella, groaning as he sat on the side of the bed, rubbing his hands over his face. The cut on his cheek was starting to scab over and he wandered into the bathroom. He looked at his reflection in the mirror, groaned again at his puffy, bloodshot eyes and gently peeled away the SteriStrips that had been holding the wound together. It was healing reasonably well but would leave a scar. He took a shower, letting the warm water flow over his head and down his back, reviving his dulled senses. The revelations of last night seemed surreal in the cold light of day.

He brushed his teeth, then slurped cold water from the tap. He combed his hair and shaved with an electric razor as he wandered back into the bedroom. The dogs had barely moved but Maisie had gone downstairs. He heard the cat flap snap shut – she'd either just gone out or come back in.

He picked out a pair of SpongeBob SquarePants boxers that Fay had given him a few birthdays ago and pulled on denim jeans and threaded a wide, hand-studded leather belt through. Then he pulled on his favourite powder blue T-shirt with the PQRST trace of a heart beat running along the chest.

He called the dogs and they dutifully followed him downstairs. He opened the kitchen door and the two of them bounded up the garden. Chester bent into a play bow and Ella mirrored him, her soggy toy, Eddie, in her mouth. The two dogs leapt around on the lawn while Daniel fed Maisie, changed her water and made himself some toast with lashings of butter and strong instant coffee with cream.

His mind was numb as he finished his breakfast. It was as if the horror of the revelations in Fay's journal had created a stunned inertia in his brain. He had to get out for a walk and get some fresh air into his lungs. He had to think.

He called the dogs, grabbed their leads, his iPhone and the burner, then locked the kitchen door. They walked around the side of the house, past the row of detached houses to the kissing gate that led into acres of farms and woodland beyond. There had been no sign of Jane, the nosey neighbour that had helped Melissa with her viscous lies. He didn't care if he ever saw her again.

They reached the woodland. The dogs twisted their bodies around the metal gate and went bounding along the woodland path. Ella barked at a squirrel but knew better than to chase it.

Daniel walked at a fast pace and took deep breaths of clean, country air. He could smell a mix of moss and soil, with the delicate scents of woodland flowers – foxglove, red campion, ox-eye daisy and an abundance of honeysuckle in the hedgerows. There were patches of lilac buddleia laden with butterflies and bees and he could hear the drone of insects as they darted from flower to flower. The path skirted the edge of a mixed woodland with farmland to the left. The fields were dotted with sheep and cattle – a landscape washed in sunshine.

It seemed like a world away from Fay's letters to Sophie in her journal. He now understood, with more clarity, her grief and the path to anger that her mind had taken – but to kill. That was a horrifying and truly disturbing revelation. It was as if, in her grief, she had suffered some sort of breakdown. She certainly wasn't acting like the woman he knew and loved. It explained her increasing irritation with him over recent months and the way she had lashed out at him the other morning. It was a symptom of the far deeper anger that was festering beneath the surface.

Chester lolloped toward Daniel with a huge stick in his mouth. He placed it at his feet and Daniel picked it up and threw it for him. Ella leapt out from behind a tree and they both chased after it, carrying it together along the path for a while until something else caught their attention and it was abandoned. Daniel smiled at their antics. A few years ago, he and Fay had loved their walks up here on the weekends. They had talked about their future together and after Sophie had been born, they walked for miles with her in a baby carrier and the dogs running free. They had been a normal and very happy family. Now, their lives were in tatters.

Daniel began to wonder what he should do. He could understand Fay's anger and could even forgive her outbursts at him now he recognised how deeply her grief had tormented her. But to take human life was another matter. He had worked throughout his career to save lives and uphold the Hippocratic oath to do no harm. How could he reconcile that with the fact that his wife was a murderer?

Yet, he still loved her. He'd married Fay for better or worse, sickness or health and he couldn't simply switch off his love like turning off a tap.

Sickness or health.

Fay had surely been suffering some sort of mental breakdown to be driven to such lengths.

If he ever found Fay, what should he do? Would he be able to persuade her to turn herself in to the police? Was that the right thing to do? Hadn't she suffered enough? Her baby had been abducted and murdered in cold blood. Wouldn't that make anyone go out of their mind with rage? Yet, four people were dead because of her. Didn't they deserve to live out their lives, whatever judgements society or individuals made about the way they behaved? They had been killers too, but was it right to punish them with death? Two wrongs didn't make a right. Hadn't we abandoned capital punishment in Britain and many other countries around the world because it had become unacceptable to society?

Daniel's mind was spinning with questions and uncertainties. All he knew was that he loved Fay and had to find her. He realised that he would never be able to hide away from this. He'd tried to do that after Sophie's death but he knew it was never going to go away. The demons would follow wherever he went.

His iPhone rang and he felt it vibrate in his pocket. He looked at the screen. It was Shelly.

"Daniel. Got time for a chat? I have a clinic to run in an hour but I could come over. I'm literally five minutes away."

"Sure, I'm in the woodland with the dogs. Come up for a walk."

"Sounds perfect." Shelly ended the call.

Daniel wondered if he should tell Shelly about Fay's journal. Would it help to find her? Would it change anything? It would certainly change the women's friendship.

Maybe it would be better to keep it to himself. He couldn't see how it would help to tell Shelly about this except to give himself an opportunity to unburden. He owed it to Fay to keep her secret.

He slowed his pace, allowing Shelly to catch up. He tried to focus on finding Fay. Trying to work out where she was. Yet his mind was drawn constantly to the fact that his wife had been capable of taking a life when pushed to the absolute limits of endurance.

Behind him, he could hear footsteps running toward him. He stopped and turned to see Shelly slowing to a walk.

"Daniel," she said breathlessly.

"Everything alright?" Daniel asked.

She drew level with him and he kissed her cheek. She smelled of coconut shampoo with a hint of freshly washed linen. They walked side by side as the dogs ran and played together up ahead.

Daniel suddenly felt awkward. He was unsure what to say as his mind fought to suppress the revelations about Fay that were saturating his mind. He tried to rewind to their last conversation from yesterday.

Shelly broke the silence. "I managed to get a list of the patients in Fay's group therapy sessions." She pulled out a piece of paper from her jacket pocket and looked at the list. "There are over thirty patients in the last two years. I only know a few of them and I can't really say whether they would have a reason to harm Fay or abduct her."

"Or if they had, where they might have taken her," Daniel added.

"Exactly."

Daniel walked slowly, studying the sheep in the field and struggling to know what to say.

Shelly broke the silence again. "One thing I noticed is that two of her group therapy patients are both dead. Victims of the serial killer."

"Is that significant?" Daniel asked, feeling distinctly uncomfortable. He kept his head lowered and focused on the path ahead.

"Just an observation, I guess. I hope it doesn't mean that Fay is in danger from him too." Shelly handed Daniel the list.

Daniel's mind was numb as her words hung in the air.

They walked in companionable silence for some minutes, while Daniel looked through the list. He felt his heart beat faster as he read the names Jack Butler and Kenneth Shaw. They were just two of Fay's victims. His wife had killed them both. Jack Butler because he was a dangerous rapist and killer and Kenneth Shaw because he'd murdered several people. The other names became a blur as the confessions in Fay's journal loomed in his mind.

He tried to compose himself. He owed it to Fay to keep her secret, although it would have been so easy to tell Shelly – to share the weight of what he knew. To seek her advice. He fought the urge to blurt it out.

"Doesn't mean anything to me," Daniel lied. He pocketed the list and threw a stick for Chester.

"Any other ideas?" Shelly asked.

Daniel suddenly remembered the events of yesterday and felt a surge of relief. "I called Hayley Shepherd from the Argus. She thinks she can get some information from the police helicopter footage during the search for Jaxon Sloan."

"Did you ask DS Harper about it?"

"I did. He said he would look into it but I doubt they will involve me. I'm sure they think I've interfered enough in the investigation."

"Surely, they don't still see you as suspect?" Shelly said indignantly.

"Who knows," Daniel said, "I just get the feeling I need to do this myself." He finally looked at Shelly.

She nodded pensively. "I just hope we can find her before Wixx does."

"Me too. He's gone quiet but I have the feeling he's up to something."

"Yes, for sure. He won't give up now. He's a psychopath. He needs stimulation and excitement. The thrill of the chase. He will pursue whatever it is he wants ruthlessly and callously," Shelly explained.

"The money?"

"Yes, his parasitic lifestyle means he will exploit others mercilessly for his own gain and he is a master of deceit. But he may also be obsessed with Fay and angry that she has – in his delusional mind – escaped from him."

"I can't bear to think what he could do to Fay if he finds her before I do. What if I can't find her? I have to stop him getting to her first." He realised he may have to take on Wixx before he could even begin to look for his wife.

"Be careful, Daniel. He will be impulsive and unable to resist momentary urges or temptations – whatever they are."

Had Fay given in to a momentary urge to kill, or had she planned it? Daniel wondered as Shelly went on.

"He will be reckless, unpredictable and act without considering the consequences. He's a very dangerous individual, Daniel. Stay away from him."

"But if I can stop him –"

"How are you going to stop him? He is very likely to attack you and is capable of anything – even murder – with no controls on his behaviour. And think of it like this. If you get into more trouble with the police and end up back in custody, you're useless to Fay." Shelly sounded adamant.

Daniel needed time to think – the one thing he didn't have. Maybe it was time to come clean with the police about Wixx. The problem was, it could expose Fay and risk the police finding out about the murders. Daniel felt torn but he knew one thing. He had to get to Fay and quickly.

"You seem quiet today, Daniel. Are you OK?" Shelly turned to look at him, her eyes brimming with concern.

She was perceptive. Yet he couldn't tell her the awful truth. "I just miss Fay."

Shelly touched his arm. "You know, Daniel, whatever challenges you face with this – whatever is pulling you two apart – you will find a way back to each other. I'm sure of it." She smiled at him as if she sensed his private turmoil.

Daniel returned her smile and nodded. There was one hell of a challenge up ahead and he wasn't sure how on earth they were going to face it. What if there was no way back from it?

Shelly's mobile rang. She looked at the screen. "Sorry, I have to take this."

Daniel nodded and threw a stick into the woodland for Ella.

Shelly listened for a few moments before she spoke. "I'm on my way," Shelly said and hung up. "I have to go, Daniel. One of my patients needs to be sectioned urgently and then I have my group therapy session to run. No peace for the wicked!"

Shelly kissed Daniel on the cheek, close to the scar that was still healing. "Don't give up, Daniel. With love and patience, nothing is impossible. We'll find Fay. We will."

Daniel gave Shelly a half-hearted smile. He watched as she ran back along the path.

Shelly's words lingered in his mind. 'Whatever is pulling you apart – you will find a way back to each other.'

Could that be true? Even if he found her, could their souls find a way back to one another, even though Sophie's death had wrenched them apart? And now, the cold, hard fact that Fay had killed four people – how could they ever find a way back from that?

Daniel stood and took in the quiet stillness of the woodland and the vast openness of the fields as they rolled away into the distance. The sunlight speckled through the leaves of the trees and warmed his body. A chiffchaff called from a high branch. A moment of tranquillity. A moment of contemplation. He longed to stay there. To hide away from all that was happening in his life, to pretend that none of it was true – that it had all been some horrific nightmare. But it wasn't a dream. He knew it would never go away. It would always eat away at his soul, as Sophie's death had done. As Susan's death had done.

How could he hide from something that would always be there?

Daniel remembered a quote embroidered in cross-stitch that Fay had framed and put up on the wall in Sophie's nursery.

'There comes a point in your life when you realise who really matters, who never did and who always will.'

Daniel knew in that moment of stillness that Fay would always matter to him. He loved her deeply and he knew that whatever she had done, he would always love her. That would never go away.

Somehow, whatever challenges they would face ahead, he knew they would find a way back to each other.

EIGHTY-SIX

Saturday 24th August 2019

Daniel had called Hayley Shepherd on the walk back to the house. She said she might have something for him from the police footage and that she would call back in the next hour.

He fed Chester and Ella in the Dog House and now they were settling down in their favourite places in the living room. Chester on his sofa and Ella on the rug. Maisie was curled up in her cat hammock, clipped onto the radiator, with one fluffy paw sticking out. Above her on the wall was a framed picture, cross-stitched with the words, 'Angels don't always have wings – sometimes they have whiskers.'

Daniel wandered around, checking both his iPhone for Hayley's call and the burner for Wixx. There had been a text from Fay's mother, Emily. He texted back.

No news yet. Hope you're alright.

She didn't reply.

Daniel tidied the kitchen, loaded the dishwasher and opened the mail. There were a few bills and a letter from the bank confirming the increase on his mortgage and the loan against the car. The money had been transferred to his account.

He checked the time on the backward clock on the wall that they had received as a wedding present from one of Daniel's aunts. He worked out that it was 10.35 am.

He wandered into the living room and picked up his saxophone from the stand in the corner. He ran a finger over the dent made by the tiffany lamp. He realised he hadn't played for over a week. He wet the reed and attached it to the mouthpiece, slipped the strap around his neck and perched on the edge of the armchair. He felt the familiar weight of the instrument and placed his fingers easily over the keys. He began to play, the sound powerful and intense. He played the scale of 'C Major' a couple of times, then went into his favourite saxophone riff, 'Your Latest Trick,' from the Brothers in Arms album by Dire Straits. The rich, throaty sound of the alto sax filled the room and soothed his anxious mind. Although out of context, the words of the chorus seemed apt as he played.

'I don't know how it happened
It all took place so quick
But all I can do, is hand it to you
And your latest trick'

He got to the end of the riff and played it again, lost in the music and appreciating the short respite it gave him.

He felt his iPhone vibrate in his pocket and stopped playing. He slipped the strap from his neck and placed the saxophone on the chair next to him before answering the call. It was Hayley Shepherd.

"Dr Kendrick. My contact has been through the police footage and Sloan was seen on foot, coming out of some woodland north of the river. He stole a car from a farmhouse and picked up the Catsash road. They followed him from there to the bypass where he was stopped. You know the rest."

"Was there any sign of Fay?" Daniel asked. He was up and pacing the room now.

"No. I'm sorry. There was no sign of another person."

"Can you describe exactly where they saw him coming out of the woods?"

"Yes, I have the map coordinates here."

Daniel sighed with relief. It was something. Hayley gave him the latitude and longitude and he wrote them down on the back of an envelope.

"So, will you give me that interview now?" Hayley asked.

"I will but not this minute. Can I call you next week? I have to find my wife, urgently. I'm sure you'll understand."

There was a momentary hesitation before Hayley answered. "Yes, of course. I understand. Let's speak next week."

Daniel thanked her and ended the call.

He raced into the kitchen and spread the OS Landranger map out on the table, found the latitude and longitude and traced his index fingers to the place where Sloan had been seen on foot. It was north west of the river and a couple of miles west of the Hallbrook Manor tea rooms. There was a small, unnamed lake surrounded by acres of mixed woodland and a small orchard. It looked like private land. There were no houses for several miles but there was a single-track lane leading to the woodland that led off from a winding 'B' road. He could get to it from the main road that tracked north from Riverbeke. He noted down a couple of landmarks on the envelope. He was confident he could find it. But was Fay there? All he knew was that Sloan had seen her and it must have been before the police search helicopter had spotted him.

Daniel thought for a moment, trying to control his mounting excitement. He could get there in less than an hour. What would he need to take with him? Fay could be cold and hungry. He ran upstairs and grabbed a thick sweater and a blanket, grabbed a sweater for himself, ran downstairs, three at a time and threw them by the front door. Then he went into the kitchen and grabbed some breakfast bars from the cupboard, a bag of nuts, a bottle of water from the fridge and a couple of bananas from the fruit bowl. He pushed them into a carrier bag and put them with the rest of the things by the door. Then he got Chester and Ella out into the Dog House and settled them in their beds. If he was longer than a couple of hours, he could call Rosie to pick them up for him.

Thinking of calls, he decided to call Shelly. She would want to know that he'd made some progress in finding Fay. At least, he hoped it would be progress. He found her number and called. It rang five times then went to voicemail. He left a message.

"Shelly. It's Daniel. The police footage shows Sloan coming out of a privately owned woodland north west of the river. I think that's where Fay might be. It's almost 11.30 am and I'm on my way there now. I'll call you later." He gave her the map coordinates and pocketed his iPhone. He checked the burner. Still nothing from Wixx.

He hoped more than anything he could get to Fay before he did.

EIGHTY-SEVEN

Saturday 24th August 2019

Wixx began gathering a selection of weapons. One of his uncle's Japanese Tanto daggers, a length of rope for strangulation purposes and a forged steel twelve-inch wrench. He would decide on the method of attack during the drive to the hospital, although he was leaning toward the dagger – he thought it rather exotic. He threw them under a coat on the back seat of the Jaguar and began the drive to Riverbeke General Hospital. Shelly Winters would be finishing up her group therapy session soon, he thought.

Then he would strike.

Wixx had been fantasising about the money. A million pounds. He could never have dreamed of having that sort of cash when he'd been growing up in care homes. He should have asked for more. If Daniel Kendrick wanted his wife back in one piece, a resourceful man like that would find a way to get it. He'd show Daniel what he was capable of with an intimidating display of power. Shelly Winters would be an easy enough target if he could get her on her own.

He eased his uncle's Jaguar through the town. Saturday mornings were always busy in Riverbeke. The town was teeming with shoppers and many of the roads were blocked off with the weekend outdoor market. He was growing impatient and blasted his horn at a cyclist, then swore at an elderly gentleman that was crossing the street. He cursed and cussed his way along the main road as his irritation reached bursting point. Then he accelerated through a traffic light that had just turned red and was forced to swerve around a stream of traffic coming from his right. Someone blasted a horn at him and he blasted back.

Finally, Wixx arrived and parked at the hospital. He reached for the dagger, concealing it in a long inside pocket of his jacket. He locked the car and strode over to the front entrance. The concourse of the hospital was fairly quiet on the weekend and he glanced around furtively, checking there was nobody around that would recognise him. He saw only strangers.

He took the lift then walked the length of the corridor to the new psychiatric wing. The place was deserted. He heard voices coming from a room ahead and to his right. The door was ajar as he slowly crept past, craning his neck to look inside. He could see a group of about six people sat in hard-backed chairs in a semicircle inside a large meeting room. Then he saw Dr Winters. She was leading the therapy group. He listened in for a few minutes, then it seemed as if the session was coming to a close as she asked if there were any final comments. No one spoke and he heard her wrap it up and dismiss the group.

Wixx scuttled down the corridor and stood near a stairwell. He hid behind a wall. He heard footsteps and voices recede down the corridor in the opposite direction. Then he peered around the corner to see Shelly walk to the other side of the corridor and disappear into her office. He didn't hear the door close but heard her voice and that of a man. He couldn't make out what they were saying.

Then he crept slowly back down the corridor toward Shelly's office. He hid inside the doorway of the meeting room and could see Shelly's back from his vantage point. A tall man was walking back and forth to the window. Then Shelly picked up her phone, tapped a couple of keys and listened for a few moments.

Then she spoke, sounding very animated. "Doug, it's Daniel. He thinks he may have found Fay. He just left me a message."

"Excellent. Let's hope so."

"Apparently, they saw Sloan coming out of a woodland north of the river. He said he'll call later."

"Well, fingers crossed then."

Wixx saw the man kiss Shelly. "I'll see you at home in an hour or so, then, love," he said. He started walking toward the door.

Wixx stepped back into the shadow of the room. He could hear the rustle of the man's clothing as he walked out of the office. Then the echo of his footsteps as they receded down the corridor toward the lift. He stood still and silent as he listened for the lift doors to open and close. Then, moments later, the whirring of the lift as it descended. He waited a few moments, then peered through the doorway and checked the corridor in both directions. It was deserted. Wixx pulled a pair of black driving gloves from his pocket and slipped them on, flexing his fingers inside the soft leather.

He could hear the *tap tap tap* of computer keys as Wixx inched toward the door of Shelly's office. He reached into his pocket, pulled out the dagger and turned its handle in his hand, ready to strike. He crept into the office and closed the door behind him.

Shelly didn't look up. "Did you forget something darling?" she asked, hitting a sequence of keys.

"Only how beautiful you are," Wixx said. He stood there in her office, smirking; the dagger now held low and out of sight.

Shelly startled and looked at Wixx. She quickly closed the lid of her laptop and gripped the edge of her desk. "What... what are you doing here?" Her voice was faltering.

"Well now... it sounds like you have some news. About the lovely Fay Kendrick. Where did you say she was? North of the river?" Wixx let his eyes roam over Shelly's body. She was an attractive woman for her age.

"You know I won't tell you. Now get out of my office or I'll call security."

Shelly was trying to sound firm and in control but Wixx could see through the pretence. He simply smiled.

Shelly reached for the landline on her desk. "You'd better get out of here now, Mr Wixx".

Wixx pounced on her, grabbing her wrist roughly with his left hand, the dagger still held low in the right. "Now, don't be foolish. We both know you aren't going to call security." He released her wrist but brought her hand to his lips and kissed her fingers gently. His face was intimidatingly close to hers. He could detect the faint smell of coconut in her hair.

Shelly pulled her hand away from his gloved fingers. "Don't touch me."

Damon loomed closer, his face inches from hers. He could see the fear in Shelly's eyes. He relished the blissful feeling it gave him to see that. "Now, are you going to give me the map reference?"

"No, never. Just get out or I'll scream."

"Dr Winters. We both know that you are going to tell me." He looked deeply into her eyes with the predatory stare of a psychopath. He was well aware of how it unsettled people.

Shelly shook her head vigorously. "Not a chance. Now get out, Wixx".

Damon pulled up the dagger, the point inches from her face, the blade glinting in the light. "Perhaps this will persuade you?"

Shelly sat motionless, her eyes darting between the blade of the dagger and Wixx's eyes.

For long moments they froze. Damon was relishing the power he was wielding over the psychiatrist. The warm feeling of validation it gave him. Soon, he would have control of Fay too.

"No?" Wixx tilted his head. His smile stopped short of his eyes. "Well, let's see what Daniel has to say, shall we?" He stood, the dagger still pointed at Shelly, and tapped into her mobile phone. He accessed her voicemail and listened. Then he picked up a pen and a scrap of paper from her desk, wrote down the map coordinates and pocketed the note.

"You won't get away with this," Shelly said. Her voice now shaking with anger.

"That's where you're wrong," Wixx said. He stepped around to the other side of the desk, dagger still pointing at Shelly's face. She was following him with her eyes.

"I'll call the police. You won't get anywhere near Fay," she said.

"Is that right?" Damon smirked again. Then snapped his head toward her, the steel blade of the dagger was glinting as he wielded it close to her throat. "If I cut your throat, you wouldn't be in a position to call anyone. Is that what you want?" His voice was disturbingly calm.

Shelly looked frozen with fear but managed to shake her head slightly. She was gripping the sides of the chair, trying to squirm backwards away from the blade.

Wixx was aware that time was slipping by and that Daniel was already on his way to the lake. It was a shame but he would have to cut short his little predatory game.

Wixx stood, then suddenly grabbed Shelly roughly by the arm. He yanked her from the chair, twisted her around and pushed her face against the wall behind the desk. She cried out but he brought the dagger back and thrust it hard into her side, then pulled back and stabbed her a second time. Blood rapidly soaked the material of her dress as she slid down the wall and collapsed into a heap.

Wixx grinned, slowly wiped the blood from the blade with a handkerchief and returned the dagger to the inside pocket of his jacket. He looked at Shelly. She was motionless.

He grabbed a chocolate bar from Shelly's desk, unwrapped it and bit into it as he strolled back out into the corridor.

EIGHTY-EIGHT

Saturday 24th August 2019

Daniel put on some old walking boots, locked the back door, grabbed the map, his car keys and the stuff he'd gathered together for Fay. He double-checked the front door was locked and threw the things into the boot of his BMW.

He was feeling fired up with renewed energy and hope as he drove toward Riverbeke. Shelly had been right. Whatever challenges he and Fay would face – they would find a way back to each other.

His iPhone rang. He glanced over to see Shelly's number showing on the screen. He pulled over and answered.

"Daniel…" Shelly sounded breathless; her voice weak, as if she could barely speak.

"Shelly, what's the matter. Where are you?"

"My… office. Wixx… stabbed me," her voice was fading and broken.

"Oh my God. Have you called for help?" Daniel felt his heart thumping.

Shelly mumbled something incoherent. He couldn't make out what it was.

"I'll be right there, Shelly. Just hold on."

"No… wait. Wixx…" Shelly's voice was barely audible.

The phone went dead.

"Shit."

Daniel knew he had to get to Shelly. If she had been stabbed, she would have massive internal bleeding. He was a surgeon. His instincts were to save life. He owed it to her to do all he could to save her. He couldn't just leave her now – bleeding to death in her office.

Daniel called the A&E Department that was just a few blocks away in the old part of the hospital. It would be quicker than calling 999. They said they were on their way. He turned the car around and raced back toward the hospital. The traffic was heavy and slow going but he managed to take a short-cut down a side street and made it to the hospital within ten minutes. He parked and sprinted to the A&E Department. He looked around frantically, checking each cubicle, searching for Shelly. Then he saw her being wheeled into one of the large bays in the resuscitation area. He ran over to her.

"Shelly? Shelly, are you alright?" He was frantic.

She looked up at him, her blue eyes dark with fear and pain. An oxygen mask covered her nose and mouth but he could just make out what she was saying.

"OK… I'll be… alright."

He held her hand as an SHO and three nurses settled her into the cubicle, hooking up the mainline oxygen, attaching electrodes to her chest and setting up an intravenous infusion.

She reached up and feebly pulled the oxygen mask down from her face. She tried to speak. "Wixx… he…"

"Don't try to talk, Shelly. Just rest." Daniel replaced the mask over her nose and mouth.

Daniel turned to the SHO, who he knew slightly. "What's the damage?"

"Looks like a laceration to the right kidney but we'll have to do a laparotomy," the doctor said.

Daniel knew Shelly could lose her kidney if the damage was too extensive to repair. He felt responsible and anxious. Shelly could easily have been killed.

Just then Doug came racing into the cubicle. "Darling. Oh my God, what the hell happened?"

Daniel looked up to see a frightened man, beside himself with worry. He reached a hand toward him. "Doug, Shelly was stabbed in her office."

"Stabbed? What the hell do you mean? Who stabbed her?" Doug's eyes were wild and searching Shelly's face. He reached out to touch her.

"It was Damon Wixx." Daniel said quietly.

"What? That damned scumbag. How the blazes did this happen?" He shot an accusing look at Daniel.

"I don't know the details, I'm sorry," Daniel said as gently as he could.

Doug spun around to face Daniel, his full height suddenly baring down on him. "This is your fault, Daniel bloody Kendrick. Your fault. Why the hell did you involve my wife in all this?" His eyes were dark and angry.

Daniel felt a stab of shame. He had asked Shelly for help and now she was seriously injured because of him. "I... I'm so sorry." It was all he could say.

Doug turned back to Shelly, tying to soothe her. "It's alright, darling. It will be alright."

Shelly pulled the mask from her face again and reached toward Daniel. He took her hand.

"Wixx... he... he knows... listened to your... message." Her voice was barely a whisper.

Daniel looked at Doug and back to Shelly. "What do you mean? That he knows the map coordinates I gave you?"

Shelly nodded as Doug replaced the oxygen mask.

Shit. Wixx could be on his way to the lake – to Fay.

Shelly mumbled through the mask, "you... must... go. Fay needs... you."

"I can't leave you like this, Shelly," Daniel said. He felt torn, guilty and out of control.

The SHO turned to Daniel. "It's alright Mr Kendrick. We'll take care of her. Colin Mathias is on his way over. He'll be operating."

Just then, Daniel felt a phone vibrate in his pocket. He took it out. It was the burner.

"I have to take this," Daniel said. He went out into the corridor and answered the phone, his hand over his weak ear to block out the noise of the busy department.

Wixx sounded pleased with himself. "I hope you have the money ready. A million pounds in cash, remember."

"What did you do to Shelly, you bastard?" Daniel was incensed.

"Ah, so, now you know how serious I am. You know your lovely wife will get the same treatment if I don't have that money by this evening. Let's see – I'll give you until 6 pm – not a second longer."

"Where are you, Wixx?"

"I'll tell you where to bring the money in a few hours. I want it all in cash, in a plain bag and if you go to the police, your lovely wife will lose a lot more than a kidney."

"You don't have Fay," Daniel bluffed.

"Do you want to bet her life on that?"

"Let me speak to her."

"Tick tock, doctor."

Click. The phone went dead.

Daniel slowly pocketed the phone. He wasn't sure whether Wixx had his wife or whether he was bluffing for a second time but he couldn't take the chance. He had to get out there and find Fay before Wixx got to her. He would undoubtedly carry out his threats this time.

He went back into the cubicle and took Shelly's hand once more. "That was Wixx. I have to go." He searched Shelly's face.

She nodded and squeezed his hand "Take care…"

Doug said nothing but turned slightly and gave Daniel a thin smile that told him he was sorry.

EIGHTY-NINE

Saturday 24th August 2019

Damon Wixx was pleased with himself. It looked like his plan was going to work. Daniel had sounded as if he believed him, despite his objections and Shelly Winters was either dead or badly injured. He guessed at the very least, she would lose a kidney with his well-aimed knifing.

He had driven the Jaguar through town and was parked in a layby north of Riverbeke. Now he had Daniel's attention and the million was on the way – things were looking up. As a bonus, he also had Fay's probable location. He reached in his pocket for the latitude and longitude that he'd scribbled down. How good of Dr Kendrick to give that to him, he thought. It couldn't be more ironic.

He grabbed the OS map, opened it up and found the location. There was the lake. It had to be Otterbrook. He traced the roads back to where he was parked up. It would be an easy ten-minute drive from here – then a tramp on foot through the woodland. He put the nearest landmark, The Riverbeke Falls tearoom, near Hallbrook Manor into the sat nav on his phone, pulled out into the traffic and drove north, following the directions. He would turn right onto a 'B' road just after the tea rooms.

Wixx was feeling confident and upbeat. He had enjoyed tormenting and stabbing Shelly Winters and re-lived it in his mind. The fear in her eyes, the tremble in her voice, the resistance of the blade as he thrust it into her side. The feeling of power and control he had over her was like a drug. His urge to kill was becoming irresistible.

He anticipated killing Daniel. He would likely put up a fight but that was all part of the challenge. Shelly had been an easy target but Daniel was fit and strong – a physical match to himself – like two stags in the rutting season. But mentally, Damon knew he had the upper hand. He would also soon have Fay. A life to bargain with.

The sat nav told Wixx he was about to reach his destination. The tea rooms. He switched it off and looked out for the 'B' road that was on the map. He found it after half a mile and took the turning. The road narrowed to a single-track lane with few passing places. He slowed the Jaguar. Somewhere, there would be an entrance into the woodland. Another mile on, he noticed an abandoned car on his left. A silver Mercedes SLK that was nose-down in a ditch. It looked like it had a flat tyre. He drove on and just a few hundred metres along the lane, he saw a muddy footpath twisting its way through the trees. He stopped and checked the map. Yes, this must be it. He inched the car along a little further and parked on the muddy verge at the edge of the woodland.

He checked the map again. The lake he was heading for was quite a way to the north. A long walk through dense woodland. Yet, if he followed the lane around the edge of the woodland, he might find a closer entrance. He decided to try that before traipsing for miles in the mud. Nature had never been his thing.

He inched the Jaguar along the narrow, unmade lane and skirted the woodland. There were 'Private Property' notices at intervals along the whole length of the woodland boundary. Finally, he reached a T-junction and turned right. He was at the tip of the woodland, the nearest section to the lake. He parked on a muddy verge, got out of the car and changed into some old training shoes he'd left in the boot. He still had the Tanto dagger in his pocket and grabbed the long length of rope from the back seat – coiling it and placing it around his neck.

Damon climbed a sheep fence and began walking through dense woodland. It had obviously been neglected for some years. Wixx checked the compass on his mobile phone. He was heading south east, toward the lake. It couldn't be far, according to the map. His mobile signal was coming and going but he had at least one bar. Wixx looked around him. He was enveloped by trees and dense shrub. Without his compass, he'd have been completely disorientated.

He briefly wondered what the hell he was doing there. Would it lead to Fay? He wasn't sure, but if he did find her, he would have a valuable hostage. He kept walking, his clothes becoming clammy with the heat and unaccustomed exercise.

Then, Wixx stopped dead in his tracks. Up ahead, he saw a large body of water – it must be Otterbrook Lake. On the other side, he could see a rustic wooden cabin. He watched for a while.

Then he saw her.

Fay Kendrick.

She looked dishevelled, not her usual well-groomed appearance but it was definitely her. He recognised the way she held herself. Then she tried to walk but was limping badly.

His spirits soared. He had found what he was looking for and what a bonus – she was wounded prey and very definitely, an easy target.

NINETY

Damon watched Fay for several minutes. He was planning his strategy. She was a slight woman and would be easily overpowered if she struggled. He watched as she limped very slowly inside the cabin.

He skirted the lake toward the cabin, keeping within the cover of the trees. Fay was still inside. Coots were calling on the lake and a flotilla of mallards with their ducklings were swimming in a 'V' formation across the water. The sun was high and bright in a cloudless blue sky. Damon reached the cabin and stood in the open doorway. Fay was standing on one leg, with her back to him near a large wooden table in the centre of a square, dimly lit room. There were several wooden chairs around the table and what looked like a home-made wooden dresser along the far wall, crammed with crockery and ornaments.

Damon smiled and leaned against the doorway; his arms folded. Her long hair was tangled and her dress had splashes of dried mud along the hem. Her bare feet were dirty from the dusty ground. Then she turned, startled to see him standing there.

"Dr Kendrick... Fay. How nice to see you again. I was beginning to think you'd run away from me." Damon smiled thinly.

Fay gripped the table for support. A hand flew to her mouth in surprise. "What..."

"You hadn't run away, now, had you?" Damon fingered the rope that was coiled around his neck.

"Damon Wixx," Fay said as if she had only just remembered him.

"That's right. You hadn't forgotten me already, had you? That's a shame. I hadn't forgotten you," Damon said, "in fact, I've thought about you a lot." He admired her delicate features, her pale, flawless skin, her narrow waist. He remembered how he had idolised her.

Fay looked puzzled for a moment, then a fleeting recognition shadowed her face. "Yes, you're one of my patients." She paused, as if she was trying to recall something. Then she limped backward, her hand running along the table. Her eyes were wide and staring, darting around as if she was searching for an exit.

Damon stood and took a step toward her. He sensed her fear of him. A fear he'd never seen before. In her clinic, her domain, she had always been in control. She hid behind a professional facade. Here, she was powerless, exposed and vulnerable. He liked that. He liked it very much.

"Now Fay, let's just sit down and talk. We haven't done that for a while, have we?" Damon indicated a chair near the table.

Fay inched away from him, shaking her head.

Damon suddenly lurched toward her, grabbing her arm. He reached for a chair, turned it and shoved her into the seat. "Sit down and we'll have a nice little chat. Just you and I."

Fay cried out and tried to get away from him.

Damon pushed her back into the seat. He half sat on the table in front of her, his legs either side of hers, blocking her from getting up. He leered, noticing how the curls of her hair fell around her shoulders. How her breasts heaved as her breath quickened.

"What do you want from me, Damon?" Fay asked. She looked up into his eyes. He could see a steely determination in them now.

He watched her silently for a moment, his eyes locked into hers in a predatory stare. He could feel a sense of power growing inside him.

"Well now, let's see. What do I want?" He drawled out the words as he reached out to touch her hair. His fingers trailed along her collar bone and traced the neckline of her dress as it plunged between her breasts.

Fay shrugged his hand away. She continued to hold his gaze but said nothing.

Damon withdrew his hand, then bent to place it on her thigh. He could feel the large muscle tense beneath the thin material of her dress. He could feel her warm breath on his cheek. He caressed her thigh with the flat of his hand. It would be easy for him to defile her right there. To take whatever he wanted from her. He leered at her again but slowly, teasingly, withdrew his hand.

Deep beneath the lecherous urges, he could feel a far more potent driver – one that was fiery, vital and commanding. A passion that defined his whole existence. A ruthlessness that gave him his power.

Idealise, devalue, abuse and discard.

That was the psychopathic bond he had with his victims. Now he had Fay, he would feed on her fear like an emotional vampire.

Fay looked at him, her chin jutted forward in defiance.

He liked her feistiness. It challenged him. "What do I want..." he said again. "I want your husband to hand over the million pounds he promised me." He watched coldly for her response.

Fay gave a small, sarcastic laugh. "So, you want me as a hostage. Daniel hasn't got a million pounds, especially for the likes of you."

"That's where you're wrong. Your sweet little worthless life depends upon it." Wixx was sneering now. "In fact, it's time I called him."

Wixx pulled a phone from his pocket. There were two bars of signal. Just enough. He tapped 'call' and waited; his eyes locked into Fay's.

Daniel answered. "Where are you Wixx?" He sounded irritated.

"That's a very good question, Daniel Kendrick." Wixx paused, enjoying Fay's reaction. "I have your good lady wife here with me." He waited.

"You're lying."

"Perhaps you'd like me to prove it to you." Wixx reached for the dagger in his pocket and held the point of the blade against Fay's stomach.

Fay screamed.

Wixx pressed the blade harder. A tiny spot of blood seeped through her dress.

Fay shouted, "Daniel." She recoiled backwards into the chair.

Wixx withdrew the dagger and slowly trailed the point of the blade upward, toward her throat to silence her. "You see, your wife is right here beside me with a knife to her pretty, delicate throat. It would be so easy for the blade to slip, just as it did for poor Shelly. How is she? Dead, I wonder?"

"Fay? My God, Fay, is that you?" Irritation had turned to fear as Daniel shouted into the burner.

Wixx's face twisted into a self-satisfied smirk as he held the phone to Fay's lips. "Say hello to your husband, Fay."

Fay's head was thrust back by the pressure from the blade but she managed to whisper, "Daniel, don't give him the –"

Wixx snatched the phone away from her. "Get the million in cash, Daniel, or you won't get to see your lovely wife again. Oh, and don't even think of contacting the police or I will cut her fingers off one by one."

"You bastard, Wixx."

"Now, now, doctor. That won't do at all. Get the money and I'll call you later with an address to take it to." He trailed the point of the dagger along Fay's jaw, resting it on her cheek.

"I know where you are – you're at the lake."

"Not for long. I will be taking Fay away from here shortly and if you want to see her alive again, you'd better comply with my wishes. Now get the million, in cash, and wait for my instructions."

Wixx ended the call and pocketed the phone.

He turned his attention back to Fay. "Now do you believe me?"

Fay nodded imperceptibly.

Wixx stood and circled Fay, trailing the cold, metallic dagger around her neck as if he were drawing a line ready to make a cut. She sat still and silent in the chair. He felt the comforting warmth of smug supremacy surge through his veins. His plan was working out very nicely and soon he would have the money.

Then, he would kill Daniel.

But first, he and Fay would have a little chat.

NINETY-ONE

Saturday 24th August 2019

Daniel threw the burner on the passenger seat of his BMW. Shit. Wixx had got to Fay. He had a knife – probably the same knife he'd used to stab Shelly. Dear God, what the hell was he going to do to her?

It had been a relief to hear Fay's voice. She was alive, at least. Now he had to comply with Wixx's demands or he would be putting Fay's life at risk. Should he go to DS Harper now – get the professionals involved? They would have skilled negotiators that could deal with Wixx. Daniel felt out of his depth but then recalled Wixx's chilling words.

"Don't even think of contacting the police or I will cut her fingers off one by one."

He had no choice. Wixx would know if he went to the police. One thing he realised for certain – he had to get the money. Without it, he had no leverage.

"Get the million in cash, Daniel, or you won't get to see your lovely wife again."

Daniel had left Shelly at the hospital. His instinct had been to drive straight to Otterbrook Lake to try to find Fay before Wixx got to her. Now it was too late. It would be pointless to try to get to the lake now. Wixx had said he was taking Fay somewhere. He had no choice but to wait. In the meantime, he should get the money together.

He was sat in traffic. It was bumper to bumper all the way through town. He would just have to find somewhere to park and get to the bank to withdraw the £880,000 he'd managed to pull together from various savings accounts, premium bonds, the re-mortgage on the house and a loan against the car. He had already given the bank the required twenty-four hours' notice. He couldn't manage the million pounds that Wixx had demanded but he reasoned he wasn't going to sit there and count it. It would have to be enough.

If he didn't get to the bank in the next thirty minutes, the branch would be closed and he'd have to wait until Monday. Fay didn't have two more days. If he couldn't hand over the money in cash by 6 pm, God knows what Wixx would do to her. It didn't bear thinking about.

Daniel managed to park in the main street and walked to the bank. He thought about how he was going to carry that much money and called in to an overpriced department store and bought a lightweight black suitcase on wheels. He made it to the bank with minutes to spare before closing time.

"I've arranged to take out a large sum of money," Daniel said, handing over his debit card at the counter.

"How much did you want?" the woman asked.

Daniel leaned closer to the Perspex screen and lowered his voice. "Eight hundred and eighty-eight thousand pounds."

The woman looked stunned. "Just a minute." She went off into the back of the bank and emerged a few minutes later with the manager, an older man with a shock of white hair and an ingratiating sneer.

"Yes, Mr Kendrick. I remember you requested this yesterday morning. We will need ID."

"Of course," Daniel said.

He was ushered into a private office.

Daniel had forgotten to put his passport ready but managed to find his driving licence with photo ID and a couple of other bank cards that proved he was a customer. He was asked a number of security questions before the clerk took the suitcase from him and disappeared.

The manager sat with Daniel and made irritating small-talk until the clerk appeared several minutes later wheeling the suitcase behind her.

They showed Daniel the cash, which was bundled up into one thousand-pound wads, a mixture of £50 and £20 notes, as he'd requested. The clerk passed him an authorisation note, which he signed. He'd never seen that much cash before and was surprized at how much physical space it occupied. It would be painful handing over this much money to a villain like Wixx – he could ill afford it – but what choice did he have? Maybe the police would track him down when Fay was safe and he would get it back. He could only hope so.

He thanked the bank staff and walked back to the car, wheeling the cash behind him. It felt surreal to be walking through a crowded street with almost nine hundred thousand pounds in cash. He glanced behind to check that nobody had followed him. The street was filled with Saturday shoppers, none paying him the slightest attention.

He got back to the car and put the suitcase in the boot, locked it and checked the time, almost 1.30 pm. All he could do was wait until Wixx called. It could be hours yet.

He decided to wait at home.

NINETY-TWO

Saturday 24th August 2019

Wixx circled Fay, the point of the dagger trailing over her shoulder, down her arm. She had the sense to stay perfectly still. He loved the way the light glinted on the shiny metal of the blade and how it contrasted with the matt of her pale skin and the colourful flowers in the material of her dress. But now he was tired of this game. He wanted to talk. He wanted to delve into the brain of the woman he'd idolised, to feed on her mind; her emotions.

Wixx abruptly slammed the point of the dagger into the middle of the wooden table – a slick move meant to unnerve his victim. The handle reverberated as he let it go. He turned to see Fay shudder then stiffen in the chair. It'd had the desired effect.

"So, what brings you here, Fay, to this lake? How did you get here?" He was circling her again, tormenting her.

"I don't know." Her voice was quiet; weak.

He stood behind her, knowing it would intimidate her. "Don't lie to me. Of course, you know how you got here."

"What I mean is, I lost my memory. Somehow, I ended up here."

He noticed a scar on the side of her head and a little dried blood in her hair. "You hit your head?"

She nodded. "Yes, I think so. In my clinic."

"Why here? What has this place got to do with you?" Wixx glanced at the dagger, its point wedged in the table. It served as a symbol of his power.

"It belongs to my aunt. I used to come here as a child."

"Your safe place. Your sanctuary." Wixx remembered the words Fay had written on her manuscript.

"Yes." She was trying to turn to look at him. Squirming uneasily in the chair.

Wixx remembered his own inner sanctuary – the feelings that gave him courage, strength and release. He was driven to kill. He would kill again. The attack on Shelly had reignited his desire and it was urging him to take another life. Soon, he would have money and power.

He wondered what it would feel like.

"You're a forensic psychiatrist. Tell me what you know about serial killers?"

"Why do you want to know?" Fay asked.

Wixx circled around her, drew up a chair and straddled it with its back between him and Fay. He placed his forearms on the back of the chair and stared at her – a long, steady predatory gaze.

"Just tell me," he said.

"A serial killer is someone who kills three or more people…"

Wixx cut in, "about their state of mind. Tell me what goes on in their heads."

"Some may show signs of mental illness or psychopathy. Some hear voices in their head telling them to kill." Fay glanced at Wixx.

"Go on," he said. He knew he had been branded as a psychopath but he wanted to know more. To understand what makes a serial killer tick. He took the coil of rope from around his neck and threw it onto the table.

Fay looked away, taking a moment to gather her thoughts. "They may be thrill seekers and seem quite normal, yet show a lack of remorse. A callousness." Again, she looked at Wixx.

He smirked. "And…"

Fay turned away and closed her eyes momentarily, as if she was trying to block him out. Block out the situation she found herself in. "They have a need for control and exhibit predatory behaviour. They may have been abused as children, bullied or socially isolated."

"But how do they feel? What goes on inside their heads?"

Fay turned and looked into Wixx's eyes. "Anger – hatred and anger." Her eyes lingered a moment too long before she looked away.

Wixx saw something in Fay's eyes. A darkness he recognised in himself. "You and I are so alike, Fay. Have you ever wanted to kill? Ever wanted to take someone's life for your own pleasure?" He stared at Fay.

She looked back at him, pure revulsion in her eyes. "I would kill you, you scumbag."

Damon smiled. "I think you would." He liked her insolence. He stared, looking deeper into her eyes, sensing there was something more than retaliation for his comments.

"You have killed someone, haven't you?"

Fay glared at him and he knew his instinct was right. He was looking at a mirror image – into the eyes of a killer. "Who did you kill, Fay? I want to know. What did it feel like? Did you enjoy watching the life drain from your victim?"

"I'm not like you, Wixx. You kill for your own gratification."

"Are you saying you didn't enjoy killing? That you needed to kill… wait, you killed out of revenge, didn't you? For the murder of your baby. A vigilante killing." Wixx thought for a moment, trying to recall a news story he'd heard. "You killed that prisoner, the paedophile, Paula Bishop, didn't you? The woman that gave birth in the hospital and then was murdered. It was you, wasn't it?"

Fay flinched and he knew he was right. Damon realised it made perfect sense – for Fay to want to rid the world of people that may have been responsible for her child's death. He continued to stare at her.

Fay's eyes held his. "If I could bring her back to life, I'd kill her again."

Damon liked that. Dr Fay Kendrick – the woman that had shown him such compassion was capable of taking a life. "And there were others?"

"I had a reason for killing. You just kill for your own enjoyment, your own sense of power and control."

"We can all be pushed to the limits of our endurance." Damon remembered some of the therapy sessions he'd had with Fay. "You said yourself that my childhood, my sense of separation and emotional stress could be triggers for violent fantasies and my urges to kill. The irony is that all the time you were counselling me – trying to 'cure' me of my psychopathy and prevent me from killing, you were taking life yourself." Wixx smiled, marvelling at the paradox.

Fay glared at Wixx in silence.

Wixx continued, "you have taken life in anger, in retaliation for something that happened. I have an inherent need to kill. It is part of me – an escape from the reality of my wretched existence. Don't you think I would prefer to be 'normal', to live the sort of life that others have?"

"You mean the normality that you despise with such utter contempt?"

"It's true, I don't trust the world to fulfil my needs. That doesn't mean I don't want more from life."

"I could choose not to kill. You will always be a murderer." Fay spat the words at him.

Wixx nodded. He knew the violent fantasies that occupied his broken mind would follow him always. He would constantly feel the need to act out the murderous deeds he dreamed of.

He had accepted and embraced that. He wanted to be a killer –
chose to take the lives of others.

He turned his arm to show the inside of his wrist; the two
death head moth tattoos. He stroked the smaller one. "You
know that I'm going to kill your husband, don't you Fay?"

She glared at him.

"I'm going to kill Daniel and then we can be together.
We could be murderers together." He reached out and gently
stroked her hair.

Fay twisted her head away. Her face contorted with disgust.
"That will never happen," she spat the words.

Wixx smiled. He was about to shatter Fay's world for his
own entertainment.

Idealise, devalue, abuse and discard.

"And do you know what else?"

She looked at him, her eyes cold and dark as if she sensed
what he was about to say.

"I murdered your baby."

NINETY-THREE

Saturday 24th August 2019

Fay leapt from the chair; her fingers lashed wildly at Wixx; her nails catching his face. She desperately wanted to strangle him with her bare hands. But he was ready for her and caught both her wrists. His grip was strong, crushing, painful. She tried to pull away, to make him let go, but he restrained her as she howled in anger and frustration. She tried to kick out at him but Wixx's chair was between them. She lacerated her shin on the wooden seat as she tried to reach him with her foot.

"You bastard. You fucking bastard. You should burn in hell for this." She was screaming – an uncontrollable, frantic rage possessed her.

Wixx kept hold of her wrists. He was standing now – towering over her. His face twisted into a self-satisfied grin.

She tried to pull away, wrenching her arms in a desperate bid to get free, struggling to put weight on her injured ankle. His grip tightened further.

"My baby – you murdered my baby. You evil fucking sonofabitch." Fay screamed obscenities at him as she pulled and railed against him.

Then he pushed her downward, toward the chair she had been sitting in. She tried to pull away from his grasp but she was weakening against his strength. She felt her arms being pushed backward, behind the chair, Wixx leaning over her. She could smell his fetid breath, feel the damp heat of his body. She hated him with every last fibre of her being.

Finally, physically defeated, she hung her head and wailed, "Sophie... Sophie... my baby..." her voice trailed off as her throat choked with anguish and grief.

She barely noticed as Wixx reached for the coil of rope on the table and began tying her to the chair. The rope dug painfully into her wrists as he tied them firmly behind her. Her legs were lashed to the legs of the chair and the rope was wound tightly around her torso. She was trapped.

Wixx had murdered Sophie. How was it that she didn't know? How could she not have realised it was him? She was a killer herself after all.

She looked up to see Damon Wixx through a veil of tears. He was standing over her, a self-satisfied smirk across his thin lips. He pulled the dagger from the table and held it briefly to her face, the blade pressing menacingly into her skin.

"I'll be back once I've killed your husband."

NINETY-FOUR

Saturday 24th August 2019

Daniel paced his living room. It was gone 2 pm and he was waiting for the call on the burner from Wixx.

The first thing he had done when he got home was to call the hospital to check on Shelly. He had spoken to Colin Mathias, who had just come out of theatre. Shelly's kidney had been too badly damaged to repair and had to be removed. They agreed that she was otherwise healthy and that she would recover and be able to function normally with one kidney. Nonetheless, Daniel felt responsible. He would visit when he had Fay safely home.

He had fed Chester, Ella and Maisie early, so he would be ready to leave at a moment's notice. He was on tenterhooks waiting for the call from Wixx. The suitcase of money was locked in the boot of the car and he'd left the food, water, sweaters and a blanket in there in case they were needed. He longed to get Fay home, so they could go on with their lives – whatever the future would hold for them.

Yet, he felt a strange mixture of excitement and trepidation. It would be a relief to have Fay safely home and this whole grisly business over with but he knew they had some serious talking to do. Fay was still a murderer, by her own confession, and it would take honesty and courage for him to come to terms with that. He also had to face the fact that his wife could be spending the rest of her life behind bars. He hadn't really considered that. Would she cope in prison? Would he have the resilience and patience to deal with it?

He paced the room, went over to the window. The street was deserted except for a lone pheasant strolling up the middle of the road. Life was going on as usual and yet his reality was being turned upside down.

He felt strangely nervous about seeing Fay again. It had only been a few days since their row on Monday morning but a lot had happened in that time. He felt as if his whole worldview had changed.

He checked the time again, 2.15 pm. He paced the room, then made some coffee but was so nauseous with worry, he couldn't drink it. He still considered whether he should call DS Harper and let the professionals deal with the situation but Wixx's chilling words haunted him.

"Don't even think of contacting the police or I will cut her fingers off one by one."

Daniel spent the next hour pacing the house – up and down the stairs, back and forth to the kitchen, checking the street through the windows, checking the time over and over again. He couldn't settle to anything – even playing his saxophone. Usually, the sound of the instrument would soothe his tattered nerves but anything he did that was an ordinary, everyday activity seemed like a betrayal of Fay. That it somehow diminished the gravity of what was happening. All that mattered was getting her home safely.

His head was swimming with images of Fay being tortured at the hands of Damon Wixx. The sound of her scream echoed in his mind over and over again.

Then, finally, the burner rang. Daniel pounced on it, his heart racing.

"You have the money?" Wixx asked coldly.

"Let me speak to Fay."

"The money, doctor. Do you have the money?"

"Yes."

"A million in cash?"

"Yes, it's all ready." Daniel knew that Wixx wouldn't realise it was short when he saw the suitcase full of cash.

"Good. Then bring it to this address." Wixx gave the postcode and directions to Auchenblae, his uncle's house.

Daniel scribbled down the details on a piece of paper he had placed near the phone.

"I need to speak to my wife," Daniel said, tapping the pen on the table.

"You'll see her soon enough. First, bring the money. I'm waiting."

The phone clicked; then silence.

This was it; he was about to get Fay back. He suddenly felt nervous.

Daniel shepherded Chester and Ella into the Dog House, grabbed the note with the address, both phones and his car keys. He locked up, typed the postcode into the sat nav and reversed the BMW out of the drive, the tyres screeching on tarmac.

Daniel followed the directions to the outskirts of Riverbeke, then headed south of the river, to an area he knew only slightly. He drove within the speed limit, wary of being stopped by the police. His heart was racing as he thought about seeing Fay again.

Twenty minutes later, the sat nav announced he had reached his destination and he saw the house name, 'Auchenblae' on the front of a large detached bungalow. He pulled up in the driveway, gravel scrunching under the tyres.

Daniel switched off the engine. The quiet stillness of the car cocooned him in a fleeting, dreamlike moment of peace.

Then he saw Wixx standing in the doorway of the bungalow. He looked out of place there. Why here? Why not the flat at Bridgeman Tower?

Daniel took a deep breath and stepped out of the car. He opened the boot and took out the suitcase. He carried it toward the door.

"Come in doctor." Wixx looked relaxed, smiling. As if this was an everyday occurrence and he was in complete control.

Daniel felt his heart racing as he stepped past Wixx and into the hallway. The place reeked of cannabis. His eyes were darting around, looking for Fay. He called out to her, but there was no reply. He knew in his gut that she wasn't there.

"Where's my wife, Wixx?" He clutched the suitcase tighter.

Wixx ushered him into the kitchen. Daniel could see the piles of dirty dishes, the overflowing bin, the broken glass on the floor – remains of what looked like a vase, an ashtray full of dog-ends. Then he saw on the table a sheaf of papers; a manuscript typed and annotated with Fay's handwriting.

Daniel spun around to face Wixx. "Where's my wife, you bastard?"

Wixx grinned. "She's safe," he said coolly, leaning against the kitchen counter.

"Where is she?"

Wixx eyed the suitcase. "The million first."

Daniel hesitated. He knew he should see Fay, prove to himself that she was unharmed before he handed over the cash but Wixx pushed him aside and snatched the suitcase from him. He set it down on the table and unzipped the soft cover.

Daniel watched as Wixx trailed a hand over the money. Then he grabbed a handful, flicked through the notes with his thumb and checked the layers beneath. He sneered at Daniel, then, apparently satisfied, he replaced the money and zipped up the suitcase.

"My wife. Where is she?"

"She's not here," Wixx said flatly.

"What do you mean – I thought we had a deal. A million pounds in cash for the safe return of my wife. Now it's time for you to honour your end of the bargain." Daniel felt the heat of anger simmer in his veins.

Wixx laughed. "Honour. What a quaint concept. Do you think I am an honourable man, doctor?"

Daniel didn't dignify that with an answer. "Where is my wife?" He hated Wixx; the smugness of his expression; the callous contempt of the man.

"She's waiting for me." Wixx laughed again – a smug, hollow snicker. "Don't you see, doctor, Fay belongs to me now."

"She's at the lake, isn't she? What have you done to her?" Daniel's mind was racing.

He saw the tiny flicker of Wixx's raised brow and knew he was right. Wixx had left her at the lake.

Wixx took a step toward Daniel, reaching into his jacket with his right hand.

Daniel saw the glint of the steel blade and reacted instinctively, grabbing Wixx's arm with his left hand. He squeezed Wixx's wrist, dug his fingers deep into the flesh, forcing him to drop the dagger. It went clattering to the floor.

Daniel tried to push Wixx away but he came at him with the full force of his weight. He pushed Daniel against the wall, winding him briefly, then brought his arm back and punched Daniel in the stomach.

Daniel groaned and doubled over with pain but recovered in time to dodge another of Wixx's punches. Wixx's knuckles hit the wall behind him. Daniel raised his right arm and brought the side of his fist down on Wixx's back but Wixx stood and pushed Daniel against the door frame. Daniel grunted as a searing pain tore into his ribcage but he managed to recover from the blow and staggered backward through the kitchen door. He glanced at the dagger as it lay on the floor behind Wixx but it was out of reach.

Wixx came after him, rage etched in to his face, his eyes dark and bulging with fury. Wixx bludgeoned into Daniel and slammed him against the grandfather clock in the hallway. The clock crashed to the floor, the clang of the broken mechanism ringing in his ears.

Daniel managed to recover and grabbed the doorframe that led to the living room. Wixx came barrelling after him once again and shoved Daniel into the room. Daniel regained his balance and threw a punch. It connected with Wixx's jaw, knocking his head sideways. Wixx turned back and punched Daniel, his fist connecting with his cheek, re-opening the wound that ran along it.

Daniel dabbed his cheek and saw the blood. In desperation, he surged toward Wixx, lashing out at his eyes with his hands. Then he saw a familiar gold-coloured cat ornament on the side table and made a grab for it. He raised his arm and brought it down on the side of Wixx face.

He could see Wixx wince in pain then roar with rage and frustration. Then Wixx grabbed Daniel by the front of his T-shirt, pushed him backwards into the hallway and slammed him against the wall, forcing him to drop the ornament. Daniel felt the reverberations through his body; the air was forced from his lungs but he recovered and pushed Wixx away.

Daniel managed to punch Wixx in the stomach and he doubled over, groaning. Wixx came back at him, lashing out furiously. Daniel fought back, giving Wixx a bloody nose, then he hacked the side of his neck with the side of his hand. Wixx staggered and fell against one of the bedroom doors, the wood crashing against the wall under his weight, the sound of plaster falling into the cavity.

Wixx stayed against the door momentarily, then glanced across at the bed. Daniel saw the glee in Wixx's eyes, then the glint of steel as Wixx grabbed the handle of the Samurai sword and wielded it high above his head.

Daniel tried to back away but stumbled into the hallway. He regained his footing, turned and tried to run, sensing he was no match for the sword.

Then Wixx, with both hands around the handle, brought the blade down toward Daniel, slicing his leg down to the muscle. Daniel fell as the searing pain shot through his leg. He saw the blood pour from the open wound in his thigh. Then he saw the curved steel blade fly toward him once again, slamming obliquely into his side. He felt another searing stab of pain but sensed the thick leather belt on his jeans had prevented the blade from slicing deep into his abdomen.

The room was spinning, then Daniel felt himself fall...

He heard the receding sound of Wixx's triumphant laughter, just before he was enveloped by the dark oblivion of unconsciousness.

NINETY-FIVE

Saturday 24th August 2019

Damon Wixx laughed as Daniel fell to the ground. He was sure he was dead. He kicked him with the toe of his boot and there was no reaction. He had accomplished what he'd set out to do.

To kill Fay's husband.

It felt fulfilling. He revelled in the warm afterglow of satisfaction – of satiation. He had gratified those dark urges for the time being but he knew they would return like a heroin addict needed his next fix.

He glanced around the bungalow. He would come back later and dispose of Daniel's body – he wasn't going anywhere, he mused.

Wixx took a couple of paracetamols from the bathroom cabinet. Daniel had certainly packed a punch. His stomach and the side of his neck was sore and tender. He looked at his reflection in the mirror and mopped away the blood from his nose. It could well be broken.

Despite the discomfort, Wixx realised with glee that he had a better life ahead of him. The money and a future as a serial killer. He aspired to join the ranks of Sutcliff, Shipman, Nilsen.

His name would go down in history as a notorious murderer. In that moment, he needed no one except his next victim.

Wixx wandered into the kitchen and rolled himself a celebratory splif, cracked open a beer from the fridge and took the suitcase full of cash out to the boot of the Jaguar, stopping to right his uncle's grandfather clock that was now blocking the doorway. He contemplated taking Daniel's BMW but decided he liked the old Jag for now. He would buy himself an Aston Martin or maybe a Lamborghini along with a mansion and a swimming pool with his million pounds. Taking a hostage for a ransom had proved easier than he'd imagined.

Maybe he would plan another and ask for two million... three... four. Limitless possibilities lay before him. His mind was awash with the previously unattainable dreams he'd nurtured since adolescence.

Wixx sparked up his splif and drove back to the woodland and Otterbrook Lake. His mind began to settle and contemplate his future. He thought of Fay but already, he was becoming bored with her. With his sights set on new ambitions, he was beginning to see her with the contempt that dominated his whole identity and perception of the world.

Wixx parked alongside the woodland and hiked toward the cabin. The only sounds he heard was the splashing and quacking of ducks on the lake. He reached the cabin and went inside.

Fay was still tied to the chair, her head hanging low in defeat. She looked up at Wixx with pure molten hatred in her eyes.

"You bastard," she spat the words at him, straining against the rope.

Wixx wandered around the room. He flexed his fist – it felt stiff and swollen after punching the wall.

He looked at the woman before him. His mask of sanity had shattered before her and Fay had seen the darkness in his soul. Perhaps the predatory game he had played with her for so long had run its course. He no longer needed her. No longer wanted to feed on her emotions. He had discovered his true calling in life – to take the lives of others.

Idealise, devalue, abuse and discard.

He, like all psychopaths, was a misanthrope – a loner. His core emotion was one of contempt for the individuals he used and abused as well as for every human being on the planet. His need for stimulation, for thrill and excitement was beginning to grow once more. Throughout his life he had become bored easily. He rarely finished the tasks he set out to do. He moved from one meaningless diversion to the next in an endless cycle of disappointment and frustration.

He looked at Fay. Beautiful, dishevelled Fay. What would he do with her, he wondered? Now Daniel was dead, the element of competition that had once excited him had gone.

She would never forgive him for murdering her baby. His impulsive confession, a momentary urge to hurt her along with his lack of deliberation about the consequences of his actions had robbed him of his advantage.

He looked into her sad, desperate eyes. The fun was gone. It was time to discard her, to destroy her, body and soul.

NINETY-SIX

Saturday 24th August 2019

Daniel slowly focused on the fuzzy outline of the grandfather clock along the hallway. He tried to lift his head. He felt woozy and disorientated. There was an agonising throbbing pain in his left thigh and he could feel the wet, stickiness of the blood that drenched his jeans. His face was caked with congealed blood from the cut that had re-opened on his cheek.

He saw, abandoned on the floor beside him, the bloodied Samurai sword that Wixx had used to slash his leg. He lifted his T-shirt and ran a palm along the side of his waist and abdomen and craned his head to look. The was some bleeding from a superficial wound but his belt and the awkward angle that the blade had caught him had saved him from a serious penetrating injury.

He remembered Fay with a jolt of adrenaline. He had to get to her before Wixx did.

Daniel gradually hauled himself to his feet, trying to shake away the dizziness in his head. He had to think. Had to get up and drive to the lake. He felt a fresh oozing of blood as he stood and his head was spinning. He would need a tourniquet.

He looked around but could see nothing he could improvise with. Then he remembered his belt, pulled it off and wrapped it tightly around the top of his leg, compressing the femoral artery and veins.

He tried to walk. An agonising pain shot through his leg as he tried to put weight on it but he had to walk. He had to. Fay's life was at risk.

He managed to limp toward the front door. He glanced into the kitchen. The suitcase and the money were gone and there was no sign of Wixx.

Maybe it was time to call the police? He checked his phone but there was barely one bar of signal. He picked up the receiver on the landline in the hallway but the phone had been disconnected. All he could think of was getting to Fay.

Daniel limped to the car and forced himself into the driver seat. He reset the sat nav for the lake and reversed out of the driveway. The pain in his thigh was agonising.

He followed the directions and drove north, over the river bridge and took a right then a left-hand turn onto the 'B' road that led to the woodland. The sat nav directed him onto an unmade road and he slowed as the lane became narrow and rough. On his left he saw Fay's car abandoned in a ditch.

She was here. He could sense it. But was she still alive?

Daniel continued along the edge of the woodland until he spotted the black Jaguar, he'd seen on Wixx's driveway.

Shit. He had got here before him.

Daniel parked on the verge and struggled out of the driver's seat. Dragging his injured leg, he limped into the woodland and headed south east to where the map had indicated the lake was situated.

He struggled to climb a sheep fence, wincing in pain as his injured leg was forced to take his full weight.

Finally, he reached the lake and skirted around the edge of the water, staying hidden in the shadow of the trees.

As he crept closer to the wooden cabin, he could hear a man's low voice and see a glimpse, through the open door. Wixx was standing with his back to him. He got a little closer and saw Fay sitting in front of Wixx. He strained to see clearly into the gloom but he was sure she was tied to a chair.

He crept closer still. The pain in his leg was agonising but he tried to block it out. He had to focus. Had to get to Fay.

He realised he had no weapon to defend himself or Fay when Wixx inevitably attacked again. He should have brought the samurai sword. He looked around and found a large branch that had fallen to the ground. He picked it up, weighing it in his hands. It was solid. It would be enough to knock Wixx out cold if he got his aim right.

Daniel limped closer still and could hear Wixx's voice more clearly now; low and menacing. Then he heard Fay shout obscenities at him. He limped to the side of the door, concealing himself behind the frame. Neither Fay nor Wixx had seen him. He peered around the corner and could see Wixx still had his back to him. He adjusted his stance to take account of his injured leg, then pounced, bringing the branch crashing down on Wixx's back.

Wixx stumbled and fell heavily on the floor of the cabin.

Fay screamed.

"Fay – it's me – it's Daniel."

"Thank God."

She looked dreadful. Her hair hung in tangles, her face was haggard with exhaustion and her eyes looked haunted and desperate.

Daniel threw the branch on the table and rushed over to her, stepping over Wixx's slumped body. He cradled her head in his arms. She leaned into him.

"Let's get you out of here," Daniel said, reaching to untie the rope.

Fay cried out. She'd seen Wixx rise from the floor, turning onto his hands and knees as he recovered from the blow.

Fay looked up at Daniel. "He killed Sophie. That fucking bastard killed our baby."

Daniel turned to look at Wixx.

Wixx twisted his head and stared into Daniel's eyes, a smirk playing on his lips. Daniel saw, for a fleeting moment, the frigid darkness of his soul, the sinister callousness that had driven him to kill.

Abruptly, and without warning, the darkest hatred Daniel had ever known exploded into a blistering inferno of rage. His whole body ignited with anger like the backdraft from a raging fire. His mind was a maelstrom of fury, abhorrence and loathing for the monster that had murdered their baby.

He launched himself at Wixx.

Wixx leapt to his feet and grabbed the branch from the table, wielding it in the air.

Wixx eyed the gash in Daniel's thigh and the blood on his face. "So, you're still alive… only just, by the look of you."

"You killed our baby. You fucking sonofabitch." Daniel spat the words at Wixx. He could feel his heart pounding against his chest as a surge of adrenaline pumped around his body.

Wixx sneered.

Daniel was reeling from the explosion of hatred at the vile, contemptuous creature before him.

He'd killed Sophie and didn't deserve to live.

With renewed strength from a firestorm of anger, Daniel lurched at Wixx again. Wixx aimed and brought down the branch but missed and hit the table. There was the sound of wood splintering. Wixx tossed the broken branch on the floor.

Daniel could hear Fay calling out to him. "Daniel, be careful." She was straining against the rope that tied her to the chair, desperate to be free.

Wixx lashed out with his feet and caught Daniel's injured leg.

Daniel went down in an agonising blast of pain.

Wixx looked at Fay, then at Daniel and slowly took out a box of matches from the tin in his pocket. He looked around the room, saw what he wanted near the couch and took a handful of old papers, twisting them into a taper.

Daniel tried to get up but Wixx kicked him back onto the floor with his foot.

He grabbed the oil lamp from the side table near the door and smashed iy onto the wooden floor, exuding a slick of oil.

Fay was screaming. "Stop, for God's sake stop... Damon... please... no..."

Wixx coolly struck a match and ignited the taper. He looked at Fay, his cold eyes reflected the heat of the flames like a devil in the fires of hell, then tossed it onto the floor. The oil from the lamp ignited. Hot sparks scattered and flames burst into the room, catching the curtains, the cushions and the blankets in its fiery trail. Smoke was billowing up to the ceiling and curling back into the room.

Wixx stepped outside, smirking with arrogant self-righteousness as the cabin burned. The old, dry wood went up like a tinderbox. Flames danced up the walls, consumed the dresser, and the floor burst into a maelstrom of fire.

The sound of Fay's desperate, choking scream pierced through the roar of the fire.

Daniel struggled to his feet through a flash of pain, fighting to breathe through the hot smoke. "Hold on, I've got you... I've got you..."

With no time to untie the ropes before they were engulfed in flames, he managed to drag the chair and Fay along the floor of the cabin to the outside, just as the fire consumed the walls and roof of the cabin.

Daniel pulled Fay to safety, beat out the threatening flames from the smouldering material of her dress and fumbled to untie the rope that bound her to the chair. Once her wrists were free, the rope fell away and he pulled it clear.

433

Daniel turned to see Wixx strolling toward the lake, nonchalantly rolling a joint. He limped after him, filled with an avalanche of pure hatred for what he had done. With the roar of the fire behind him, he wound the rope around his hands, testing its strength, then, as he closed the gap between them, he lunged at Wixx, throwing the rope over his head and pulling it taught against his throat.

Wixx pulled against it and made a grab for the rope but Daniel was dragging it tighter and tighter around his neck – the searing heat of anger that raged inside him urging him on. Wixx tried to pull forward again but Daniel tightened his grip. Wixx pushed backward against Daniel and they both fell to the ground. Daniel's grip loosened only briefly but it was enough to allow Wixx to pull the rope free. He lay choking for several moments, coughing; his hand to his throat.

Daniel stumbled to his feet, ready to take on Wixx again. He glanced over to see the rope had been tossed aside and out of reach.

Wixx got up falteringly. He turned to face Daniel but was slumped and gasping for breath. As he tried to stand, Daniel grasped him by the throat with both hands, throttling him with all the strength he could muster. Rage for Sophie's murder still burned like a broiling inferno inside him. He could feel the muscles in Wixx's neck tense beneath his hands, he saw the fear in his eyes as he gasped for breath. He glanced past Wixx; the lake was just feet away. He squeezed harder, his thumbs digging onto his windpipe as he propelled Wixx backward, step by step, toward the water.

Daniel could feel Wixx weakening. He bore down on him and Wixx fell, his head and shoulders now over the lake; the distorted reflection of the fire rippling on the water behind him. Daniel looked into the steel grey eyes of Sophie's killer and saw the black shadow of evil.

"This is for my little girl," he said before he thrust Wixx's head under the water, his hands constricting like a noose around his neck.

Daniel could feel Wixx weakening against him, his arms flailing uselessly, head straining to free himself from Daniel's grip. Somewhere, from the fathomless depths of his soul, Daniel found a raw molten rage he didn't recognise in himself. An imperative need for revenge against the sadistic killer that had murdered their daughter.

As the lifeforce ebbed from Wixx's body, Daniel howled with the full force of his grief, the grief that he had denied. The heartache that had festered, buried beneath the shallow façade of his life for so long. The desolation, the hollow emptiness, the wretchedness he had tried so hard to escape.

Then Daniel looked down at Damon Wixx's face beneath the orange glow of the water, into the black void of his lifeless eyes. He sensed the limp stillness of his body and knew he was dead.

Raw anger slowly began to recede and in its place a peace, of sorts. He sensed a deep, silent, primordial release.

Daniel stood; his heart racing; his breathing laboured; his body wracked with pain.

He had killed Damon Wixx. The callous monster that had murdered their baby, the debased creature that had stolen her life from her. From them.

The struggle was over.

He looked at Fay; at the woman he loved. As she stood there, now next to him, haunted by what she had seen, he saw the anguish in her eyes and finally understood the pain and torment she must have gone through.

He knew the raw anger and desperation that had driven her to kill.

He vowed to protect his wife, the woman he'd always loved. He couldn't let her go to prison for something she had done in the madness of her grief. She had wanted justice for Sophie.

He wanted that too.

They would let Damon Wixx take the blame for the serial killings. He would tell the police that Wixx had confessed to the murders.

They fell into each other's arms. He tilted her face toward him, looked into her eyes and saw the deep, quiet strength of hope.

He held her tightly in his arms and knew, for all they had been through, they would find a way back to each other.